Praise for *Bright of the Sky*

". . . a splendid fantasy quest as compelling as anything by Stephen R. Donaldson, Philip José Farmer, or yes, J. R. R. Tolkien."

Washington Post

"At the start of this riveting launch of a new far-future SF series from Kenyon (*Tropic of Creation*), a disastrous mishap during interstellar space travel catapults pilot Titus Quinn with his wife, Johanna Arlis, and nine-year-old daughter, Sydney, into a parallel universe called the Entire. Titus makes it back to this dimension, his hair turned white, his memory gone, his family presumed dead, and his reputation ruined with the corporation that employed him. The corporation (in search of radical space travel methods) sends Titus (in search of Johanna and Sydney) back through the space-time warp. There, he gradually, painfully regains knowledge of its rulers, the cruel, alien Tarig; its subordinate, Chinese-inspired humanoid population, the Chalin; and his daughter's enslavement. Titus's transformative odyssey to reclaim Sydney reveals a Tarig plan whose ramifications will be felt far beyond his immediate family. Kenyon's deft prose, high-stakes suspense, and skilled, thorough world building will have readers anxious for the next installment."

Publishers Weekly Starred Review

"[A] star-maker, a magnificent book that should establish its author's reputation as among the very best in the field today. Deservedly so, because it's that good . . . a classic piece of world-making. . . . [H]ere is another of those grand worlds whose mere idea invites us in to share in the wonder. *Bright of the Sky* enchants on the scale of your first encounter with the world inside of *Rama*, or the immense history behind the deserts of *Dune*, or the unbridled audacity of *Riverworld*. It's an enormous stage demanding a grand story and, so far, Kenyon is telling it with style and substance. The characters are as solid as the world they live in, and Kenyon's prose sweeps you up and never lets go. On its own, [it] could very well be the book of the year. If the rest of the series measures up, it will be one for the ages."

SFSite.com

"The author of *The Seeds of Time* imagines a dystopic version of our own world. Reminiscent of the groundbreaking novels of Philip K. Dick, Philip José Farmer, and Dan Simmons, her latest volume belongs in most libraries."

Library Journal

"In a fascinating and gratifying feat of world building, Kenyon unfolds the wonders and the dangers of the Entire and an almost-Chinese culture that should remain engaging throughout what promises to be a grand epic, indeed."

Booklist

"With a rich and vivid setting, peopled with believable and sympathetic characters and fascinating aliens, Kay Kenyon has launched an impressive saga with *Bright of the Sky*."

SFFWorld.com

"Kay Kenyon has created a dark, colorful, richly imagined world that works as both science fiction and fantasy, a classic space opera that recalls the novels of Dan Simmons. Titus Quinn bestrides *Bright of the Sky* in the great tradition of larger-than-life heroes, an engaging, romantic, unforgettable character. The stakes are high in this book, the characters memorable, the world complex and fascinating. A terrific story!"

Louise Marley, author of *Singer in the Snow*

"Kenyon writes beautifully, her characters are multilayered and complex, and her extrasolar worlds are real and nuanced while at the same time truly alien."

Robert J. Sawyer

Hugo and Nebula Award–winning author of *Rollback* and *Mindscan*

"Kay Kenyon takes the nuts and bolts of SF and weaves pure magic around them. The brilliance of her imagination is matched only by the beauty of her prose. You should buy *Bright of the Sky* immediately. It's astounding!"

Sean Williams, author of *The Crooked Letter* and *Saturn Returns*

BRIGHT OF THE SKY

KAY KENYON

BOOK ONE *of* THE ENTIRE AND THE ROSE

an imprint of Prometheus Books
Amherst, NY

Published 2008 by Pyr®, an imprint of Prometheus Books

Inquiries should be addressed to
Pyr
59 John Glenn Drive
Amherst, New York 14228–2119
VOICE: 716–691–0133, ext. 210
FAX: 716–691–0137
WWW.PYRSF.COM

12 11 10 09 08 5 4 3 2

Library of Congress Cataloging-in-Publication Data

Kenyon, Kay.
Bright of the sky / Kay Kenyon.
p. cm. — (The entire and the rose ; bk. 1)
ISBN 978–1–59102–541–2 (hardcover : alk. paper)
ISBN 978–1–59102–601–3 (paperback : alk. paper)
I. Title.

PS3561.E5544B75 2007
813'.6—dc22

2007001608

Printed in the United States on acid-free paper

For Mike Resnick

ACKNOWLEDGMENTS

MANY THANKS TO THE EARLY READERS of this manuscript: Karen Fishler; Barry Fishler; Gary Nunn; Barry Lyga; and, as always, my husband, Tom Overcast. Their comments and suggestions greatly improved the story and saved me from embarrassing lapses. Bravo for those who take on a first read! Barry Lyga was kind enough to read the novel twice, and my husband, well—we've lost count. I am grateful for the insights offered by Robert Metzger, although I took liberties with the science above and beyond all advice. I am indebted to my agent, Donald Maass, for big-picture perspectives that can be lost in the tangle of pages. His belief in this story played a major role in keeping me on task in writing the first book and keeping faith with the coming three. During these years of concentration on The Entire and the Rose, I benefited greatly from the support and wisdom of Mike Resnick. Coincidentally, it was Mike who first collaborated with me on a short story sold to an editor I hadn't worked with before, Lou Anders. I am delighted to team with Lou and Pyr for the debut of my first series.

Storm wall, hold up the bright,
Storm wall, dark as Rose night,
Storm wall, where none can pass,
Storm wall, always to last.

—a child's verse

PART I

WHERE NONE CAN PASS

CHAPTER ONE

Marcus Sund came awake all at once. "Lights," he said.

The cabin remained dark. "Lights," he repeated, louder this time, but with the same result. He sat up. The station hummed with life support—the ProFabber engines churned in their colossal duties—but something was missing from that profound vibration.

He dressed hurriedly, toggling the operations deck as he yanked his shirt on. "Report."

"Sir, we have some minor failures in noncritical functions. We're on it."

Marcus left his cabin and hurried down the corridor. The lights browned and surged back again. The station exec knew his rig, down to the last bolt and data structure, and therefore he could feel through the soles of his feet that the hum was wrong, the vibration of the carbon polysteel deck plates a few cycles off. That worried him far more than the flickering lights.

The station's military-grade ProFabber engines simultaneously churned out artificial gravity and monitored the Kardashev tunnel, calming it for company business—the business of interstellar travel. With such critical functions, the engines were under the control of the on-station machine sapient. Thus, if engine performance fell even slightly, and if the system hadn't alerted Marcus Sund by now, that meant the mSap—the station's sole machine sapient—was not paying attention. It was unthinkable that the machine sapient was not paying attention.

They were far from home. The Appian II space platform orbited a stellar-mass black hole, stabilizing it. From their position deep in the Sagittarius arm of the Milky Way near the Eagle nebula, the Earth's sun appeared as a mere dot in the constellation Taurus. Even with Kardashev tunnel transport, the Appian II depended utterly on the station and the twenty-third century AI that ran it. The platform contained living quarters for 103 crew, an advanced research laboratory, and Marcus Sund's entire career.

As Marcus approached station ops, twenty-year-old Helice Maki met him in the corridor. Six years ago she had been the youngest graduate in the history of the Stanford sapience engineering program, a fact that she mentioned with annoying frequency. He didn't like her, but he needed her now. By the expression on her face, she felt it too—that something was wrong.

"I'm going in," she said, nodding at the Deep Room, site of the interface with the quantum sapient.

"Go," he said. The sapient had better not be in trouble, but if it was, Helice Maki could deal with it.

With a sickening blare, the klaxons burst to life. As Helice disappeared into the Deep Room, Marcus rushed to the operations suite a few doors down. Here, tenders were on task, deadly serious. The deputy exec reported that in the last two minutes, the ProFabber engines had powered down to maintenance level, abandoning the K-tunnel. It could hardly be worse news, not because the tunnel had to work, but because the mSap had to. They were dead without it.

"Lock out the mSap from expert systems," Marcus ordered. He had to nod at his deputy to reinforce the order. They were isolating themselves from their central computation resource, a logic device with perhaps limitless capabilities. Now they must fall back on the workhorse savants—simple tronic computers, wickedly fast, duller than stumps. The K-tunnel as a transport route was off-limits for now, but they could clean it up later. They could get through this, Marcus thought, while the word *runaway* kept stabbing at him.

From the Deep Room, Helice's voice came over the comm, throaty with emotion. "Get in here, Marcus."

Ops was erupting with reports from all stations, all decks: *Tronic systems failing; K-tunnel functions, off-line; extravehicular communication arrays, off-line; life-support systems moved to auxiliary power. Onboard host experiments terminated; memory caches dumping data, slaved to the mSap for incoming data.*

The deputy exec turned to Marcus. "The mSap is hijacking storage capacity from every embedded data structure on station, and slaving it to itself, commanding all station power, and locking out both human and savant overrides."

Runaway. Marcus brushed the thought aside.

But people in the room heard the assessment, and exchanged glances of disbelief. Not one of them, including Marcus, had ever seen a rogue machine sapient. Stories had it that once an mSap got away from its handlers, it could quickly form goals of its own—a chaotic state known as *obsession*. Pray God this mSap had not acquired one.

Leaving his deputy in charge, Marcus hurried down the corridor to the sapient domain, took a chair in the anteroom, and punched up a screen so that he could see Helice Maki at work inside the Deep Room.

She came on-screen, talking to him as she worked the sapient. "Secure this channel." He obeyed.

Surrounded by the simulated quantum output, and talking in the sapient code language, she pointed her indexed thumb at sections of the sapient's mind-field. To Marcus, it looked like she was dancing—or conducting a symphony.

In between code talk, Helice spoke softly to him: "It's an incursion. We have a worm loose in here."

"That's not possible," Marcus snapped. He'd never used such a tone with Helice Maki before, especially given the rumors of her impending installation as a company partner.

She ignored him. "There are missing responses, rogue strands. I'm beginning error correction."

"Don't do that; we'll lose everything." It had taken three years to coach this mSap to oversee a space platform. Retraining it would be an ugly smear on his reputation.

"We've already lost everything. It's on a mission, and it's not mine. Or yours. Isolate the savants from this rogue."

"I've already done that."

"Okay, okay," she said, preoccupied. She pointed her hand where she wished to retrain, talking the gibberish of the sapient engineer, looking almost ecstatic, like a believer getting a dose of Jesus.

As he waited for her, he tapped into the comm. "Report."

"Marcus, we've got an imminent life-support failure on deck four. If we evacuate, we'll lose connection with the main nutrition fabber."

Food was the least of his worries right now. "Evacuate. Take all self-contained life suits off the deck." He knew how that sounded. Like they'd need them.

The sapient grooming staff trickled in, leaning against the wall in the small anteroom, waiting to help—or to throw themselves on the funeral pyre. Anjelika Denhov arrived first, with three postdocs trailing her, looking ill. Their research had been running on the mSap. They could pray they hadn't touched off this disaster.

Marcus saw his career imploding. He thought they'd live through this—Christ, this was a Minerva Company main K-tunnel station, of course they would survive—but his career was over. On his watch, they were abandoning a deck, yanking critical science lab work, dumping all data, and, worst, retraining an mSap. His stomach tumbled in free fall, like his career, heading to a permanent landing in the warrens of the damned. There, the majority of people were unemployed, living off the dole, feeding on the Basic Standard of Living and virtual entertainments, sustained by the wealth of the Companies—the behemoth economic blocs that fueled the world. His parents took the dole, and all his siblings, and all his cousins. He was the only one who had tested strongly enough to groom the sapients, and then, groom the groomers. He had risen high. Looking down, he could see how high.

From the screen, Helice had stopped her dance. "Oh my God."

After a beat Marcus prodded, "What, what is it?"

She stepped in closer to the knot in the display, a tangle of virtual quantum waves. She mumbled something in code. Then: "It's a simple evolutionary." She turned toward the optic and said, "Someone's let loose a goddamned evolutionary program. And it's in its three hundred and ninth generation."

Marcus leaned into the audio pickup. "That could be EoSap, it still could be," he said, wanting to blame Minerva's arch competitor and not one of their own crew.

"No. This is a basic vector that any groomer could deliver to the sapient. Somebody sat in your chair out there, Marcus, and goddamn typed in an evolutionary training sequence."

"If it's simple, then yank it out," Marcus pleaded.

She glared into the optic. "It's not simple anymore." She turned back to the cocoon of light surrounding her, mesmerized by the visions she saw in the Deep Field.

Runaway, Marcus thought again. If the mSap had broken out of control, it was in danger of grabbing every resource, every qubit it needed for whatever it was doing. Such things had been seen before. The Jakarta runaway, for one, when an evolution-driven mSap had nearly taken over the world's entire fleet of orbiting comm satellites. Korea had responded with nuclear strikes, leaving the island of Java a radioactive slag heap.

"Who's had access here?" Marcus glanced at Anjelika Denhov, who had better know what her postdocs were up to. The people in this room were the only ones who could have interfaced with the mSap.

Anjelika turned to her three gangly charges. "Well?" She eyed them each in turn.

No movement. The team looked slightly green in the glow from the Deep Field room.

"Anybody got a theory?"

Under her stare the newest of them, Luc Diers, swallowed hard. "It was me," he said.

Marcus turned on the youngster. "Talk. Talk fast."

"I was just trying to salvage my program." Luc glanced at Anjelika, his PhD adviser. "I didn't want to fail." Realizing that he still had the room's attention, he stumbled on: "I kept getting nonsense readings, and I couldn't fix it. I had no idea the mSap would take an interest. Would commandeer everything."

Marcus didn't know if he was relieved or sickened that it was one of his own crew.

Luc told about his simple, evolving program that was supposed to reconfigure his experiment on fundamental extragalactic particles so that it was back on track and not outputting data on impossible particles. Particles never seen before. Luc was going home next week. He wouldn't have time to restart the program. It was just a minor program running on the mSap. He thought no one would notice.

Listening in, Helice exploded. "You thought no one would *notice?* You let go of your program goal and assigned it to my sapient?" Luc stared at the floor, and Helice turned away in disgust, concentrating again on the Deep Field.

They all watched, transfixed by the sight of a woman trying to tame a quantum monster. The eerie light flickered on her face like a tormented mind probing for comfort from the one person on-station who could understand it. She murmured, "It's analyzing an anomalous structure. A profound goal that it can't reach. And it's getting lost."

"God help us," Marcus said. He leaned into the comm. "Call Mayday."

The audio responded, "Sending." The nearest help was weeks out of the system.

Helice walked out of the Deep Room, pulling off her data rings. Glancing at Anjelika, she asked, "Which one?" Anjelika nodded at the unfortunate postdoc, who cringed under Helice's predatory stare. "Name?"

"Luc Diers."

"All right, Luc," she said in a too-smooth voice, "describe the anomalous readings that you retrained my sapient to fix."

Luc winced hearing this characterization of his crime. "Neutrinos," he said.

The group stared at him, waiting. He plunged on. "I had impossible neutrinos. Wrong angular momentum, wrong spin state. Reversed, actually."

"Meaning?" Marcus snapped.

Anjelika broke in: "Think of it like the direction of corkscrewing. Neutrinos go to the left."

Luc added, "And the ones I kept registering went to the right, if you want to think of it that way. And the readings were coming from everywhere at once. So it was garbage. Unless it was evidence of another dimension, it was garbage."

Helice put up a hand to stop others from interrupting. "What do you mean, *dimension?*"

"Space-time construct. Universe." Meeting blank stares, he went on, "Nature creates symmetry all over the place, except at the subatomic scale. So some folks figure the missing symmetry is in other universes. Like right-turning neutrinos are in the fifth dimension, and orthopositroniums' missing energy is there. It's all in other dimensions."

Marcus stood and fixed a blank and hopeless gaze on Luc Diers. "Kiss your ass good-bye, son."

Luc nodded. "Yes, sir."

Helice said, "Get out of here, all of you. Except Marcus and Luc. Make yourselves useful somewhere." When they left, she said, "The mSap wants this station, Marcus. And it's taking it."

He nodded, strangely calm, now that he knew the worst. *Runaway*. He glanced at the Deep Room. "Kill it."

"And kill the station?"

A small moan came from Luc as the reality of their disaster sunk in.

"Maybe we can still salvage life-support systems," Marcus said.

"You can't. It's dissolved your networks. You don't have any networks left."

"We've got expert systems."

"That can't talk to each other."

He glanced at the room again. "Kill it, Helice." If they could. There was the Jakarta runaway. It had copied itself into a thousand home computers moments before decoherence.

"First I'm downloading the mSap output." Leaning over the keyboard, she shunted the data into a high-storage optical cube. She was taking it home. She was leaving. "Prime the shuttle and get us a pilot. You can assign whoever you want in the remaining seats." She cocked her head at Luc. "He's coming with me." Her face softened. "You come too, Marcus."

He heard her as in a dream. "Put the sapient down, Helice."

She looked at him a long moment. "Putting down the mSap." She leaned over the control board and typed in the command to collapse wave function. To blow its quantum nature, that of being in several places at once, they needed to shatter the quantum isolation. Turning on the lights inside the domain could do it.

And did. In an instant, the $1.3 billion demigod snapped into decoherence.

A soft whine came from the Deep Room, high-pitched and eerie. Aside from terror, Marcus felt relief. At least they could still kill it.

As they opened the door into the corridor, the sickening blare of the klaxons ballooned louder.

"Meet me at the shuttle bay," she said, already heading out the door.

In automatic problem-solving mode, Marcus began prioritizing the remaining shuttle seats. Send home nonessential personnel. The researchers, the support techs, the . . . he let a wave of nausea pass through him. He decided on the six people who'd fill the remaining shuttle seats. He wasn't among them.

His rig. His watch.

Hurrying down the corridor, Helice had Luc by the arm, heading for the shuttle bay, avoiding running but wasting no time. She clutched the data cube. The quantum platforms didn't travel, of course. Too leaky, too vulnerable.

"I'm sorry," Luc whispered.

Helice nodded. "Yes. Yes you are." Sorry was only the beginning of his troubles. But first they had to launch out of here. With the mSap down and the savants isolated from each other, the station now ran on human-powered thought, which, as the case of Luc Diers demonstrated, often went awry. Hurrying down the corridor, she debriefed Luc, wringing the salient details from him, of his research gone wrong.

Then, herding him into the domain of the executive quarters, she made a quick stop for Guinevere, her pet macaw.

"Carry this," she told Luc, passing the hooded cage to him. Guinevere gave a harsh bleat of protest as they rushed on to the launch bay.

A pilot, disheveled and pale, joined them there. Four others trickled in to join them, their faces betraying wild-eyed panic.

As they began finding their seats, she went forward to talk to the pilot. "Before you do anything," she told him, "isolate your onboards from all station contact." At his confused expression, she said, "Sapient's got an obsession. It'll eat your tronics for a snack." The mSap was dead, with any luck. But it hadn't been a lucky day so far. He nodded, somber.

"And go, go now."

"Still waiting on two more passengers, Ms. Maki."

"Not any more. Get out of here if you want to save the passengers you have."

Back in the passenger cabin, she strapped Guinevere's cage into one of the seats, then herself, as the engines hummed to life. Luc followed suit, looking stunned. She held her hands in a firm clasp to keep them from shaking. She didn't give the station a snowball's chance in hell. Go, go, she urged the pilot.

They launched, easing out of the bay, vernier thrusters working.

Holding the cube in her hand, Helice stared at it. She'd made a snap decision that Luc's discovery was real. Because the mSap had taken right-corkscrewing neutrinos seriously. Because it had marshaled the entire resources of the station to cache its output, pursuing a problem so deep and long that it must be the toughest question in the history of quantum sapients. Helice had known all this, standing in the Deep Field, gazing into the obsession. It suggested not a sapient run amok, but a sapient probing the most astonishing question: Where had the right-turning neutrinos come from? And how could the source's mass exceed that of the universe?

With the shuttle under way, she looked out the viewport, seeing the lights dim on the top deck of the station. Then another. Deck by deck, the platform was powering down. They would freeze to death before their air ran out. She tried not to think about the dying, but the two empty seats next to her kept the thought fresh. She patted Guinevere's cage absently, seeking comfort.

They sped homeward. She clutched the data cube in her pocket, all that remained of the mSap and its journey next door. Into an infinite land.

CHAPTER TWO

ON A CLIFF OVERLOOKING THE PACIFIC OCEAN, Lamar Gelde sat in his sport vehicle, straining to see the panoramic view of the breakers and distant horizon. His car headlights tunneled a blind light into the fog, in a socked-in December landscape, dominated by saturated low clouds and the pounding surf. It had been decades since Lamar had seen the ocean; and he wasn't going to see it today, either. Instead he was going to see one of the most difficult men in the Western Hemisphere: Titus Quinn.

He brought good news, but Titus might not see it in that light. No telling how the man might react, especially as reclusive as he'd become these last couple of years. Lamar loved Titus Quinn like a son, and hated watching him throw his life away, here on this godforsaken coast where it rained forty-five inches a year and the nearest neighbor was fifteen miles away.

But this isolation was precisely why Titus Quinn retreated to the Oregon coast, to escape the company of his fellow men and women and to stay a universe away from black hole interstellar transport and the destinations that implied. Lamar carefully backed into the whiteout conditions on the road and sped toward his meeting, one that would take Titus by surprise. Titus's own fault. The man never answered the phone.

In the warmth of the car, Lamar drew off his gloves and gripped the steering wheel of the custom ZXI 600, loaded with after-market options, gliding through the hairpin turns with a surge of power from the precision engine, worth a year's salary of a member of the Minerva board of directors. Retired or not, he could still afford it, even without the Minerva stipend that kept him on retainer. Now, Minerva had a little task for him, one Lamar intended accomplish, both for Minerva and for the sake of Titus Quinn's immortal soul. At thirty-four, Titus was too young to be living in the past. Today, Lamar hoped to recall him to life. That was how Lamar saw it, though he was pretty sure Titus would see it differently. He gunned the engine and grabbed roadway down the straightaway, wiping sweat from his hands so he wouldn't lose his grip on the wheel. He hadn't seen Titus for over a year. He hoped Titus had mellowed a bit.

Keep Out, More Private Than You Can Imagine. The sign on the sagging split log fence had been freshly redrawn. Turning down the rutted drive, Lamar squinted at the warning signs nailed to trees. *Not Interested, Go Away.* In another few yards: *Contrary to What You Believe, You Are NOT an Exception.* The road descended into green-black trees, dripping with moss and rain. *Last Turn Around. Land Mines Ahead.* Lamar sighed. He knew Titus had booby-trapped the property, but he trusted that Titus had not yet stooped to land mines.

Parking the car under a giant tree heavy with pea-green fans of cedar, Lamar struggled out of the low-slung car, hating the indignities of old bones and sagging muscles. He pulled his jacket close around him and tucked in his head against the rain that had now begun to patter through the overhead branches. *Cold, soggy, godforsaken* were the words that came to mind as he slogged down the path toward Titus's beach house.

A high whine needled at his hearing, followed closely by a crunch and the fall of a giant branch across his path. Still waving from the jolt of hitting the ground, a wood sign proclaimed: *My Dogs Are Hungry.* Lamar stepped over the crude barrier and shouted, "Titus? It's Lamar. Stop this nonsense, will you?"

Fog rolled through the treetops, blobs of congealed wool. Through them, he could see the melted yellow of the sun, thin and cross-looking. It was high noon, ten days before Christmas. A miserable time of year to be on the coast. Ahead he saw the beach house, two stories, brown shingles, looking like a hole in the forest and not a proper residence. Rain trickled down Lamar's neck as he hurried down the path, surrounded by sounds of small explosions and the accompanying release of foul smells. No, Titus Quinn was not growing mellow. If anything, his property was worse than ever. Christ, we should visit the man more often. Keep him tethered to reality. "Titus?" he shouted.

Up ahead Lamar heard, "Who the hell is it?" A shutter slammed open on the second story of the cottage, and someone's head poked out. Titus.

"It's Lamar, for Christ's sake."

"Go away." Titus disappeared from view.

Lamar shook his head. He'd known this was not going to be easy.

The porch that usually overlooked the ocean on the four days a year when one could actually see the ocean in this dreadful climate felt slick as snot, causing Lamar to grip the handrail and jam a Paul Bunyan–sized sliver into his hand. God damn, he thought, rapping on the front door, the things I do for Minerva Company.

He rapped again, this time using the oddly fashioned door knocker in the shape of a face. Eventually Titus answered the door. He looked resigned at seeing his old friend. But it was not a friendly greeting—in fact, no greeting at all.

"How did you get past my defenses?" Titus asked, turning back into his living room and leaving his guest to close the door.

Coming inside and throwing his gloves on the side table, Lamar said, "You can't keep the world away forever, you know."

"Doing okay so far."

Doing okay would not be how Lamar would describe it.

But despite his reclusive lifestyle, Titus did look fit. A couple inches over six feet and athletically built, he hadn't yet gone soft. He was handsome still, despite the white hair that had prematurely come upon him. He kept it clipped short, and it might as easily have been blond. In fact, except for the baggy plaid shirt, he might still be mistaken for Minerva's top interstellar pilot, a man who'd won the heart of Johanna Arlis—a tough woman to please.

A whining sound from the direction of the dining room caused Lamar to flinch.

"Don't worry, it's not an incoming missile. It's my new St. Paul Olympian locomotive."

Titus flipped on a light, revealing what Lamar had not noticed before: that the entire living and dining rooms were crisscrossed with miniature train tracks, both at floor level and elevated. One snaked by Lamar's feet, making a turn at the lamp, past a miniature semaphore and telegraph post.

"The Blue Comet," Titus said, as though Lamar should be impressed. The line of cars stretched into the back hallway.

Titus hit another button, and a sparkling green-and-gold locomotive came clacking around the sofa. "A new acquisition. Lionel 381, all steel, with brass inserts plus the original box. Paid eleven thousand bucks for it." He frowned at Lamar. "Suppose I overpaid?"

Lamar well knew that Titus could afford to squander a damn sight more than that. Minerva made sure Titus needed no money. That he need never succumb to selling his story to the newsTides, or to the insatiable fan base of those who believed that Titus Quinn had traveled to another universe. Two years ago. A lifetime ago.

Lamar reached out to touch the locomotive, now stopped at a crossing.

"Uh-uh," Titus warned. "Gets skin oils on the moving parts." Lamar retracted his hand and unbuttoned his coat instead. Removing his jacket, he looked for a place to put it amid the furniture cluttered with cast-off clothing, dirty dishes, and packing boxes for model trains. Lamar hung the coat over a lamp.

"Titus," he began.

A hand came up, stopping him. "I go by Quinn now." Titus Quinn fussed with the Olympian, adjusting the switch in the tracks, ignoring Lamar, the man who was his last link to Minerva, who had been watching out for Titus's interests since the man himself didn't seem to care.

"I wouldn't have disturbed you if it wasn't important."

Titus took the locomotive to the dining room table covered with miniature tools and boxes of spare parts. "Sometimes the wheel alignments need a few tweaks. It's three hundred years old, so I don't begrudge it a little tune-up."

Lamar looked around at the place. Even in Johanna's time, it had never been tidy. Johanna had had canvases stored everywhere, and tubes of paint . . . but now, it was clearly a bachelor place.

"They've found it," Lamar said softly.

Tinkering. Titus used the small screwdriver with surprising precision for someone with large hands, and for working, as he was, in the gloom.

Lamar went on. "A way through, Quinn. To the other place."

Titus didn't flinch or look up, but he stood immobile, screwdriver in hand.

Lamar let that statement settle. Looking around, he saw pictures of the family collecting dust on the fireplace mantel. At least Titus hadn't turned the cottage into a shrine. As pitiful as he was, he'd made something new for himself. Lamar resolved to be patient.

Titus turned the model over in his hand, as though seeing it for the first time. "Still got the original screwdriver-assembly kit. Otherwise I would only have paid half as much."

Lamar looked about for a place to sit down, then gave up. "It was a fluke, really. Some physics geek let a program go haywire, and they found themselves in a barrage of impossible subatomic particles. Minerva thinks the source of those particles is quite . . . big."

Titus's icy blue eyes met his own. When they did, Lamar said, "The source is large. Infinitely large. We think it might be the place you went."

A lopsided smile came to Titus's mouth. "The place I went."

"Yes."

An eyebrow went up. "You mean, Minerva thinks I *went someplace*? You mean instead of abandoning my ship and hightailing it off to some backwater planet, I actually *went someplace*?"

Lamar coughed. "Minerva owes you some apologies. I've always thought so."

But Titus was still talking: "You mean you think you've found the other universe, and that I wasn't lying and crazy after all? You mean you think you've found Johanna?" He slammed the locomotive down on the table.

Lamar winced. Eleven thousand dollars . . .

"And Sydney," Titus whispered.

Sydney had been nine at the time of the ship disaster. She was their only child.

Titus stood near his chair, body tensed, but with nothing to hit. Except maybe Lamar, and Lamar was practically his only friend.

"I'm telling you that they've found what *may* be the other place. Nobody knows what it is, much less who might be there." He hated to bring up Stefan Polich's name, but he couldn't tiptoe around forever, and it was, after all, Minerva's CEO who'd sent Lamar here in the first place. "Stefan thinks we know the way in."

From another room came the faint rumble of an electric train looping through the cottage. Lamar wondered just how extensive this hobby had gotten.

Finally, Titus blinked. "Would you like a cheese sandwich?"

Lamar closed his mouth. Then nodded. "That would be fine. Thank you." He followed Titus into the kitchen, ducking under a two-track bridge overpass supported by pillars made of door moldings.

Titus leaned into the refrigerator, pulling out plastic containers with strange colors inside, and finally found a hunk of cheese to his liking. Lamar shook his head. Here was the man who once commanded colony ships through the stabilized Kardashev tunnels, who could run navigational equations in his head and repair cranky lithium heat exchangers at the same time. Living off moldy food. Playing with train sets.

He'd been a family man once. No one had ever thought Titus Quinn would settle down, but when he met Johanna Arlis, she'd tamed him before the colony ship that he'd met her on reached its destination. Well, neither of them were what you might call *tame*. Johanna was dark, flamboyant, passionate, and irreverent. Only Johanna had ever matched Titus's appetites, and he'd not looked at another woman for the nine years they'd been married. Still didn't, though Johanna was dead, tragically dead, and her daughter with her. On Titus's ship, the *Vesta*, along with every other passenger. All dead, except Titus. For which Minerva had fired him, and for which Titus had never forgiven himself.

The sandwich sat in front of Lamar, remarkably appealing. And Titus tucked into his own sandwich with gusto, despite just having been told that the human race had discovered a parallel universe. One that, a couple of years ago, to the general derision of the civilized world, Titus had claimed existed.

Titus swallowed another mouthful of sandwich. "Why should I believe any of this?"

"Because one of Minerva's favorite sapients believed it, that's why. Killed off an entire orbiting space platform to prove it."

"Oh. A crazy mSap thought it found another universe." He shrugged.

"Stupid machines with quantum foam for brains. I've had collies that were smarter."

"They're as smart as they're supposed to be, without taking over the world." After the Jakarta Event, the World Alliance had developed firewalls to forestall runaway machine intelligence. To forestall a posthuman world. Those firewalls apparently needed some rethinking.

Titus muttered, "So Minerva's taken over the world instead. You and all the half-assed geniuses. Gee, why don't I feel all proud and happy?"

Lamar glanced away. He himself was one of those geniuses, a *savvy*, in the vernacular. Able to outthink a computing savant. That fact conferred on him status and privilege beyond the dreams of the average smart—and far beyond all the rest. Titus had scored at the right level, of course, but had squandered his opportunity for the life of a pilot.

"I thought you'd be more interested," Lamar said. He took a bite of his sandwich.

Across the kitchen table Titus eyed him with a hot, blue stare. "*Stefan Polich* thought I'd be interested."

Of course Stefan Polich was behind all this. The president of Minerva Company would have to be. Lamar spoke through a mouthful of sandwich. "He's said that he made a mistake. For a man like Stefan, that's a big step."

Titus licked his fingers and wiped them on his wool pants. "Well, fine. We're all settled then." He stood up, carrying his plate to the sink. "Stefan Polich—"

Lamar interrupted. "I know what you're—"

"*Stefan Polich*," Titus repeated, somewhat louder, swinging around, his eyes glinting, "has decided to ask my pardon, eh? So sorry Titus, old man. So sorry you lost the one damn job you were any good at. So sorry I said you murdered your wife, that we put the word out that you went nuts and that you made up cock-and-bull stories about some flaming fantasy world." Titus was still holding his lunch plate like he wanted to crack it on someone's head. "So sorry that nutcases come traipsing onto your property, lurking about, hoping for a glimpse of the man who claims to have been the privileged visitor to another cosmos or what they're secretly hoping for—their favorite gaming universe!"

At the present volume of discourse, Lamar checked out escape options through the kitchen door, where two room-long trains were just passing over the bridge.

"And now," Titus continued, "if I don't mind, he'd like *me* to be interested in *his* new interest in the little universe next door!" He stared at the plate, then turned to the sink, ran water over the plate, and left it on the counter, his movements precise, tense.

Lamar had to get the whole story out now, before Titus got further worked up. "One thing more. He wants you to go back."

Titus stared at him with eyes like old pack ice. "Get out, Lamar."

Lamar gazed at Titus, thinking how much he looked like his father, Donnel, the old man—for Christ's sake, Lamar's contemporary—who used to be in business with Lamar, who'd asked Lamar to take care of his boys when he died too young and no one remained to care for them. Lamar had done his best. And now Titus was throwing him out of his house. Probably he deserved it. They all deserved it—Stefan Polich most of all—for not standing by Titus when he needed it.

After the ship broke apart in the Kardashev tunnel, Titus put his wife and daughter in an escape capsule, and the forty other survivors in numerous small pods, and sent them off. Then, at the last moment, when he'd done all he could to save the ship, he found that Johanna had kept her own capsule attached to the ship. He boarded and they launched just in time to watch the *Vesta* blow apart. The next thing Minerva knew, six months later, after all hope of survivors had been abandoned, Titus showed up on the planet Lyra, disoriented and his memory gone. Hair gone white. Tales of a barely remembered world. Claims that wife and child were there. That he had been there for years, though he'd only been missing six months. No wonder Minerva distanced itself. But for some reason Lamar himself had believed Titus. That was one reason why he was no longer on the board of directors.

Not that he expected any gratitude for that little act of faith.

"Get out," Titus repeated.

Lamar looked around at the cottage stuffed with Titus's old life and with his new hobby. "What have you got to lose? An expensive hobby that's taken over your living room? What are you afraid of, anyway?" But he was backing up as Titus herded him around the sofa and toward the front door.

Titus smiled, not necessarily a nice sight right now. "Not afraid, Lamar. Just tired of Minerva's nervous twitches."

"Twitches?"

"Yes, twitches. Makes you guys nervous, doesn't it, all the attention I get, all the crazies coming by, sniffing for the real scoop on invisible worlds. You're terrified that I'm finally going to give an interview on the global newsTide, really cash in, reveal what a piece of shit that ship was, that you sold as safe to all those colonists who died. Aren't you?" He grabbed Lamar's coat and shoved it at him. "Be somewhat easier if I just walked out a ship hatchway into the void. Regrettable space accident. Former pilot tragically dead in same K-tunnel where his family was lost. Make a nice, tidy ending to the sorry tale, wouldn't it?"

"Christ, Titus, you think we're trying to *kill* you? You think—"

"Don't call me Titus. That person's dead now." The gloves were shoved in his face, and the door opened before him.

Titus's face had lost its anger, the expression replaced now with a kind of thousand-yard stare. Lamar waited until Titus said, "You really think I'm going to believe you've found *that place* after all this time? After I begged you to search, to pay attention? Now, all of a sudden, Stefan has *taken the big step* of saying he was wrong?" He shook his head in some mirth. "Pardon me, Lamar, but that's such bullshit."

It was time to convey the last piece of information. "Your brother," Lamar said. Damn, this was distasteful. It made even Lamar hate Stefan Polich. "Rob's turned forty. The only reason the Company keeps him is that he's your brother. I'll do all I can for him, Titus, I swear it. But they'll let him go, you know they will." He felt like an ass.

Quinn's voice was eerily quiet when he said, "If you touch my brother or his job, I'm going to put my trains away and come after you. All of you."

From the yard came a crash, perhaps some jury-rigged tree limb, or a smoke bomb. As the sun broke through a tattered cloud, Titus's eyes glinted. "Now then. I'll turn off the system for three minutes. By then, you'd better be gone." The door slammed shut.

Lamar was left standing on the porch, staring at the door knocker in the shape of an oddly thin and sculpted face, both beautiful and disturbing.

Lamar spoke so that Titus would hear him through the door.

"Titus . . ." No, not Titus any longer; he wanted to be called Quinn. "Quinn, for Johanna's sake. I thought, for her sake . . ."

From inside he heard the tinny hoot of the St. Paul Olympian racing through the living room.

Along with the damp cold, a sense of dread crept through Lamar's jacket. Quinn was wrong if he thought this was the end of it. As far as Minerva was concerned, it was just the beginning.

CHAPTER THREE

A CRASH CAME OVER THE BOW OF QUINN'S KAYAK. A patchy, thin fog tore now and then to reveal a sky the color of what Johanna used to call cerulean. He sped northward, lulled by the rhythm of paddling. Brief glimpses of the horizon drew his gaze outward, to the limit of sight. Some days he thought he would try to reach that horizon, just paddle without stopping. He'd thought of that more and more lately. He'd even fantasized that he'd find—somewhere past the horizon—the place that eluded him, that kept Johanna and Sydney. The place that Lamar Gelde claimed was now found.

He kept up a brutal pace, propelling the kayak through the chop. It was no coincidence that Lamar Gelde had shown up just when the newsTides were nosing around to do a major story on Titus Quinn, one that would bring unwelcome attention to Minerva's stellar transport losses. To protect his coveted privacy, Quinn had no intention of giving an interview, but Stefan Polich couldn't know that. The man would do anything to shut him up, even concoct a story that they might have a lead on Johanna and Sydney.

He sliced the paddle again and again into the waves, reaching for exhaustion, for peace. Not that peace was that easy to come by.

The ocean always conjured that other place, but when he tried to summon the details, all he grasped was fog. And a vast emptiness. In that vastness were his lost memories. This was the reason he couldn't move beyond what had happened. Because he didn't know what had happened.

A wisp of fog descended over him. On its fuzzy screen he imagined a strange river flowing. It moved slowly, more like lava than water, more silver than blue. . . . And the things that *rode* the river . . . The image receded, leaving him no wiser. Somewhere in the murk lay his memories of the other place. Ten or so years of memories. But the tests had all shown he was the same age as when he left Earth, still thirty-four years old. Of course, these contradictions only existed if one held to strict rules of logic. And Quinn's hold on strict rules had always been loose.

Up the beach he could see someone on his property. Paddling fast, he got close enough to see that it was his brother Rob. Caitlin and the kids were with him. They hadn't spotted him yet. He could still evade them, as he had been doing for two years now, for reasons not entirely clear to him. Rob with his normal family. Those kids. He was becoming a lousy uncle—eccentric, unpredictable, unavailable. He wearily paddled to shore. For Caitlin's sake, because she always thought the best of him, and he hated to prove her wrong.

As he pulled the kayak up the beach, his brother and Caitlin came down to help. Quinn nodded at them. "I thought you weren't coming until the twenty-third."

Rob smirked. "Merry Christmas to you, too."

Caitlin gave Quinn a big hug, which he returned with feeling. Her face always lit up when she saw him, the last human being who seemed to look forward to seeing him. She wore her light brown hair pulled casually back from her face—round, where Johanna's was oval, green eyes where Johanna's were deep brown. He couldn't understand what a fine woman like that saw in his brother, though he liked Rob, too, after a fashion.

"Uncle Titus," Mateo shouted, "I found a dead bird!" Down the beach, Mateo was holding a mass of greasy feathers.

"Good!" Quinn shouted. "Give it to your little sister!"

Mateo began chasing Emily with the bird as Caitlin hustled down the sand to forestall a sibling fight.

Quinn gazed at his brother, seeing a mirror image of himself: big-boned, deep blue eyes—but gone a little soft with that desk job he liked so much. "I thought you said you were coming on Friday."

"This *is* Friday." Rob gestured at the porch with his armload of presents. "Let's get these inside." He stared at his brother. "We *are* invited in? We drove three hours from Portland, Titus."

"I haven't got any food or anything. For the kids." Well, there were some hard candies left over from *last* Christmas.

"Caitlin brought the food, naturally. You don't think we'd let *you* cook a turkey, do you?"

Quinn helped to carry the presents, feeling like an ass that, again this year, he had more or less forgotten about Christmas. He cut a glance at Rob—Rob doing the brotherly thing, reaching out, doing Christmas. Rob the stalwart, the steady.

Rob hanging by a thread at the company.

Quinn began the unlocking procedures on his front door, fiddling with mechanisms he'd designed himself. Also he'd designed his door knocker. In the shape of an impossibly long face, with finely formed lips and brows, it was cast in bronze from his own carving. Rob took in the view. "It's nice here."

"Yes. No one around for miles."

"That's not what I meant."

To avoid a rerun of the lecture on becoming a hermit, Quinn made a show of bundling the packages inside and looking for a place to stow them. He dumped the parcels on the couch, on top of the kayak equipment he'd been cleaning that morning, while Rob carried bags of food into the kitchen. Thunderous jolts from the porch announced the arrival of Mateo and Emily, hollering and streaming sand.

Caitlin managed to grab Mateo by the collar. "Shoes off," she ordered.

Quinn waved at them. "Don't bother." He looked around at the mess. "Little sand can't hurt the place."

Emily was drawn to the dining room table, where the Ives New York Central locomotive sat prior to the new headlight installation Quinn had planned for that afternoon. Before his brother showed up a day early.

"Uh-uh," Quinn said. "Don't touch, remember?" His heart crimped a little looking at his niece, his memories of Sydney at that age poking up as always when Emily was around.

Emily nodded sagely. "Espensith."

Quinn smiled. "Very espensith hobby."

From the kitchen came his brother's voice. "My God."

"Oh, that thing in the sink?" Quinn said. "It's a jellyfish." He got Mateo's attention. "Ever seen one? You can see their innards through their skin."

Mateo dashed into the kitchen to confirm this marvel.

Looking around the living room, Quinn realized he should have picked up a little. He started lifting items off chairs, then spun around looking for where to put them.

"It's all right, Titus," Caitlin said. "Really. We don't need to sit." She took the pile from his hands and plopped it at the base of a pole lamp. Then, checking that Emily wasn't listening, she looked him square in the eyes. "How are you? Tell me the truth."

Quinn cocked his head and put on a jaunty smile. "Good. I'm good."

"You are not."

"Am too."

"We haven't seen you for months." The words were reproachful, but her tone made it go down just fine.

"Guess I've been too wrapped up in the hobby. You said I should take an interest in things."

"I meant *people*, Titus."

"Oh. Well. People are harder." He noted that the Lionel Coral Isle was going into the curve at the sofa a little fast and flicked his right hand into the digit commands that controlled his railroading models. He could have used a voice-actuated system, but he liked hand controls. He'd always been good with his hands, and wearing the three tiny rings on his right hand, he could manipulate the timing and performance of eight trains on five tracks, no problem.

Mateo was back. "Can I hold the new engine? The one that cost eleven thousand dollars?"

Pointing at the St. Paul Olympian just emerging from the back bedroom, Quinn said, "Just for watching, Ace, not for touching."

Mateo eyed the sleek train with its brass and die-cast trim pieces as it raced under the dining room hutch. "I wish I had a toy like that."

"It's not a toy," Quinn said, rummaging in the coat closet for the presents he'd mail-ordered for the kids.

"Then what is it, if it's not a toy?" Mateo asked.

Rob had returned from the kitchen. "It's an escape."

Emily pronounced, "It's a *hob-by*."

Retrieving the cardboard boxes from the closet, Quinn responded, "It's a way to keep from thinking." Then, seeing the worry on his sister-in-law's face, he put on a cheery grin. "Merry Christmas, to my favorite nephew and favorite niece."

Mateo rolled his eyes at the old ploy. "We're your *only* nephew and niece."

"Well, there you go, then." Quinn handed the presents to the kids, who received a nod from Rob as to opening them now. They tugged open the boxes, filled with tronic gadgets five years in advance of what either of them could figure out.

"Didn't have any wrapping paper," Quinn said.

"That's okay—" Caitlin was saying, but Rob interrupted. "For God's sake, Titus." He looked like he'd say more, then glanced at the kids.

Caitlin's hand came onto his arm again. Like a dog handler, Quinn thought. Why didn't she just let Rob have his say? He knew what his brother thought of him. Of his hobby, his crappy little cottage.

Instead of the expected rebuke, Rob said, "Join us for Christmas, Titus."

Christ, the man had no idea what lay just around the corner, at his cushy little job.

The kids were punching buttons and causing lights to flash on their respective gifts.

Quinn managed a smile. "I'll try."

Mateo, still fiddling with his present, said, "Kiss of death."

"Out of the mouths of babes," Rob said. He locked a gaze on Quinn. "You aren't going to come. Why don't you just say so, save us all from waiting up for you?"

Quinn shrugged. "Okay, then."

Rob snapped, "Fine with me." Kneeling next to the kids, he started repacking the gifts, shoving paper into the boxes while the kids watched in dismay.

Emily said, "I thought we were staying."

"So did I," her father murmured.

Caitlin watched this familiar interaction play itself out, knowing better than to step between them until they'd each taken a hunk of flesh. If they didn't love each other, it wouldn't matter if Titus came for Christmas, but Titus could infuriate her husband in ten seconds flat, without even trying.

"Kids," she said, "play outside for a few minutes before we head back." She was letting her husband's edict stand, and Rob looked surprised.

"I'll keep them from drowning," Rob said, knowing when to get some distance from the heat of an argument.

You do that dear, Caitlin thought. You could look at the Pacific Ocean as a drowning pool or a beach adventure. Rob would be watching for beach logs in the surf every time.

Titus was smiling. Damn his blue eyes, anyway.

"I just don't do Christmas," he said, engaging and wry. But it wasn't going to work on her this time.

"You're slipping away, Titus. From us." As he started to shake his head, she added, "From yourself."

He looked around his living room as though assessing whether this could be true or not. But it *was* true. No jollying the kids along, no earnest hobbies could hide the fact that her second-favorite man in the world was becoming one of her least favorite.

Titus's face relaxed, grew serious. "I don't much care anymore, Caitlin."

She shook her head. "That'll be true in another year. It's not true right now."

"It's not?" He looked hopeful that she was right.

He was giving her some power over him with that simple utterance, and it was a heady gift. "No," she said, "it's not. That's why you're coming for Christmas." He didn't answer, but she hoped he'd come. It would be a small gesture—for Rob, for the kids. She hoped her request wasn't just for herself. She always worried that she was the only one who felt electricity in any room where Titus Quinn stood.

Happy screams from the beach drew their attention to the open door, where they could see Rob looking at them from the shore. He wouldn't like her begging Titus to come. So she hadn't. She'd commanded him. And Titus was at least listening to her, listening with a blue-eyed intensity that held her transfixed. She let herself imagine that he liked a woman who could match his strong will. Not that Caitlin would ever compare herself to Johanna, a woman she'd both loved and deeply envied. They'd been friends: the beauty and the plain Jane. The flamboyant and the responsible. Just once, Caitlin would have liked to trade places.

She picked up one of the toy boxes, using that moment to cover the heat that had come into her face. Standing, she put her hand on Titus's arm. "Say you'll come."

He didn't answer, but he looked at her, all defenses gone. "I miss them, Caitlin."

"I know." Let them go, she wanted to say, but hadn't the heart.

He reached toward her, and for a moment her breath caught on a snag, but he was taking the gift box from her grasp. "I'll put these in a bag," he said, and the moment was gone.

"Titus, at least see us off. Rob will take that for amends."

"Which it won't be."

She grinned. "No, of course not."

At last they were packed and on their way. Quinn watched as Rob's truck climbed the steep driveway. The kids waved from foggy windows, and Rob honked the horn. All was patched up until it fell apart again. Quinn reflected that Caitlin was the best thing that ever happened to his brother. He hoped Rob knew that, or he'd have to give him a black eye.

As the truck disappeared up the road, he snapped on the juice to the property defenses. He always looked forward to seeing Caitlin, but he was glad she was gone. For a moment there, she had looked so much like Johanna.

In a heavy rain, the copter swooped down the approach to Minerva/Portland, skimming over a vast and uniform lattice of Company buildings, a land-devouring sprawl that—combined with the other corporate holdings of EoSap and TidalSphere—stretched from Portland to Eugene. Helice Maki gazed out the rain-splashed canopy at the squat office buildings glued together with parking lots and roads.

Banking, the copter provided a view of the Columbia River slinking through the city, and in the distance, Mount Hood's white cone. These were the only things that hadn't changed about Portland, covered as it was with Company warrens stretching from here to the horizon. Dense canyons of office buildings might be smarter use of the land, but the masses preferred ample parking for their custom transport rigs. Helice shook her head. As the ultramodern world spun toward its sapient destiny, some things remained impervious to good planning and higher math.

In the cool cabin, her business suit sent a surge of warmth to maintain her comfort zone, but her hands were clammy from nerves. This was her first board meeting at Minerva, the Earth's fourth-richest Company. Slipping into fifth position, as Stefan Polich had admitted over drinks. Helice thought the events on the Appian II would change all that, but only if managed wisely, a task CEO Stefan Polich might fumble.

Approaching for landing, the copter sped toward the roof pad of a cavernous building housing at least eight thousand workers. As the craft settled on the roof, security crew sprinted across the pad to open the hatch, then stood back as Helice hopped out, ignoring helping hands. A short distance off, Stefan Polich stood, so lean he looked like he might disappear if he stood sideways.

He hurried forward, waving at the pilot, calling him by name. Helice winced. It was the wrong name. Stefan was starting to lose his edge.

"Helice, how was the ride on the beanstalk?" He held an umbrella for her, ushering her into the building. Stefan handed the dripping umbrella to a staffer.

"It was fun." The space elevator *was* fun and had given her some time to prepare herself to meet the company on new terms—equal terms, as Minerva's latest partner. And to begin to put her stamp on things—starting with the proper handling of Titus Quinn.

Dismissing the security staff, Stefan led the way in his blue jogging suit and sneakers, making Helice feel overdressed. The black fabric of her suit sparkled now and then with little computing tasks. She stranded the data from her suit into the company data tide, that omnipresent stream of data cached in data structures embedded in the walls and carried by light beams through the work environment.

Amid his long strides, Stefan glanced at her. "He said no."

"I know he said no. Titus will change his mind." It was essential. They needed his experience with the adjoining region, as it had been dubbed. Minerva's great hope was that the adjoining region, if it existed beyond the quantum level and if they could penetrate it—mighty ifs, no doubt—that it might be a path, plunging through the universe in a warped course, giving access to the stars. An access that might not rip apart a stellar transport like a barn in a tornado.

Stefan said, "He likes to be called Quinn, now."

"I heard." Why did people insist on telling her things she already knew?

Stefan kept up a good pace, in his habit of using the Company's long corridors to stay in shape. "He ran Lamar off the property."

"I know that," Helice said. "Even the threat about the brother . . . what was his name?"

"Bob."

"Even that made no difference. But we'll let him stew a few days. He'll come around." When he did, when he agreed to go, Helice would go with him. Somebody had to make the business judgments. Minerva wouldn't let him go alone, Stefan had already said as much.

The validity of the find was becoming more convincing every day. Earthside mSaps—tightly under control—confirmed the optical cube data Helice had salvaged. At irregular points in time and locale, Minerva sensors detected quantum particles that mirrored the proper quantum orientation. Shunning ordinary matter, they were devilishly hard to register. But the mSaps reasoned—with the nonchalance of machine sapience—that beyond the horizon of our universe lay another. It was incredible. And she wanted to see it for herself—wanted it with a fierce hunger that had slowly crept upon her during the three-day descent on the space elevator. She didn't know who Stefan was considering for the junket, but she had to make her pitch now—now that she had him alone.

They power-walked through the savant warehouse, packed with technicians tending the savants and tabulators that in turn tended Minerva's data tide. Every tender aspired to administer to the mSaps, but that privilege fell only to the savvies, those who could, for example, solve complex equations on the back of a napkin, or even without a pencil at all. Like Helice herself.

Here in the warehouse, young scientists on the make had only a few months to prove themselves. Failing in the Company, they might find a menial job—but most would opt for the dole, the guaranteed BSL, the Basic

Standard of Living. Just shoot me, Helice thought, if I ever sit drooling in front of a Deep Vision screen.

The savant warehouse led to the central warrens, where the work cubes formed a vast lattice. Stefan broke into a jog and Helice followed. The occupants barely took note of the owners passing by, intent on their data entry quotas. This was where the data cycle began, where the information strands wound onto the skeins of the nonquantum tronics forming the broad base of the computing pyramid that embodied Minerva's collective knowledge. This scene was repeated at similar company nests at Generics, EoSap, ChinaKor, and TidalSphere.

And now Helice Maki was at the top of that pyramid. She took a moment to savor this, but the taste ran thin. The region next door towered in her imagination, casting a long shadow on the day.

She glanced at Stefan, "Still got a fix on the emissions? Three locales, right?"

After the destruction of the Appian II, every Minerva installation in commercial space had joined in the search for anomalous particles. They'd found them in three other locations, across several parsecs of space, now that Minerva knew what to look for, and how to look, using a next-generation program of the one Luc Diers had inadvertently set in motion.

"One locale," Stefan answered. "Two of them dried up."

Helice knew about the shifting coordinates. "That just reinforces my thesis. It's not merely a quantum reality. If it was, the readings would be constant. So it's a universe of greater than Planck length."

"Right, it's bigger than that, but smaller than our universe. And it's not always in the same place." He banked around a corner and sprinted up a stairway, his face starting to redden.

On the first landing, Stefan bent over, hands on knees. He shook his head. "Damn, but I'd like to believe all this, Helice."

"I know you would." He'd been a worried man since the day she'd met him. She'd heard that he used to be a driving force, but these days he was afraid of risks, looking for proof before making decisions. This was not the man to lead Minerva, or manage the real estate next door.

He puffed, catching his breath. "Hell. What makes you so cocksure?"

"No guarantees," Helice said, "but try thinking of it this way. How come we live in a perfect universe? Ever think of that, how we just happen to live in a space-time where things are stable and tend to support life? We just happen to have the exact force of gravity, the exact force of the strong nuclear force so that things cohere rather than not. That's a lot of fine-tuning for our convenience. Religion says that God arranged it that way. Nice answer, except it kind of stops further discussion."

Stefan unfolded from the bent-over position and leaned against a railing. She had his attention.

"So you could say, *of course* the universe is finely tuned for us. If it weren't, we wouldn't be here to wonder about it. But then it leads to the idea that there must be other space-times where things aren't perfect for life. Where the fundamental particles have different values, and some universes—maybe the majority—will be cold and dark. And some, like ours, won't."

"Right. The multiverse has some scientific logic behind it, if not scientific evidence."

"No evidence. Until now."

Stefan smiled. On his thin face, it looked more like a crack than a grin. "Wait until you see what we've got at the meeting."

Frowning, Helice realized he'd kept something from her. "Tell me now, Stefan." She hated secrets. All her life she'd had a horror of people whispering, knowing things she didn't, talking behind her back. Being smart could be a curse in a world where intelligence measured your worth. Being smarter than her parents had been the worst, when they couldn't follow where she went, when she outgrew them before she'd even grown up.

Stefan started the next flight, a little slower now.

Helice didn't move from the landing. "Stefan."

He turned, waiting. This was her last chance to get him on her side.

"I'm your best thinker. Your best strategist. I'm young, in great shape. I don't have a family to hold me back. I'm new, and willing to put myself on the line to prove my worth." She wouldn't beg. But she could argue.

He let the words settle. "And if true?"

She didn't like the hostile tone, but she pressed on. "I want to go. With Titus. As his handler." She walked up to join him, standing finally on the same step, but he still towered over her. If he sided with her, she would be the first—along with Titus—to know what the new universe held. How could *knowing* mean so much? And yet it did.

"It'll be dangerous, Helice. Titus might not come back."

"I've said I'm willing to risk a lot."

"Maybe I need you here."

She forestalled a harangue by a declaration: "I won't be content to stay behind."

He watched her with narrowed eyes, appraising her. "I'll consider it." He turned and, breath returned, ran up the steps, leaving her to follow. Leaving her with hope, though not much.

She and Stefan arrived at the boardroom, and all faces, real and virtual, turned to them.

Around a smart table sat the other partners: Dane Wellinger, Suzene Gninenko, Peter DeFanti, Sherman Pitts, Lizza Molina, and special projects manager Booth Waller. Twelve others shunted in virtually, and their chairs silvered with their images. Looking at Booth Waller, Helice stopped and touched Stefan's arm. "I thought it was just the partners."

"Booth is on track for partnership. You knew that."

She hadn't known. Booth was an easy man to underestimate, a mistake she wouldn't make again.

The board members welcomed Helice with nods. She thought that one or two might even be sincere. She brought prestige to Minerva at a time when they needed it. And she'd brought them the Appian II. That was the contribution that really earned her the expedition. It was, after all, *her* region. She'd salvaged it from the Appian, ensuring its discovery wasn't lost to an obsessed mSap.

Stefan said, "We've made a little progress while you were in transit." He nodded, a motion that made his face look even more like a hatchet than it normally did. He voiced the table display, and in front of each board member appeared a V-sim projection of a small circle.

"It doesn't look like much at first," Stefan said. "Booth, take us through this thing."

Booth rubbed his hands on his thighs and started to stand. Then, thinking better of it, remained seated. "It's not always in the same place, so we had trouble getting a lock on it. We finally got this result at the Ceres Platform," he said, referring to another K-tunnel outpost. "The physics team says we're bumping up against the membrane of another universe. Think of it like a bubble within a bubble, where reality is on the surface, or the brane. Sometimes the branes touch."

Helice rolled her eyes. To be lectured on brane theory by this guy . . .

Booth noted her impatience and went on: "Anyway, at one of these brane interfaces we went in about nine hundred nanometers. We've consistently gotten in at least that far, proceeding a nanometer at a time, and recording the sights. We're confident we can transfer in a mass, but we're not to that point yet. We're using ultra-high-energy quantum implosions, followed by an inflation to macroscopic size." He shrugged. "If you want the gruesome details, we'll bring in the physics guys. But for now, think of it as a simulation of the big bang. But instead of creating a universe, we're punching through to one that already exists. Apparently exists."

Helice tried to keep her voice even. "We *know* this, Booth."

"Okay, then," he said, "what you're looking at is the picture so far."

"The picture of what?"

"The other place." Booth got the reaction he was hoping for. "I thought you'd be surprised." As the board members leaned in to squint at the display, he added, "We've been busy, as I said."

Booth enlarged the sim until the center of the circle looked grayish, like a fried egg seen in negative. Vertical slashes appeared in the gray center. To Helice it looked like chromosomes in a nucleus. He enlarged the display again. Some of the vertical slashes were askew, or bent over. Booth pointed a wand at the display, changing angles of view, from the vector of the pointer. The scene began to look familiar, but not quite . . .

"We're not sure if the color spectrum is distorted, or how the transmission degrades through our interface."

Helice peered at the V-sim. "Are you saying that this is a *visual*? Not just a graphic representation?"

Booth coughed. "Yes. It's the adjoining region. What we've seen so far."

Helice stared, and stared hard. They'd been talking about a mirror universe, a place, and until now—even as intriguing as those words were—it had just been talk. But here was a visual. It staggered her. The board members, silver and real, remained silent for a long while.

Then, from down the table Suzene Gninenko asked, "So what exactly are we looking at?"

Stefan made a sweeping gesture at Booth. "And the answer is?"

Booth's voice squeaked as he said, "Well, actually, our best guess is . . . that it's grass."

It could not have been a more remarkable utterance if Booth had claimed to see angels dancing on the head of a pin.

The board members exchanged glances. Suzene Gninenko peered at the V-sim like she'd never seen a blade of grass before.

"Grass," Helice said. Now that the suggestion was planted, the picture did look like blades of grass.

Face beaming, Stefan looked at Helice. "Apparently the universe next door is not dark, barren, or chaotic. It has an atmosphere. It possesses life."

"The blades aren't green," Helice murmured, still strangely moved by the presence of those brave shoots of grass.

"We don't know what light is falling on it, or what the photosynthesis analog might be. Chlorophyll isn't the only option."

"What are the chances that grass would look so similar—over there?" She controlled her elation with difficulty. She had believed in it before anyone else. It shouldn't come as such a surprise. But the implications of grass, of life, were almost beyond comprehension—as few things were to Helice Maki.

Stefan smiled, enjoying her reaction. "Maybe God plays in more than one realm."

Along with every other member of the board, Helice stared at the bent-over blades of grass. She murmured, "Yes, but which god?"

She intended to find out.

CHAPTER FOUR

THEY CALLED SUCH THINGS OUT-OF-BODY EXPERIENCES. From Quinn's research, he knew them to be illusions. An OBE was the impression of being detached from one's body and seeing it from above, now proved—to the scientifically minded, at least—to be the result of body-related processing in the medial temporal lobe of the brain.

His body was giving him such an illusion now.

He lay on his couch, having fallen asleep there well after midnight, and now awoke to the OBE. *A man stood below him, standing on the edge of a platform, looking down. By scrunching forward a bit, Quinn could look over the man's shoulder. His stomach convulsed at the sight of the thirty-thousand-foot plunge to the planet below. Beyond the man's shoulders and fluttering hair, Quinn could see a vast ocean, a gaping maw into which the man might step at any moment. The man was thinking of jumping; the ocean beckoned with silvery indifference.*

It was always the same OBE. Quinn knew the next thing he would do was look up. He fought this inclination.

The man below him was himself. Neither of them spoke, by mutual consent or by the rules and vows of this illusory place.

Then he did look up. *There, in all its wrongful horror, stretched a river of fire as broad as the world. It must not be there. It must not be silent and stable. But it was. It had eaten the Sun. It* was *the Sun.*

Quinn turned away, facing down—almost as bad. He descended, becoming one with the man standing on the platform. No longer the superior, knowing, separate mind, he now had truly become Titus Quinn, indivisible. And he so wished not to be.

The scene faded, as it always did, leaving him feeling light-headed and disturbed. Was this the phenomenon known as OBE, or had he actually been dreaming? Of far more interest: was this a memory? Two years ago he'd known the answer. He'd been someplace, a place that had kept him a long time. He had snippets of memory that amounted to little more than dreamscape images. He didn't know what happened to his wife and daughter. For a few months after he had regained consciousness on Lyra, a settled planet on the rim of known space, he had strongly believed that he'd been in an alternate world. Gradually he'd come to doubt his experience, his shattered memories, though there was no explanation for how he had come to be on Lyra. Ignoring his claims, Minerva treated him like a disoriented survivor of a terrible event, the ship's explosion and the death of its passengers and crew.

Thus it was of the utmost importance whether the vision of the man on the platform between bright ocean and flaming sky was a memory or not. Because if it was a memory, then that was *the other place.*

He heard noises outside. In an instant he realized it was what had kicked him out of his dream. There were sounds outside, in the yard.

Now fully awake, he sat up, throwing off the coverlet. From the next room, through the kitchen window, he spied one of his defensive lights strobing. Another light caught his eye through the window near the dining room hutch. His feet found his shoes in the dark, a knack carried over from the old days when he had often been summoned to the flight deck in the middle of a sleep shift. He was instantly awake, also a carryover, all senses on alert. As he passed the laser gun propped up against the bookcase, he grabbed it and made for the back door, already fully dressed, having fallen asleep that way.

Outside, the fog dumped a load of moisture onto his warm body, quickly leveling the heat gradient between him and the Pacific Northwest air. He crouched near the door and listened. It was Christmas Eve. A soggy, dangerous one.

The cedar trees dripped rain from limb to limb, a patter so light it might have been the background radiation of the universe. A drift of lavender smoke slid through the woods, like the cremated remains of unwanted visitors. Quinn waited for them to reveal their positions.

It was easier to trespass in a soggy wood than a dry one, since every fallen stick was likely rotted and willing to bend rather than snap. But that very fact would lead people to move too quickly, and sooner or later, Quinn would hear them. A spike of noise off to the left, a chuffing of breath, or the soft scrape of cedar fingers against a wool cap . . . Quinn rose and, avoiding the squeaky middle plank of the deck, crept down the stairs into the woods.

His falling-down cottage by the sea held little worth stealing. Most of what he had, he'd be happy to give any truly needy burglar. But he would die to protect his trains. He'd spent two years of his life assembling the most intricate standard-gauge model railroad in the history of the bungalow hobbyist. The fact that it was probably worth almost $400,000 was not the point. It was the care with which he had hand-selected every piece, maintained the precious antique system with the sweat of his brow, and the fact that his house without it would be intolerably empty. The idea that someone would break in and summarily dump his Lionel 381 Olympian into a duffel bag filled him with a simmering resentment. He'd show them, by God. Clutching his shotgun, with the dual modes of paint spray and hot laser stream, he crept forward, swiveling his head, listening.

He keyed the gun to view his integrated communications environment protecting his five acres. The system had triangulated the intruder's position through sound patterns. By the graph on his gun's display, he was fifteen yards to the southeast of Quinn's position, moving toward the road. He keyed in the scope, looking in the infrared. Yes, a figure moving.

He advanced. He'd give him a dousing of orange paint to brand him for a guaranteed six days, according to the fabber's warranty.

Carving through the mist came a river of golden smoke, knifing up his nose and tracing a bitter gully down his throat. He couldn't help it; he coughed.

Now the woods grew unnaturally quiet. Even the perpetual dripping of the trees ceased.

Then a block of shadow emerged from the night, moving fast, some thirty feet away. Having given away his position already, Quinn shouted, "Stop where you are. Or you're a dead man."

Someone laughed.

Then he was crashing after the shadow. As it fled toward the road, Quinn hurdled over fallen logs, propelled by adrenaline. As the moon took sudden command of a blank spot in the canopy, he could see a figure trying to make it up the steep embankment by the road.

"Stop!" he yelled again, and then he brought the nozzle of his gun up, determined to paint the fellow before he got to his car. He pulled the trigger, and by sound, he knew he'd sent off a lethal stream of laser instead of paint. The intruder was down, hit by the mistaken blast of laser, lying wounded, possibly dead. Quinn's heart coiled, and he broke into a sweat that made him simultaneously hot and cold. He saw the end of his life before him: a virtual courtroom, a real-time cell.

Shaking, he came closer to the form, now lying immobile in the rotting leaves. He reached down and flung the body over to face him.

He called for lights, and they bloomed from his hidden illumination network.

Before him lay a girl in city clothes, ripped and dirty. She was staring in consternation at his gun. He'd missed.

"Jesus," was all he could say. She was young. Maybe fifteen. Lord God, he had almost killed a child. He let the gun fall to forest floor.

"I'm sorry," she said, and tears were just behind the words.

"Jesus," he repeated. He was frozen to the spot, unable to move, but not because she looked afraid, but because she looked familiar. Her eyes were dark, with flat slashes of eyebrows pointing to a long straight nose and a wide mouth that looked like it could smile as broad as the world. She looked just like Sydney. Like Sydney would have—if she were still alive. His throat tightened so hard it might strangle him.

He looked down at the shotgun, lying in the rotting leaves. It made him weak to think of it.

The girl stood up, eyeing him warily. Now, as he saw her expression and the blue eyes, she didn't look like Sydney, except insofar as all young people evoked all young people, for those who loved specifically.

At a movement from the road, Quinn looked up. "Your boyfriend's a coward," he said. "Why isn't he down here helping you?"

She shrugged. "Sorry we bothered you. We just wanted to see . . ." She paused, and now tears did come. "See you for real."

"Okay," he said, surprising himself. "Here I am." He watched her watch him, imagined what she would be seeing. A guy with rumpled clothes, no space hero.

Maybe she did look like Sydney. That dark hair . . . But the terrible truth was, he was having trouble remembering what Sydney looked like, except for her pictures.

"So you wanted to see me for real," Quinn said.

The girl lay inert on the ground, eyes big.

"Thing is? I'm not real. In a sense, I'm not really here at all." She was watching him with more intensity now that she had concluded he wasn't going to shoot her. "I haven't been here since I got here. Since I got back from that place. And no, I don't know where it was. I'm not holding back secrets. There are no secrets, no conspiracies. I don't remember anything. Sorry to disappoint you. I know you want to believe things." He held up a hand. "Never mind what it is you want to believe; that's your business. But don't pin it on me. I'm not really here. Anymore."

She hadn't moved from the hillside, nor did she now.

But she was listening.

"Do you understand?" he asked her, knowing she couldn't have the slightest idea what he was talking about, but needing, suddenly and with a strange intensity, for her to understand.

And then she gave him the gift. She said, "Yes. Yes, I do. I'm terribly sorry, Mr. Quinn."

He nodded at her, unable to speak. But her words unlocked him. Yes, I understand. The young girl gazed at him with the look of wisdom and blankness that children sometimes had. She knew she was talking to a ghost, a man who had slipped away from himself. Who had almost killed a child.

The girl rose to her feet and, with the swift recovery of the young, scrambled up the embankment.

When the car squealed off down the road, he shouted after her, "And lose that miserable boyfriend of yours, will you? Where was he when you needed him?"

He picked up the gun and trudged back to the house, dousing the tree lights as he went by, feeling dazed by what he'd almost done.

Caitlin, he thought. What's happening to me?

In his bedroom, he felt under his bed for the duffel bag, hauling it out, still packed from the last trip he'd made.

He didn't want Rob's noisy household right now.

But, he was very sure, he needed it.

Past 1:00 AM, Quinn's car sped along the rutted dirt road, murky with coastal fog. Pebbles and rocks kicked up, denting the paint job. But by the time he reached the first Mesh, the dents would be pearling back smooth. He drove fast, eager to be out of the woods, to separate himself from some darkness he could hardly identify. He swung into a curve, accelerating out of it, driving hard before he changed his mind. He conjured up the expression on Emily and Mateo's faces when he showed up for Christmas after all. Maybe even Rob would smile, that brother of his who thought Quinn had squandered his future. Even before the star ship disaster.

Quinn and Rob had both tested at the same time, even though, at eight years old, Quinn was taking the test early. They walked into the test as two bright, active young boys. Quinn walked out as a fast-track boy. A *savvy*, as the term went. His brother, as a middle-track child. A *middie*. To his credit, Rob never begrudged his brother's genius-level score. But to Quinn's enduring annoyance, Rob had expected Quinn to *do* something with it. Quinn could have made his fortune by now, but all he had wanted was to pilot the K-ships. It was the best job in the universe. Johanna had understood that, and never tried to change him. Went along on his trips.

Went along on his trips. He swerved from those thoughts. Reaching the paved road with its smart surface, he floored the accelerator, an action that the car's savant overruled, assuming control, establishing an annoyingly safe speed.

In the darkness, the car headlights created a white tunnel, at the end of which Quinn could now see the Mesh platform, where a platoon of cars was just forming up. At this time of night it was a small fleet that would mesh together for as long a ride as their respective passengers shared common destinations. Joining front to back in the modern—and, in Quinn's mind, damn inferior—version of trains, they'd zoom onto the highways at super speeds, conserving highway space and protecting against highway slaughter with mSap control. Quinn felt the bump of his car as it meshed with the one in front.

As sapient-run transport, PMT—Personal Meshed Transport—was efficient and private. People overwhelmingly preferred personal transport to communal buses—or rail cars for that matter. It was a damn shame. What must it have been like to ride the Southern Pacific's Coast Starlight into Los Angeles, with the porters, dining cars, and the full-length tavern-coach?

Easing into the short queue at the station, Quinn noted that the platform was deserted except for washes of fog and pools of lamplight.

Through one of these pools stepped a woman wearing a black tunic, her hair piled into a holiday coiffure. She ducked into a for-hire PMT in front of Quinn's, eyeing him as she did so, revealing a stark and lovely face. Party over. Going home.

The platoon set off, quickly reaching top speed on the intercorridor between Portland and points west. Now that his vehicle was meshed and his attention to driving was no longer needed, the newsTide streamed onto the dashboard, a recap of the latest protests from South America, where an antitech junta had banished all foreign and domestic Company holdings and proclaimed the people's right to traditional jobs and life off the dole. A Catholic priest in Argentina, Mother Felice Hernandez, was taking things even farther, threatening secession of indigenous peoples from their national governments and proposing a ban on technology imports and even the world tides of news and information.

Poor bastards. Only ten percent of South Americans finished even a sixth-grade education. The vast majority were mired in the twentieth century, maintaining a fatalistic resistance to the data-fed world. They must think their old lives preferable to digital delights and underemployment in the data warrens of South American tronic giants.

Thinking of his brother holding on by the skin of his teeth to just such a life with Minerva, Quinn thought that the United States could use a Mother Hernandez of its own.

He rested his head on the back of the cushioned seat. He could sleep for an hour, except for the fact that he was unnaturally awake. The windows curving in front and back of the cars allowed him to see straight down the platoon, into each car.

Through his forward window, he could see that the passenger in front of him had turned around and was looking at him. Her auburn hair had fallen down to her shoulders, framing her face, giving her a siren beauty.

The woman parted her tunic, baring naked breasts. He reached forward to opaque the window, but stopped, and instead touched her full breasts through the layer of polyscreen. Her eyes closed and she pressed harder into the window. A jolt of erotic energy spiked into him. It surprised him how quickly she had summoned him. Placing his hands on his side of the window, he insisted she look at him. Finally she did, driving up the heat in the car. In her left eye he saw the glint of bioware; she might be recording this for later enjoyment. She was one of those modern women, unafraid of bodily adaptation, insisting on direct access to the tideflow, despite the infamous failures of machine-body interface.

Even so, he wanted her. Even if it was through a window. This was closer than he'd been to a woman in two years, and he was man of appetite, or used to be. Her eyes softened, and he thought that perhaps she too was lonely, locked in her compartment as he was in his.

There was an emergency release on the window. She saw him glance at it, and nodded. They had plenty of time. It wouldn't be rushed. He hesitated. Why not? Why not take some comfort?

Outside, clusters of tract houses sped by, where people lived and made love . . . but the moment passed. He pulled away from the window, seeing the hurt in the woman's eyes. His lips formed the words *I'm sorry.* He blacked out the window, leaning back in his seat. At least he still felt something. Even if it was for a stranger. That might be progress if, as Caitlin said, he'd been slipping away.

But there could be no one new, not even like this, for the body alone. He owed Johanna that much, and he meant to stick by it.

Caitlin made up a bed for him on the couch. In her bathrobe, with her hair crunched up by sleep, she looked sweet. And relieved to see him.

"I need to talk to you," he said.

But then Rob came into the room, shuffling out to see what the commotion was, and Quinn thought that it could wait until morning, because he wanted to talk to Caitlin alone.

He lay down, weary at last.

Caitlin turned at the door, as though she would have said something. But, "Good night," she whispered, and left him to toss on the hard couch until sleep came.

In the morning, in the children's room, he and Mateo tinkered with a broken savant action figure. The lower-level tronic figure wouldn't activate the battlefield pieces of the invading hordes that Mateo needed as backdrop for his battle queen, the lovely and formidable Jasmine Star.

The kid had imagination to burn. He'd announced at age five that he'd be a virtual environment designer. Quinn didn't know if he had the talent, but Caitlin claimed he did. More to the point, would a Company think so? But the kid was eleven years old. He didn't need to worry about the Standard Test for a couple years.

Emily lolled on the bed on her stomach, watching the proceedings. "I can't step on the battlefield, or my feet will get smuffed."

Quinn angled the tronic probe into the savant's circuits. "Smuffed?"

Mateo shrugged. "She's been warned."

Appearing in the doorway, Rob said, "Maybe Santa Claus has some solutions wrapped up under the tree."

Quinn almost had the kink worked out. "Santa Claus will get smuffed if he tries to fly over this tactical ground."

"Yezzz," Mateo said, "tactical ground."

Rob watched for a few minutes more, and then headed back to the kitchen to help Caitlin with breakfast.

With the smells of real cooking and the quiet play of the children, Quinn felt a pang of envy for this domestic peace. And a decided unease that it might be shattered. At forty, Rob was in no position to start over. Or Caitlin, either. The dole would ensure they'd be warm and entertained, but it was a comfortable hell that Quinn would despise, and so would Rob.

From the lanai of his brother's apartment twenty stories high, Quinn could barely hear the street noises. At this distance, the road grid was lit up, looking Christmasy in the white and red lights. From the street, sirens pierced the heights as security converged on some scene of violence. The ground level was no place to loiter, and the higher the apartment, the more expensive it was. Rob and Caitlin had worked their way up as their fortunes improved. But it was still a miserably small four-room hive of a place, one that made Quinn antsy to be gone, even as his mind churned.

They want you to go back, Titus, Lamar had said. *They've found it. The other place.* And what if they had found it?

Sipping his dessert coffee, he looked across Portland's sprawl, with its ocean of prefabber residential boxes. These boxes might be uniform, but their walls carried the tideflow, bearing virtual schools, markets, information, social contact, entertainment. By the Blix-Poole Act, each citizen was guaranteed a basic standard of living that included housing, food, and EDE, Electronic Domain Entitlements. The Companies paid the taxes that kept the world fed and housed. Educated, if need be. With such deep wealth, they could afford it. They couldn't afford not to, not after the Troubles had brought civilization to the brink of darkness, when the starving told the well-fed that those gradients must pass. So in a way, the dreds—those with IQs of one hundred or less—had changed the world.

Caitlin and Rob lived considerably better than what Blix-Poole managed to dole out. Rob tended savants for Minerva. For now. Quinn looked south, toward the cramped apartment blocks where occupants upgraded the EDE basic services with every piece of gear they could afford. These diversions, selected by each occupant and reinforced by data agents, created a feedback loop that created odd, individual realities. Psychoneurologists claimed that people were unaware of choices—that their subconscious generated the "choices" using its hidden logic. By this theory, people were biological machines, driven by subconscious processes always a half second ahead of what we consciously "chose" to think. So you could walk into any child's bedroom, any couple's parlor and, by seeing their virtual environment, look into the jungle of their minds. Quinn's cottage, though, didn't have live walls, his reality being on hold.

Caitlin opened the sliding door and joined him on the lanai, handing him a glass with an inch of amber in the bottom. "The good stuff," she said, raising her own glass.

They toasted each other. Behind her in the living room, Rob was settling in to the evening newsTide.

She gestured toward the city. "Not as nice a view as yours, but not bad, for a guy with a master's degree and a wife who likes to stay home." After a moment she said, "Want to talk about it?"

"About what?"

"About whatever it is that brought you to see us last night."

"Maybe I came to spread holiday cheer."

"Try again."

"To annoy my brother by tinkering with toys?"

"Bingo," Caitlin said, tossing off her drink. She'd brought the bottle, though.

They settled into two stiff chairs that barely fit on the lanai. "Now, talk. I want to hear what's going on, and I don't want any bullshit this time, Titus Quinn. I don't know who you think you're fooling, but it ain't me."

"Half my pleasure in life comes from fooling you, Sister-in-law."

"Half of nothing is still nothing, Titus."

Quinn held his glass out. Received a splash. "I haven't thrown myself into the surf yet, for God's sakes." He looked over at her, but she wasn't letting go. Nor would she, now that he'd come to her.

"It's Minerva," he said. "They're back meddling with me. They said they'll shit-can Rob if I don't do what they say."

She leaned forward, worried. "What more can they possibly want from you? You've already given them everything."

"Not quite everything." He told her about what Minerva claimed to have found, and what they wanted him to do. He didn't know what to make of it. But a needle of hope was thrusting up from his innards, and it was drawing blood as it came. What if they were right?

Caitlin took an angry swig from her glass. "Sons of bitches. This came from Lamar?" He nodded. "You don't believe them, do you?"

He didn't answer. Maybe he did believe it; maybe he needed to believe. But Caitlin would have a hard time accepting the idea. He'd never asked her whether she believed his claims of where he'd been. He assumed she didn't, and he forgave her for that. But he didn't want to hear it outright.

Caitlin stood and went to the railing, gripping it. "Damn, but this makes me mad. Look at you. I see that look in your eyes, Titus, and it makes me real mad. They've done the worst thing to you that they possibly could have done. They've made you hope again."

Caitlin wrapped her sweater more closely around her in the chill December air. Just when she thought there might be a future for Titus, the past threatened to swallow him up once more. She'd be damned if she'd let that happen.

She went to him, sitting down knee to knee with him and taking his hands in hers. What to say to a man who heard only what he wanted to, whose stubbornness was as strong a legend as his sojourn in another realm?

Taking a deep breath, she said, "I wish I could change things for you. But they're gone, Titus. It hurts so bad, but they're gone for good. I'd jump off this porch for you if I could make it different. But nothing, nothing will bring them back."

She searched his face for a response, but she was talking to a man who'd piloted star ships. So of course he wasn't listening to cautions. Why should he? Was this safe little apartment with a safe little wife the sum of his dreams? No, not even close. It was what she loved about the man, and what sometimes stirred her to imagine a bigger life, even while fearing it.

She noted his glance as he looked back at Rob in the living room. Pouring another splash, she said, "We'll get by, Rob and me. I've still got a degree in engineering that I can do something with. We'll get by; don't you worry about us." But Titus's eyes were stoked with some pale fire, and her words slid away from him. "God damn you, Titus, if you go and get yourself killed."

"Thanks," he said, eyes mock large.

"Don't get goofy with me, Titus. I mean this."

"Yes ma'am."

From somewhere, perhaps the apartment below, came the tinny refrain of a Christmas carol.

Quinn knew she meant it. But the harder she pushed, the more he went opposite, and the more he said to himself, What if they *had* found the other place? And why was hope the worst thing that could happen to him? Even if it was a mirage, wasn't it better than—than what he had?

She shook her head. "I read you like a book. You aren't listening to me."

He put a hand on her arm. "I am listening to you, Sister-in-law. But I might not mind what you say."

She wavered, finally smiling. "No, you never minded. Lamar told me all the stories. You never listened." She looked more wistful than he'd ever seen her. He didn't like disappointing her, his staunchest ally in his war against, quite possibly, the whole world.

Caitlin vowed not to share the Minerva news with Rob, at least until after Quinn went home. He didn't want to argue with his brother, though he'd have to, eventually. When he and Caitlin entered the parlor, they found Rob asleep in front of the silvered wall.

Then, tiptoeing into the kids' room, Quinn checked on his favorite niece and nephew.

From a dark corner of the room came the voice of the toy savant, Jasmine Star. Her program activated by motion sensors, her mechanized voice exclaimed: "Come to do battle, pagan scum?"

Emily was sleeping with her hands thrown over her head like she was jumping into a lake. Mateo was dreaming hard, twitching.

Maybe it was true that Caitlin and Rob could take care of themselves, as his sister-in-law had said. They didn't need a benevolent brother holding the world off with bloody fists. But what if that brother had brought players onto the field that would never have noticed Rob Quinn, one savant tender among thousands? What if Rob was about to suffer just because of having the wrong brother?

Emily's face had a faint sheen of perspiration, as though dreaming were hard work. The room swelled around him, full of big things like justice and innocence and rage. He was going. Of course he was. The decision felt like fog evaporating off the ocean. He wasn't going to watch this family suffer. He'd walked into the room having decided, but not realizing it. Now, it was clear.

As the breath he was holding left him, he felt weak with relief. He'd wanted to go from the moment Lamar asked him—he'd just hated going at Minerva's request. But the truth was, he'd go any way he had to.

Mateo stirred, knotting his blankets around him like armor.

Okay, then. *I'm going.*

On his way out of the bedroom, he cast a glance at Jasmine Star, sitting in her cardboard box.

"Yes," Quinn answered her at last. "Heading into the fray."

In the darkness, he thought he heard a far-off din, as though he were hearing, across endless plains, a thousand voices raised in a desperate battle.

CHAPTER FIVE

STEFAN POLICH HELD THE SILVER KNIFE, WIDE AND SHARP. "I am expected to do the honors," he told his guests seated behind their too-thin china and too-thick wine goblets. He surveyed his fourteen dinner guests, including Lamar Gelde, Helice Maki, his mother in her dotage, a remote hanger-on uncle, and various acquaintances to complete the table. None of them could be called friends.

His wife, Dea, sat some distance away, virtually present, pretending to partake of the first course, which in her case was taro root, as she sat in her tent in Papua New Guinea, on her latest foray in search of rare flowers on Sori Island.

Amid applause, his cook entered, bringing the main course: a sparkling ham armored with cloves.

Stefan carved the ruby meat, producing the first serving for his mother, who might or might not remember which fork to use. Next to her sat Lamar Gelde, who was to help her should her manners lapse.

As he carved, Stefan tried to summon the Christmas spirit. The penthouse apartment was bedecked and fragrant, the women in their jeweled colors, the men in black and white, capturing the season with elegance. Behind him, in the sparkling view out to the city's heart, Stefan's aerie stood eye-to-eye with the tallest of Portland's office towers. He missed Dea's real presence. You couldn't hold a holographic woman. She searched for the ultimate Christmas present: her own name on an exotic natural orchid. He'd given her everything else, so now, he supposed, she must search for a gift worthy of herself.

Helice smiled at him as he filled her plate. She looked awful in blue. Her neck and décolletage—such as it was—held a yellow pallor. Without makeup she looked like she'd just stepped out of the shower and was ready for a jog. But damn lucky to have her. She could have gone with Generics last year, with that signing bonus they'd offered. Minerva had to offer partnership to get her. Cheap at any price. She was a few points to the right of ultrasmart, and he counted on her strategic wizardry to salvage Minerva's fortunes.

Because the ships were falling apart. Replacement costs would be staggering. Replacing any of them would suggest that they all should be replaced, since they'd all been built at the same time, back in his grandfather's day when Minerva had the depth to create an interstellar fleet and command the K-tunnels. Hoarding the technology of black hole stabilization, Minerva had preserved their monopolistic control of the star routes. Now the K-tunnels looked more like rat holes, eating capital, breaking ships down midvoyage, stranding passengers. The public perceived that the black holes were not as controllable as Minerva claimed. There was the perception that people were dying.

Stefan Polich had the perception that he was lunchmeat. He'd be out on his ass faster than Lamar Gelde when he rose from his boardroom chair and argued in favor of Titus Quinn's delusional rantings.

And now came the last chance to recover: with an alternate route to the stars.

No one, looking at the data from the Appian II runaway, would have thought of *path to the stars*, not right away. But put the physicists' interpretations of the radiation into the same bag with Quinn's claim of a hidden dimension—where he claimed to have spent *ten years*—and one suddenly had a hypothesis worth testing.

It was the *ten years* part that intrigued Stefan the most. Even without any evidence of aging, Quinn was adamant that he'd been there a number of years. So if that place existed, time might be warped there. And since space and time were but two ends of a continuum, the space aspect of it, three-dimensional space, might be warped as well—warped to humanity's benefit. The other place might be a shortcut to the stars. And if it was, it might allow Minerva to abandon the Kardashev black holes that many people saw as suicide holes. Very few people who weren't physicists ever believed that they were *tunnels*. The original designation was *black hole*, and the name had stuck. Now there was a fleeting possibility of a new lease on life. If the new universe could be leased, by God, Minerva's lawyers would nail it.

He looked down on his plate of glazed ham and felt ill.

"A new species of spathulata," Dea was saying, shimmering in her chair, eating from a half coconut shell. "Imagine my disappointment when I found out that Jordy found it already, and named it after his Pomeranian."

"You'll find your orchid," Helice said. "Some of those jungles have never seen a human footprint. It almost makes me want to go have a look-see."

Stefan groaned inwardly. The last thing Dea needed was competition from twenty-year-olds. He intervened. "More ham?"

She smiled, patting her waistline. "Don't be mean."

Meanwhile his mother was slapping at Lamar. "Stop helping me. When did you become such a fussy eater, Lamar?"

Mother was having a lucid moment, glaring at Lamar, who, approaching seventy-five, looked like a ruin, his former robust frame now crumpled in on itself like a partially deflated balloon.

A crash came from the foyer. One of the servants caught Stefan's look and exited to check.

In another moment the sounds intensified with shuffling feet and someone's harsh voice raised. Stefan put his napkin down and rose from his chair just in time to see Titus Quinn appear in the doorway along with the doorman, who struggled to keep hold of his arm.

"Let go of him," Stefan said. The doorman reluctantly released his grip, and, at a nod from Stefan, retreated.

Quinn wore a white home-knit fisherman's sweater, and gray wool pants a couple inches too short. He stood blinking in the brightly lit room, surveying the guests, the table, and Stefan.

Stefan exchanged glances with Helice. How the hell had the man gotten into this secure building? "Titus," he said. "Merry Christmas, man, glad to see you."

"Cheers, yourself."

"We'll set another place. Come in." Stefan gestured the servers to create another place setting, but Quinn held up a hand.

"No, can't stay. Places to go." He was staring at the chandelier now, as though hypnotized.

Dea asked from her pup tent, "Stefan, who is this person in the badly fitting sweater?"

Helice said pointedly, "Perhaps the two of you would enjoy a sherry on the porch, Stefan. I'll host the table. We can get along without you, don't worry."

Quinn approached the table. "Lamar," he said, eyeing the man. "Sorry about the other day. Not your fault. It's just that I'm a little sensitive about *family*." He smiled. "Don't like to hear them threatened with ruin." He turned to Stefan. "That was the gist of it, wasn't it? Ruin?"

Stefan was at his side, taking him by the arm. "Let's have a drink. Alcohol covers a lot of sins. Even mine."

Letting himself be led to the sliding doors, Quinn muttered, "Probably we won't want to talk about *sin*, Stefan. I might have to kill you."

Chuckling, Stefan nodded at the butler. "Two sherries," he said, and crossed through the window wall onto the terrace.

They walked out into a perpetual summer, thanks to the climate modifiers that controlled for wind and temperature.

Quinn followed Stefan through a rooftop garden of exotic plants, all in darkness now, so as not to ruin the city view from the dining room table. As flower fragrances hovered, they snaked through frondy palms, and topiary firs in the shape of mythical beasts.

He passed a rosebush, the blooms gray in the darkness.

"I didn't think roses grew outside in winter," Quinn said, following Stefan to the railing.

"They can be forced." He led Quinn to the railing where he could show off his view.

"She's a wonder, that wife of yours."

Stefan looked surprised. "Oh. Well, she has gardeners now. Used to do it all herself, but now she's . . ." He paused. "I never know what to say to you, Quinn. Everything seems wrong. Why is that?"

A servant appeared with their sherries. Quinn slugged his back, put it back on the tray, empty. "You might try not killing people, Stefan. Makes a bad impression every time."

Stefan kept his sherry, sipping at it, eyeing Quinn as the servant retreated.

Quinn moved to the patio edge and looked down—not out at the view of the city, but down at the sixty-three-story drop. Formidable, but dwarfed by the miles-high drop to the silver ocean of his dream.

When he looked back at his host again, Stefan looked worried. "Think I was going to jump?" Quinn cocked his head. "Disappointed?"

Stefan sighed. "Ah yes, the theory that we are trying to murder you." A crumpled smile started across his face, then stopped.

Quinn said, "I have a fee." At Stefan's nod, Quinn went on, "Forty million. Deposited prior to my departure in the account of Rob and Caitlin Quinn."

"Forty million. Christ."

"Okay, twenty million."

Now a genuine smile lit up Stefan's face. "You always were a lousy negotiator."

"I'm not negotiating. I'm just trying to go home." What was he saying? Why had he called the other place *home*? Maybe because his family was there.

"You'll agree then? To go?" Stefan blinked as though he'd just woken up.

"Smarter than you look, Stefan." Quinn leaned on the railing and looked down once more. He envisioned Caitlin falling, her long hair flailing overhead, screaming in spite of her resolve to sacrifice herself for him. He saw little Emily falling, her hands forming a prayer in front of her as she dove.

"Sign me up."

"For the whole shebang?" A woman was standing amid the date palms.

Quinn faced her, trying to remember who she was. "Um. Am I supposed to know you?"

"Yes. You're supposed to know Helice Maki." She came forward to reveal herself as a youngster in a grown-up gown and a sporty haircut.

He did remember this woman's name. She was the youngster with too many degrees. The one who was nuts about animals and could let a hundred people die on a space platform.

"Yes," Quinn said, "whole shebang. Price okay?"

Stefan hesitated. "Twenty million . . ."

"You've got the checkbook," Helice said.

Stefan nodded. Just the slightest tilt of his chin.

God, but Quinn disliked the sight of the man. "Okay, then." He turned to go.

"Wait," Stefan said. "You don't even have your marching orders yet. For twenty million dollars, I think we have the right to some product delivery."

Quinn turned back. Oh, right, they expected that if he survived, he would accomplish something for them. The mission that would make it worth their while. The thing he'd have to pretend to care about delivering.

"Send Lamar to brief me. I've used up my Stefan Polich time." He tried and failed to keep the sneer out of his voice. "I'm on a strict Stefan Polich diet."

Helice cocked her head at him. "You already look pretty trim to me."

Jesus, was the girl flirting with him? He looked beyond her, into the rooftop jungle, wondering if he could find his way out of here for a breath of fresh air. He did need a good, cleansing breath, because it was starting to hit home. He was going. Everything would change—his whole life, with any luck at all. But no, he didn't want to think about luck, or hope, or bringing back what was gone. Yet the thought filled him with a slow, banked fire.

Okay, I'm hoping, he thought. Damn it, Caitlin, I'm hoping. The twenty million is just for show. I'd go for nothing. Probably Stefan Polich knows that, so it just kills him to have to pay it.

"You'll be part of a team, of course," Stefan said.

"Team?"

"You'll be along as expert guide. But I'm sending one of our own to evaluate the prospects."

Helice drew closer to Quinn. "Didn't Lamar tell you we'd want our own representative?"

"No."

Stefan drew himself up, so tall that he looked almost inhuman. "Booth Waller is going with you."

"Booth . . ." Quinn said. "Your henchman with the beady eyes?"

Helice heard Booth's name with incredulity. Booth Waller? No, that was ludicrous. But here Stefan had decided on Booth without telling her, without giving her a chance to weigh in. She caught Stefan's eyes, and he had the decency to look contrite. But *Booth Waller*. In her kingdom. It was all she could do to control her reaction. Stefan hadn't even had the decency to inform her first. She loathed him.

"Booth?" she said, stepping into the fray, advancing on Stefan.

"The decision's been made. He's ready." Stefan refused to meet her eyes.

Shame and disappointment warred within her. Then, a cool hope of revenge replaced them. She would make sure Stefan fell from grace, and she would make sure he knew she was the one who had pushed him.

A servant appeared on the patio carrying a drink tray, but Stefan waved him away. The three of them stood silently for a few moments.

Then Quinn said, "Nope. I go alone. The *only* way I'm going."

"For twenty mil—," Stefan began.

Quinn stepped forward, grabbing Stefan by the tux collar. "I don't want to hear you talk anymore. If you say another word, the deal's off." He held up a warning finger. "One word. You know how crazy I am. So trust me, one word."

Helice didn't care if he took Stefan's face off, but she wanted Titus Quinn alone. She took him by the arm and tugged him away. "We'll stroll out together, shall we?"

Quinn released Stefan, who straightened his tux.

Helice guided him through the fragrant potted plants to a side door, where she stopped. "Lamar should have prepared you. It's not a good beginning, and I apologize. I didn't know about the Booth Waller decision." He didn't respond, but he was listening with a casual intensity that both warned and intrigued her. "I could go instead. If you insisted. I'm young. I could keep up."

"Going alone," Quinn said.

"You're sure."

He smiled, a maddening, easy smile. "Yeah, I'm sure. Nothing against you personally—but you wouldn't last an hour where I'm going."

Holding his gaze, she said. "Oh, I'd last."

He sized her up. "Nah."

The remark drilled into her, sharp and piercing. He had dismissed her hopes, just like that. She took him by the elbow and steered him into the foyer.

Frowning the doorman away, she opened the door herself. "Titus, I just want you to know that if you don't come back, if you decide that the other place is more to your liking than this one—wife, daughter, all that jazz—

well, we've got our sights on nephew Mateo. Coming up for the Standard Test in a few months, I believe. Sometimes the bureaucrats transcribe the scores inaccurately. Hate to see wasted potential, don't you?"

His smile faded, and he turned a new look on her. She didn't back up, though it might have been wise. "I guess there's another thing people didn't tell you," he said. "I'm an expert at rigging explosives. Lots of experience, dotty as hell, you never know what I might do. Better check your yard, Helice. And learn some manners."

She watched him leave with a mixture of resentment and envy. He was going alone, to her discovered land. She had not the slightest doubt that he would betray them all.

CHAPTER SIX

Lamar Gelde put his hand on the portal, eclipsing the star field outside. The Ceres Platform was an industrial environment, stripped down, devoid of proper windows. Perhaps that was for the best. It gave him an ominous feeling to see black space, to think of the pitiful tin can protecting him from the void. He didn't have the constitution of an explorer. By rights, at his age, he shouldn't even be here.

But Quinn had insisted he come along, and Minerva agreed, eager to keep the man happy while he waited here, hiding out until they were ready for him. Earth-side, agents of other companies had come sniffing around Minerva, sensing a kill. Minerva wanted no competing deals, no personnel raids. So Quinn had agreed to wait it out in the comparative isolation of the space platform. Not for long, they promised; they were almost ready.

The problem was, Quinn wasn't doing so hot, and the platform made it worse.

Quinn had stopped admitting to Lamar that he was having visitations from the past. The more he withdrew, though, the more Lamar guessed that he suffered from the return of his memories. The crew on the platform thought Quinn was odd, with his way of stopping in the middle of conversations and staring past a person's shoulder. Pretty soon the board would think Quinn *too* odd, and find another test subject. For Quinn's sake, Lamar didn't want that to happen. The man needed to go. But Minerva wasn't ready. The probes went through, never heard from again.

Helice emerged from the lab module where the probes were staged. "Damn, we lost it," she said.

"I have to talk to you," Lamar blurted out.

She drew off her disposable outer suit, now wearing one of those body suits that only the young could manage.

She led the way out of the science lab into the main corridor, bulky with cables and pipes, color-coded like an invasion of alien growths. The place was designed to be ugly, to remind the crew that they were in space, to force caution and attentive occupation. Things could go wrong. For Lamar, the point didn't need emphasis.

They settled into her suite: a ten-by-ten cubicle alive with data structures, more like living in a machine than a room.

"He's ready to go, Helice. We should send him. Now."

She poured herself a glass of purified water and sipped. "Can't. We lost the latest one."

"I think Quinn is willing to take the chance." He related the OBE events, and their effect on Quinn. He was obsessed. Anyone would be.

Helice shook her head. "It isn't just that we lost the *probe*. We lost the *place*." She nodded at him. "Right. We don't have a fix from here anymore."

"Then for Christ's sake let's find another one."

"Good idea, Lamar. I never thought of that."

Lamar would not want to be the one sitting next to Quinn during the trip home, everything canceled because the Minerva shrinks deemed Quinn unstable. The damn doctors had a distorted view of sanity. They wanted to see calm, patience, normalcy. Christ, if they'd wanted *that*, why had they picked Titus Quinn?

"His memories are coming back," Lamar said. "It's enormously stressful. Keeps him awake nights. It's time."

Helice took a swig of water and voiced the wall to show the latest probe launch.

On-screen came a small metal arm from which wires dangled, holding a small tube suspended below. Inside the tube, Lamar knew, were living nematodes. Best to practice on worms, first.

"What are the wires for?" Lamar asked.

"We have better luck if the specimen isn't touching anything."

The tube looked like it was melting. It slid sideways. Or perhaps it was backwards. It slithered. Elsewhere. It was gone. The wires didn't even stir.

Helice grimaced. "We lost it immediately."

"I'm no engineer, Helice, but maybe there isn't any interaction between there and here. Maybe readings aren't possible."

"Right. But sometimes we get a four-picosecond feedback from it. A picosecond is damned short, but we've taken that time interval as an indicator. Today, the probe vanished instantly. One moment we had a fix on the other place, getting a stream of particles, and by the time the sapient kicked the launch, the place vanished."

"Where did the probe go, then?"

Helice shrugged. "Vacuum space. Want that to happen to Quinn?"

Lamar sighed. In truth, it would be more humane than keeping him waiting like this. He said quietly, "If I ask him, I know what he'll say." He rose and paced in the small confines of the box. He couldn't make any demands. He wasn't on the board anymore.

"I agree we need to go soon. Before others stake their claims."

If others did, they'd have a jump on Minerva. They'd have a chance to break Minerva's monopoly on interstellar travel. The shortcut that was implied by Quinn's otherwise inexplicable appearance two years ago on a planet he couldn't have reached without a starship.

"You think the Companies are going to beat us to it?" Lamar asked.

"They're lagging behind, but who knows how far? After all, they had Luc Diers for a while."

The youngster who stumbled on the neutrinos. "He's just a grad student."

"Was. He died in a car accident last week."

A few moments of silence crept in. Lamar didn't want to know more.

Helice had the grace to avert her eyes. She murmured, "The firm that hired him is good. I know. They almost netted me." She appeared to contemplate that enormous loss for the competition. Then she said, "A few more tests, then we'll punch him through. Stake our claim."

"For Christ's sake, Helice, don't test it to death. Remember, he went there once, and he came back. Let him try again." From the expression on Helice's face, he thought he was losing the argument. "I always believed Quinn. I practically raised him, you know."

Helice said softly, "I believe him too. And not because of some soft fuzzy feeling."

Lamar would never have accused Helice of soft and fuzzy.

"It's because of this." She voiced, "Recording, Quinn."

From the silver wall came the sounds of a man babbling. The language was unfamiliar to Lamar. Lilting and glottal. The man was distressed, speaking rapidly. And then a familiar word emerged. *Sydney.*

Lamar froze. "My God. Is that Quinn speaking?" The voice continued, a rush of words, desperation, and, at times, anguish.

Helice lowered the volume. "Yes." She shifted uncomfortably under Lamar's stare. "Yes, the Company recorded his deliriums when they first found him."

"And never bothered to tell anyone."

"Stefan knew. The way I heard it, you were on your way out." She shrugged. "People knew. It's just that it didn't matter. Nobody could figure out whether this was a real language or delirium from a man who'd just seen his child die."

Lamar bit his cheek. They had known. They'd had proof . . . and they'd still treated Quinn like he was a dred, without the neurons that God gave a Dalmatian.

She stared at her glass of water. "We had our best linguists on it. We let the *sapients* at it. Nothing. It was gibberish."

"That's bullshit, Helice. Minerva just didn't try very hard."

Their eyes found each other, but she didn't waver. "Well, we're paying more attention now. We've cracked the grammar."

Closing his eyes, Lamar rubbed them. Stefan's sins were many, and frankly unforgivable. "Go on."

"He's saying, 'No. Oh my God, no. I'll kill you, come closer, I'll kill you.' Things like that. It's not in any family of languages we've ever seen. In fact, it's in a language that couldn't be Earth-based." She rolled the water in her mouth like excellent wine. "That's why I believe him."

Lamar's voice came in a whisper. "What else does he say?"

"He wails Sydney's name, and throws out phrases that we think are curses. He's in a rage."

But to Lamar's ears it sounded more like weeping.

She brought the volume up, and now it was clearly Quinn's voice, amid the sibilant consonants and deep-throated vowels. *Sydney*, came the moan.

"My God," Lamar said, listening to the despair in the man's voice. The recording deteriorated into a sustained sob, one so deep-seated that Lamar hung his head, touched to his core. He finally glanced up at Helice, who looked like she, too, had been affected. He asked, "How bad is this place?"

"It doesn't need to be nice. Just useful."

Lamar frowned "But he's got to make it back here."

"He will. I've chatted with him, and he's got resolve."

"Then we'll send him? No more delays?"

She smiled. "Tell him to pack. As soon as we get a new reading, we'll hang him from the wires."

Lamar swallowed, hard. The recording went on, relentlessly presenting Titus Quinn's bad dreams. The dreams to which Quinn so desperately hoped to return.

Be careful what you wish for, Lamar thought.

"Take a deep breath," the surgeon said. "What do you smell?"

He sat on the edge of the gurney, wearing a poly-paper gown, getting last instructions as he headed to the lab module and the harness.

"What do you smell?" Every time Quinn opened his mouth it hurt. And brought a flood of smells.

"Antisepsis, from that open vial on the table," Quinn replied. "Something acrid from the carpet." He shrugged, looking at the doc. "I can smell your skin."

"What else?"

Quinn opened his mouth a little wider, letting the air currents flow over the newly implanted Jacobson's organ in the roof of his mouth. "Something stinks over there," he said, turning to the counter.

"Be more specific."

Quinn closed his eyes, sniffing. "It's rotten. Mold."

The doc smiled, lifting a towel off a small dish of mold. "Good for you. But don't close your eyes. Learn to access your heightened sense of smell without shutting down other senses. It's there for you. But you have to trust it."

Trust the docs to modify him for survival in the other place. Trust them to have implanted the rebreather without screwing up his esophagus; trust them to give him the olfactory sense of a chimpanzee.

"Right," he said, trying to make nice to the people who could still ground him. The docs needed to clear him—despite the fact that he'd lived for *years* over there without any help breathing or help selecting food that wouldn't throw him into anaphylactic shock. The docs wanted to play, and Minerva wanted him to have every advantage, and Quinn wanted to get going, just get going. He'd waited two years, but these last few minutes stretched interminably.

The door opened, and Helice Maki sailed into the exam room, greeting him with a nod. It annoyed Quinn to have such a perky enemy. Five foot four inches tall and sporty-looking, except for the fangs. The youngster who ratcheted up the penalty for dying on the other side . . . moving past the threat to Rob and going for the kid. Well, he was coming back, by God, and Helice Maki might just live to wish he hadn't. The doc acknowledged Helice, then continued, "It won't be foolproof, but let your sense of smell guide you to high nutrient content, steer you away from toxins. If you can't smell the food, put it into your mouth and suck on it for a second or two. Puncture it if you have to. That should kick in the Jacobson's, if nothing else will. When you're revolted by the smell or taste, don't imbibe." The doc gestured for Quinn to open his mouth and peered in, lighting his way with a small wand. "In a way," he said, speaking with the leisure of a dentist having a long conversation with someone whose mouth is stuffed with gauze, "in a way, we're going backward to go forward. Adopting our primate cousin's ability to forage through the chemical minefield of the plant world. Minerva doesn't want any tech on this mission, so you've got to make do with naked flesh."

"Eggsept iss all upgrazes," Quinn gargled.

Helice said, "Yes, upgrades that look ordinary. We don't want to call attention to you, in case you need local cover. You've got to be your own nutritionist and pharmacist. We don't know how you got by before—maybe you won't need any of this. But considering all the things that might kill you, we can't have you starving to death or ingesting poisons."

The doc withdrew the probe from Quinn's mouth. "Even on Earth, lots of compounds can kill you. I assume where you're going will be as chemically charged. There'll be a lineup of alkaloids, phenolics, tannins, cyanogenic glycosides, and terpenoids—or their other-side equivalents. We're counting on your body's enhanced chemical knowledge to steer you to the edibles."

Other-side equivalents. Quinn knew there would be plenty of those, and not just plant compounds, either.

Anticipation had kept him awake for the past two nights, though he *might* have slept, dreaming that he couldn't sleep. It was all mixed up now: OBEs, sleep, memories, projections, fantasies. Now the hour had come, and he'd get the reality. Oddly, he was calm as a statue, whether from exhaustion or a state of grace, facing death, facing the *other place*, which could be the kingdom of God, after all. If Quinn were religious—as Johanna had been—now would be a good time for a prayer. But he was hopeless when it came to religion. What was the point, when life was all you wanted? He'd asked Johanna once why she went to Mass. It was all so illogical. She'd answered, "To be captured by it." She thought that answer enough, and offered no other. Everything she said was so deeply *her*. He was captured by her. So perhaps he did know why she went to mass.

"Okay," the doc said. "You're excused. Any questions?"

"Weapons."

Helice shook her head. "No. If you need them, your mission is over anyway."

Quinn looked into her perky face. So easy to be a pacifist when you're twenty.

He went to the next item on his list. "My pictures." They'd already told him no personal objects. "I want my pictures." Johanna and Sydney were fading. The pictures were important.

Helice bit her lip and glanced at the doc. *Is he stable, do you think?*

The doc patted his shoulder. "I think you remember what they look like."

Quinn looked at the hand, which was quickly withdrawn. He jumped down from the gurney.

They led him through a side door to the sterilizing booth, where he'd lose a few nanometers of skin by the time the sonic shower was done. Nearby he could smell Helice Maki, her underarm deodorant—flowery—and a faint whiff of breakfast still on her tongue. Other smells, woman-things. He didn't want to know what he was smelling. He didn't want Helice in his thoughts at this moment.

"Where's Lamar?" he asked.

"Right here," came the voice from a side chair. Lamar stood up, came over to say his good-byes.

"Private moment," Quinn said, eyeing Helice and the doc. They stepped aside.

Now Quinn faced Lamar, a face he knew, a man grown older than he remembered, seeming to age every week that passed. As of course, he was.

Lamar put out his hand, and Quinn shook it. The old man nodded, overcome.

"Your promise," Quinn said.

"On my honor."

The kids would suffer no harm. Could Lamar protect them? Was he any match for a twenty-year-old intent on controlling the world? He shuddered from the chill of the room.

"On your honor, then." Quinn peeled off the paper robe. He looked at the door to the sterilizing booth. "I feel like I'm going to be shot out of a cannon."

From the look of distress on Lamar's face, he thought so too.

Lamar pasted up a manly smile, trying to put a brave face on the fact that they were sending this man into the quantum foam without a clue where he'd be and when.

"Quinn," came Helice's voice. When he looked at her, she said, "Godspeed." She actually looked concerned for him. Hell, they all did.

Quinn walked into the booth naked, except for the photos taped to the soles of his feet.

The smell was pungent, earthy, heavy with ozone and antiseptics. The brew of chemicals revolted him, as the doc had said, meaning he should avoid this place.

Well, he knew that much. He was eager to be done with this side of reality.

Scoured and sore, he emerged into the main tube leading to the transition module, a modification to the space platform built for just this purpose. They called it interfacing; but he'd also heard the techs calling it *punching through.* In the access tube he was met by two paper-suited figures who escorted him toward the transition module, as though he might bolt at the last minute. A heavy door parted before them, and they emerged into the module with its racks of electronics, cabling, and wires surrounding a small platform where an empty harness hung suspended.

It was all, at this point, unreal, with his senses hideously alert, and his mind damped down. It might have been lack of sleep, or some unguessed-at depth of terror. He found himself wondering if the pictures had survived the sonic cleansing. He wanted to have a profound thought or two, but instead he was blank and numb.

They helped him into a simple costume of plain woven wool: loose trousers and a fitted shirt. He drew on socks and boots, careful to avoid crinkling noises from the pictures. Then he stepped onto the platform, where an attendant helped him thread his arms through the sleeves of the harness, high on his shoulder, for the brief suspension. The attendants left the module. Now they would wait for a lock on that place, that place that shifted, constantly shifted. The very act of finding it tended to push it away. So when the sapient pierced it to three hundred nanometers, they would instantly lock on, and throw the power on, send him into a state frighteningly called *decoherence*.

He waited. It was cold. They would hoist him two seconds before launch. Already his arms were taut, held up at an uncomfortable angle. It was so cold in there. Mercifully they weren't talking to him over the audio.

So quiet. He waited. Licked his lips. Dry mouth.

He stood spread-eagled, a sacrificial lamb, a sacrificial man.

He began to worry that they had already thrown the switch and he would be lost forever in this harness, waiting for the world.

Then it came.

The hoist lifted. The cannon shot.

But silently. No noise, but the *smell*. He was in a world of olfactory nonsense. Things he had no name for. The smell of the world dissolving, the smell of the quark-filled universe. He saw his own arm hanging out at his side. Saw the pulse of blood through an artery. He followed the movement of blood, traversing his upper arm with the stately pace of a glacier. At this rate, the blood would never make it back for reoxygenation in time to . . .

He couldn't remember what blood was for.

His arms were gone. *Uh-oh. Floating ahead of the rest of him.* He hoped that didn't mean a screw-up. He looked through the harness, and his torso was drifting suspended, armless, through the corridors of the Ceres Platform. Picking up speed, coming to the end of the corridor, an impossibly long corridor, where the wall up ahead was about to have a very personal interaction with his face.

Tearing through the wall, past the foam of insulation, data structures, carbon nano hull. Waiting to explode in vacuum space. Looking back at the hole in the space platform, people frozen in midstride. Better close the hole, he thought. He saw people changing positions. They weren't frozen, they were just moving so *slowly*. It made him sick, watching how slowly they moved, when his life was speeding faster and faster. He turned around, to look where he was going.

Ahead was vast, black, capturing space. He submitted himself to it.

The universe rewarded him by knocking him senseless.

PART II

HOLD UP THE BRIGHT

CHAPTER SEVEN

WEN AN WAS OLD, past the age when she expected to see miracles, or even the unexpected. A life of 50,000 days ensured that you had seen most everything at least twice. But looking into the eyes of the stranger, she knew that an old woman had just been given the gift of surprise. Of course, it might be a fatal one.

Now, as she led the beku down the valley, the stranger lay on the palanquin, still delirious. His head injury would heal, but he would not last long once they reached the village. So she must decide whether to cast him to his fate, or protect him. God not looking at me, she thought crossly. I haven't asked to be surprised; I've never hoped to make high decisions, nor ever looked to be garroted by a bright lord.

All of these things appeared likely to happen, because of the appearance on her doorstop of an out-of-place man.

She'd found him during her walk, shortly after rising. The stranger lay at the foot of a rock outcropping, as though he had fallen from its height, though why a man should climb a rock in the far reach of a dusty minoral was incomprehensible. Lugging him by beku to her outpost, she had cleaned his head wound, attempting to analyze it for infection, but the stone well could make nothing of his blood sample. When his eyes fluttered open for a moment, she understood why.

Blue eyes. After sitting a moment digesting this discovery, she leaned forward and picked up his left eyelid to confirm the impossible. Yes, blue.

It was no absolute proof that he was from the Rose. But combined with the odd clothes she drew a scholar's conclusion. All these years of peering through the veil at the Rose, eking out the merest snips of knowledge, and now she had a Rose specimen lying in her bed. The implications for scholarship staggered her. However, by bond law, her life was forfeit unless she turned him in. So much for scholarship.

"Heaven give us few surprises," she muttered now as she led the beku by a rope. How had the man made the crossing? And why? He'd come with no army of invasion, nor in any brightship, to penetrate the great wall. The man groaned now and then, and the beku's ears twitched as though the beast wasn't used to moans in that strange tongue. She thought he spoke English, but she couldn't be sure, her Rose studies having focused on Mandarin, Cantonese, and Latin.

In the purse tied to her belt were the lenses she'd made for his eyes. She'd worked through the ebb forming them in case she decided to save his life. Now she must decide whether to give him to the lords or exploit his knowledge. Better, far better than squinting at the Rose universe through the veil, now she might ask this man directly, *What is your world? How does it work? How do you live?* Many scholars wished to know these things, and were allowed to study them, provided no one of the Rose ever guessed they were being looked at. This was the immutable vow of the realm: to hide, always hide, from the Rose. Some disagreed. Some wanted converse with the Rose, even a few of her own Chalin people. Wen An's position had long been that the worlds should have discourse and learn from each other. Until now, she'd assumed she would have her grave flag before that ever happened. It was well to stay far from politics. And treason.

If she was caught, the eye lenses she'd made would condemn her to lie at the feet of the bright lords. It wasn't too late to cast them away, to be innocent of breaking the vows. Yes, perhaps she should do that. She was too old to embark on new scholarship, to become an important personage. She was a minor scholar, of course; why else would she be stuck at this piddling, dusty reach, working alone and without decent help? She'd grown used to her routines, with her Rose gleanings filling a redstone every day, or every arc at the least. Why strive at her age? On the other hand, she might live to reach 100,000 days, and that meant she was only in the middling years of her life. Hadn't Master Yulin's wife Caiji just died at exactly 100,000 days? Yes, there was still time for important work. She glanced back at the unconscious man.

But the fool spoke English, so again, this opportunity was not for her. It was a relief to decide this. Let those who wanted God's notice strive for importance. She would give the stranger up and have done with it.

Who to give him to, though—the lords or Master Yulin? Yes, Yulin might take it amiss for her to deal directly with the bright lords. She had family ties to Yulin's household; there was that as well. Yulin's oldest wife Suzong was Wen An's distant cousin. She knew enough of that exalted lady to suspect that Suzong did not love the Tarig, so let her grapple with the problem. People in high places had high responsibilities, and those in low didn't. She liked the justice of it. There's an end to it then: Let the man go to the Tarig, through the hands of Yulin, and leave her in peace.

Her feet hurt, treading on the rocky minoral floor. She sighed, feeling cowardly and also cross for having to walk six hours with the breath of a beku on her neck.

She turned to see the man stirring on the riding platform. A shame to have saved his life only to see the Tarig take it from him again. Or perhaps as with that other Rose visitor, the bright lords would keep him in a cage for their amusement, or so the story went, that a man of the Rose had been spared for the sake of the bright lady Chiron, who found him a source of amusement—though, of course, the Tarig didn't laugh.

As the Heart of Day cast its fiery heat over the trail, Wen An plodded onward, looking for a good resting spot now that the man was stirring.

Lying blind, his head riddled with pain, Quinn probed his surroundings with his sense of smell. A complex, pollen-filled breeze, tangy and fragrant; an organic musk of an animal. Underneath all other smells lay the memory-laden scent of cloves.

He hovered on the edge of consciousness, clinging to a hard platform that rocked under the swaying plod of some beast of transport. The smells of the beast staggered him. Hundreds, maybe thousands of compounds, churning, churning.

Under an impossible sky.

He rode in an open-sided tent. Sprawled against a hard backrest, he lay staring at a woven cloth sparkling here and there with defects through which the day needled at his eyes. They had stopped.

A woman peered in at him, old and strangely dressed. She spoke to him in a jumble of sounds, then handed him a cup of what smelled like water. He leaned on his side to slake his thirst, and this brought him closer to the edge of the overhead canopy. Gaping at the sight of the sky, he dropped the cup, drawing a blameful stare from the woman. She left, and his view widened.

The sky was on fire. High, stratified clouds boiled in a blue-white fire. It seemed as though it should blind him, but after the initial shock, he realized the fire was both gentle and bright. Why didn't the woman look up and remark on the clouds being on fire? But even as he thought the question, he knew the answer.

Because it was always like this: the sky, on fire.

It wasn't until that moment, as his transport beast crouched on the ground, and as the woman brought him another cup of water, that he was certain he was back. "Back," he croaked, using his voice for the first time. His eyes watered, perhaps from too much sky-gazing, and a longing welled up in him. To see Sydney once again. To bring her and her mother home. If they were here, that thin hope that had become thick with repetition.

The woman narrowed her eyes, watching him drink.

He slept. When he woke, they were on the march again. The woman led a beast, massive in the shoulders and head, through a gilded landscape of yellows and brownish golds. When he scratched a wound on his temple, bits of dried blood flecked onto his hand. Punching through had been a rough journey—either that or he'd landed badly.

His guide saw him stir but, with little more than a backward glance, continued in front, holding the beast's lead. Her cloak, frosted with the gloaming light above, fluttered in a stiff, warm breeze. On either side, low desert hills hunched up, confining their path to a narrow track.

He was in a new land. He was *back*. There would be time enough to make sense of the fiery sky, and whether he had a friend or foe walking ahead of him. It was curious that the woman was human. How could there be humans here, in this place of strange grasses and alien beasts? Once he had known the answer. With this question began the great struggle that would engage him for the rest of his days: wrestling with his mind, with his soul, for what he'd known and what he had been. Before.

In time the beast stopped, and in a convoluted process of collapse, settled onto its knees. With some difficulty, Quinn dismounted and regarded the creature.

The animal munched on grass, reaching the clumps from its great height by virtue of a long but powerfully built neck. Topping the massive, scoop-jawed head was a small cranium and dainty ears. The four long, meaty legs ended in the broad-hooved pads of its feet. Coarse hairs on its hide sheltered small critters catching a free ride, or a free meal.

The woman rummaged in one of the animal's saddlebags. Presently she presented a few tidbits of food on a cloth, but they smelled inadvisable. Of more interest was the woman herself, her white eyebrows and golden eyes giving her an albino appearance. She wore Asian-style pants and a short jacket, silken and sturdy. Around her neck was a string of red, irregular stones. On her head she wore a wrap of silken cloth that slightly overhung her eyes, protecting them from the sun. From the sky-bright. He called it that, for lack of a better word.

From her packs the woman retrieved a new food offering. This was a kind of cereal that she mixed into a cup of water. He took the proffered cup, liking its smell already. Gulping it down, he held out the cup for more. She refilled it, smiling. He knew the word that was called for.

"Nahil," he found himself saying. *Thank you.*

At this, the woman froze. Her lips parted to say something, then closed as she stared at him.

He had just revealed that he spoke at least a little of her language.

Finally she uttered a short phrase, a mash of words anchored by heavy glottals.

He didn't understand. The language lay buried inside him. Yet he'd said *nahil.*

His utterance had staggered her. She walked away, gazing down the valley, standing immobile for a long while.

Had he just made a drastic mistake? What a fool he was, to reveal something so important. But couldn't he be a stranger from another nation, who knew only limited words in her language? He waited, letting her make the next move.

Coming back, she looked up into his eyes and said something in her language.

He shook his head. *I don't understand.*

She squinted her eyes at him, perhaps disbelieving him, that he knew a word of her language, but not others. But why was this so disturbing?

Then it became clear. If he hadn't been so addled, he would have known instantly: She had known from the beginning that he wasn't of this world; and when he said thank you, she knew he'd been here before. Evidently this was not good news.

She turned away, then sat on a rock, staring at the dust. From time to time she glanced up irritably at him, muttering.

This woman had saved his life. Where would he have found water in this barren place? But where was she taking him? He was not ready to face others in this state: weak, disoriented, confused. And now he appeared to be a less-than-welcome guest. If he could just *remember*. Whatever had transpired the last time he was here, it was an unclaimed territory: deep inside of him yet out of reach.

At last the woman rose and, coming close, scrutinized his face. She nodded, pursing her lips, as though she'd just swallowed something distasteful. She turned to the pack beast and retrieved a length of cloth. By her gestures, he realized she wanted to drape his head. He kneeled as she wound the cloth and tucked it in.

This accomplished, she brought out a small box, opening it to reveal a remarkable thing: two small golden lenses. With gestures she showed him how to wear them.

He hesitated to put them on.

Her mouth formed a sneer of impatience. She gripped her neck and made a choking gesture. Evidently there was danger in being blue-eyed. He had little choice but to trust her, and he knelt down to cradle the box and insert the lenses into his eyes. Annoyingly, his vision clouded, but he was not uncomfortable.

The woman nodded with satisfaction. "Nahil," she said.

He decided to trust her for now. She had revealed that he was in danger, and that she would help him. Even so little information was priceless.

They set out again, his guide insisting that he ride. Quinn felt a new energy, even an exultation. His strength was returning. He had survived. So far, he had survived.

At length they and their pack beast emerged from the narrow valley down which they had been traveling for hours. Before them lay a sight that both thrilled and sobered him: a colossal plain, relentlessly flat. Spanning it all, the heavens sparkled, forming an endless bright cloud to the limits of vision. In the sky's soft folds he perceived just the slightest dimming into lavender.

As they descended onto the plains, he saw that at the edge of the flatlands was a towering wall of blue-black that stretched to the limit of sight. The valley they had just come down—perhaps five miles wide—pierced that wall like a tributary. They had been in a minor valley. Now they were in the heart of things.

The wall was a dark escarpment, appearing to form the boundary of the world itself. At an awful height, it bore down on them, bringing a feeling of chaos restrained. It raced toward them over the dry mud pans. . . . But even as his eyes told him this, he knew the wall didn't move.

Later. He would understand it later.

Several people with pack beasts passed them on their route. The road was little more than a dusty track. If they knew how to make eye lenses, he thought it strange they used no mechanized transport.

One man turned around to take a second look at Quinn, but otherwise he did not draw attention. His skin was slightly darker than most others here, but there were variations in skin tone, and he thought he might pass as long as he didn't have to speak.

The clouds overhead were cooling toward a time that might be dusk. It seemed that the day had been many hours too long already, yet still the sky-bright churned. They were approaching an inhabited place.

They came upon a corral of pack beasts like his own. Beyond this, a dusty but clean settlement—little more than three dozen or so huts, made of an irregular, molded material of an indescribable color somewhere between black and gold.

The people here conveyed an impression of lean physicality, precise of movement with little wasted on gestures. He would have said fighters, though he saw no arms. By their behavior they appeared more like traders—ones who knew a fair price and meant to fetch it. He had difficulty distinguishing men from women at a casual glance, for their dress had no obvious gender markers.

Into one of the huts his companion went barefoot; when she emerged, she presented him with a quilted jacket to go over his shirt. Peering into the doorway, Quinn saw goods laid out. Cottage industry.

His guide glanced ahead, and her face took on a look of alarm. In their path was a small crowd. This seemed to confound his guide, who looked to the left and right for a way to pass. But the line of huts funneled them toward the gathering, and it would draw attention to pause. As they moved closer, they heard voices raised.

They moved closer. In the midst of the small crowd lay a man, garroted. A device of sticks and wire was wound around his neck, and he was dragging air in between swollen lips. His hands bled as he pulled on the wires, to no avail.

Astride him, standing perhaps seven feet tall, was an extraordinary creature.

Thin, almost impossibly elongated, the being wore a long, narrow skirt, sleeveless tunic, and elaborately silvered vest. His powerful muscles declared his gender, when otherwise he might be mistaken for female. His face was deeply sculpted, and his lips, sensual and fine.

Quinn locked in on that face. It was the one on his door knocker. He felt the shock hit deep, into his bones. Here, beyond doubt, was the thing he must hide from.

Every aspect of this creature—his stature, bearing, and motions—was oddly beautiful. Beside him, the villagers looked fleshy and sordid. The creature's skin was a deep bronze, darker by far than any of those who stood staring at the victim, one of their own. The executioner straightened from his task and skimmed the crowd with his eyes, stopping for a moment on Quinn.

The creature held him under a dark gaze. Quinn fought for standing, wrestled for control, until the gaze dismissed him. To such a being, Quinn was not interesting.

Then the creature strode off, with a grace of movement unlikely in one so tall. The crowd parted for him swiftly, but no one would meet the creature's eyes. As the crowd dispersed, Quinn watched for the figure, but it had disappeared.

A tugging at his arm got Quinn moving again, despite a sense that he had just been given a clue to some profound puzzle.

They went past the strangling victim, who lay, one knee raised up, hands clutching at his throat, staring at the sky-bright. Those watching him lost interest, leaving him in his agony.

This vision clung to Quinn. Then the woman was leading him off to the side, down an alley with wagon ruts carved in the golden soil. He followed her, feeling drained by the day's irreconcilable images. He held the pack beast's reins as his companion made yet another house call. This time, though, she came back outside and motioned him to enter.

One look at the four men inside, and Quinn knew they were lying in wait for him. He landed the first blow, sending one of them crashing. The hut was small, and he was confined amid the three remaining men and the woman, all of whom rushed him. Filled with a savage will to escape, he spun around, lashing out again and again. He jabbed backward with an elbow and connected with flesh, but as he swung around to complete the assault, his stomach met a fist even larger than his own. The man looked surprised when Quinn managed a knee to his groin. But then Quinn was down on one knee, and they had his arms behind his back.

Looking up from the floor where they were securing ropes around his wrists, he gazed into the eyes of the woman who'd saved him from the desert. She slowly unwound her head scarf, then pulled her hands through her hair in a casual gesture of one home from a trying journey. Her hair was startlingly white.

They had been traveling for many days. Gagged and bound, Quinn was imprisoned in a tall jar with breathing holes at the top. His kicks could not shatter it. With no vision of the outside world, he couldn't gauge the passing of days, and slept between bouts of shouting for release. All ignored.

The jar was bad, but he could bide his time. They hadn't killed him, nor delivered him to the bronze creature. They had taken his boots and his pictures. At intervals they let him out to take food and walk and relieve himself, under guard. So he was not dead yet.

Sometimes he fell to thinking that he had gone mad at last. That this impossible world was his final refuge from sanity. He had seen unearthly creatures, and an unearthly sky. The black wall that rose like a tidal wave. Yet it was a consistent madness; and in his better moments he knew just where he was.

On his brief reprieves from the jar, he found never-ending desert—all hard yellow soil, without landmark or habitation. No trees grew on these plains, increasing its look of blasted flatness. Once, he saw a few round shapes floating in the sky. With no way to judge distance he couldn't tell if they were large or small. Dirigibles, he guessed. He listened to every word the guards spoke. The sounds of some words were familiar, and now and then a bit of meaning coalesced and shredded under his scrutiny.

When his captors tried to put him back in the jar, he fought them, even weak as he was from inactivity. Since they avoided hitting him, he presumed that they wanted to keep him healthy. He held on to this thread of hope—that they were permitting him to live—for all the reasons that he had to live: for Sydney, here, and for Mateo, there. Both in jeopardy because of Titus Quinn.

For a time he was sure that he was traveling on a train, or at least some kind of rolling transport. He tried learning about his captors and his surroundings by smell. He had taken to standing in a half crouch, with his fingers gripped through the holes in the top of the jar. There, the air was freshened, laden with scents other than his own. He let the air flow over his tongue, under the roof of his mouth. As he concentrated on the smells, an odd thing began to happen. Wisps of memory came riding on the smells. Faces of people, structures. Emotions, not all of them bad.

They let him out for a meal. The train was gone, nor were there tracks or any evidence for the conveyance. The journey continued in a cart pulled by two beasts such as he had seen before.

Not once in all his out-of-jar intervals did he ever witness night. The sky, he remembered, never ceased, and it never dimmed except to a twilight. Effortlessly, the word sailed into his consciousness. *Bright.* The river of the sky was called the bright.

The jar began to crack open. A fork of light blasted into Quinn's eyes as the jar parted slowly, pulling strands of viscous material with it. The two halves fell of their own weight, and he saw that he was in a forest: dim but, compared to the jar, gloriously brilliant. Animal screams and twitters and the musk of organics assaulted him.

A man stood before him, his white hair pulled into a topknot. Combined with his quilted clothing, he looked like a Chinese nobleman. From long ago.

He led Quinn a short distance to the shore of a small lake, perhaps three hundred yards across. Hugging its shore and screening further views, graceful trees and shrubs formed a tidy collar. Across the lake, Quinn could just make out the top of a grand edifice, its masonry sparkling under the furnace glare of the bright.

The Chinese-dressed man picked at an edge of Quinn's clothing, wrinkling his nose.

Quinn bathed in the lake. And the glory of it made him laugh. When he emerged, he received quilted pants, a cropped jacket, and soled slippers. He dressed, and when he put his feet into the shoes, they enlarged, molding to his feet. The technology of this place confused him, with its mixture of backward and advanced.

Around him the lush garden crowded his senses, smelling of moist soil, complex organics, and mildew-laden spores. In a tumult of growths, an upper story soared with spindly gold and cinnamon-colored fronds; crouching beneath, an understory of black, thick-leafed shrubs. Animal whoops and chitters announced other dwellers. Quinn ignored all this for now, concentrating instead on his visitor: young and fit and rich.

The young man led Quinn into a hut, where he gestured for Quinn to sit on a bench and offered a cup of water for Quinn to drink.

He drank, gratefully, but his attention drifted to a cylinder on the floor of the hut from which came the aroma of edibles.

The man noticed his glance. He fetched the cylinder, a stack of three round boxes. In each were different types of what might be dumplings. The man watched closely as Quinn brought each one to his nose and inhaled. Although thrown off by the many acrid odors of the jungle, he made some judgments about the food. He ate everything in the first two boxes, leaving the last untouched.

Then the young man spoke. In Chinese, Quinn guessed. *Chinese.* Quinn was certain the influence here was Chinese, although there was no epicanthic fold near the eyes, and the skin tones were too pale.

Quinn shook his head. *I don't understand.*

"We shall try this language next," his jailer said, in deeply accent English.

Stunned, Quinn nodded his understanding. The man's utterance was even more preposterous than the Chinese version. Why would these people speak such languages? "Where am I?" Quinn asked. "What is this place?"

"Master Yulin's palace garden," came the answer.

"Who is Master Yulin? And who are you?"

"I'm of no importance. But my name is Sen Tai." He looked more closely at Quinn, frowning. "You hide your eyes. Why?"

He was referring to the lenses. "I don't know," Quinn said truthfully. "A woman gave them to me, then forced me to go with the bandits who put me in a jar."

A smile hovered at the edge of Sen Tai's mouth. "They weren't bandits. Take the coverings out."

Quinn bent over his hand and popped the lenses out, relieved to be done with them. He wiped a wash of tears away as his eyes adjusted. When he looked up, Sen Tai was staring at him.

"Who is Master Yulin?" Quinn repeated.

"He is master of this sway, of this garden, and of your life."

"I have a message for Master Yulin. I will convey it only to him."

Sen Tai was very still. An animal screeched from some hidden place, as though laughing at Quinn's pretensions.

"I've come a long way to convey this message," Quinn said.

"It's not so far to Wen An's reach, where you fell."

"Farther than that."

Sen Tai nodded slowly. He stepped over to the hut wall, where a glossy rope lay coiled. He spoke into the end of the rope, using the language that Quinn should know, and didn't.

Then he turned and announced, "My lord will come to the lake, where we will meet him." He gestured to the door.

Master Yulin would come. Quinn hoped *the master of the sway* was not one of the bronze creatures he'd seen.

But he was out of the jar. Somehow, his stature had climbed. Would he still have stature when they discovered the truth? Quinn hoped so. The truth was his game plan.

Snugged up to the shore was a small raft, bare except for a pole, shackles, and a large block.

"I must bind you to these for the safety of my master," Sen Tai said apologetically. But the shackles were attached to a heavy block. Noting Quinn's glance, Sen Tai said, "He's very cautious."

"My own master will not be happy to think me so treated," Quinn said.

"Your master does not rule here, I think."

Quinn submitted, remembering the jar and how much worse his position might be.

As the young man poled him onto the lake, Quinn saw it was shallow, perhaps fifteen feet deep. As they glided to the middle of the lake, he got a clearer view of the garden. He spied cages here and there, from which wrong-looking animals peered at him. One cage was spacious, and held flying insects that formed chains of themselves, and dispersed again, as though spelling out answers for him in letters he had forgotten.

Across the lake a barge had set out.

As it approached, Quinn saw a rotund man poling it. Richly dressed, the man poled with an athletic grace. From his upper lip drooped a long white mustache. When he reached the lake's center, the master lifted his pole and plunged it into the lake bottom with a mighty downstroke. He held the pole, keeping his barge in place. Quinn's boatman did the same.

The man known as Master Yulin looked at Quinn with narrowed eyes.

Standing face-to-face, Yulin was by far the shorter of the two. He glanced at Quinn's boatman, speaking to him in their tongue.

Sen Tai said, "My master wishes you to answer three questions. Each one is worth your life."

Quinn was listening. In the back of his mind he understood that the conversation would be through an interpreter. But his eyes were only on the master. "Ask, then."

The master did, and the interpreter said, "Look at these pictures and tell who they are."

On the other barge, the man held in his fat fingers the pictures of Johanna and Sydney. The little squares were creased and smeared, but still, seeing them in this place filled Quinn with a bright spear of courage.

"They are my wife and daughter."

As this was translated, the master remained utterly still, his face taking on a golden glint from the water where the seething sky cast its image. A large carp roamed through the gilded water near Quinn's raft. The forest seemed to hold its breath.

Then, the second question: "What is your name?"

"Titus Quinn."

After a pause, came the third question: "Why can you not speak the Lucent tongue, if you are Titus Quinn?"

So he *did* know their language. He had been here long enough to speak this exotic tongue. "I think I can speak it. I've just forgotten." Beneath his feet, the platform rocked as he changed his stance. The chains chafed at his ankles.

The interpreter spoke softly, then, relaying the master's next words: "If you are truly he, then it would be far better for you to be at the bottom of this lake."

The master, still unmoving, gazed at Quinn with a baleful stare.

Taking advantage of this pause, Quinn delivered the speech he had composed over his long days of confinement in the jar. He turned to the interpreter. "Tell this to your lord: You can drown me, but my people will come. They will come and they will ask permission to travel here, traveling to distant places in our world, using your world to shorten our journeys. You can hope to control them, and they will pay you well. But you can't stop them."

The master stood, still holding his pole, as though it anchored him to the kingdom he was about to lose.

"What do you want?" came the question.

"My pictures back, for starters."

Yulin's full mouth compressed flat. Then he looked at Sen Tai for the first time.

From behind Quinn came the translation: "Kill him."

For an instant, Quinn thought Sen Tai was being told to kill him. But by Sen Tai's stricken look when Quinn turned around, this was not the case. After another exchange in their language, Sen Tai said in a whisper, "My master directs you to kill me."

Gazing at Yulin, Quinn said, "Kill him yourself."

After another order from Yulin, Sen Tai bent to unlock Quinn's shackles.

Then he bound them to his own ankles. Sen Tai dragged the block to the side of the raft, and Quinn stepped to the other side to keep the platform from tipping. The young man looked up into the sky for a few moments. Then he bent down and maneuvered the block so close to the edge that it almost toppled into the lake. Finally, it did topple, yanking him into the water, and into its depths.

Quinn looked in fury at Yulin. "Let me release him."

The master shook his head, saying no, no, to whatever Quinn was asking.

At the bottom of the shallow lake, Quinn could see the man's white topknot as he stood there, bubbles streaming up to the surface.

A rage settled into Quinn's chest, cold and heavy. Yulin was a barbarian, and a cruel one.

After satisfying himself that the bubbles had ceased, Yulin yanked his pole from the mud. Turning a lofty glance on his prisoner, he pointed in the direction of the hut, directing Quinn to remain there. Then he pushed his barge off in the direction of the opposite shore.

Quinn forced himself to look into the water. He had no way to release the chain, and now, in any case, it was too late. Why kill Sen Tai? He thought it was because the interpreter now knew who Quinn was, and that information was valuable or dangerous, or both.

Sickened, Quinn thrust the pole into the water, pushing the raft back the way he'd come. This was a violent world. In such a place, could Johanna and Sydney have survived long? A fierce protectiveness swept through him, especially for his daughter—only nine years old, for God's sakes. However old she was now, she had been a child among these barbarians.

Poling to the shore, he felt eyes on him as animals peered from the forest thickets, some in cages, some free. He knew which state described him. But at least he was not in the jar.

They would have to kill him to put him in another jar.

CHAPTER EIGHT

NOW THAT YULIN HAD DECIDED TO DROWN TITUS QUINN, he was at peace.

The death of a sentient must never be undertaken lightly, nor did the master of the sway easily require such deaths. The Tarig lords alone took life, and then only seldom. It was just and fair.

Sometimes justice came in the back door, of course.

"Uncle," came the girl's voice as she knelt in front of his dais.

He had almost forgotten about Anzi, trembling before him, face on the stone tiles, not daring to look at him.

Ignoring her, Yulin reviewed his decision with satisfaction.

Titus Quinn had come to him in a jar, the terrible gift of Wen An the scholar, who sought to transfer her bad fortune to him. May she fry in the bright, he thought. Thus, all unlooked-for, the man of the Rose was now living in his animal compound, and the sooner he stood at the bottom of the lake the better, the safer. Yulin took a dumpling from the tray and chewed it with pleasure. Yes, it was gratifying to have made the decision. The man had thrown him off course when he said that his people would come anyway. He congratulated himself on the shrewd insight that this alarming statement had nothing to do with his own predicament of playing host to the fugitive. Those who came next could never know the man's fate, or the identity of his executioner. Let them come. And may they arrive in some other sway and torment some other master.

Yulin arranged his robes to lie more loosely around his girth. They must all die. The man of the Rose, his village captors, the gardeners, and Wen An.

He had considered turning him over to Lord Hadenth, the lord Titus Quinn had so grievously injured. But suspicion would still fall on Yulin, even if he sent word immediately to the Ascendancy. The fiends would ask, why had Wen An sent the man here? And the answer lay groveling before Yulin: Ji Anzi, his worthless niece.

As though divining his thoughts, Anzi spoke again. "Uncle of my deliverance? May I speak?"

"No."

Yulin looked down at the portraits lying in his lap. The wife. The daughter. Their fates were unfortunate, irrevocable. In the cause of his wife and child, the man of the Rose would make no end of trouble, even if the lords never found him. Yulin had heard about human attachments, and the chaos brought by a surfeit of emotion. Such as Titus Quinn so amply displayed his first sojourn here. No. The lake for this man. Sen Tai would perhaps be glad of company.

Picking at his gums with an ivory toothpick, Yulin thought that his favorite wife Suzong would be pleased with his resolve. Yulin sighed, staring out the window that faced his garden. Soon, he could stroll alone in his sanctuary, where now the despicable stranger stalked the grounds. There he could once again enjoy his collection of exotic animals, free from his wives' complaints and his subjects' demands.

Ji Anzi coughed softly, forcing Yulin's thoughts back to the present, and the question of whether or not to endure her protestations. He had sent for her, thinking she might aid his deliberations, but in the event, she had not been needed.

"Rise, then, Niece. I am finished with you."

She stood, smoothing her jacket, looking properly deferential, and yet flushed with excitement. Best to quash her schemes before she could launch them.

"He is not welcome, Niece." He locked a gaze on her so that she would know his intention. "It shall not be."

Yulin nodded, feeling a moment's pity. "Go now, and find occupation for your energies." He added, "Somewhere far from here." He liked her well enough, but she brought misfortune, as even his late wife Caiji had admitted.

"And the others who have seen him come here?"

"They shall not be welcome, either."

Her face reflected her inner strife, but to her credit, she held silent. Then she blurted: "But Wen An is your wife's cousin."

"Even so."

"A shame to kill Suzong's cousin for no reason." Her next words came in a rush. "Wen An is utterly loyal to you. She spends all her days in a minoral no one has ever heard of, and travels only by beku. She will die with her mouth shut, yes, Uncle."

Perhaps she was right, that Wen An might be spared. . . .

Her voice needled at him: "And Suzong loves her so."

His voice rose. "Do you decide when my orders are obeyed and when they are not?"

She fell to her knees, speaking into the floor once more. "No, Uncle of my deliverance." He pulled at his mustache, thinking how she had brought disquiet and uncertainty to a day that had begun so well. Her voice was barely a whisper. "But such a waste, to kill Titus Quinn."

"Eh?" What was this, a plea for the breaker of vows as well? He'd already given his ruling: They all die. Except, perhaps Wen An. Wife's cousin. Cause no end of trouble.

Her voice hovered like a swarm of gnats. "And Titus Quinn?"

He glanced around the audience chamber—private enough, but not impervious to spies: "His name, until I drown him, shall be Dai Shen. Never speak his Rose name again."

"Yes, One Who Shines."

This whole situation was her fault, if one went back far enough to find first causes. But he had long ago forgiven her. That is, until this man of the Rose had returned to haunt them.

Still, he took pity on her distress. "Rise, Anzi. You are in disfavor, but you may stand if you behave."

As she rose, she met his eyes, and he saw that in the many days since he'd last seen her she had become a strong young woman, no longer gawky and too tall. Well, perhaps taller than a short man could wish, but her face was fine enough. Perhaps Suzong should be thinking of a suitable first husband for the girl. . . .

"This man—Dai Shen," Anzi was saying. "Perhaps we might yet wring advantage from him, learn from him. Learn what the Rose intends, now that they will come."

Yes, a husband for the girl, and then a child. Either that or send her to the Long War, where she would learn the value of life, instead of living spoiled and demanding, as he had taught her to be. After her parents had died, she had been just another brat around the palace, but one he'd liked, and it was his own fault how she'd turned out.

She was still prattling on. "Everything will change, Uncle. The people of the Rose know us now. They will come here, as he has said. In your lifetime, you will see them come. Since many things will change, might you advance because of it? Better to plan than to be caught unawares." She bowed quickly at his glare.

He murmured, "Well, I can kill him and then plan what to do when the rest come." Why was he bothering to argue with her? She was a minor niece, and not in his counsels. This was a matter of high state that threatened his rule, his family, and his sway. Why argue with a girl who was so unlucky and of so little consequence?

Her voice became soothing and less confrontational. "Yes, you might want to kill him, eventually. But not until he's told you all he knows. Uncle, think of what he knows! You can gauge what the Rose will do, and plan with extreme delicacy how best to prosper."

Waving her words away, he shook his head. Too dangerous.

Her face betrayed her misery. "I beg you, Uncle."

He surged to his feet, upsetting the tray of dumplings, sending it clattering to the floor. "You dare to beg?"

She fell to the floor, burying her head.

He stormed toward her. "You dare to push me thus? To presume on my favor, after I have forgiven and protected you?" He looked down on her abject form, his face hot with rage, that she could be so base as to beg him.

Because of you, he thought, we almost died at the feet of the bright lords, that day now long past. Yet I hid you, protected you, and in a thousand days peace returned, and the Tarig were no wiser. And then the man of the Rose tried to kill a lord, and the nightmare began again. The lives of my family trembled on the tip of a branch, like a drop of water ready to fall with a nudge. And then it all passed, and life returned. Until now. May God look at Wen An and curse her.

He stared down at Anzi, the dumplings in his gut turning to stone. He took a calming breath. Many things, he thought, are this worthless niece's fault. But not Titus Quinn's return. To be fair, that's not her fault. And she gives good counsel about exploiting future events. Who does the man of the Rose serve, and what do his masters intend? I'd like to know the answers. I can always kill the man later.

"Sorry, so sorry, Uncle. Forgive me." She huddled, still shrinking from his anger.

"If," he began, "*if* I spare him for a few days, and we learn from him, I still doubt that I will welcome him in my sway."

Even in his private chambers, he preferred not to use the words *kill*, *murder*, *drown*.

"Yes, Uncle. Just a few days, then decide. Very wise."

He snorted. Craven flattery.

Turning her head, she looked at him from her crouch.

"Rise," he said, weary of her, and less peaceful of mind now than before.

When she stood before him and raised her face to look at him, he saw her happiness, and it struck him with some force how temporary that state was likely to be. But in a long life, he noted philosophically, pain was no more than a ripple of water under a passing breeze.

"Anzi," he said, "you speak the dark languages. I have in mind to assign you to bring forth Dai Shen's memories of how to speak proper Lucent. Why he has forgotten, we do not know. But you will teach him again."

"Yes, Uncle of my deliverance." In her eyes he saw the veneration. One day soon it would be sorrow, when the day came that Dai Shen joined Sen Tai at the bottom of the lake. That was the problem with Ji Anzi. She was too easily impressed, too susceptible to kindness.

The sooner she learned to be cruel, the happier she would be.

Quinn had exchanged the prison of the jar for the prison of the garden. He could, with difficulty, climb the smooth compound walls, but an impenetrable, invisible barrier at the top thwarted attempts to pass over.

He paced, longing to be away from here rather than wait for the one called Yulin to decide his fate. The vision of Sen Tai standing on the bottom of the lake haunted him, for its useless cruelty. It was better, the fat lord had said, for Titus Quinn to be dead than to have come back. He was unwelcome, and in danger. He'd gleaned as much from the old woman with the pack beast. He had a history here, and a bad one. Had it saved his life so far or jeopardized it?

He had been in this world nine days. Perhaps that interval was not nine days on Earth, nor even one day. But what *was* the relation of time between this place and home? Einstein had proven time was malleable. Did time pass at a different speed here? And was that relative speed constant? He might guess that fewer hours had passed on Earth in his absence. But wasn't it actually as likely that the progression of time was unpredictable—just as the location of the Entire was uncertain, shifting in Minerva's sensors? Whatever the relation between home and here, he hoped that Helice Maki had not had enough time as yet to set her gun sights on young Mateo.

The sky waxed and ebbed, disorienting him. Night and day were no such thing here. In an approximation of night, the sky cooled to bluish gray, ushering in a twilight of several hours. Then the sky burned white again. These were his nights and days. While Quinn slept, someone left food in stacked baskets outside his hut. He saw no one except the gardeners, who avoided him.

During the day he roamed the garden, examining the profusion of plants and Yulin's collection of animals. The smells were a thick soup, rich and jumbled, augmented by the sharp scents of dung. The animals paced in their pens, fluttering petaled flanks or tossing heads crowned with elaborate horns. For all their alien aspect, they were side-by-side with Earth animals: pandas and a pair of tigers. He kept casting about for theories to explain what he saw. The Chinese, he thought, had come here long ago, as had beings from other worlds. The world was a collection, perhaps, as this zoological garden was.

On the sixth day of his sojourn in Yulin's garden, he paced restlessly in a remote corner of the garden, coming unexpectedly on a gardener feeding a long-necked biped through the bars of its cage. The gardener, young and with a malformed hip, looked at Quinn in alarm and, dropping his pail of slops, fled into a dense stand of trees.

"Excuse me," Quinn said. And then louder, after the man's retreating form, "Come back." Using English, so it was useless. He'd grown tired of the isolation and wondered if the man might speak with him, might know Earth languages as others here did. But the gardeners acted afraid of him, so it was no use to try and engage them. Wearily, he continued his rounds of the walled park.

The screams of the animals in nearby cages set up a furor from deeper in the garden. Feeding time always created tension in the cages, and now the beasts seemed to sense that their meal would be late.

But these matters were far from the mind of the animal steward as he hurried to put distance between himself and the patient.

Chizu's loping gate compensated for his short right leg, and carried him swiftly if not gracefully. Hiding from the patient was Chizu's only thought. He had been foolish to let the man sneak up on him, so to endanger his position as animal steward of the second rank. Chizu's wage would hardly support a godder much less a demanding wife and hungry baby, but his side income as the eyes and ears of Preconsul Zai Gan, Yulin's brother and enemy, was sufficient to make him a most careful follower of Yulin's rules. The rules being, do not disturb patient, do not speak with patient, do not show yourself to patient except at a distance.

Chizu was so distressed at the near encounter that he voided his bladder right at the base of a sangwan tree, one of Yulin's favorites. He directed the stream up the fuzzy bark for good measure, pretending it was Yulin's hairy chest. One last pulse from his faucet for good measure, the old bastard.

Calm now, Chizu tried to absorb the startling new discovery: that the patient spoke a strange language. If the man were a scholar, dark languages could be at his command; but the man—Dai Shen his name was—was a soldier of Ahnenhoon, a remote son of Yulin by a mistress of another sway. Well, the Long War had delivered this Dai Shen of a head wound, stealing his ability to speak and remember who he was, and in his goodness Yulin had brought him here to speed his healing, for which he needed happy peace and no disturbing or clanking of food pails. But if the man was a scholar—speaking dark languages, after all!—then why put out the story that he was a soldier? For whatever the fat master wished to hide, that was a matter of interest to the fat master's brother.

True enough, if the patient were addled, he might babble outrageous words. But in truth he didn't act crazy, except for looking at common things as though startled that plants grew and animals screeched. Chizu and the others had been ready to believe he was gone in the head, since the patient wandered through the grounds like a child, like one stunned from a blow of a beku's hoof. But not raving.

He rubbed his hip absently, bringing blood to the gnarled joint. Would Zai Gan pay for this tidbit?

Zai Gan was Yulin's younger brother, and might rise to master of the sway if Yulin should fall from worthiness, perhaps disgracing himself. As a lofty preconsul of the Magisterium at the Ascendancy, Zai Gan was in position to lead, except for Yulin blocking the way. Of course, there was also the matter of Yulin's many daughters and sons, also eager to replace him, the consequence of Yulin's bedding of a thousand women, Yulin being a fountain of inexhaustible waters. This long line of replacements caused Yulin never to leave his house except in extreme necessity, as must have been the case when he fathered Dai Shen, since the mother's name was unknown in these parts, and no one had heard of this bastard son either. So Zai Gan had his spies, and waited for favorable events, of which this patient might be one.

What had the man said? *Kum bak?* Chizu memorized these words. *Kum bak*, and something else that he couldn't remember because he was a cursed animal steward and not a farting preconsul or a fat master of the sway. So he had perhaps not yet earned a reward from Zai Gan. No sense to risk a communication with the preconsul if the surmise that the patient was not a patient was unimportant, much less false.

Chizu rubbed his hip and frowned, considering. He could imagine the look on Zai Gan's face when the preconsul easily explained how the patient came to say this odd thing, and how Chizu had broken silence for no good reason and might be blind eyes and deaf ears and unworthy of Zai Gan's confidence.

Yes, better to wait and lurk, watching from a discreet distance this Dai Shen of the addled head.

He made his way to the low garden gate, the one even Yulin, very short, must bow down to pass through. The hinge squeaked as the Door of Eight Serenities swung closed behind him and locked.

In the lavender time, the twilight that passed for night, Quinn found he could gaze at the sky and watch its fires without straining his eyes. In the narrow patch above the canopy of trees, the sky-bright was a river, constantly changing, yet always the same. It settled him to watch it. Despite his hard start, and the death of the interpreter, he felt a barely controlled elation. The world beyond the ocean's horizon, the world no one had believed in but him, existed. He was standing in it. He was *back*. His brother would be dumbfounded. See, Rob? The universe is larger and more strange than you believed. And your brother isn't as strange as you thought.

Sleeping, he dreamed of the alien being in the village, staring at him, approaching with the garrote. Quinn stepped closer, engaging with the creature, eight inches taller, with a reach a yard long. I will kill him, he thought. The creature gazed at him with black eyes, without fear. Waking in the middle of the time-that-passed-for-night, he tried to remember what had happened to him here. But at his probings, the strands of memory dissolved.

In the morning, he woke with a start, feeling watched.

There on the edge of the clearing stood a woman. Even at this distance, her hair was iridescent in the morning light. She wore it at chin length, and was dressed in the same quilted, squarish jacket and pants that Sen Tai had worn. Standing to meet her, he saw she was tall for a woman. She regarded him a long time without speaking. He let her stare at him, because he was frankly staring at *her*. The strength of her face gave her years, but without lines, he thought her young. Her skin was very pale, and would have seemed chalky except for its fine tone. He couldn't decide whether she was beautiful—but striking, certainly.

Reaching into a deep pocket on the front of her jacket, she withdrew something and held it out to him.

His pictures.

He took them. Though creased and grayed, Johanna's likeness looked out at him with her half-playful, half-ironic expression. Her expression held strength, the kind she would have needed here, the kind he had so loved in her.

"Nahil," he said. *Thank you.* He tucked the photos in his own jacket pocket. This was a small triumph—to demand his pictures, and to receive them.

The woman bowed slightly from the waist. Then she said in heavily accented English, "I am called Anzi. I will teach you to speak. When you speak Lucent words, then you leave the cage." She gestured at the walled garden.

The man who could kill him wished instead to teach him. Perhaps Yulin had absorbed the message that humans were on their way. And that one of them had already arrived.

Quinn said, "I have forgotten your words."

Anzi nodded. "You forget. You remember, soon." She gestured for him to follow her as she turned down a path.

The overhead canopy closed in, obscuring the sky, tingeing the understory with a false twilight. Now and then she stopped to point at something, and utter its foreign name. She was pleased when he began to repeat the sounds after her.

He pointed to the sky, describing its fullness with a wave of his hand.

"The bright," she said.

"What is the bright?"

She frowned. "Bright is . . ." She struggled for a moment, then said, "Above us."

Her linguistic compromise brought a smile to his face.

She joined in, smiled broadly. Then the smile vanished, as though their endeavor were more serious in nature. She began naming things closer to the ground. Some sounded familiar.

Once, when she pointed at something, he gave the name on his own, from the Lucent tongue, as they called it. This brought a clap from Anzi. He thought it strange that the language these Chinese-seeming people spoke was not Chinese, if he was any judge, but some tongue with origins he couldn't even guess.

He stopped on the path, unable to wait any longer with the foremost question on his mind. Anzi turned, waiting for him.

"Where is my daughter?"

She didn't respond. To make it clear, he brought out Sydney's picture. "Where?"

She pointed over the wall, a gesture that thrilled him. "Long way ago," she said.

"But she is here. Johanna is here." He pointed over the garden wall. "Far away?"

"Wait for asking, yes, please." She continued walking, and he joined her, struggling to restrain his questions.

Nearby, a long patch of leaf mold humped up, revealing a black snake a yard long, slithering away from them. She spoke its name, then added, in English, "Like Earth, you remember?"

It startled him to hear this, though he'd known he was not on Earth. Just where in all the cosmos *was* he, then?

He put the question to her: "Where am I?"

She told him in the Lucent tongue. Then in English: "Master Yulin's garden of animals."

"No." He waved his hands large around him. "Where am I, where is Master Yulin, where is the sky?"

She looked up at the sky, and she understood him. She spoke a phrase in her language. Then in English, she said, "You will remember. This is All. This is, you may say, the Entire."

The Entire. Yes. That seemed right. It seemed like memory. "But how can you look the same as me? How can you be human?"

"We copy you. You were copied. We had such choice, how to look. We chose . . . that culture of long ago."

"Chinese," he said.

"Yes. Chinese. It was so important a sway once, when lords create the All. We chose such form."

Imperfectly, Quinn thought. They've blurred some distinctions—around the eyes, the hair color . . .

Anzi went on: "Also, we chose such culture, but since have improved it, as all things are improved in the Entire."

"All created by the lords . . . ," he repeated, looking around him, at the trees, the sky, and Anzi.

"Yes, certainly."

"They are the tall creatures, with sculpted faces?"

Her expression became more alert. "You remember?"

"I saw a lord, in a village."

"Yes, Tarig," she said.

Tarig. The word seemed right, seemed awful. He asked, "They have powerful technology, beyond that of my people, beyond that of the Rose?"

She shook her head, not understanding. *Technology.*

"Science, manipulating forces of nature."

Brightening, she nodded. "Yes. Such scientific arts are beyond you. None of us know such powers. They give knowledge to us, here and there. Crumbs from their large table." Raising her arm, she pointed in a direction through the trees. "Long way. Don't fear."

He didn't fear. But he remembered. *Tarig. The face, long and beautiful. It crouched, looking down at him, its sinews sculpted from some bronze metal, one hand raised, four-fingered, becoming a blade, slicing the air toward him. . . . He stepped forward, muttering, "You will die now. It's over." Then he turned, delivering a backward kick, thrusting hard into the Tarig's midsection, sending him staggering to his knees. In front of his eyes, he saw his fists bearing down on his enemy, and a great raptorlike scream erupted. . . .*

Anzi was standing in front of him, looking worried.

"I was a prisoner among the Tarig."

Solemnly, she nodded, as though it saddened her. As though it were an awful thing.

"Hadenth," Quinn continued. "He died." The creature's name was Hadenth. He was a prince of the Tarig. Felled by Quinn's hand after the terrible thing that happened.

"No," Anzi said. "He not dying. Wounding. He remember you."

The prince was hurt, but still smiling. The memory faded. "What did Hadenth do to me that I tried to kill him?"

Anzi shook her head. "Ask later, please."

"No, tell me now."

Her face hardened. "Later. Master Yulin says later."

He grabbed her arm. "I say now."

Anzi freed herself in a swift move that wrenched his arm. Her eyes cooled. "Never touch one trained as warrior. I will teach you how not." She moved into a fighting stance. With lightning speed, her foot swiped out and knocked him to the ground.

He stood, slapping off the dust from his fall. Normally, it would have stopped there. She was a woman, and he had a big advantage of strength. But this was not a normal time. Blood boiled under the surface, and he lunged at her. Pivoting out of his way, she yanked on his arm, using his own momentum to send him staggering. Her strength took him completely by surprise. She followed up with a kick that hammered his shoulder.

When he collected himself again, she was standing, hands in front of her, ready to punch. She said evenly, "You do not fight yet. You do not speak yet. You are not free. Yet."

Taunting as this was, she stated the truth. He'd just lost a fight with her. It galled him, but he couldn't afford to alienate her like this—not when he needed her to inform him. "Tell me," he said. "Tell me what happened." She stared coldly at him. "Tell me, and then I'll practice your language. Not before." He needed to learn the language, so it was a bluff to negotiate, but he guessed she was under pressure to teach him, and he could exploit that.

She frowned at his demand. "You must learn following Path. We all, even Master Yulin, following Radiant Path. Learn obedience, yes please."

"I have a different path, I think."

They faced off for a long time. Her face was as still as porcelain. "You have path; I have path. But now one, you must know."

He doubted that. He might be in the Entire, but he was of Earth, of his own path. These things could wait, but knowing his past couldn't. "Anzi. Tell me."

She glanced into the glen, as though worried Master Yulin would hear her. But she relented.

"Tarig sending Titus Quinn daughter away to far land where beings are who Tarig wish to be happy. They are the Inyx, rough creatures—of herd. One may ride upon such. And Inyx wish sentients to ride them. Daughter is a fine gift to the Inyx. The Inyx accept this gift. Long ago. But one thing they wish to be happy for . . ." She shook her head, wavering.

"Tell me."

"That she must be a gift without sight. This the Tarig did. Took her sight."

Quinn listened to the words, trying to process them. "Her sight?"

"She is blind."

He paused, trying to register the words. "They blinded her?" He looked at her, waiting for her to retract this statement, but she didn't. "Blinded her?" he repeated. Then he whispered, "How?"

"We have no knowing. Tarig are surgeons. They do this. But we hear Inyx riders keeping their own eyes, though not the sight in them."

A bellow came up from his throat. He kicked savagely at a thick sapling, and it snapped in two, sending a crack into the forest like a rifle shot. Anzi watched this without flinching.

She waited as he demolished several other of the master's plantings.

Finally he rested his forehead on the trunk of a tree that was more than a match for him.

His youngster, his sweet daughter. He gazed into the garden depths, whispering, "So I attacked the Tarig prince."

From a distance, he heard Anzi say, "We heard. We are long way ago."

"And now? Sydney still dwells there? With the Inaks?"

"Inyx, they are named. Perhaps she is there."

He would get it all out now, quickly. "And Johanna?"

There was a very long silence. Quinn continued to stare into the forest, seeing trees and leaves and cages hidden among them, for the most dangerous animals. Like himself. They hadn't discovered all the harm he could do. "And my wife?" he repeated.

Silence still.

He couldn't bear to stretch it out. "Dead, then?"

"Dead."

He heard her say this, perhaps in English, perhaps in her tongue. The dread that had been lurking in shadow now came into clear and awful light. He leaned against the tree looking at this odd girl, all white, all cold, mouthing words he desperately didn't want to hear, and must.

"How did she die?"

Anzi couldn't meet his gaze. "Of sadness, they saying."

He whispered, "How do you know?"

"Everyone knows, of her dying of sad."

She was dead. Had been, for many years. He closed his eyes. So now, how could it hurt this much? Such old news, and so fresh.

Quinn stared into the dark forest. He placed his hand on his pocket, feeling the paper inside. He pressed his hand against his chest, hanging his head.

Sydney. Blind, enslaved. What kind of hell was this, where a child was torn from her mother and blinded? Where a woman could be left to die of grief? Whatever this place was, it had kept Sydney too long, far too long. He would find this Inyx sway. And bring his daughter home.

"I promise," he whispered. "Sydney, I promise."

He wandered the garden a long while, avoiding Anzi, who followed him the rest of that day. When the twilight came he slept inside the hut, where it was almost dark. In misery, he tossed and fought with dreams.

Anzi woke him as the bright streamed through the window of his hut. He opened his eyes, wondering what the terrible thing was that had plagued his sleep. When he remembered Johanna and Sydney, he groaned, and clenched his eyes against the pain.

His keeper would have none of this. She'd brought hot food, and removed the top lid to entice him. To placate her, he took a few pieces of safe edibles.

She said, "We practice talk."

He left the hut to go to the lake. Washing, he heard a new sound, a discordant music. Perhaps it came from the master's house, though it seemed far away. Somewhere, people laughed and had music. Somewhere, perhaps Sydney laughed, heard music. She lived, at least. He held on to that.

When Quinn came back to the hut, Anzi rose, bowing. This bowing was odd. Good food, bowing. All to please a prisoner. He picked up the pictures that had lain beside him during the twilight, and tucked them in his pocket.

Anzi watched this, narrowing her eyes. "We now talk," she said.

"Not today."

"Yes, today." Eyes cold, she challenged him. Would she fight him, to make him a good student?

She gestured for him to come with her. "I show you something new."

Giving up on privacy, he followed her in a new direction into the garden. From the depths came alien cries as creatures woke up and screamed for their pails. From one nearby pen, hidden by foliage, issued a haunting, ululating scream that could belong to no Earth creature.

Anzi walked ahead, saying the name of a plant. When he didn't repeat it, she stopped and pinned him with a stare. "You learn faster, Dai Shen."

"Good. Glad you're pleased."

"I *not* pleased. You not pleased. Not when Master Yulin putting you in his lake." She stopped, glaring at him. "Deep in."

"Maybe I'm a slow learner."

"Master Yulin not yet decide, if killing you." She raised a finger like a schoolteacher. "But may. If not learning."

"I had a translator. He spoke my language. Yulin drowned him."

Anzi bowed her head. "Unfortunate."

At this breezy comment, Quinn snapped. "Now your master will have to wait for his slow student." He was depressed by the death in this place. He'd only been here a short while, but already, there were three deaths, and one was Johanna.

"You not wanting your life, Dai Shen?"

He paused. That depended. Today, he was not so sure. "Why are you calling me that name?"

She continued deeper into the woods. Her voice trailed back as he reluctantly followed. "You can have new name. We conceal you from bright lords. Dai Shen is name for you, so saying Master Yulin."

He thought that he'd found a crack in Yulin's armor. If he was hiding Quinn from the Tarig, Yulin was no doubt straying from the Radiant Path. Maybe the crack could be widened.

They came to a tall cage within which birds, some furred, some bald, flew to perches in treetops.

"We climb," Anzi said, jumping up to the first strut where she could gain a foothold. Without waiting for him, she began to climb up the cage, using the cross-pieces where the birds roosted. He followed her.

"Keep fingers away," came her voice.

Too late. A ochre-colored bird dove at his hand, narrowly missing it with its spiky teeth. After that, Quinn paid more attention, finally emerging on the lid of the aviary, above the treetops.

Here was a view of the limitless plain that Quinn had seen before. In the foreground, on every side, stretched a city, grand and dense, one that might house a million people. Above, the unending bright threw its blanket across the sky. The smell of the lavender grasses of the great plain came to his senses in a rush of clove-tinged perfume. The expanse lay devoid of any geological feature, or tree, or settlement besides the immense city beneath him. Whatever the towering gray walls had been that he'd seen before, they were invisible from here. The staggering emptiness of this land conveyed less a sense of isolation than of power. There was land enough to squander.

Anzi gestured. "Great city of Chalin sway," she said. "Yulin's city of Xi." She crouched in the center, where a top mast formed a pinnacle. Quinn crept closer to her, stepping carefully on the struts, below which lay a hundred-foot fall. "Chalin, that is people here. Outside"—she gestured to the plains—"is many sways, not all Chalin."

She pointed to a palatial building layered into a hillside. "Master Yulin house."

Yulin's dwelling was a sprawling palace, hewn from the same golden-black material as Quinn's own hut. Its architecture was one of rounded forms: domed roofs and half-circle porticos. The master's fine black stone gave way, in the rest of the city, to deep browns and golds, sparkling under the bright. "Yulin rules here?" Quinn asked.

"Master care for sway as please the Tarig to do so."

The noises of the city came easily to this perch, and Quinn heard the music that had caught his attention earlier. Anzi pointed to a plaza, where a line of people wound through in a bedecked procession. The bright gleamed in raised cymbals and polished horns.

"This day of sadness, for Caiji, she dead. This her . . ." she search for a word. "Her funeral line."

They watched the procession thread through an open space crowded with hundreds, perhaps thousands, of people.

"Who is Caiji?"

"Caiji of master's many wife. Very near oldest of all wife."

"Are you also the master's wife?"

Anzi looked startled at this. "No, you would say, niece to master. One of many nieces. Smallest niece."

Quinn had not had time to wonder who Anzi was. Now he thought he knew why Yulin had sent him one who couldn't speak his language well. Because he trusted her, being a relative. He didn't trust his interpreter. Not with the news that Quinn had brought.

She sat with ease, perched on the aviary. Her jacket sleeve fell back from her wrist as she held onto the center plinth, showing her muscular forearm. In profile, Anzi looked to be about twenty years old. But her poise was of one older.

"Tarig come to Xi, sometime. They roam here, sometime there. Looking."

"Looking for me?"

Anzi's eyes grew wide. "No. Lord of heaven give us not looking!"

"What do they look for?"

"Tarig do what they do."

"When I was a prisoner among them, why did they send my wife and daughter away?"

Her face fell into sadness, as it had once before when he spoke of his imprisonment. "For controlling you better, we hearing. Separation was a grief. They use such grief. We hearing." She thought for a moment. Then: "Also, girl and woman great gifts for those they wishing to please. And girl and woman, not being scholars, tell little that can be interesting to lords."

So the lords wanted scholarship. . . . Despite Quinn's distinct impression of their great power, the Tarig did lack some things. "Do the Tarig know about Earth?"

Far below his perch on the aviary, he noticed that people in the funeral procession threw things to the crowds. A few children dashed forward to snatch these offerings.

He continued, "You know about Earth, Anzi. Does Master Yulin? Do the Tarig?"

Watching the procession, Anzi said, "Everyone know of Rose. But we vow that Rose not know us. This why Tarig kill you." She looked pointedly at him. "Unless Master Yulin hide you well, which you learn to speak also."

"Rose? You call it Rose?"

"Yes, long time call so. On Earth there is a plant call rose?" When he nodded, she said, "We have no plants shaped thus here. Nothing like such a creation as rose."

A breeze lifted Quinn's hair, bringing to his nostrils the smell of dust and cooking and a tangle of chemicals that might be natural or manufactured. Anzi herself smelled like a human woman. And, if copied, *was* she human? He ran his hand through his hair, now growing beyond its usual cropped cut. It was, he knew, the same color as Anzi's: a hot white. Surely the sky didn't bleach all hair this color. Someone altered him to look like one of the Chalin people. Perhaps even the first visit here, he had to hide.

"Tell me my story, Anzi."

She turned to look at him. Her face was sad. "Better if I speak better. When that story is said."

"Say the story, now, Anzi. I'm ready."

She crouched silently, looking over the city to the plain beyond.

He hated to wait on her whims, and he hated the constant effort of trying to remember. A lid pressed down on his past. He wondered who had clamped it there.

After a long while Anzi began to speak. "You came here," she said. In her voice was an overlay of regret. "You came from the Rose, behind the veil. Long time we always know of Rose, the place of young death, and many wars. At the . . . reaches . . . our scholars study Rose. Long time. But never touched Rose, nor Rose touch us."

The music of the procession still came to their high perch, but more faintly now, as the mourners wound from sight. He already had questions, but he feared interrupting her.

Anzi went on: "Then you come. In ship. Very confused time. Tarig want you, and keep you. Does Rose know about Entire? This Tarig ask. What powers dwell in Rose? Difficult to know what Rose understands. Our views of you are small, visions in a shattered glass. Tarig hope that you do not know us, but how to be sure? They wish to know enemy, and so keep you and asking questions. Send wife and daughter away, to keep you to please them. You please them if you think someday wife and daughter give back to you." She shook her head, over and over. "Never give back to you."

He listened to her words, memorizing them.

"Tarig are pleased. Learn that Rose is ignorant. Not fear so much Rose, since Rose not understand there is the All. Entire of all things. You please them. They keep you."

"How long?" He couldn't help but ask.

She flattened her mouth, thinking. "Four thousand days, is possible."

Four thousand days, that was almost eleven years, close to what he'd always thought.

Anzi went on: "Then one time you strike Hadenth, the high lord. We hearing this, but hard believe to strike a Tarig. So Tarig hunt you. But you go back? You gone back?"

He shook his head. "I don't know what I did. I think I went back then. I can't remember." He glanced at her. "How would I have gone back?"

"This we wondered. How can Titus Quinn disappear among us? If gone back, how go back and not die in the black space? So I thought—we all thought—that you have died." She seemed sad, recounting this, and Quinn thought perhaps he had not just made enemies in this place. She continued, "We hear that to not submit to high lords, you ended your days." She smiled tentatively. "Not true, I see."

Unexpectedly, she seemed genuinely glad, and he was touched. Perhaps the story of his capture was known, and some people rooted for him. He would ask later.

"So I was here four thousand days. And then disappeared . . . How long have I been gone?"

Anzi frowned, considering. "One hundred days. Not long. But long enough for us to wonder where Titus Quinn is."

This proved it then, that there was no constant relation of time between here and there, between Anzi's land and his own. Back on Earth he'd languished two years without his family. Here only a few months had elapsed. A ratio of seven to one. Far different from the time when Earth registered his absence from the K-tunnel as a half year, and he'd experienced Entire time as ten years. A ratio of one to twenty.

He finished the most important computation: His daughter would be nineteen or twenty years old. Her childhood gone. He had been among the Tarig for her whole childhood.

"Why can't I remember, Anzi?"

"This we wonder also." She smiled again, a very pleasant expression on her usually stern face. "But you will remember. No one can have your past, take same from you. You will recover it, yes." The smile faded. "When you do, you must remember to forgive."

"First, justice."

"Entire justice is thing to learn. You are here now, so learn our justice. It begins with vow to keep invisible to our enemies, of which you, I am sorry, are one. In view of Tarig. Some of us not sure to see you as enemy. I am one of these, you must know."

He would not argue this just now. There was too much to digest. *Ten years . . .*

"Dai Shen," Anzi said, turning toward him to regain his attention, which was wandering to Johanna and the time before. "Here is thing to learn. It is most big thing, I believe. Caiji, who now dead, took her life on one hundred thousandth day of life. She lived long, and wishes to have remembering as Caiji of one hundred thousand days. You understand how long is one hundred thousand days?"

After a quick calculation, Quinn said, "About three hundred of Earth years." He added, "The time it takes Earth to travel around its sun."

"Yes. Suns." She paused, as though considering this odd word. "We have no years, yet days we have, and count thus. Caiji lived as long as I may live, but you will not see one hundred thousand days, Dai Shen. This is thing to know. Your life is not so long. Yet all peoples in Rose would live long. Yes? So to come here, they are pleased to have one hundred thousand days or more. That is why the Tarig fear you. To take our All. To be longer than you are."

"Are your lives truly so long, Anzi? Time might flow differently here, making it only seem that way."

She seemed unperturbed. "No. The lords say your world has only short lives: thirty thousand days, not many more, of health and strength. But the lords extend our lives, by their grace. Some say that the night kills you, but believing thus is hard. It is more likely, and the lords say it, that the bright sustains us."

The bright. If it was some function of the bright, then that was why, if humans came, they might be recipients of the long life Anzi claimed could be found here.

She began to climb down then, and he followed her. At the foot of the aviary, she turned to him. "Because of such long life, you perceive why you must never be here. First vow, which breaking is to die, we must withhold knowing of Entire from Rose."

"Too late now, I expect."

She closed her eyes. "I fear so."

"Master Yulin won't want humans here."

"To come with your many people? Your wars? No."

"Or to pass through? To shorten Rose travel?"

She frowned. "Such travel is not possible, we are thinking. I am sorry."

"I traveled here. The first time by accident, the second time deliberately. And back again. So it *is* possible."

"No, it is a game of chance, especially going to the dark universe, your universe. You cross over to the Rose, but likely into black space. Most of the Rose is empty . . . you say, *vacuum*? No one knows how to pick place of arrival. Not even Master Yulin, nor all the Chalin scholars know this."

Easy to claim that safe travel wasn't possible, but this was a matter to discuss with Yulin, not Yulin's niece.

She resumed leading him through the garden, naming things, drilling him in the Lucent tongue. "You learn more words," she said. "So please Master Yulin."

She was relentless. But he was also grateful for her. He did need to learn the Lucent tongue, and quickly. For Sydney's sake. For when he took her home.

CHAPTER NINE

This is how All began.

Once the Tarig lived in a realm outside. It was the first created realm, the Heart. No one but lords could live there, and they dwelt alone in their magnificence. After many archons, they saw that a realm was forming in a new place. They watched as the realm grew and formed a vast land of dwelling. Thus the Entire was born, but in barrenness, with no wonders of life.

The Tarig sent simulacra, automatons with no need for food or air, to explore. The simulacra reported on all that they had seen. The Entire was barren, they said. But outside the Entire could be seen another place, where many round worlds existed in black air warmed by balls of fire. This was the Rose. Living there were many sentient creatures and wondrous animals, all living their brief and sorrowful lives.

The Tarig, being gracious lords, decreed that the new realm would become enlivened with life and sentients, but superior in every way to the beings of the Rose. The Entire would be, they said, a realm of great brightness, perfect peace, and long life. They bestowed the thousand gifts, creating sky and land and many sentient beings according to forms seen in the Rose, as many as pleased them.

The simulacra asked to be fashioned in the image of beings in a sway on a minor world they admired. In reward of their high service, the gracious lords granted this, creating the great Chalin people. Then with their retinue, the gracious lords descended from the Heart into the Entire, and began the reign of the bright.

—from *The Book of the Thousand Gifts*

QUINN HAD LEARNED AN ASTONISHING THING. He could read.

Anzi had been telling him about the Entire—that it was a habitat of cosmic dimensions, and that the River Nigh, the great transport system, conquered these distances. How it worked was another question Anzi couldn't answer. The lords knew. They knew all. She kept asking if he remembered any of these things. He didn't.

Mulling over these imponderables, Quinn asked for books—and receiving scrolls instead, he opened one. The letters formed words, words he knew.

He could read the Lucent tongue. The effect was astonishing, leaving him almost breathless as the words on the scrolls became meaningful.

Once he and Anzi discovered this, he began reading simple texts, children's books, devouring the words and the knowledge, pouring over enlivened scrolls that streamed printed narratives.

After a day and a half of reading, the barriers broke, and the spoken language came to him, first haltingly, and then in a flood. He could understand Anzi as she spoke the Lucent tongue. Not all words, but most were there for the taking. Anzi talked as fast as she could, her eyes wide, and Quinn kept saying, *sett*, *sett.* Yes.

He could barely sleep, but paced Yulin's garden with great energy, trying unsuccessfully to engage even the zookeepers in conversation. These attempts failed, as they shrank from him and averted their eyes. Returning to his scrolls, he read all he could of things pertaining to the *reaches* where, he learned, the barrier between the Entire and the Rose was thin and, as Anzi had said, observations could be made. The scrolls never so much as hinted that one might *step through*, but it was the most logical place to make a crossing. He could imagine it. He could almost remember it. The secret of the reaches was the thing Stefan Polich coveted, if it would provide star routes. And it might. But most important, it would provide the route home—for Sydney.

Speaking was harder than reading. He had to trust that he knew how to speak. By Anzi's face, by her excitement in hearing him use the Lucent tongue, he learned that trust.

Keen to understand how the Chalin viewed their universe, and what physical laws governed it, he called for books on science and mathematics. His vocabulary wasn't up to the bewildering texts. In any case, it didn't appear that Chalin science attempted to explain fundamental things: what the Entire was, its walls, its sky. What powered them. How they could exist.

But the jar had broken. He practiced the language, and as he did so, there came trailing pieces of memory.

An old man with a hawklike nose, bent over scribbling with a pen.

A silvery ocean far below him as he stood on a platform looking down.

Riding a giant bird through the air, the creature begging for freedom.

Pressing his hands against a glittering wall, pleading for release.

The memories triggered more questions. He told Anzi, "I knew an old man. A Chalin scholar." The face had been coming into focus. Someone he knew well.

Correcting his grammar, Anzi nodded.

"Who is the old man, the scholar?"

"Perhaps the scholar Bei," she answered. "Because he knew your language, the Tarig used him to interrogate you. Once, he was high in rank, but when you fled, we heard he was in disgrace. He retired to a far reach."

Quinn tried to wring out a drop more of memory. Bei was there. Over and over. "I keep seeing his face, hearing his words."

"That was your life for a time: interrogations. The lords wondered why you appeared. What you knew."

"Bei was my enemy, then."

"It is hard to say who are friends, who are enemies."

Not to Quinn. He usually had that squarely pegged. "Why is it hard?"

Anzi's voice fell to a whisper, and she looked away. "Sometimes, those who meant well did not do well. I am sorry."

She didn't know much on this score. She hadn't been at the Ascendancy.

He was the only one who had his complete past. Perhaps that past would emerge as language had. But there was more to this story of Bei, he was sure. "Do you know what happened between me and Bei? Was it something worse than interrogation?"

"Truly, Dai Shen, I don't know."

Nevertheless, his progress was so rapid that at their midday meal, she pronounced, "Soon you can leave the master's garden of animals, Dai Shen."

"I'm ready to leave now."

"So you must think, Dai Shen." She smiled. "But you must become more perfect if you are not to arouse curiosity." He had learned some protocols to use when near Master Yulin, and his titles, and the names of his wives. To prepare him to enter the palace unremarked upon, she had tried to comb his hair back to form a tail, but so far it was too short.

"Am I so odd a Chalin?"

Her face became earnest. "I would not like to say 'odd,' Dai Shen. Only that more perfections are needed."

"This might be as perfect as I get."

She looked askance. "It will not go well for any who see you make a mistake. They would have to be destroyed."

"But even the gardeners know I'm here. You can't kill everyone."

With a shake of her head, Anzi said, "Oh, but the keepers of these grounds must die."

Quinn looked out at the forest, where four or five servants had quietly fed him and the animals these many days. "You're going to kill these men?"

She must have noted that his expression changed, because hers did too. "Master Yulin must cloak your identity from the high lords. Remember that you attacked Lord Hadenth. If he were to discover that you are hidden here . . . It is necessary that the keepers remain silent."

Quinn shook his head. He was getting tired of Yulin's death sentences. He remembered the air bubbles bursting at the surface of the lake as Sen Tai released his last breath, chained to the muddy bottom.

"Why didn't you remove the caretakers from the garden, if seeing me meant they'd be killed?"

"But who would feed the animals, then?"

"I could feed them, for God's sake!"

"You had more important work."

He rose, pacing away from her, trying and failing to summon patience. He turned back to her. "Take me to Yulin. I'm done waiting. Tell him I'm not happy about the gardeners."

She stood also, anger flickering at the edges of her mouth. "No one is happy to kill them. You think we kill so easily? It's all for you."

He stared at her a moment, grappling with these cultural differences that seemed awful to him and normal to her. "Tell him, if the gardeners die, I will never speak another word of Lucent."

"So, now you threaten the master?"

Perhaps a show of defiance would gain Yulin's attention. "Tell him that I've had enough death." It was true.

Anzi stood slowly and bowed. "I will bring him your plea."

"Better bring him more than that."

She scowled and left, leaving Quinn uneasy as to how much he could push this man, used to unquestioned obedience. But Yulin hadn't killed him yet. There must be some reason, but it might be a profoundly small one. Quinn looked out over the tended park scanning for the gardeners, whose reticence he now understood.

When Anzi came back later, he could tell by her expression that Yulin hadn't budged.

Quinn considered his bargaining position. It was appallingly weak. Still, he found himself striding away toward the lakeshore. There he took the raft and poled out alone to the middle of the lake, bringing a scroll with him. He meant to stay as long as it took. Anzi stood on the shore periodically cajoling and upbraiding him.

"Dai Shen, you have no food."

"Dai Shen, the Master is not pleased with you. You should want to please him."

"Dai Shen, you are ruining all I set out to do for you. You are ungrateful."

The bright waxed and waned, shedding exotic images on the surface of the lake. He stayed on the raft, not answering Anzi. Sometimes he felt cold, and wished he'd remembered to bring a blanket from his hut. Sometimes orange carp came sniffing around the raft, and he thought of catching them to eat; but he didn't like the smell of them. Now and then, at the lake's edge, he saw a gardener in the undergrowth, the one with the halting walk, but the man faded back once Quinn looked at him. Too late—he must die according to the master of the sway.

To pass the time Quinn read the scroll he had selected, one that described the place called Ahnenhoon, the place of Johanna's former imprisonment. It was the site of a war with a sentient species called the Paion that had been ongoing for six archons. Somehow he instinctively new that six archons was equal to thousands of years in Rose time. This everlasting war had taken many lives, many of them Chalin lives—and Inyx lives, those herd-beings who wanted their riders blind.

"Blind riders," he said in the Lucent tongue. Speaking out loud brought more of the language to his command. He practiced what he would say to Yulin. How he would argue for the gardeners' freedom, and his own. Because it was time for both. Having the language, and having it fluently, gave Quinn a strange sense of elation. He would make Yulin listen to him, to secure him as an ally, not a warden. It could be done, and Quinn thought he knew how.

At the brightening of the third day, Anzi came to the shore bearing a set of folded silks over her arm.

His clothes for the interview with Yulin.

As he poled back, he kept the smile off his face. But Anzi smiled. He thought her a graceful loser. And he thought that she was beginning to understand him.

At the shore, he tied up the raft and was grateful to see a basket of food waiting as well, and a small pot of steaming oba. The clothes she'd brought were similar to what he'd worn before: a square jacket and pants gathered at the waist. But this set was moss green stitched with red thread, a style Anzi had sometimes worn.

He transferred his pictures into one of the silk pockets. He was ready.

She cut a glance at him, smiling though disapproving. "You are stubborn," she said, giving him a small square hat to mask his too-short hair.

"Yes." It was what most people said about him, but he thought of the quality as steadfastness. Once he set his sights on something, he was not easily put off. But Anzi, like his sister-in-law before her, wished that Titus Quinn were more pliable—amenable to reason, or at least her own reasoning. Of all the women he'd ever met, it was only Johanna who'd loved him for what he was.

They walked to a curiously small gate, one that Anzi unlocked with a touch. Bending down, Quinn went through.

Watching them approach the Door of Eight Serenities, Chizu drank in the sight of Ji Anzi, lovely niece of the fat master. She walked with an athletic grace, her hair swinging just beneath her chin, hovering there as Chizu longed to hover, caressing her face.

After Dai Shen had passed through the gate, Chizu stepped out of the bushes to catch Anzi's attention. He bowed low.

She frowned and gave a cursory nod, shattering Chizu's moment of peace in which he thought that, given her beauty, she might shed a moment's splendor on him, insignificant as he was, if he bowed low enough.

The gate clicked shut behind her, leaving Chizu with a bitter stomach.

So, too good are we? Too good for the steward of second rank, unworthy of even a proper bow. The *crippled* steward of second rank, good only for pissing on trees and hauling slop buckets. Yes, Ji Anzi, too good, now that you are the tutor of the wounded soldier who is no soldier.

His resolve fell into place. It gave him a refuge from the snub, the compensation afforded by revenge. I will complicate your life, fine lady, he thought. Yes, I will report to Yulin's brother some things I've seen. Then we will see you and your fat master bow low.

Quinn stood before Master Yulin in the Hall of Wives, a large chamber, its walls carved in tiny patterns of a bearlike animal, Yulin's icon. At the master's side sat Suzong, his favorite wife, and an old one. She wore a red silk gown that made her skin look as pale as a fish belly. From an open porch, the glow of the day spilled across the floor, backlighting the two chairs where Yulin and Suzong sat.

"You have learned to speak," Yulin said by way of greeting. His voice was a vibrant rumble from a man who looked like he could wrestle a beku to the ground. Despite his brocaded robes, Yulin reminded Quinn of the strong and plodding pack beast he'd ridden on his first day back.

"The Lucent tongue is among my languages now," Quinn answered. He had bowed to Yulin, but he was not going to scrape. Behind him, he heard Anzi's soft cough. He had neglected to say "One Who Shines," or another of Yulin's honorifics.

"The suppliant reads children's scrolls," Suzong said, to put him in his place.

"Yes. Though I am dumb as a beku, of course."

Suzong's buck teeth showed for a moment in an abrupt laugh.

"I have heard," Yulin said, "of a petition to save gardeners' lives. I would have thought your human masters had higher concerns."

"They do. But I have discretion to please myself, Master Yulin." It was one reason why he insisted on returning to this world alone, and not with a Minerva handler.

"Would it please you to take the slow death from the hands of Lord Hadenth?"

"No one wants to die. I don't, and your servants don't. I'm not pleased to be the cause of the gardeners' deaths." Quinn held Yulin's gaze. "Maybe death means more in my land than yours."

Yulin murmured, "To take a long life is more than to take a short one."

"Then let them live, Master Yulin. They don't know me. To them, I'm Dai Shen who had a head injury."

"Who was kept in the palace garden for some strange reason."

Quinn spread his hands. "Who knows what the One Who Shines may decide, in his wisdom, to do?"

Yulin rumbled with laughter, and the hall echoed with it. Suzong petted her collar, now revealed as a small animal curled up around her neck. Two eyes blinked open from the furry mass.

Yulin stood, stepping off two carved stones his feet had been resting on, saying, "Cunning, Dai Shen, but unconvincing."

He strolled toward Anzi, his movements graceful for one so heavy. "Your opinion, Niece?"

Anzi didn't hesitate. "A compromise, Uncle." Receiving his nod, she went on: "Let the gardeners live forever in the garden, not to mix with others." She glanced at Quinn. "No deaths."

Yulin drew himself up, gazing as near to straight-on to Anzi as he could manage. "It shall be so."

Quinn frowned. "Life in a prison?"

Yulin held up a warning finger. "It is my last word on gardeners."

Suzong muttered and reached for a cup next to her, slurping loudly while her collar went back to sleep.

Under Anzi's pointed stare, Quinn managed to say, "Thank you, Master Yulin." It wasn't good enough, but it was an improvement. "Now we may move to the more important matters."

"Matters," Yulin repeated. "Such matters are?" He swung around to accuse Anzi. "Have I no *matters* pending, that I must have *matters* from a suppliant?"

Anzi hurried forward to pull on Quinn's sleeve, trying to restrain him. "You said nothing of matters before," she murmured to him.

"My daughter is a *matter*." He turned to Yulin. "Help me to find her." Did Anzi and Yulin hope that he'd forget why he'd come here?

Yulin's face remained impassive, his wispy mustache framing a disdainful mouth. One man's daughter could have no value to this master of the sway. Pity would not move him, nor threats. What threats could a prisoner make?

But Quinn was not just a prisoner. He was also an emissary: emissary of the Rose, if he dared claim such a thing. And he could. Who else could speak for his world? Not Stefan Polich, or Helice Maki. They were left behind. Titus Quinn was the one who'd come—alone, as he'd known he must. And he'd arrived with a powerful message: *Humans will come.* From his first confrontation with Yulin on the lake, he'd understood that that message was his one power in this place.

Now he would use that power to bend Yulin to his goals.

"Master Yulin, Lady Suzong," he began, "you've sheltered me in your palace, and taught me your language. For these things I'm grateful. It's been a good beginning." It had been an ugly beginning, and someday he hoped to repay the fat master for his time spent in a jar and the death of Sen Tai the translator. But not yet.

He continued, "My people sent me here to bring home the child. This is the matter we have to discuss. It's the first condition of peace between us. The Tarig offer no road to peace, so I turn to you. I know it won't be an easy thing, or a safe thing. It requires that we break the Tarig law that bans contact.

"That law is already useless. I've come here twice, and others will come after me. Humans will come. If you hear nothing else from me today, hear this. Perhaps someday you'll think yourselves fortunate, that you heard it first, and not your enemies." He didn't know who Yulin's enemies were, but he was sure he had some.

"To safely return the human child to her home, I have to learn the way back, which only you of the Entire can know. Bringing her safely home will be proof that my people can travel to and from your land and also that we can traverse great distances in the Rose universe. So this child and travel routes are linked. Helping me will prove your friendship."

"Friends of the Rose?" Yulin shook his head. "We must walk into the River Nigh with our pockets full of stones."

"If there's no help here, then we'll have to find another sway to help us."

Yulin exchanged glances with Suzong, then muttered, "How can the Entire provide traveling in the Rose?"

Quinn answered, "When I returned home the first time I came here, I arrived at a world very far from Earth."

"Ah yes. Worlds. Balls of mud in the air, scattered far and wide. I have heard of these things. You wish to arrive at such a place with the small daughter. When you leave."

"My masters are eager to know these routes. It's their condition of alliance."

Suzong leaned forward, her collar's eyes wide open in a green glare. "What kind of ally can humans be? What can the evanescent possibly give to the immortal?"

Quinn turned to her, seeing an irritable old consort who listened more carefully than she pretended to. He was grateful for the remark, even clothed as it was in disdain, because it gave him a chance to argue his side. "Wealth," he answered. "Trade. Power. You're the mistress of a sway humans will take note of. The Chalin people are close in nature and temperament to humans. There'll be rich trade, and it'll begin here."

He turned back to Yulin. "My people know the way in, now. That knowledge can't be put back in a jar."

Yulin smoothed his mustache with a jeweled hand. "You think the lords can't put your people in any jar they please?"

Suzong watched the man of the Rose, every nuance of his gestures and speech. He was the first to come into the Entire. The first to strike a Tarig lord and live. Improbably, he had come back again, and now stood before them, a man to reckon with. His people would never be put off. They would leak into the realm, slowly or all at once, and this man was their high servant. Humans were coming, yes. And how would they come? Why, through the reaches. And once here, they would keep following, and then the Chalin would be the suppliants, being small in numbers compared to the beasts of the Rose. Better to befriend such invaders, to wring advantage from the hands of disaster. Her husband thought that when things changed it was time to retreat. Yulin had retreated his whole life until now he was a prisoner in his own house, afraid of the city, afraid even of his own relatives. If it weren't for Suzong, he would long since have composed the saying for his grave flag, and that great fart in a barrel, Zai Gan, would be sitting in his chair.

Beyond the open terrace, the city lay spread out, the ancestral city of the Chalin. Today, Suzong found that sight small indeed. The bright lords granted Yulin governance of the sway, and in return Yulin was loyal. But scratch that surface devotion and one would find timidity. No wonder he looked like a man straining with constipation. He had to decide for or against treason.

The To and From the Rose Door was open, figuratively left ajar by this man Titus Quinn. Now she must watch Yulin throw his bulk against that door, striving in vain to shut it. When he was done pushing, then perhaps Suzong would have a small suggestion or two.

From the open terrace, a languid breeze brought the scent of hot dust and cloves mingled with the juices of a million people.

Quinn knew that this city, its very existence in an impossible universe, was an emblem of power. The Tarig had created this universe. But for all their power, the Tarig were afraid. They were afraid to be known by the Rose. They fear us, he thought with mounting confidence. The Tarig, somehow, are vulnerable.

Yulin's question lingered. *You think the lords can't put your people in any jar they please?*

"No," he answered at last. "The lords can't contain us. Understanding this, they fear us. It's why for so long they've forbidden us to know each other. Because they're afraid."

Pausing, he saw that he had Yulin's keen attention. And Suzong's. Evidently the idea of the Tarig fearing someone was a totally new thought to them. And an appealing one. He could almost see Yulin's mind weighing and scheming, whether to gamble or not.

Yulin's response, when it came, was a low rumble. "What do you ask of me?"

"Set me free. Be my ally."

Yulin shook his head. "Free? Free to hunt your daughter? The lords will find you in the same way as before. You will fall at their feet, and I will fall with you."

"No. We won't fail. You'll make sure of that."

The One Who Shines turned a darkened stare on him, then spat out, "You may snatch this daughter from the Inyx—although it exceeds the imagination to think how—but you will have no way back. No quick exit through the veils. While you wait, the Tarig, in all their power, will hunt for you."

"As they did last time. And failed."

Yulin snorted. "No man can win this game twice. Here is what I believe: You will attempt to bring your daughter out of the Inyx sway. You will stumble—perhaps in a small way, for not all disasters come from large errors. Then you will expose yourself, and me, that I hid you in the garden." He turned to Anzi. "I kept him for your sake. Now, my niece, you see the trouble he brings."

Anzi averted her eyes under the rebuke.

Quinn looked at her. "For her sake? Why for her sake?"

Yulin stroked his chin, saying, "Humans are held in high regard by some. Anzi is such a one."

Quinn looked at Anzi, wondering how strongly she had already argued for him.

Yulin muttered, "She is in awe of you, like a useless scholar peering through the veil, hoping for a glimpse of the ancient race." He looked at Quinn. "Yes, your race is ancient, but the Tarig are older yet, as all children know."

"I know this, Master Yulin. That's why I need your help. When I leave here, I have to pass as Chalin, and you can show me how. If you are my ally, help me. And if you know how to cross over to the Rose, tell me."

Yulin waved his hand in dismissal. "Cross over and die. The gamble is where the exit point leads, and it may well be into eternal darkness." He held up a hand to stop Quinn's protest. Then, rising from his chair, he beckoned Suzong to join him, and he walked onto the terrace. Quinn and Anzi followed.

Here, the bright shone at full, creating an impression of a sparkling lid over the world. "Look out at my world," Yulin said, stretching his hands out to display the city of Xi. "We live in peace, side by side, except for one war, far away. We have all the comforts we could wish. Now you urge me to throw all this away for the promise of alliance with people whom I have not even seen."

Yes, that was Yulin's dilemma. Quinn could see he wasn't a gambling man, and he racked his mind for a way to sweeten the pot.

Suzong murmured at Yulin side, "But they will come anyway." Her collar had moved up to wrap tightly around her neck, like a velvet noose.

Yulin turned to fix Quinn with a troubled gaze. "For the sake of travel? Is this their great hope?"

"To be free to travel, yes."

Yulin gazed over the city as though even now seeing it overrun with evanescent humans. "One can die of too much travel."

"One dies anyway."

Yulin shook his head. "I know nothing of the ways to and from. I have kept the vows. Perhaps others . . . scholars, traitorous ones." He glanced at Quinn. "But no doubt you will go looking. There's no containing you." The master sighed, as though despairing of his houseguest. "The future is changing."

Suzong drew closer. "It always was. The garden walls, my husband, were only a temporary refuge."

Yulin was perched on that wall. And needed a push. Quinn summoned all his wits. He had studied for one week. What did he know of the Chalin? What of the Entire? But he knew more than he could logically summon.

He let himself speak from the heart: "Maybe you'll gain a new future for your people. The Tarig made this world. They also made you subservient. They require you to fight the Long War against the Paion at Ahnenhoon."

He went on, "Why don't the Tarig, with all their power, end the Long War? Because they have little to lose. They don't fight, but require the sways to send their conscripts by the thousands, by the tens of thousands."

"And they die," Yulin murmured.

"Yes," Suzong said. "Die early and often. Our young warriors, the best of us." Suzong's bright amber eyes looked like jewels, afire in the furnace glare of the sun.

The room was heavy with silence. Anzi looked like she was afraid to move, for fear of toppling the conversation in the wrong direction. He had the attention of Yulin and Suzong, had their imagination. And it was lit. He followed some underground stream of logic. It was all he could do, as ignorant as he was. It might even be true that the Tarig were invulnerable. But even if they were, Quinn would use them, would use Yulin, to take back what was his.

"What would the Chalin people rise to, given their lead, given a chance to say how they wanted to live?" Quinn plunged on. "You're comfortable, Master Yulin, but not free." In desperation, he turned to Suzong. Not everyone quailed before the bright lords. Yulin was a loyalist; but Suzong—ah, Suzong hated them. He said to her, "Do you want to serve the Tarig all your days?"

Yulin waited for her to answer Quinn's challenge, and Anzi watched with wide eyes.

Suzong's mouth quavered. "Serve them?" she whispered. "Who could wish to shovel the dung of beku?" She added, her mouth widening into a lively smile, "When one can ride them instead?"

Standing still as a mountain, Yulin had narrowed his eyes as he regarded his favorite wife. Perhaps he was thinking of trade and riches rather than defeat of the Tarig. But even if so, that might be enough to secure his allegiance.

At last Yulin nodded. "So be it, then."

Quinn nodded. Yes. The garden can't protect you anymore. For all the lies I've told, I know that much is true. In triumph, he stole a glance at Anzi, whose look took on a disturbing cast of adoration.

Warming to his decision, Yulin said, "We will find this small girl. And send her home." He said it softly, as though hoping the lords wouldn't hear.

An almost-invisible smile played at the corner of Suzong's mouth, and Quinn let himself breathe at last.

It was then that his training began, that very afternoon. Anzi led him to a small courtyard, its soil hard-packed and raked. Here, she began instructing him in all that he should know for that false identity they had chosen for him, that of a soldier of Ahnenhoon. It would be expected that he could fight with Chalín skills, using staffs and short knives, and the weapons of his hands, feet, and body. He and Anzi knew it was likely he *would* fight, even in this peaceful realm where so much was ordered. So, when he fought, it must be like a Chalin warrior.

He must, in all ways, become a more perfect Chalin man. Because he must pass under the very noses of his enemies. He must, Yulin said, travel to the Ascendancy first, before attempting to reach the Inyx sway.

No one came to that remote sway without official business, such as delivery of prisoners. The Inyx precincts were tight, clannish, and suspicious, not welcoming—and hardly permitting—visitors. Under these circumstances, Quinn would need an approved mission.

Yulin said that only one purpose would logically originate with him: one having to do with the protocols of leadership on the death fields before Ahnenhoon. Yulin was, in title, commander of the Chalin-led forces of the Long War. He would therefore provide a new decree that allowed Inyx to have leadership roles in battle for the first time. Such a decree, called a clarity, would be brought to the Inyx personally by Dai Shen. A brilliant stroke on Yulin's part, the new clarity offered a chance to curry favor with the Inyx, a matter of the first importance to the Tarig, even if Chalin legates considered the Inyx barbarians.

But first, the matter must be approved by the legates governing affairs, and the center of this vast administration was the Magisterium embedded in the heart of the Ascendancy. This meant that it would be necessary for Dai Shen to meet with Cixi, the high prefect—unfortunate because she had once known Titus Quinn at the Ascendancy, so his disguise must be more than adequate. It must be perfect.

The rest of his false identity was one he had already been using, that he was Dai Shen, a child of Yulin by a minor concubine. Dai Shen's sloth had earned him a banishment to the Long War, where he had earned a measure of respect, and he had now come back to his father, seeking to be useful. As a token of his father's new regard, Dai Shen was given the mission to the Inyx.

In this way, Master Yulin would earn the goodwill of the humans who would be coming. Quinn knew that this was not exactly true, and that Minerva would in fact think this a betrayal of their own mission. But they must pay attention to an influential prince such as Yulin who had established friendly relations. So it wasn't all lies, and might indeed be the best thing Yulin could have done for his future prospects.

Knowing that he would return to the Ascendancy, to that place that had been his prison, filled Quinn with both elation and disquiet. He wasn't done with the place, of course. It held all his memories of the time before. It held his enemies. The prospect of deceiving them and snatching from them a victory was not unwelcome, even with all its dangers.

Through their daily fight drills, Quinn learned that he wasn't in as good a shape as he had presumed. Being faster and more skilled, Anzi usually won their matches, and in hopes of regaining his pride, he worked hard to advance.

Some days his teacher was Ci Dehai, Yulin's general of battle. Ci Dehai and Yulin had been friends since their early days on the fields of Ahnenhoon, and Yulin trusted him completely, even with this act of treason, the training of a man of the Rose. The general, in advanced middle age, was hardened in muscle and outlook, with a face to intimidate the enemy. One side of his face was horribly disfigured, with an eye gone, the gap hidden amid folds of sagging skin. The other side looked mean.

Being taught by a top officer of battle was a great privilege, Anzi had told him, but Quinn thought that Yulin had little choice. The master's fear of betrayal extended even to his own family, leaving his inner circle composed of three good wives, his niece, and Ci Dehai—none of whom could logically succeed him, and all of whom would suffer any defeat at his side.

Ci Dehai took him through the hall of weapons, asking which ones Quinn could use. Quinn admired one short knife with a carved handle. Pleased to have that blade remarked upon, Ci Dehai held it out, letting Quinn balance it in his hand. The weapon was a favorite of Ci Dehai's, one he'd named Going Over. Quinn had never fought with knives, or any weapon; in his youthful sparring days, his big fists had been enough. A knife, though; that would take skill.

Mornings were for physical training, and afternoons for language, both of which Anzi pursued with a relentless zeal, leaving him little time to savor his victory over Yulin, or to worry about next steps. They would travel by train. This would bring close inspection by a multitude of sentients, and Dai Shen must arouse no notice. He was glad to think that Anzi would accompany him. It was a promise of sorts. Yulin wouldn't betray him with Anzi along, and, in addition, Quinn was coming to like her.

By ebb-time, his fighting lessons usually brought him a pleasant weariness, and he slept deeply during the night phase of the Entire. Because of this, he'd been startled one night when a touch on his arm awakened him. At first he thought the girl at his side was Anzi, but Anzi slept in Yulin's house, and this person was younger, with long hair pulled back and hanging to her waist. Making a sign for silence, the girl led him through the garden, avoiding the cages of animals lest their screams alert the animal stewards. He followed her, ready for trouble, remembering the ambush in the village, when he'd first arrived. Although Anzi said that the woman who'd brought him to the village, Wen An, had done him a favor, he couldn't thank her for the misery of the jar.

The girl led him to a wall-less hut like a gazebo near a short door that was called the Door of Eight Serenities, being Yulin's entrance to his garden. There, Suzong was waiting for him. Nearby, the girl kept watch just out of hearing.

Suzong had shed her usual red garments for a suit of gray, helping her blend into the hushed tones of the garden. Her black upswept hair was anchored in place by a sour paste that hit his Jacobson's organ strongly at such close range.

"I am not here," Yulin's wife began. "It is your imagination."

He bowed, receiving her nod in return. "I have a vivid imagination, Mistress."

"Yes. You do." Suzong gestured for him to sit, and she did so herself, kneeling on the bare wood floor. "One that I favor."

Insect noises from the garden lay a net over their conversation, but still, they whispered. He wondered why she had come here, and concluded it was to avoid Yulin's notice. So if he spoke to her, he was colluding. But it would be worthwhile to see what she offered. For someone with as little as he had, every offer was interesting.

"First," she began, "without *imagination*, tell me why your masters wish routes through our land. Is this true, or a ruse?" Her face in the semidark of the gazebo looked decades younger, but her voice was cracked with age.

"True, Mistress Suzong. My people have a strong drive, to voyage, to explore. . . ."

"To conquer?" Said sweetly.

"Yes, sometimes. Not always. Not where trade is a better option."

"You believe there are routes through our land because, when you went home once before, you were in a far reach of your universe?"

"Yes, and because when I came home, I was not much older than when I left. But I was sure I'd been here . . . a thousand days," he said, using the vernacular term for *a moderately long time*. "If time passes differently here, we reasoned, then space might be twisted as well. We hoped. My masters hoped. There was little to lose, sending me to find out."

Suzong smirked. "Only your life. Are you held in low regard, to be thus expendable?"

"No. It was a privilege to come. Others fought me for the chance."

She let that lie. "And will soon follow, as you say." She sighed. "The Entire is riven with holes. We watch you through the holes."

He knew this. The *reaches* were places where the barrier between universes was thin, and the Rose could be seen.

She continued, "You and I live side by side, yes? You had only to stretch a little in our direction to find us. We did marvel that you remained in darkness."

Despite the twilight of the ebb he could see her smile, not a pretty sight when she meant, as now, to put him in his place. "To us," Suzong said, "you are the dark. Dark space, dark night, dark thoughts. You are a gloomy people, riddled with death. We pity you."

"No need, excuse me, mistress."

She shrugged. "To the mole without eyes there is no dark." She held up a finger. "There will be no agreeing between us on this. But there will be time enough to discuss philosophy when your people come in numbers, yes?"

"I look forward to that, Red Mistress," he said, daring one of her more intimate titles.

The name seemed to please her, because she smiled, more easily this time. "So you do claim that your wish is to pass through?"

"But first, my wish is to take my daughter home."

Suzong sucked on her teeth as she regarded him. "Yes the small daughter who is not small anymore, of course."

"Yes." He must remember that.

"But once you have summoned the daughter to the Rose, you still wish to . . . come and go. To pass through." She nodded. "Perhaps I will prove to you that we are more than a temporary ally."

She had his attention. All of it.

She murmured, "You will bring home, if you can, a prize past all reckoning." She cut a glance at him, and her mouth curled in a voiceless laugh. "Not the daughter. The passages. Such power you will have among your former masters. You could demand your own sway, and many consorts. They will bow low indeed, if you find the passages you require." Talking almost to herself, she examined the palm of her hand. "Oh to be young once more and hold such power." Her fingers closed.

Watching Suzong with a startled intensity, Quinn thought about that *prize past all reckoning*. The prize Stefan Polich desired more than anything. In Quinn's long-standing contempt of Stefan, he had not much cared about routes to the stars, except as it would affect Sydney's escape. But now he sank into a new realization. *You could demand your own sway. . . . They will bow low.*

. . . He couldn't imagine Stefan or Helice bowing in any way—but wouldn't they do just that? Because of this power, wouldn't they give him anything he wanted? They couldn't threaten his family ever again. Rob would be safe—if he wanted the desk job—and Mateo . . . no one would dare touch the nephew of the man who had knowledge of the *passages*, as Suzong called them. Minerva couldn't ride him any longer. He would be free.

He looked up at the old consort, riveted by her insight.

At that moment she turned her head to listen for something. In the back of her lacquered hair, sticks protruded in a prickly array, some with tassels. Turning back to him, she continued in more haste: "You will learn soon enough if you don't already know, that our world is shaped by the Three Vows. The First Vow is to withhold the knowledge of the Entire from the non-Entire."

He thought that this cat was well out of the bag, but refrained from saying so. Suzong watched him carefully, and her voice lowered so that he had to bend forward to hear her. "So now I give you this power over me, that I break the vow and say that, as to routes between, there is one who may know a direction."

The girl standing watch had come to the foot of the steps. Suzong waved her away. He thought for a moment that Suzong would have to postpone her secret, the one she'd come here to tell, and he almost placed a hand on her arm to restrain her.

"Bei," she whispered, bending close to him. "Su Bei. You remember your translator from long ago?" When Quinn nodded, she went on, "Find a purpose to go to him. You have proven by your presence here that it is possible to forge passage. Even a Chalin wife knows this much. But *when* can one pass? Ah, that is the question. Twice you have been lucky. Twice you came into the Entire, and survived. But the real problem is how to go in the other direction, of course. Because the Rose is inhospitable. Dark, and full of death. We must ask, When does a reach connect with a place you would wish to go? You might wait until your hair turned black with age and never find safe passage. But Su Bei told me once that there may be someone with profound knowledge of the timing of these routes."

Quinn whispered, "Bei knows?"

"He knows where the knowledge lies. With one who resides in the bright city."

"The Ascendancy."

She nodded. "It is said. I'm glad I know no more." She held up a finger. "But, you will soon be in that high city. You can now go there with a double purpose, yes?"

He saw a movement in the garden, and Suzong's servant appeared again at the bottom of the stairs, looking concerned. Urgently, he whispered, "How can I find Bei to question him further?"

"Anzi can find him." With surprising agility, Suzong stood up, and smoothed her jacket.

Quinn rose too. His good fortune made him suspicious for a moment. "Why, mistress? Why are you telling me this?"

"When humans come"—she looked up at the bright as though envisioning the ships that would bear the invaders—"they will grind the bones of the Tarig under their boots." She smiled. "Oh yes, I have seen your wars. Very good ones."

She turned away and walked to the stairway. Before she descended, she said, "I have never come here."

"I never saw you," he said, bowing. When he straightened again, she was gone.

He left the gazebo, feeling dazed. The passages. It wasn't just about Stefan's routes, saving his star fleet from disaster. It was about feeding the dragon, satisfying Stefan at last, with the prize past all reckoning. It would put Quinn on an equal footing with Minerva. *Earning him a sway of his own,* Suzong had said.

He looked at the palm of his hand, silver in the gloaming light of the sky's embers.

Oh yes, Sydney, he thought. We're going home. And when we do, we'll have a safe haven where no one will ever own us again.

CHAPTER TEN

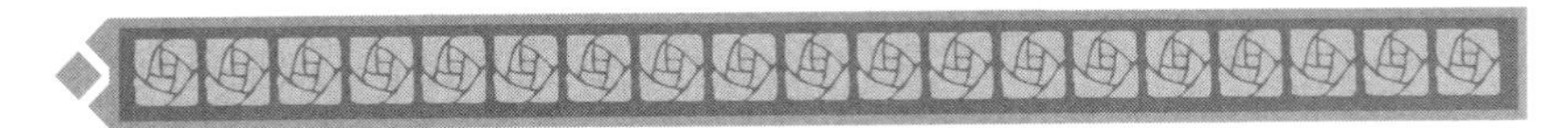

To keep the harmony of the Entire, the gracious lords set forth the Radiant Path. By keeping to the Radiant Path, all beings may rise to a station of happiness.

The path is comprised of the vows, the bonds, and the clarities. Each child must learn the Three Vows and the Thousand Bonds. The legates keep the great pandect of the laws at the bright city, within the Magisterium.

This is the Radiant Path. When all walk together, no sentient being is without hope. All may become masters, magistrates, prefects, soldiers of the Long War, legates, consuls, factors, and stewards, according to ability. No master may deny the least sentient his hope to do and be as he wishes, within the Path. No sentient, crossing from one sway to another, becomes a servant by reason of being a stranger. There are no strangers on the Radiant Path, not even the Inyx, who cannot speak.

All may be legates and scholars, according to their gifts. This is decreed by the gracious lords, that no sway bring violence to another sway. Thus is the Peace of the Entire assured.

—from *The Book of the Thousand Gifts*

DUST BOILING, HOOVES CRASHING, the two of them sped over the flat land, exulting in the noise and speed.

Sydney rode the thundering beast, whipping his sides with her crop, because he enjoyed the blows and liked his rider to like it. She'd pay for the pain she'd inflicted when they got back to the encampment. This was their twisted relationship, but it, or something like it, was all a prisoner of the Inyx could hope for. They wanted no equals. The Inyx wanted to run, and be ridden. Sydney was a good match for them in one crucial way: She loved to ride.

Glovid's hooves spit stones as he galloped, his ears flattened against the wind, his eyes mere slits against the glint of the bright. They had been running a long while, and still the hard-packed dunes were as distant as ever, so Glovid's eyes told his rider.

Blind since childhood, Sydney saw through the beast's eyes a flickering version of the world—fragmentary, yet vivid. Assimilating those volatile projections was a skill all riders learned from necessity. By this means she saw the far-flung steppe, roamlands of the Inyx. No one came to this sway unless they were bonded to an Inyx, and all came blind, because the stinking beasts wanted their riders dependent on them.

She held tight to the rear horn on Glovid's spine. It had been whittled down, or her hands would be red meat by now. His row of forward-curving horns would serve Glovid well when he fought for a mate. Next time perhaps a female Inyx would cull him permanently from the herd with her even longer horns.

Her knees tucked into the creature's sides as they entered a pockmarked terrain where, if she fell, she could break her head open on the rocks. A saddle would have helped stability, but Glovid disliked the feel of them.

"Haagh!" she cried, lashing the beast's flank, and he galloped mightily, excited by her excitement, pleased by her lust for speed.

She felt his exultation. She would have denied him the pleasure of knowing her mind. But there was no way to hide her thoughts from Glovid, or any other Inyx who cared to take a peek. Though, in truth, the beasts didn't pay much attention to the thoughts of their riders, any more than, once, Sydney had cared what her pet hamster was thinking . . . in that other life, lived far away.

Glovid stumbled. In the next second she was flying over Glovid's head, crashing to the ground. She landed hard, but rolled out of it, stunned. The wind flattened her hair, blowing grit into her eyes.

Her mount trumpeted in pain. Following this sound, she found him collapsed, with one leg shattered at the fetlock. Bone protruded, Glovid's terrified vision told her. So. He would never join the herd again. His burial mound would be here.

Kneeling next to him, she imagined his horsey face, the liquid green eyes, his long neck with its curving horns, a being once powerful, now cringing. A dozen taunts came to mind, but they lost their flavor as Glovid grew nauseated with pain. She felt some of it as her own, bringing her the sudden insight that the herd's solidarity sprang from shared pain as well as shared thoughts.

Kill me, Glovid said.

She'd known he would ask that, but she hesitated. He could possibly be mended. The sway would have to send for a Tarig physician, because this break was beyond the surgeons in the roamlands. The camp's healer, Adikar, would never try to set an Inyx compound fracture.

At the thought of a Tarig doctor, Glovid sent, *Kill me, I said.*

No one would blame her. They knew Glovid commanded it. Stepping forward, she unsheathed the knife at her belt. "Lay your head on the ground." She would have to press down with both hands to sever the thick tendons in his neck.

Glovid obeyed. *Many days to you, small rose*, he thought to her.

He knew she hated that nickname. Small rose. Somehow, in his twisted mind, he thought she was proud of her sway. He was wrong. But now her mind was on the thing she had to do.

"Good-bye, Glovid," she said. "That last ride was very good."

Placing her hands first on his neck to feel the throb of the large artery, she carefully lifted the knife straight up and then she plunged it down, ripping through his hide. Twisting the blade, she sawed at the throat until the blade hit the artery.

He bled swiftly, losing consciousness. In a few moments he was beyond his days.

She wiped the blade and her reeking hands on Glovid's hide. Kneeling on the hard pan, she gathered her thoughts. Soon another mount would lay claim to her. He might be better or worse than Glovid, but what did that matter? Nothing was truly bad, except the lords of this world. She had hated them from her first glimpse of their stretched bodies, their skin like polished copper, and faces as cruel as their hands. Their hands. One hand could hold a small child immobile, while the other hand was free to be cruel . . . with great precision, taking her sight, cradling her in an elbow joint like a vise.

No, the Inyx were nothing compared to the mantis lords.

After the day of her blinding, she had longed to die. Her parents were dead, she thought, leaving her alone in a hated world. She hadn't seen them since the Tarig captured them in the underground place where they were hiding and where they had pierced the Entire. A good way to die would be to throw herself from the outer deck of the Ascendancy.

The old woman had been summoned the day that Sydney stood on the edge of the balcony, having crossed the barrier, and held on fiercely as the winds yanked at her. The woman spoke a halting English, and promised her that no Tarig would approach her. She said that if Sydney came away from the rim, she could have a pet to keep; and then, if she still wished to jump, she could do so tomorrow. So Sydney went with her and learned that the woman, who was barely taller than herself, was named Cixi, and that she was important. It was Cixi who taught her of her father's betrayal, and her mother's, when it came, and that they weren't worth dying for. She also taught her never to call the bright lords bad names, although when Sydney was sent to the Inyx, Cixi broke down and called them *fiends*.

Now, sitting next to Glovid's body, she tilted her head to the sky, to judge the time of day by the heat of the bright. It was Heart of Day, she guessed. The system of time was based on eighths. Eight phases of the bright, each with a name: *Early*, *Prime*, *Heart*, and *Last*. And then of ebb-time, *Twilight*, *Shadow*, *Deep*, and *Between*. And each of the phases was four hours long. All sentients could judge the time of day, and the time of ebb, by internal design. All except Sydney.

Now, deep onto the steppe-lands, she was riderless and in jeopardy. She hefted her water bag to calculate her water supply. Not enough. She could wait until Twilight to walk back, to conserve water loss. But which direction? Flickers of the herd came to her, without directionality. They sent their thoughts to her, and also lapped at her mind. She was passive in these interactions. She knew that the stronger her feelings, the more likely they were to listen to her thoughts. So she could attract their attention, but not truly send.

One thing was clear. They knew that Glovid had fallen.

She began walking, perhaps even in the right direction, by the wind, by the strength of the herd's sendings. She doubted the herd would come for her.

The mounts had once thought her worth the trouble. But that was long ago, before they grew weary of her. Priov, chief of the Inyx, kept her to avoid offending the Tarig. But few wanted her. Glovid was the latest to give her a try. Seeing how he ended up, perhaps he would be the last.

The wind was shifting around to blow from heartward, the center of the Entire, which was a radial universe. The topography of the world was burned into her mind. Someday she would need a good map, and her mind was constructing it, piece by piece.

The geometries of the Entire were simple. The main forms were the five *primacies*. This primacy was called the Long Gaze of Fire, enormous beyond comprehending, beyond traveling, beyond hope. Here she was as far from the Tarig in their city as Earth was from the pole star. The primacies radiated outward from a central core. She thought that such a land as this must somehow exist within the Rose universe, side by side with it, or tunneling through it. But some of her fellow riders claimed that the Entire could not extend *through* something, since it was All that existed. They scoffed at the idea of the other universe, although they held in their midst one who was born there. Truly, her fellow stablemates were dumb as dreds in the Rose.

Branching from the primacies were the small *minorals*. Narrow and deserted, the minorals were occupied only sporadically, and only at the tips, the reaches, where scholars worked.

Smaller still than a minoral were the *nascences*, growing out of the minorals like root hairs. Highly unstable, they could close up quickly, or lie crackling with energy for thousands of days. If you wished to kill yourself, that was a good place to go. But in the Entire, death was easier to come by than that.

Each primacy had a great river along one wall. In all primacies, it was called the River Nigh, the mysterious flow that, together with the bright, was the Tarig's invention, to allow normal life and travel, in this land as vast as a universe. Such things had seemed a story when she was nine, and newly born into the immortal realm. By now, it was the map of her world, the only world worth knowing about. So, by her internal map, she was heading away from the River Nigh, and down-primacy. By these crude calculations she could walk for a thousand days and not see another soul.

But *a thousand days* was just a turn of phrase. In reality, one could never walk the length of a primacy. A primacy had no absolute length. Around the campfire, in the ebb, the riders talked of regions of twisted space-land—the Empty Lands—where geography was distorted into ever-changing patterns. You might cross a plain in ten days or in ten thousand. But you would never arrive on the other side, so it might as well be an eternity. Only the Nigh could bring you to the ends of the Entire. But of the lands where one *could* walk, even these were endless, and mostly empty, although countless billions of sentients called the Entire home.

Already her feet hurt. She wasn't used to walking. *Yes, my feet hurt, you stinking, stupid beasts.* She couldn't send her thoughts to them, but it was her habit to try.

The plains hummed. In the soles of her feet she felt a gentle throb. Gradually, it became more insistent. So they were coming for her, after all. That would save a very long walk. Despite herself, she was glad—even counting all the injuries from them that she had recorded in her book.

At length she could hear them, the drumming of their hooves on the hard pan. Finally, she smelled the dust rise up, and then the sweat of their bodies around her.

It was a small pack of them, perhaps forty mounts. Some of them bore riders, the scum of the sways—a filthy and course mixture of species. Emotions, thoughts, and images assaulted her from all sides. The Inyx peppered her with thoughts, and relayed their riders' thoughts, and it came into Sydney's mind as noise, with a few spikes of clarity.

The mounts with riders sped past her, heading for Glovid's body, but a few solo Inyx stayed. She heard them snort to catch their breaths. One of them sent, *You are unbonded now.*

"Yes." She wouldn't beg. Some of the riders who'd lost mounts were content to stay in the stables and eke out an existence. But Sydney wanted to ride. Some of the mounts knew this.

A hoof struck the ground. One Inyx had already decided to bid for her. A powerful surge of emotion came to her. Riod, the creature's name was. Not a good prospect. He was a renegade who often was crossways with Priov, sniffing at the edges of Priov's band of mares. No, Riod was crazy. Young, brash, and hated by Priov and others who thought he didn't know his place.

Again, the hoof struck the ground.

She waited. Other Inyx stood there with him. Four others, she guessed. Why had they come, unless they were interested in competing for her? But there was no jostling and mock fighting. Only Riod signaled his intention.

As Sydney stood before the giant mounts, her legs stiffened and grew tired. She tasted the wind, and the scents of the Inyx. She must respond to this offer from Riod. If one of them wanted you, and you weren't bonded already, then it was in your best interests to ride that mount. You would learn to care for it. Most of the riders preferred male mounts, because they could offer more protection, being stronger and not subject to the bearing of foal, as infrequent as that was.

Riod stomped again. But Sydney was waiting for him to woo her.

On her long walk she'd decided to never again accept a mount like Glovid, who was course and mean. Let any mount who desired her make his case.

So she stood immobile. And waited.

Behind her came the sounds of the mounts returning from the place where Glovid had fallen. Now they surrounded her, creating a wall of sweating, breathing Inyx. You could not be unaware of their power. Their heads towered over hers, an arm's span above. She was, as near as she could tell, diminutive. She had taken her mother's frame, and her father's athleticism. It was all she had taken from them, and she would have given even that much back if she could. Aware that her mother had always worn her dark hair long, Sydney cut her own dark hair very short. She was nothing like any Quinn, nor any Rose being.

For starters, she did not bow the knee to enslavers. "Why do you want me?" she asked Riod.

Sitting astride their mounts, the riders were silent, and kept their emotions in check. If they felt anything, they knew to keep it submerged at a time like this.

Finally Riod answered, *I choose you.*

"But why?"

You ride well.

He had said more than Glovid had ever done. Yet she wasn't satisfied.

In impatience, the Inyx began snorting and shaking their heads. But still she stood, defiant.

Riod stomped the ground once more. *Hear me, human woman: I choose the best rider in the sway.*

Sydney moved in the direction of his stomping noises. She placed her hand on the side of Riod's strong face. He stood quietly, allowing her to touch his hide, hot and sweating. She liked what he had said.

His words came vividly: *When the best rider in the sway swings onto my back, none will be faster on the plains than we.*

A vision leapt into her mind, of a furious gallop across the tundra, Riod's hooves spitting sand and rocks behind them, the wind lashing her face, the Entire coming to meet them. She saw herself hunched forward, hanging on lightly, her body synchronized to the rolling gait, the joy of the ride clinging to them both.

The joy of a very fast ride.

Riod dipped his head, impatient for her to climb on. From the circle of Inyx, one sent her an image of a hoof cracking against her skull.

She laughed out loud. That was one mount who didn't know how to persuade her. She turned to Riod. But here was one who did. "Yes," she said. "I choose you, too."

A tension left the circle, and the Inyx began to mill around Sydney as she reached up for Riod's postern horn. He dipped his forelegs down enough that she could swing up, and she did so, in an easy leap.

He spun in a circle, as though eyeing the other Inyx. A triumphant mood came from him, a mood that hit her hard and sweet, surprising her. Fending off this weakness, she dug her knees into his side and he sprang forward, reaching for ground, speeding away from the others, hooves pounding, as though eager to prove what he could do.

She tossed away her crop. With this one, she wouldn't need it.

CHAPTER ELEVEN

This is all that can be said of God:
Shun Him.
—from *The Twelve Wisdoms*

QUINN FELL HARD, smacking his shoulder into the ground, having taken a savage kick from his combat teacher. He rolled to his feet and faced the man.

Ci Dehai beckoned him, with a flick of his fingers from his open palm. But Quinn didn't need that gesture to come at his opponent. Ci Dehai was leading with his right, and might not expect an assault from the left. He began his lunge, but before he had gotten far, his mouth was full of dust.

So it had gone for the last few days, as Ci Dehai had beaten and berated Quinn into his version of a Chalin warrior. One who might have been away at the Long War, to account for Dai Shen suddenly appearing in the sway. Before long he would be transformed in another way: they planned to alter his face—surgeries they seemed more confident about than he was—which was necessary since at the Ascendancy, if not in the Inyx sway, he would be among those who would recognize his old face.

His Chalin teacher said, "You have too much passion. Find the river, Dai Shen, and it will carry you." He summoned Quinn, palms up, fingers beckoning.

Quinn circled, breathing, imagining a river. Imagining punching Ci Dehai senseless. Ci Dehai was as big as Quinn, but faster.

Anzi stood at the edge of the circle, her arms folded over her chest, clearly hoping her student would make a better showing than he was.

A heavy dew had moved in early in the morning, dumping moisture on the outbuildings and drenching the combatants. Quinn rubbed his hands dry on his tunic pants and closed with Ci Dehai, forcing his teacher to step back, leaving an opening for him to punch with the side of his hand. Delivering the blow to empty space sent him falling once again. The breath left him. Ci Dehai should be vulnerable on his blind side, but so far he wasn't.

Ci Dehai looked down at him, unimpressed. "Let go of winning. Use your reflexive mind. Your body knows what to do."

Quinn stood, slapping himself off, squinting at his opponent, a man who'd taken terrible blows, most likely from the Paion themselves, since the Entire had no other wars. Evidently the Paion hadn't let go of winning.

Standing in the dusty yard, Ci Dehai scowled. "Master Yulin will have a story that you fought at Ahnenhoon. So far, it's hard to credit." He looked over his shoulder at the high wall forming Yulin's personal training courtyard. Beyond it lay the barracks where, no doubt, Ci Dehai preferred to be, presiding over the battle training of ten thousand men and women. Anzi had said their numbers were ten thousand, but by now Quinn knew that was just their way of saying *many*. Or their way of not disclosing real numbers.

The general beckoned Quinn to close with him.

Moving in on his opponent, Quinn delivered a short punch to the jaw, careful not to expose himself too much.

Ci Dehai easily deflected him, striking Quinn a glancing blow with his elbow as Quinn's momentum carried him by. "Clumsy and obvious," he pronounced. "Since you are overmatched, you must conserve energy, watch for my openings."

"Do you have any?"

"So you are blind as well as clumsy?"

Quinn lunged, receiving a painful chop to his neck.

Ci Dehai's lecture continued. "Induce fear by striking at the *three*: eyes, neck, and groin."

Quinn blocked a punch and followed up with a near miss to his opponent's eyes.

"Good," his teacher said. "But you are dead. Behind you is the post where I will fling you, smashing open your head." Sweeping his foot, he took Quinn down within inches of the training ground's center post.

Looking down at Quinn, he said, "You care too much." He shrugged. "A human failing."

Still sitting in the dust, Quinn caught his breath. "How do you stop caring?"

"By accepting. By releasing. By forgetting."

"I can't forget." He hadn't intended to discuss personal feelings with a Chalin general, but the general had seen into the core of him and called him on what he saw.

With a careless tone Ci Dehai murmured, "An immortal must forget, or carry a heavy load." He looked at Quinn, well aware that his student was not of the Entire. For these practices Quinn had been told to take out his eye lenses since their imperfections hampered his training. But Ci Dehai was calling him to be of the Entire, at least in combat.

Quinn got up, slapping the dust from his pants. "Maybe forgetting is a Chalin failing." If you forgot who you were, how could you care enough to go on?

The single eye glinted in the bright. "There is a river in you, Dai Shen. But it should run forward, not backward." He walked to a covered gallery that bounded the practice field, where he took a drink.

Anzi came forward with a damp towel for Quinn. "How am I doing?" Quinn asked. She caught his ironic smile and allowed herself a smile in return as he accepted the towel, wiping down the sweat from his bare arms and chest.

"Ci Dehai is teaching you how little you know. So that is good."

A movement on the rooftop caught his eye. Two people stood on the palace roof, watching the courtyard—one stout and short, the other slight and dressed in red. Over them, the bright cast a blurry light, obscured as it was this morning by a haze of moisture.

Quinn bowed in that direction. Yulin nodded to him.

The dew that had been heavy when the lesson began was now thinning to a mere gauze, and Suzong's red silks caught stabs of light. He hoped that he had read her correctly: that she craved autonomy from the Tarig. And that the reason she had come to him in secret that night was to break the First Vow without Yulin's complicity, in case the treason should be discovered. He felt a fierce gratitude for her willingness to commit that treason.

He bowed again, in Suzong's direction, and she returned it.

Ci Dehai took a long drink of water, then placed the empty cup next to his discarded shirt and the tangle of his necklaces. Quinn had seen that style of ornament before, on Wen An the scholar.

Ci Dehai beckoned Anzi into the yard, saying, "Now watch, Dai Shen."

The two of them faced off. Anzi circled the general, diving close to slap his lower arms, retreating, advancing, and slapping. Quinn noted that the forays allowed her to keep her balance while punishing her opponent's arms. Ci Dehai began blocking her slaps, finally catching one, and in a swift move, twisted her to her knees.

"Here, I break her arm," Ci Dehai said. He held her immobile, then released her.

"Again."

Anzi began her slapping advances as before, this time sweetening her approach with a side kick that sent Ci Dehai to one side to evade the foot. Before he could face her squarely, she'd punched a slicing thrust at his elbow.

"Good. When fighting someone better, ruin his arms and hands." Quinn saw that this was Anzi's tactic. The only part of Ci Dehai she could get near were his arms. At her first chance she attacked an elbow, even more vulnerable.

"When overmatched, be content with small harms. Small adds up to large."

She came again, then was up in the air and crashing to the ground. It was too swift to know what had happened. Rolling away, she used her momentum to rise to her feet.

"Spend little time on the ground," Ci Dehai said with only a hint of sarcasm.

Their session over, Quinn joined the master at the gallery, taking the proffered cup of water and looking more closely at the ravaged face. It had healed well, from the looks of the depth of the wound.

Anzi came up, adjusting her fighting tunic, unfazed by her fall. She smiled at Quinn.

"Ci Dehai has fought the Paion at Ahnenhoon and suffered his terrible wound at their hands. I'm not ashamed to lose a match with him."

There was something of propaganda in her statement, but he needed to know more about the Paion, not least because they were enemy to the Tarig. "Who are the Paion, Anzi?"

Ci Dehai answered, drinking a long draft of water. "No one ever knows." He looked off, beyond the palace within which their deserted square lay. "Nor has any living sentient ever seen one. They ride on the backs of mechanical simulacra, under carapaces of battle, and if we split one open, they dissolve, confounding our desire to see their forms and faces. They are foreigners under the bright—not of the Entire, neither are they of the Rose. So our scholars have it." He paused. "Perhaps it is well for a military man to have a fine enemy, for there are none in the bright realm."

"What are they fighting about?" The books had not been clear.

He scrunched up the movable side of his face. "No one ever knows."

Ci Dehai wiped down with a wet towel and then took his necklaces from the bench, dropping them in place over his head. The redstones rested on his broad chest like a jeweled collar on a boar.

"Tomorrow then," Ci Dehai said, and turned to leave, but Quinn stopped him.

"General." As Ci Dehai turned back, Quinn said, "I'm privileged to have such a teacher. You have larger concerns than me, yes?"

Ci Dehai nodded. "I do. But perhaps a general rides too often, when he should walk." He patted his ample belly, and he gave the half-smile his face was capable of, one that was large, even so.

Quinn bowed. "*Nahil*, Ci Dehai."

Anzi bowed as well, and then they were alone in the courtyard, with Yulin and Suzong departing from the roof. Anzi waved happily to her uncle. In that unguarded moment, when her face was relaxed and free of serious duty, Quinn thought that he knew her from another time and place. The unwelcome thought came to him that there was no particular reason to trust Anzi.

Twilight had dimmed the bright, and Quinn was in the gardens once more, sharing a meal with Anzi by the lake. He liked to stare at the flat sheen of the pond, where occasionally he conjured memories. But, like the out-of-body experiences he'd once had, these visions were hard to follow—and believe in. It was as though someone else lived inside his skin. At times he resented that person, the one who remembered.

In the lake's smooth surface, he saw Johanna, her black hair disheveled, her eyes distant. *Without the young girl.* Haunted by a world that never had a night.

I'll bring her home, Johanna, he thought. He had come here to bring Johanna home, too, but that was not to be.

Twilight deepened into Shadow time, and the pool lost its faces.

Anzi stood. "I've brought you something. In the hut." She led the way and entered his one-room living quarters, then knelt beside a box that she had left in the middle of the floor. "This is something you remember, Dai Shen?"

It was an adobe-colored flat-sided container, about as long as her forearm.

"A stone well," he said, bringing forth the term from that reservoir within him. But until he'd seen this box, he'd forgotten that the sways had computing devices. Very odd ones.

"Yes. A well of keeping and releasing." She reached into her tunic pocket and brought out a thong on which hung a small, irregular redstone. Untying the end knot, she pulled the redstone off the string and thumbed a nodule on the top.

A hole opened. She dropped the stone into the hole, which closed up.

Anzi cradled the box in her arms to bring it closer to Quinn's view. They waited. These things took time. The data rock must dissolve, and the molecular material must dock onto the locking sites, recognizing other molecules by shape. Computing work would result. It was pattern recognition based on shape-fitting. A uniquely Tarig twist to computer processing.

A picture formed on the forward face of the box. It was a wide plain, with an army massing. There were thousands of warriors, wearing armored suits in colors that may have signified branch of service. Great transport beasts stomped the ground, horselike animals with curved horns down their necks. Creatures rode them, creatures even stranger than their mounts.

"The Inyx," Anzi said, pointing to the horse-creatures.

Quinn peered more closely. He had heard descriptions of these beasts. So, here were the native beings that ruled the Inyx sway. Incredible to think that Sydney lived among such creatures. Sentient creatures, he had to remind himself.

On the stone well screen, he noted a boiling black mass sliding down the flanks of distant, low hills. "Paion?" he asked, and Anzi nodded.

Quinn saw Ci Dehai standing on a platform with his lieutenants, pointing and directing. Behind him lay a dark and enormous keep.

"The Repel of Ahnenhoon," Anzi whispered.

The stone well emitted a salty smell, bringing a flood of memory, of larger wells, and a labyrinth of rooms, where legates hunched over their labors. The Magisterium, he realized.

"Where did you get the redstone, Anzi?"

She watched as a contingent of tall Inyx mounts formed up next to the reviewing stand. But she didn't answer.

"Is this from Ci Dehai? He gave you the redstone?"

She shook her head, still watching the scene, and pointing at things Quinn should notice, like a Tarig lord who stood well back, watching, wrapped in a long cloak.

"Anzi?"

She looked into his eyes with her trademark calm. "For you, Dai Shen," she said. "I borrowed it for you."

Quinn thought that Ci Dehai had not given it willingly. "You'll get in trouble."

"If he notices it gone, only then," she said. "He has many stones."

They watched the scene change as the bright dimmed over the battlefield, and the fight continued somewhere in the distance, where a clash of arms could be heard. But Quinn could only stare at the fortress. "Ahnenhoon," he said.

"Yes. The fortress of the Long War. The Paion have come for many archons, beating on its doors. So far, our armies have kept them out."

"Who lives at Ahnenhoon?" Besides—once—my wife, he thought.

"It's the station of Lord Inweer." She glanced in the direction of the figure on the well screen.

He remembered that name. The Lord Inweer. His wife's jailer. Lord Inweer who looked so much like Lord Hadenth. It had taken Quinn years to figure out the difference between them. By temperament was the surest way. Hadenth was half-mad, for one thing.

The scene faded, and the stone budded out at the bottom of the box, falling into a small cup. It was still wet, but it looked exactly as it had before, despite having been dissolved. Anzi began threading it back on the thong.

"You stole it," Quinn said.

"Yes." She smiled as she threaded the stone on its string. "But I wanted you to see the battlefield. So you can almost have been there, which is the lie that must persuade others."

Yes. So it would seem probable that Yulin had a son whom no one in the palace household had ever seen.

Anzi had grown still, and now her head turned slowly to face the open doorway. She rose, moving to the opening.

"Listen," she said.

There was nothing. Then he realized the animals were silent. The treetops rustled in a breeze, but no bird cried from the aviary. No animal screamed or chittered. Even the lake was unnaturally placid. He and Anzi made eye contact, and he rose swiftly, joining her at the door. Tugging at his arm, Anzi led the way across the clearing, looking back as she hurried.

Then, in the shelter of the forest brush, they crouched down, watching. On the other side of the clearing, he spied a movement. A gardener moved among the bushes there, stealthily, and with the lurching gate of one whom Quinn recognized. The gardener, come to warn them of something?

As though in answer, Anzi looked at Quinn, shaking her head and frowning. She pulled his sleeve, urging him to follow her. "Quiet," she whispered. They slowly moved out of their hiding place, retreating farther into the brush. They had barely spoken during these few minutes of flight, but by Anzi's alarm, he understood they were in peril. She led him to a cage where a door lay ajar, and nothing lay within but overgrown vines.

Quinn checked behind them. A line of sight gave him a clear view of the top of the great aviary. There on the cage summit, against the dimming bright, an impossibly tall figure stood watch, its skin glinting bronze.

Anzi hissed at him. He followed her, helping her lift a heavy plate from the ground. The two of them managed to raise it, though it was covered with soil and plants. She motioned for him to crawl in, and she came close behind, lowering the trap door.

They were in a tunnel, in complete blackness.

"Made for Master Yulin to escape," Anzi explained. "Hurry."

Quinn followed her, heart pounding. She had said the Tarig come and go, looking . . . But why now? Had the gardeners betrayed him after all? Or Yulin himself?

"It's the Tarig, Anzi. I saw one."

"Yes," she answered. "We are betrayed."

The blackness of the underground passage was absolute. After so many days in a world where it never darkened, he was startled by the blackness, and the blind dash through the earthen tunnel. Yet, in that perfect blankness came a memory, keen and whole:

The escape capsule, heavily buffeted. Johanna at the controls, the ship breaking up, Sydney hunkering under a control panel while Quinn lurched forward, taking control of the navigation that didn't respond. Dead controls, screens breaking up, the capsule thrashing. He reached for Johanna, thinking it would be their last moment. As he reached out she took his hand, pulling herself toward him; and as he looked into her face, it stretched and twisted. He saw her face slide sideways. *Sydney*, he called, but no answer, until, as he lost consciousness, he heard her voice, far away, saying, *Father. Father.* Growing more faint. After hours or days or moments, he awoke to a patch of light. He saw a woman with startlingly white hair. It had been Anzi, he now realized. She stepped back, retreating so far she was pressed against the wall of a strange alcove. She looked like she'd just seen the face of God.

Quinn stopped cold in the tunnel. "I know you."

After a pause, came a small voice from up ahead. "Yes."

"Who are you?"

"No time, Dai Shen. The Tarig—"

"The hell with the Tarig. Who are you?"

"Please, Dai Shen. I'll tell you everything. First, run."

But should he put himself in her hands? Where was she leading him? To more captors, as the other Chalin woman had? A sound close by. She had crept back to him, and he latched onto her, pressing her against the dirt wall. "Not until you tell me who you are."

Her voice quavered. "Dai Shen, forgive me." He waited to learn what for.

She continued: "I took you here, into the All. It was my error, all my error. I am sorry." She grew limp under his hands, sinking to the floor.

He crouched next to her. "You took me?"

"Yes, at the reach. Everything that befell you was my fault, because I saw you in your peril, and brought you into a worse one."

"How? How did you bring me here?" He gripped her arm.

"The reach. At the veil. A forbidden thing, a terrible thing."

He released her. "So that's what Yulin meant, that he hid me for your sake. Because you owed me a debt."

"Yes, forgive me. I could never be happy since, knowing your sorrow."

Sounds of footfalls came from above their heads. He pushed her away. "Why should I trust you now?"

After a pause, her whisper came: "I don't know."

He leaned against the tunnel, trying to control his anger. "I don't either." Muffled, guttural voices came to them. He whispered, "Get us away from here, then."

They rushed down the tunnel, finally coming to a bright patch where the air freshened. They peered through a tangle of hanging moss at a cityscape of glinting black buildings.

Anzi reached into her tunic and took something out. A knife. "Take this," she said.

It was the knife from the armory. The Going Over blade.

He took the weapon and climbed through the opening after her, wondering what else she'd stolen, besides the redstone, the knife, and his family.

Yulin was sweating, but then, the day was warm. The pot of oba sat on a tray, steaming, adding to the suffocation of the surprise visit from Lord Echnon, a Tarig they had never met, but one whom Yulin knew was loose in the city, watching and wandering, as they increasingly did these days.

"May I offer refreshment, Bright Lord?" Suzong asked in a sweet voice, very steady.

The Tarig lord sat opposite them, his vest and long slit skirt of fine-spun metal—a tasteless display of wealth and weaving skill. With slicked-back hair, the elongated face seemed too thin to contain a fine mind, or a kind one.

When the servants had first arrived, stammering about a lone Tarig at the door, Suzong had spat at Yulin, "Mention Zai Gan, and that he does not love you. Let us discredit him as a jealous heir." She cursed Zai Gan in awful terms, always quick to blame Yulin's half brother for setbacks, and then, as the Tarig lord approached, she charged her face with a radiant smile, bowing low. It made Yulin wince inwardly to see her so frightened, and it set him more on edge than he was already.

"Oba?" Suzong asked the Tarig again. "Sorry, or I can send to the marketplace for skeel, which our kitchens lack, not expecting the honor of your visit."

Lord Echnon looked out beyond the terrace where they sat, gazing at the garden treetops. "A very pretty garden. Yes, and its wild creatures in cages. Well fed?" Yulin winced inwardly, remembering how, earlier, the lord had climbed the aviary for a better view, his long arms grabbing for the crossbars, drawing the birds to peck at him, which had caused Yulin to nearly lose his bowels with dismay. But the birds soon lost interest in Tarig meat, and the lord climbed rapidly, like a river spider.

Well fed? the lord had asked.

Yulin had been breathlessly waiting for the conversation to get under way, and now that it had, he was speechless. At Suzong's pointed stare, he replied. "Oh certainly. The gardeners take excellent care of one's collection. Thank you for your concern, Bright Lord."

He fervently hoped that by now Anzi and Quinn were well away, melted into the teeming city, or fleeing beyond it. But why had Lord Echnon come? Yulin had known that the lord was in the city, but prowling, as was their custom, not paying social calls, just watching, unnerving all who came near.

Suzong still hovered with the oba pot, not having permission to pour or not pour.

As they waited for the lord to direct the conversation, Yulin loosened his sash belt, feeling too warm. Suzong warned him with her eyes, as though to say, *Stop fidgeting.* God's beku, was he doing everything wrong?

Lord Echnon went on, "We have heard of the Chalin master's park with cages. It is even larger than our own grounds." He took pity on Suzong and nodded for her to pour.

She did so, with remarkable steadiness, spilling not a drop. Then she poured for Yulin, who gratefully slurped, wetting his throat. "Lord, it is my refuge," he said. "I have many enemies who wait for me to walk among them, so it is wiser to do my walking at home."

Echnon picked up his cup of oba, holding it with surprising delicacy for one with only four fingers, and all of them too long. He drank, slurping with polite appreciation, though it was well known that Tarig did not favor oba.

The lord turned his tar-black eyes on Yulin. The worst part of a Tarig visit was that they did not blink, so the impression of a fixed gaze was unnerving, even if one was innocent. "Terrible when enemies lie so close to one's nest, ah?"

Yulin put on a face of gloom. "Yet more terrible when they are one's own . . . relatives, Lord. As sometimes happens, of course, despite all the overtures one can make." There. He had blamed his brother, indirectly. It was all he dared to do, lest he look too obvious.

The main question was, did the lord know that a man named Dai Shen was here? If so, then better to mention Dai Shen first, to appear forthcoming. But if the lord didn't know, then no reason to mention a bastard son by a minor concubine. So Yulin dithered, wishing with all his heart that he and Suzong had had warning so they might have prepared a strategy. Now he was on his own.

"Excellent oba, Chalin wife," the lord said to Suzong.

Chalin wife was not her favorite appellation, but she sweetened her smile even further. "No, certainly not, Bright Lord, not up to the standard, nor what you deserve, but thank you." She poured again, saying, "If Zai Gan were here, we could all enjoy oba together." She sighed. "Now he will hear that we had honored company, but he was not invited. Please, if you see him, say we were distressed to not have time to summon him."

Yulin was impressed that she had managed to turn the conversation from refreshment to his brother, while suggesting that the brother was testy and jealous, and that they were sorrowful at his absence. She was adroit, and he began to breathe easier. His cup refilled, he drank to cover his lack of a follow-on remark.

"We will tell him," the lord said, implying he would be seeing Zai Gan, the poxy fat schemer. So perhaps Suzong was right, and Zai Gan was behind this visit. Meaning that Zai Gan had a spy in Yulin's house. Meaning also that it was likely the lord knew there was a man in the garden. Or did he?

"Send for cakes, Suzong," Yulin said. "Lord, may I offer food?" He hoped that this would force Echnon to come to the point.

The Tarig held up a hand. "Send for nothing. Sitting and discussing is enough, ah?"

Suzong said, "Certainly, Lord Echnon. Then, what news of the Ascendancy, if it pleases you to say? We live so far from great proceedings." She leaned closer like an old gossip with nothing on her mind but Tarig glamour and the bureaucracy of the bright city. Yulin admired her more than ever.

Echnon turned his gaze back to Suzong. "Hnnn. News of the bright city. What would it please you to know?"

"Oh, anything," Suzong chirped as though witless to be wasting the lord's time. "Lady Chiron, is she in residence? And does Cixi fare well? She is old by now, even older than this Chalin wife."

The lord put down his oba and unwrapped his long fingers from the cup. "The Chalin high prefect does not tire us with her duties, which she handles that we may be spared them. But she lives. Still. As to Lady Chiron, she is sometimes there. You cannot know where we are."

"Lord, my life in your service, I meant no disrespect. I am an old woman, too long on the margins to know fine manners."

Suzong looked at the pot of steaming oba, cursing her stupidity. She had gone too far, but the fiend would not come to the point, and she was desperate for him to be gone, or to accuse her and be done with it. If they could just keep the lord talking, perhaps Dai Shen could escape with Anzi's help.

Lord Echnon sipped his oba, and the conversation lapsed.

Suzong glanced at his handsome face, so flawless, except too long. Everything about the Tarig was long and narrow, yet she knew they were fearfully strong. It would take little for him to snap her neck, as perhaps he was considering at this moment. May he take me first, she thought passionately, so I will not see my husband go down at his feet.

The lord said, "Ji Anzi has returned to this house, hnnn? Have we been misinformed?"

Suzong was startled, but Yulin controlled himself nicely, saying, "Yes, Lord, the least of my nieces has been visiting. Thank you for your interest in so small a girl."

Suzong's blood cooled. So, Zai Gan did have a spy in their house, and had informed the lord. The spy must also have revealed their other guest. A suspicious patient in the garden was one matter, but if he were known to have blue eyes, that was quite another. But no one knew of the blue eyes except herself, Yulin, Anzi, and Ci Dehai.

Recovering, Suzong blurted, "Of course Anzi is nursing the bastard son Dai Shen, and so it is well that she happened to come home at this time. She has been useful to us."

Yulin was looking at her as though she were demented to mention Dai Shen, but in this, he was wrong. Better to tell the lord first, before being asked or accused.

"Hnnn. Dai Shen. Your son, you say?"

"A worthless progeny, Lord," Yulin said. "He hardly merits your interest."

"Now husband," Suzong said, "Dai Shen made a good soldier, since by all accounts he showed himself well at Ahnenhoon."

"No, I fear he was average," Yulin said pointedly. "Nothing whatever to brag about or dwell upon."

Suzong shook her head. "Oh, that you could say such things of your own son! True, he has not the brains of a veldt mouse, but he is loyal, and a soldier. For shame, husband."

Yulin began to catch on, saying, "Ci Dehai has been in battle a hundred times, and of all that time, only one wound. Dai Shen fights once and comes home with a dent in his head and loses what little common sense he ever had—can't even remember his own name, and now he'll be a hanger-on at court and I'll be forced to bear his presence." He turned to Echnon. "Your pardon, Bright Lord, but my son is worthless, an embarrassment, and now I have him in my garden, disturbing my peace. The only place where I had privacy. Yet we do our best even for wayward progeny, do we not, even if he's one of a hundred sons?

With growing distaste, Echnon watched Yulin prattle on. Finally he said, "We would see Anzi, to greet her." He unfolded himself from the chair and stood, towering over them.

Suzong nearly fainted. Then, recovering, she stood along with Yulin, saying, "Oh, Bright Lord, of course. She is bathing just now, but we shall send for her. It will take a few moments for her to prepare herself to see the bright lord. No trouble at all. In that case, we have ample time for a meal, and I will order it immediately."

Looking down at her, the lord remained silent, as though considering her offer. If he accepted it, their ruin would be upon them. A rivulet of sweat fell down her neck into the silk collar of her jacket.

Then, brushing the matter aside with a sweep of his hand, the lord said, "Do not disrupt the Chalin girl's bath. We have duties that await us, ah?"

Yulin bowed as though the breath had left his body. "Of course, Lord. Duties. I sympathize."

Echnon walked toward the door of the meeting chamber and paused at the threshold. "You should mend the rift with Zai Gan, Chalin master."

"Yes, Lord," Yulin said. "Immediately."

Still gazing at them from the door, the Tarig said, "He was not in the garden, this Dai Shen. Bathing also?"

Suzong simpered. "Oh, he wanders, being addled from the wound. Wanders here and there, Lord."

"Ah." Echnon nodded, and then turned, receding from them, allowing them to breathe once again.

Suzong and Yulin waited stiffly until they could no longer hear his footfalls. One did not see a Tarig to the door, since they disliked being directed and came and went as they pleased.

A sheen of perspiration gleamed on Yulin's forehead. Suzong dabbed at it with the sleeve of her jacket. "My master of the sway," she murmured with affection, glad she had not had to witness his garroting, rejoicing that Zai Gan had wasted the lord's time. But now, of course, Anzi and her patient could not return here, and Dai Shen was far from ready to walk freely among them. But at this moment it was enough that the bright lord was gone.

Still watching the door where the lord had departed, Yulin stroked his beard. When he spoke, his voice was a soft rumble, "Now, kill the gardeners."

Suzong nodded. They should have been drowned in the lake days ago, of course.

She departed to order this done, her tread wobbly now that the crisis had passed. Finding her favorite eunuch, she whispered to him, "Feed my carp a special meal from the garden this ebb." The servant's eyes narrowed, and he paused to make sure he'd understood her.

He had.

Arranged in terraces, black-and-gold dwellings descended the hill on which Yulin's mansion stood. The city enveloped Quinn, sprouting mazes at every turn. Now outside Yulin's compound, he was completely dependent on Anzi to know her way, and she led him swiftly through the tangle of streets. He suppressed the urge to keep looking behind them for the tall bronze lord, the one who might still be gazing from that high perch in the garden or striding close behind, searching the city for them.

In short order Anzi had stolen servant's clothing for him, and he followed a few steps behind her, adopting the demeanor of a servant for a lady of means.

The dark adobe buildings pressed in, rounded, mottled, unnatural. Complex smells assaulted him, from cooking and the press of bodies and the small produce gardens on the rooftops of most of the dwellings. In the center of such things, and in his rush through the town, he felt disoriented, hardly registering what he saw. He had to be wary of making assumptions in this strange place. Anzi, for instance. Not just a simple niece of Yulin. And where was she taking him?

They passed through a neighborhood where every house sold something, especially food, cooked on braziers on small covered porches. At one of these porches Anzi traded a stolen trinket for two drinks of water.

Out of earshot of the householder, Quinn said in a low voice, "Where are we going?"

"Do not talk, Dai Shen," she urged. "I know a place."

As they drank their water, Quinn noticed a small boy inside the dwelling, at his studies by the window. It was the first child he'd had a clear glimpse of in this land. In fact, so far in the city he'd seen only a few children. When you lived a long time, infrequent breeding made sense. The child stared, and Quinn turned away, thinking that perhaps his eye lenses were not as convincing as he wished.

Anzi returned the drinking cups, bowing her thanks, and led Quinn onward, down the hillside. The sky was more visible here, away from the tall trees of Yulin's preserve, and its silver expanse glittered in the Heart of Day. Spreading forever onto the plains, at times it almost looked like the sky on Earth with endless high cirrus clouds. Boiling.

Anzi stopped momentarily to pilfer another item. He thought her stealing went beyond what she needed to do, and that she enjoyed it, palming trinkets with one hand while making a show of picking one up with the other hand. It was hard to trust her. But if she and Yulin wanted to betray him, they could have easily done so earlier. Anzi's glance cut in the direction of Yulin's palace. It looked silent and quiet. Sometimes she looked at the sky, where, Quinn knew, the Tarig flew their aircraft. He had a faded memory of those exotic craft—brightships, they were called. Only the Tarig rode them. Oddly, when Quinn thought of the ships, his memory conjured a muffled, distant scream.

The vision clung to him, of the bronze-skinned creature on top of the aviary. He must flee those lords. But he must also close with them. To finish things, came the thought. Especially to finish things with Lord Hadenth, whose memory flickered just out of reach. He wasn't here for revenge, though, despite his hunger for justice. There was too much at stake to let personal enmity cloud his judgment.

"Where are we going, Anzi?" he said again.

As she walked, she murmured to him, "To hide. And while we do, to proceed with the changes to your appearance. I know a safe place; don't worry."

"Trust you, then? All will be well?"

Her face was grim as she increased their pace. "Yes. But hurry, please."

He stopped, and when she noticed he no longer followed her, she motioned him to a side street, out of the stream of foot traffic. Before she could complain, he said, "What is the plan, Anzi? I'm glad you've got one, but now I'd like to hear if it matches mine."

She looked around fretfully, then relented. "There is a friend, Jia Wa, who will help us. He must alter your face. But first we must travel to his city."

Quinn nodded. He'd been prepared for alterations to his face. "But where is this Jia Wa?" And, cautiously, he added, "And where is the scholar Su Bei?"

She told him that both men resided far away, entailing long journeys by train in opposite directions. She was beginning to gather that he would not follow passively, and she grew agitated. "We must find another way for your face surgery to happen. Since Yulin's physician is no longer available to us."

"I don't have time to go to Jia Wa, Anzi. I'm going to Su Bei instead."

"But why?"

Suzong had said he should find his own excuse for going, and he had prepared one: "I need what he has. My history of what I did when I was here before. I'll need those memories if I meet people I used to know." But most of all he needed Bei to reveal who at the Ascendancy knew of travel between the realms.

"First to Jia Wa, then to Bei." She glanced at him hopefully.

Not if they were in opposite directions. It could mean weeks of delay. "No," he said.

They stood without speaking for a while. Anzi's face was unreadable, but she held her mouth firm, and he knew she was angry. She refused to look at him.

At length she started down the street again, leaving him. When he caught up to her, he said, "Well?"

She pointed to a turret rising high about the low-slung buildings. "I must stop there." Coldly she added, "You can come or not."

So, she was playing the game too. He needed her as much as she needed him.

Without a glance backward, Anzi headed toward the turret. Finally they came upon the spire standing in the middle of a commons, deserted and fallen into weeds. The spire rose some five stories. At its foot stood a man dressed in tattered white silks.

"Wait here for me," Anzi said. "I must go into the needle."

"I'll come with you."

"No. It is a God's needle, not a good place."

"What do you need to do there?"

"The trains, Dai Shen. We need one." She added, "It would draw attention for two people to wish to approach God." She cocked her head in the direction of the man wearing white, who now was watching them. "This is a godman. He worships the god so we don't have to. Stay here."

She walked toward the needle, and despite her admonition, he followed her.

At the doorway, the godman examined the trinkets she showed him, wrinkling his prominent nose. He looked up dubiously at Quinn.

"My servant will ascend for me," Anzi said. "And I will make sure he does."

The godman looked unhappy at this proposal, but was mollified by receiving the best trinket from her assortment. He stood aside, and Anzi ducked inside the pillar, where a winding staircase ascended into the darkness. Mold and filth assailed Quinn from stairs badly in need of sweeping.

"Dai Shen," her voice came to him. "The pillar is the altar of the god. It isn't good to come here, so I wish you had not brought attention to us. Of course, you don't trust me. I've given you good reason not to. But don't doubt Master Yulin, since he will fall with you if you fall."

"What's in here, Anzi?"

"Nothing. At the top we'll look to see if a train approaches. We must take such a train, Dai Shen, to leave quickly. And yes, to Su Bei, if you demand it." Now she had stopped on the stairs, waiting for him to come abreast of her. In this shadowy place he couldn't see more than her vivid white hair.

He wanted to trust her, but it was difficult after she had misled him about herself. "Anzi, you've been lying to me. Stop lying now."

She expelled a long breath. "Yes, lying—by all that I didn't say. Forgive me, Dai Shen."

No forgiveness was in the air. He waited for her to tell the truth.

She sighed, leaning against the rounded sides of the needle. "Once I studied to be a scholar. I was a small apprentice, to my teacher Vingde, who was the Eye of Knowledge. Vingde broke the Vow of no connections to the Rose. He found a way of seizing objects in the Rose, something never done before."

Vingde had discovered a way to convey objects from the Rose to the Entire. To steal things. No wonder it appealed to Anzi.

"For approaching forbidden things, the Tarig gave him the slow death, their favorite death, garroting. After Vingde's death I went back. I wanted to see a being of the Rose. I wanted this with all my heart, but why, I don't truly know. When the Rose tunnel faltered, I brought your conveyance in."

He held up a hand, stopping her. "How did you find me? How did you happen to seize my capsule to bring it here?" Did Anzi, then, have the secret of to and from?

"It was a game of chance. I knew just enough from my studies with Vingde. I would have taken anybody, and they might have been anywhere. After waiting a long time—fifty days—I saw your craft. Afterward, I tried to hide you, but the Tarig took you, and they never found me, nor could you tell them, since you knew nothing." She averted her eyes. "I did this terrible thing, to bring you here."

Quinn most likely could have taken the escape pod safely out of the K-tunnel. No doubt she'd told herself that she was trying to save his life. Instead, she'd nearly destroyed it. He had to turn away. When he faced her again, his chest felt crushed by the column of thick air in the pillar. "And here you are again, showing up, pretending to help me."

"Not pretending. . . ."

"Are you real this time, Anzi?" He stepped back from her, controlling his temper. "Or just curious again?"

"Oh, not curious. Dai Shen, please don't say such a thing."

"Is it hard to hear, Anzi. Is it?"

Their voices had risen, especially his.

The white-garbed figure of the godman appeared on the steps below them. "Mistress?"

"Leave us. My servant is afraid to ascend. He will do so, though."

The godman retreated down the stairs.

Anzi's voice took up the thread of her story. "Master Yulin was very angry. He regretted that he gave me all the advantages, so that I learned no restraint in my life. I abased myself before Caiji of the hundred thousand days, and she persuaded my uncle to help me, which I didn't deserve. Then we heard stories of you, and stories of your wife and child. All bad. So, as you suffered, I also suffered, but all in my own mind, imagining your horror, and knowing what I had done."

"Am I supposed to feel sorry for you, Anzi? I can't." He wanted to. But for Sydney's sake, he couldn't let it pass. For Johanna's sake.

She knelt before him. "Dai Shen, you have the knife. Now you can use it to free yourself."

"Free myself?"

"From the hate you carry, and from the sadness. Then, as Ci Dehai said, you can find that river to carry you forward. To a new life." She paused. "God hates you, but it's no use to hate back. I've learned this."

She reached up, fumbling at his tunic, to free the knife. But he slapped her hand away. "Stop it. I know I have the knife. What do you think, that I'm going to kill you in a church?"

"That would be a good place, if you only knew, Dai Shen."

"Get up, Anzi." She remained kneeling. He took her arm, pulling her to her feet. "Just stop lying to me." He was tired of her voice. "Find us a train, Anzi." He pushed her ahead of him.

At the top, they emerged onto a small platform heaped with rotting fruit and offerings, including coins and jewelry. From this vantage point, Quinn surveyed the near territory, looking for the glint of bronze skin, or any hurried activity, but the city appeared untroubled.

Bowing before the offerings, Anzi placed her handful of trinkets among the rest. She intoned, "Do not look at me, do not see me, do not note my small life. Do not look at this man beside me, poor and small as he is. These gifts make us poorer by far than others more worthy of your great notice."

Here was an ominous god, one who was so malevolent even worshiping it was inadvisable. Thus the godman, to do it for them. "Do you hope He hears your prayer, or that He doesn't?"

"That is truly a scholar's question, Dai Shen." But she didn't answer. Maybe she didn't think about such things. Everyone had their self-delusions—including Titus Quinn, he thought, although he wasn't sure what those might be.

Without further ceremony, Anzi turned and scanned the plains beyond the city. Squinting, Quinn looked as well, but saw nothing. More than any other feature, the bright commanded his attention. How could this river of sky exist? It was a colossal stream of energy, without a natural explanation. It had a Tarig explanation, though, as did the Entire as a whole, a place that could not exist, and yet did. A place, if not created by the Tarig, then at least exploited by them, and enhanced to sustain living creatures. Despite such powers, they were only copiers of what the Rose had evolved. So then, their one glaring inadequacy was lack of creativity. Perhaps they had other inadequacies, as well.

"Will the sky ever burn out?" Quinn murmured.

Anzi looked up at the bright as though considering this for the first time. "Surely not, Dai Shen. How could we live?"

Well, that is never guaranteed, he thought.

Just then Anzi pointed, and he saw a crinkle in the yellow plains that she convinced him was a train approaching from far away.

"Fortunate," Anzi said, nodding with satisfaction.

"The right train?" Quinn asked.

"Who knows? But it's the one to the scholar Bei." Motioning for him to hurry, she disappeared back down the stairs.

Quinn hurried after her. He had expected her to loot the offerings, there being several fine pieces among the junk, but apparently Anzi didn't steal from God. The woman had her standards.

Waiting for the train, they shared a pilfered meal in a cemetery close to the station. The cemetery was deserted, but still, they couldn't relax. Surely the Tarig watched the trains. Small flags fluttered from shafts that pierced the graves, giving each soul a lofty-sounding name: Weaver of a Thousand Silks; Son Who Saw a Far Primacy; Aunt of a Shining Face; Soldier of Ahnenhoon (many of those); Soldier of One Arm; Child Dying on the Nigh. Now they shared their meager meal, next to the grave of One Who Laughed.

From their place, they could see thick crowds milling on the platform. "How far is it to Bei?" Quinn asked.

"An arc, at least," she said. An arc was ten days. A long time to remain undercover, trying to pass for Chalin. Anzi admitted that Bei, or those in Bei's service, could perform the alterations—although, she couldn't help but point out, it would be much preferable to go to Jia Wa and not be countermanding Master Yulin's orders.

Quinn remembered Bei's face. Frowning, netted with lines of age, the hair threaded with black. A hawk nose, and a hawk's eyes, blinking relentlessly, repeating relentlessly, "Tell me, Titus. Tell me . . ." And the old man would write, hunched over his scrolls, and Titus would listen to the *skritch skritch* of his pen.

"Do you think Bei will help us, Anzi?"

"If you must pick a destination not endorsed by Master Yulin, Su Bei is not a bad choice. He is loyal to Yulin."

"But not to me."

"Now they are the same thing."

Quinn let himself hope so. He had been fueled by hope from his first day back. There wasn't much left without it. He had a young nephew who unwittingly depended on his uncle to return from the Entire. Helice Maki had made it clear: Quinn had to come back. Preferably with good news, but he must come back. Perhaps he would come back with more than she could imagine.

A commotion on the distant train platform signaled the approach of the train. They quickly rose, eager to be under way. It was a risk to be in close quarters with the denizens of this new world, but they had no choice. Anzi had listed all the rules of riding on trains. Every few moments she thought of one more thing he should remember to do or refrain from doing. They set out across the field of graves.

Anzi caught his attention with her eyes. Someone was following them.

She murmured to him, "I will pretend to relieve myself, Dai Shen. When he approaches, I will spring at him, and you also."

He turned his back as Anzi went off a distance, crouching. And then their pursuer was upon them, taking Anzi down easily and catching Quinn's punch before it was even thrown.

Standing above them was a man with half a face. "You learned nothing," Ci Dehai said, looking sour.

Anzi brushed herself off, rising to bow before the fighting teacher.

Quinn had fallen hard, but rose with what dignity he could muster.

Handing Anzi a small pouch, Ci Dehai said, "Four hundred primals. Spend little." He fixed Anzi with a cold glare. "But spend, instead of stealing."

Anzi bowed. "Thank you, High Warrior of Ahnenhoon." The purse of money disappeared into her tunic pocket. Then, under his critical gaze, she reached into her pocket and withdrew the redstone, handing it to him.

The general took the stone, but still waited.

From his waistband, Quinn removed the knife.

Ci Dehai made no move to take it. "I would have thought my lessons better repaid than this."

Quinn nodded. It was fair to think so, but a man needed a weapon, despite Helice Maki's theory that the Entire would be nonviolent.

"The Tarig—," Anzi began.

Ci Dehai interrupted: "Wanted a tour of the famed gardens of Master Yulin. A lord, snooping—but finding nothing." He recounted the conversation of the lord and Yulin. "Best to leave now, however."

"Dai Shen insists that we see Su Bei," Anzi said. "I couldn't dissuade him."

The old warrior turned his face so that his one eye locked on Quinn. "Su Bei? No. Better to prevail on someone less conspicuous. Jia Wa, for example."

Quinn responded, "I need what Bei can tell me of my history."

"Not advisable."

"Nevertheless."

Ci Dehai looked at the man of the Rose with new concern. This Dai Shen had enticed Yulin into a ludicrous alliance: the Master of the sway and the Rose fugitive. The blackmail was explicit: *Help me, or you'll be my people's enemy.* And even Suzong of a thousand ambitions had urged her husband to comply. But to what advantage? What did it matter if Yulin was an enemy of the Rose? Since the Rose was powerless against the bright lords, why should anyone fear Dai Shen or his masters?

He looked at Dai Shen, still hoping to convince him against this new course of action. "Bei is in disgrace, and has little to offer." But Dai Shen set his mouth and wouldn't budge.

Perhaps, Ci Dehai thought, he should save his master the peril of this rash scheme by dispatching Dai Shen here and now. A small matter, to slit his throat in this field. How could the man's patrons know that Yulin hadn't cooperated, if the emissary never returned? The Rose would send other scouts who would find other personages to exploit, and he would be doing Yulin an enormous favor. He itched to take his blade from its sheath at his waist and put this man into one of these convenient graves.

His hand hovered over his knife, and he saw that Anzi saw this, and moved between Ci Dehai and Dai Shen.

As Dai Shen grew wary, Ci Dehai saw his moment evaporating, when he could make a clean kill. He had lost the advantage of surprise, all because of Yulin's worthless niece. Still, it could all easily be done within a moment.

Out of the corner of his eye, he saw the train coming into the station.

Anzi said, "I doubt that my uncle cares whether it is Bei or Wa whom we take refuge with. Both are loyal. I'm sure my uncle would permit it, Warrior of Ahnenhoon."

He relaxed his knife hand. He didn't want to hurt Anzi nor face Yulin's outrage if she was wounded. And now she was giving him an excuse not to kill Dai Shen, either. And so the moment passed when he might have killed the man. A part of him was relieved—the part that had sized up Titus Quinn in training sessions and knew him for a better man than most.

Ci Dehai turned to Quinn. "I see you are set on this course."

"I am," came the answer. "Tell Master Yulin I believe our enterprise will be safer if Su Bei can tell me my history."

In the distance, on the train platform, crowd noises surged.

Ci Dehai snorted, giving in, feeling older than his days. Time was when he wouldn't have hesitated to save his master from a troublesome individual.

He glanced at the knife Dai Shen had stolen. "Keep the blade. Use it on Master Yulin's enemies." Or on yourself if events turn bad.

He unstrapped a small pack from his back. "Here are some children's scrolls to continue your journey from ignorance. Also inside is a thong on which are strung four redstones, each one a copy of Yulin's message to the prefect." He handed the pack to Quinn, who thanked him.

Turning to Anzi, he said, "Once again you have leave to create disorder. Your uncle has given you another chance. Don't squander it, Ji Anzi."

Looking up to note the approach of the train, he said to Quinn, "If you make it to the Ascendancy, Master Yulin warns that you must, above all, win over the high prefect Cixi. But know this: She despises the One Who Shines. Master Yulin is second only to Cixi. Do you understand what this means, Dai Shen?"

Quinn nodded. "She won't welcome any chance for Yulin to succeed."

"Can you charm a dragon, then?"

"Any hints?" Quinn asked.

"No," he said. "I'm a fighter, not a diplomat." As Quinn and Anzi repeated their thanks and headed off, Ci Dehai added, "And beware of her legates. They're worse than she is."

Quinn and Anzi began hurrying toward the train platform, threading their way through the graves. "Does he like anyone?" Quinn asked Anzi.

She smiled. "He's too wise to have friends."

Carrying the pack of scrolls and data stones, he took his position behind his mistress. She assumed a regal stride, clutching the purse Ci Dehai had given her.

They approached the platform where the thing they called a train was waiting. It was very long, and here at the loading dock he couldn't see the front of the assemblage, or the rear. The surface of the compartments was smooth but mottled, looking more like cooled lava than worked metal. No wheels, and no tracks. He could almost conclude that it was not a train at all, not as he would define it. But there were coaches. Between each coach, a connecting tube.

Just before they boarded, he had time to hope that when they copied this from the Rose, they'd had the decency to keep a caboose.

CHAPTER TWELVE

The Three Vows are these:
Withhold the knowledge of the Entire from the non-Entire.
Impose the peace of the Entire.
Extend the reach of the Entire.

—from *The Radiant Way*

ALL CHILDREN LEARNED THE VOWS, as their first chant, first ditty.

It was a sober nursery song, Quinn thought as he memorized the three vows with their stark verbs: Withhold. Impose. Extend. If Suzong was right, among the officials at the Ascendancy there might be some who chafed at withholding, who wanted converse between the worlds. Su Bei knew one person, but would he reveal the name? Yes. Because Quinn wouldn't leave Bei's reach without it.

For the train ride, Anzi had booked quarters on top of a passenger car. It had half-wall sides and a small roofed section for sleeping. In the next car forward, a wealthy Hirrin camped atop her own car, and sometimes sat on the roofed section looking around. The Hirrin was a four-legged creature with a long neck and a bald face. She sat on the roof, rear legs splayed forward, her long neck turning 360 degrees as she viewed the scenery.

Anzi said there were no lords on the train, and they could relax for at least a while. He saw Anzi glancing up now and then, watching, and he imagined the crescent shape that defined a brightship—as it must appear from the ground. He had never seen one from below, only from close at hand, when he had ridden them. The memory swam in and out, of his time as a prisoner in the

Ascendancy. It was a city in the sky; he remembered that now. But every vision of the time before was hard-won, freed from oblivion only intermittently, and randomly. He felt like a rat, fed tidbits but caged from his own mind. Patience, he thought. It's coming. It's all coming to me, now that I'm here.

Quinn sat on a bench that Anzi had coaxed from the floor. Nubs on the car sides responded when she touched them, a slow process, but dependable.

Anzi fretted about the Hirrin. "She is watching us." But if they moved quarters, that would look suspicious, she concluded.

"Let her watch." To Quinn, the Hirrin seemed merely curious, and nothing to quash his exhilaration at being on the move.

Anzi said, "It's no small matter, if she doubts who we are. Since you left, all sentients have been alerted to watch for Titus Quinn. No one knows where you disappeared to, or that you went back to the Rose. It's not trivial."

"No, perhaps not. But what can we do? The less we fret, the more natural we look. And if she turns us in, then the next move is ours."

Absorbing this, Anzi said, "A contradiction. Interesting."

"What is?"

"So few days, for you of the Rose. And so careless of dying, yes?"

He hadn't thought he was careless of dying, but it was true he hadn't given it much thought. People of the Rose didn't often think of dying. Maybe it was too big to carry around. He said as much to Anzi.

She marveled at the thought. "So big, and yet it remains under cover. Or perhaps it's bravery. Yes, I think you're very brave."

"But Anzi, so are you. Being with me is an indictment all by itself."

"True. But being with you is my duty."

"And being here is mine."

She cut a glance at him. "I thought it was for love."

He'd never said that. But he liked that she'd said it. No one, not even Caitlin, had ever said outright that it was for love. Most of the time he'd heard *stubborn*, *bitter*, and *inflexible*. He smiled at Anzi and, tentatively, she smiled back.

The wind off the veldt brought a clovelike scent as the two of them watched the plains speed by, one region, or wielding, giving way to the next within the great Chalin sway. Moving without tracks, without wheels, the train hummed quietly. The material it was made of might have been metal, but it had an odd texture. There could hardly be natural deposits of metals in this world. Or petroleum. The materials were likely to be the result of molecular engineering. In a universe without stars, without a geologic history.

The train's technologies were hidden, and taken for granted by Anzi. The energy source was the bright. What generated the bright? Or the walls, for that matter? These questions were apparently far from Anzi's mind. Whatever the source, it was colossal. Perhaps infinite.

Anzi managed to convey that for the energy needs of industry, of computer stone wells, of dwellings nothing was burned, not even hydrogen. Modeled on a plant's photosynthetic reaction centers, plasma cells harvested photons. The longer the train, the more surface room for its molecular arrays, acting like antennae for the energy of the bright—no mere drizzle of photons, but a shower. The Tarig had remade photosynthesis in inorganic form. It made Earth's fusion technologies seem crass by comparison. In this universe, the likes of Helice and Stefan were not the savvies. The Tarig were.

Eventually, Quinn grew restless, saying, "I'll go down to the passenger cars, Anzi. It's a long way to the reach. We can't just sit here." There was great variety; enough variety even in Chalin skin tones for him to pass, if he stayed silent.

"No, please, Dai Shen." Other travelers might engage him in conversation he wasn't ready for, she said. Hirrin, especially, were meddlers, as proven by their neighbor who had no need to sit on her roof unless she wanted a better view into others' cars.

Anzi's caution only emphasized what he already knew, that she thought this whole undertaking one of unconscionable risk. No one had asked her what she thought, and if they had, she could hardly argue that Quinn give up his daughter. On the subject of family, Anzi knew to be quiet.

Still, he argued with her. "It attracts more attention if we never leave the roof of this car. People will wonder about us."

"Dai Shen, you have an accent. It marks you as from the Ascendancy."

This spooked him. "Since when?"

"It's been coming into your speech. People will ask you of the bright city, and you will have nothing to say."

They worked on ridding him of his accent. The subjects ranged among politics, social customs, religion, and the law. And always, the past, Quinn's past.

Anzi told how she had brought him into the Entire. Her teacher, Vingde, had been studying a gravitational phenomenon in the Rose. By Anzi's general descriptions, Quinn thought it might have been black holes. At his reach, at the tip of a minoral, Vingde had been experimenting with forbidden connections to the Rose, and had determined that passages were easier between the Entire and black holes. Vingde planned to exploit this in an experiment, but the Tarig detected his fumblings and swept down on him. Afterward, Anzi worked for a hundred days before she locked on to a Kardashev tunnel. One day she observed an intense perturbation. This was the explosion and destruction of Quinn's ship. Anzi saw the capsule and who was in it. A man, a woman, and a child. She had only a moment to decide.

He wondered if, when the time came, Vingde's reach might be an exit point to get home. Anzi said no. The Tarig had destroyed Vingde's reach, for one thing. And one reach was as good as another. Just because one entered from a certain reach, this was no reason to believe the site still correlated with home.

As they talked, the bright subsided from lush silver flames to the verge of lavender, glowing with hints of incandescence amid the embers. It was not what one could call night. One could read a book all ebb long, and never need a candle.

He was gazing at his pictures, shading them with his hands so the sky would not fade them. Johanna had been dead a long time. At some level he had known this, but now it was certain. Sydney was blind. But she was alive. It calmed him, knowing what his sorrows were instead of guessing at them.

Next to him, Anzi murmured, "Tell me about your young girl."

After a pause he said, "She liked to climb trees."

Johanna stood at the foot of the mountain ashberry tree, looking up at Sydney in the upper branches. "If you break your neck, you're grounded for a week."

Sydney's face appeared out of a nest of leaves. "It's a deal."

He began to improve the placement of his tongue for the glottal sounds.

"What else did she like?"

"Running. The color orange. Riding horses." The memories, no longer sharp knives, were still little cuts. "She had a train set."

"Did she look like you?"

"No." After a time he said in a low voice, "She looked like her mother."

Quinn tried to imagine what Sydney looked like now as a young woman. Well, he would soon find out, after Bei's reach, and after the Ascendancy—when at last he arrived at the Inyx sway at the far end of the universe. *A million lifetimes away*, Anzi had said, *but close, when we travel the River Nigh.*

We are near, Sydney, he thought. Wait for me.

The next day, sitting on his bench at the Prime of Day, Quinn could see hundreds of miles, and within that view were only the sky, the mighty veldt, and in the distance, a pillar that descended from the bright. That slender thread, called an *axis* of the bright, marked a trading center and a communication center, Anzi said. If you wished to transmit messages within the Entire, it was as easy to go there in person as to rely on the axes. And going there in person involved "a thousand days," which was the Chalin answer to almost all questions of how far things were. This was because the answer was, in terms of travel, *That depends.* The River Nigh rendered distance beside the point.

This river was no natural river, but it was a transport stream. Devised by the Tarig, it made travel possible in the Entire over galactic-scale distances, so Anzi claimed. The River Nigh bound the kingdom together, unifying the sentients and the sways. If you were determined, you could travel anywhere.

"Where is the Nigh?" Quinn asked.

Anzi pointed to the port side of the train, off into the distance. "At the storm wall. The river follows the storm wall. But one side only, and farthest from here."

"How far does the river go?"

She looked at him in surprise. "That's hard to say. Forever. It goes forever. And then, into the Sea of Arising, which is the sea above which the Ascendancy floats. And then, down each primacy, a similar river flows. Always called the Nigh. Eventually, the Nigh will bear us on its back, if God does not look on us."

His scrolls said that the key to the Nigh resided in the binds, the nexus points. But when he asked Anzi about the binds, she said, "Only the navitars understand them. The pilots." She grew sober, speaking of the navitars, creatures so distorted that they no longer had normal lives, nor allegiance to any sway. The Tarig performed the needed physical alterations at the navitars' request, granting the pilots sole powers to navigate the dimensional transport stream. From Anzi's comments, Quinn gathered that she found the navitars both morbid and sublime.

As relief from being cooped up and constantly studying, Anzi continued his fighting instruction. The swaying of the train was just enough to make them both more prone to falling. The Hirrin watched from her rooftop, then disappeared.

They soon knew why. A train magister came knocking at their berth, wondering about the fighting, saying trouble had been reported by concerned parties. Anzi said she was receiving instruction from her servant who had served at Ahnenhoon, which brought from the magister many bows in Quinn's direction. The magister left, with apologies.

Anzi hid her smile. The Hirrin was truly just a gossip, and no Tarig spy.

It was several days before the Hirrin resumed her perch. When she did, she bowed in their direction with a sweep of her long neck, a nice bow for a quadruped. Anzi bowed back, and peace between neighbors was restored.

On the fifth day out from Yulin's city of Xi, Quinn gave in to the urge to explore the train. Knowing Anzi would argue against it, he waited until she left to purchase their midday meal. Then he descended into the passenger cars. In the general melee of bodies and activity, hardly a face turned to regard him.

Among the Chalin passengers, he saw other sentient creatures, including Hirrin of lesser means than their wealthy neighbor. It seemed normal to him that these quadrupeds were sentient, because, of course, it was not the first time he'd seen them, and at some level he recognized them. He saw smaller beings he guessed might be pets, but avoided staring, and learned to watch with his peripheral vision.

Pressing on through the cabins, he went through flexible tubes between cars, passing Chalin dressed in loose pants and jackets in colorful varieties of silks. Many Chalin had the aspect of soldiers and bore the scars of battle.

There were games played on raised tables, where fingers inserted into divots created patterns of colors. Continuing through the cars and tubes, Quinn caught glimpses through the windows at the everlasting flat country. It was an oddly peaceful view. He was content to be on the move. It wasn't happiness, but it was a more solid grounding than he had known in a long while.

He came to a car where one half was crowded and the other half contained only one man in white, surrounded by empty seats.

"You won't want to go through there," the man said as Quinn headed for the tube.

Quinn turned to gaze on the plump young man, by his dress a godman. He was intent on rolling a spindle of thread in his lap. "The meat car," the godman added.

"I see." Though he didn't.

"Take my aunt's chair, if you want to rest." He nodded at a vacant seat that looked molded for a hugely broad bottom. After a pause, Quinn took the seat. The godman pulled thread from a basket at his feet. "These are the worst seats, of course." He glanced at the tube to the next car. "Can you smell them?"

"Not so bad," he said. Although he did smell something strange.

The young man looked at Quinn as though afraid he'd taken offense. "I don't say it's wrong. There are many ways within the path, of course. I may wear white, but I'm not as bad as I look. Do you think I'd be a godman if I could help it?"

Unsure of the polite reply, Quinn gave a noncommittal look. The godmen were the dregs of society, unfit for most other duties, or such misfits that they preferred vilification to ordinary society. Sometimes they were women, then called godwomen, and treated with as much loathing. To the Chalin, and perhaps to most of the Entire, the god worshiped by the godmen was a demiurge—evil, rigid, jealous, and prone to murder. If you needed a reason why bad luck happened, that would be God. There was a concept, loosely thought of as "heaven"—although not associated with life after death—that people called upon, and swore upon. It seemed to mean "the best of us all," or even for some, the bright sky itself.

But for most sentients, the best chance lay in living beneath God's notice. As to a higher being of love and compassion, the Entire was devoid of this concept, perhaps because the Tarig themselves were so powerful as to fill this role. Some individuals demonstrated such deference to the bright lords that it amounted to worship, although Anzi had said that people who could fawn in that manner possessed feeble intellects. Still, the Tarig role was godlike: They had created the world and its creatures, and had organized society to be just and prosperous by enforcing laws and dispensing technology as needed. If the Tarig wished to diminish religion, they had been wise to give God a role, a debased one.

The godman looked resentfully at the other half of the car, where passengers ignored him. "I take the attention of God off of them, so naturally I am cursed. But I bear God's attention, and I'm still alive." He looked eagerly at Quinn. "You're not afraid to sit with me?"

"I take my rest. You had a seat."

The godman nodded. "Exactly. No waiting for a seat to come up. Even if the smells are unfortunate." He twirled the spindle, content to chatter. A Chalin woman walked up to them, dropped a coin on the basket, and hurried away. Quinn thought he might be drawing attention sitting with a godman. As he rose from his seat, the godman looked crestfallen. "Leaving, then? To see the Gond? Heaven give us not seeing Gonds. Stay a while."

The godman's thread got stuck, and he opened the top of the basket, revealing an insectoid creature with a mouth spinneret, extruding a filament. He nudged the spinner, producing a mewing sound, then snapped the lid closed. The filament fed out. "They're vow breakers," he said, glancing at the tube opening. "The madness takes them. They go to their deaths, poor creatures. Through the veil. And so, after all, breaking the First Vow."

Quinn covered his surprise at hearing this. "They risk much," he said. "Discovery by the lords—"

The godman snorted. "They risk death by explosion. By the bright, an ugly way to die, for your body to erupt." He shivered.

"If their timing is wrong."

The young man drew back from him. "No time is a good time. It is not a matter of time, but of the law."

Quinn hastened to agree. "Yes, naturally."

"You are from the Ascendancy? You sound like it."

Quinn shrugged. "There and back. A long time ago."

"You are a legate?"

"A soldier." He rose, saying to the godman, "You should find better seats. The smell."

The basket lid raised up a little, and the godman tapped it shut with his foot. "Some say they're not mad at all. That they go over, and their days continue." He shuddered. "They live short lives then. But their bellies are full." Through narrowed eyes, he regarded Quinn. "Do you hear such things at the bright city?"

"Legates tell little to a soldier." Managing a smile, he began backing off. Then he left, heading back the way he had come.

At the forward end of the car was a closet that served for a latrine. He used it. When he emerged, the godman, in the company of a fat Chalin woman, was just disappearing through the tube to a forward car.

In the next moment Quinn was heading in the opposite direction, and through the tube, toward the bad smells. He would speak to these Gonds.

He found himself in an empty car where the sour smells intensified. Through the next connecting tube, he found a car with a narrow aisle between two long, open boxes. Here, without doubt, was the source of the smell: a pungent odor like ammonia, and decidedly toxic. Something was moving in the boxes. He looked over the sides, finding them full of soil. Little humping ridges marked the paths of burrowers. One hump surfaced, revealing a plump cylinder of flesh. It flopped out of the soil, showing itself to be about as long as his forearm, with the forward end bearing eyes and a slit for a mouth.

Turning around, he found that, in the other box, burrowers had lined up on the lip of the box to stare at him. As he approached, they dropped out of sight with plopping noises.

One remained. Its eyes were covered with a membrane, but they held an iris, and somehow the face managed to look like it was both infantile and wise. The little face turned to look toward the side. Eyes widening, it plopped into hiding.

As Quinn turned in that direction, he saw in the tube between cars an alarming animal.

The beast took up the entire opening. And, improbably, it was the Devil.

Quinn stepped back, and the beast cocked its head, as though interested in movements to flee.

The head was as large as a steer's. Triangular, with two horns and red, lacquered gums. Fleshy wings twitched like a leathery robe around its snake-like body. No hooves, Quinn thought, because every other thought had fled.

The creature's head turned in a jerk to one side, peering askance at the intruder. Then it spoke, in a troubling deep pitch. "You are hungry for momo."

"No," Quinn thought to say. Whatever *momo* was.

"Perhaps you eat momo, and not pay the price."

"No."

"Come closer."

Quinn stayed where he was.

"I will rip out your backbone and feed you to my momo. That is the truth."

The horns and pointed chin looked spectacularly like old, traditional images of the Devil, an association Quinn was having trouble shaking.

"Come closer. Breathe on my face. If you have not eaten momo, then we are friends. We have few friends."

The admission of unpopularity softened the creature's aspect. Quinn walked forward. He blew on the triangular head, ruffling a pointy beard that straggled from the chin.

"A meat eater," the bass voice pronounced. "Not a momo eater. Then we can have transactions." It backed up, tucking its wings about it as it squirmed through the passageway. "Come in. My sisters and I will have conversations on price. But the momo are fat, as you saw, and Gond are not fools."

The Gond disappeared into the next car. Quinn hesitated on the threshold.

The triangular head poked through with an irritated stare.

Quinn followed, thinking he would regret it. Thinking that there were many times he stood wondering if he should do something that seemed very inadvisable, but very interesting. And how the same choice always resulted.

At first it was hard to see what the next car contained. As his eyes adjusted to a dark interior, Quinn saw several huge dead tree limbs upon which rested two additional Gond creatures. He could now see the whole aspect of the Gonds' bodies. They were enormous and fleshy newtlike creatures. The first Gond rose on her muscular trunk and appeared to stand.

The Gond and her sisters watched him. He wished that they did not appear poised to jump. Quinn leaned against the doorway and folded his arms. "Well?" he said, trying to match their intimidating manner. One of them scratched herself with a wing tip.

"Where are you traveling?" the first Gond said, making the plain question seem full of meaning.

"That is of no concern," Quinn answered.

The Gond exchanged glances with her sisters, and said, more conciliatory, "Of course. We can deliver them. No concerns."

When Quinn didn't respond, the Gond continued, "Good and fat. Alive, as you saw. Very fresh upon arrival. The soils make a difference. The grubs are from the richest lands of the Ord Wielding. It imparts a flavor much admired in the great city of Xi, where you are coming from, since you weren't on the train before." The Gond dipped her head. "We watch. Through the windows."

She gazed at Quinn. "At first I took you for the train magistrate, come to bargain for momo on behalf of the dining pleasure of passengers. This has not happened. They put us and our cargo in the last cabins, and charged us, additionally, for the empty car in front." Her eyes partly closed, and her face folded inward in an impressive scowl. "Such is their hate of Gond."

Not liking the turn of mood, Quinn offered: "There are many ways on the Radiant Path."

"Quite so," the Gond said. "But some ways are said to be dark ways."

From one of the branches came a slipping noise as one of the Gonds slid with a thud to the floor of the car, leaving a slick of something on the tree limb. This Gond watched Quinn just as steadfastly as before, but with her chin resting on the floor.

"'No sentient being is beyond hope,'" Quinn quoted from *The Book of the Thousand Gifts*.

The third Gond spoke for the first time, from her tree perch, and in the same unnerving bass. "He has no money."

Without looking at her, the first Gond said, "Ignore such a speech. You will pay."

Quiet came upon the group then. Outside the day dimmed, lending a certain beauty to even this nest of devils. The bare tree trunks became graceful boughs, and the glittering wings took on a purple sheen.

During this quiet, Quinn began, "I heard a story."

The three watched him. "The story was that a madness comes upon some Gond, and the sadness is that they die in the reaches."

The first Gond showed teeth for the first time, deeply stained and long. "That is not the story you heard. You heard that we go across, and take our fill of unusual meat. Thinking meat."

Thinking meat. They ate sentient creatures. Perhaps this was approved behavior, so long as they were Rose sentient creatures.

The Gond continued, "The sways think that we must be mad to go to the Rose, and lose our days, and never come home. The madness is what keeps us from Tarig justice. They pity us."

The more he looked at this creature, the more compelling the idea became, that the Gond had come into the Rose—at least to the Earth—and spawned stories of a monster, the Devil, that took on this bizarre appearance.

"Are we mad, do you think, to throw ourselves into the Rose?" The Gond rose even higher on her body, until her head nearly touched the ceiling.

"Where is the Rose?" Quinn threw this out, to see what he caught.

The Gond boomed, "Where is the meat of the Rose? Where is the Rose? But no sentients know the correlates. That is why we are mad to go."

"Perhaps brave—to go."

The Gond lowered herself, coming closer. "The price for the meat of momo is no less, for saying such things."

Correlates. Here was a new term for the thing he sought, the secret behind crossing over to the Rose.

He risked saying, "You believe, do you, in the correlates? That they are more than a child's story?" He tried to sound casual, as though the answer made no difference.

The Gond's breath smelled of rot. It was all he could do to stand his ground. "The vows forbid," the creature said, so low it was almost out of hearing range.

"Of course." Backtracking, he said, "But children will prattle." The correlates were the charts of passage. Like the closely guarded sea manuals of medieval seafaring, they would trace the safe waters, allowing a ship to avoid dangerous shoals and false routes—like a map, perhaps, or equations that would predict timing and place of exit from the Entire.

But if there were correlates, the Gond didn't have them. "The vows forbid," the Gond repeated.

It might be prudent to leave now, but no parting comment came to mind. Then one did: "What is the price of these momo you offer for sale?"

"Ah, to the point." The Gond smiled, a disturbing sight. "I thought you long-winded, even for a trader. Twelve minors per heft." She flexed a wing. "If alive, then fifteen minors. That is fair."

"Good. I will consider your offer." Quinn turned to leave, eager to be gone, to savor what he'd learned.

A talon caught at his shoulder. The Gond shifted her weight, coming closer. "You talk strangely."

"There are many ways on the path," Quinn said, managing a steady gaze into the Gond's eyes.

"You only say what others have said. You are bad at bargaining. You are no trader."

"Well," Quinn said, shaking free of the claw. "We'll see, won't we?"

"You will buy momo?"

"My partners will decide."

The Gond's breath was hot in Quinn's face. "I will be waiting for you," she said.

As the train raced across the veldt, Quinn faced Anzi, considering his opening move in their fighting match. He swayed slightly, adjusting to the trembling floor.

They were halfway to their destination of Bei's reach, and he considered how totally dependent on her he was, isolated from even such allies as Yulin and Suzong. They had a long way to travel together, if ultimately he needed to reach the Ascendancy and then the far sway of the Inyx. He wanted to trust her, but he was having a hard time of it.

Coming at her, he pierced her defense, snapping her tunic. She blinked, surprised, moving around to his weak side, his left.

Quinn wanted to win. He wanted her to fall. He wanted her to stop withholding from him.

He darted in, receiving from her a kick that caught him on the thigh. He grabbed her foot, yanking her down. As she fell, she swiped his legs from under him, taking him down as well. They both lay winded.

"The Gond cross over to the Rose," he said, panting. "Did you know?"

She sprang up. "No. And neither do you. It's only a story."

"The Gond told me that they go. There are what she called *correlates*. They do go, I believe." He thought that perhaps Gond were not the only monsters to appear in the Rose from the Entire. Any nonhominid that went over would seem a monster on Earth.

She circled him, watching for an opening. "They go, but only fling themselves through the veil. That's not going to and from. It's suicide." Anzi whipped out a knife from her tunic. "What to do, Dai Shen, when one has a weapon and you do not?" She feinted a few jabs at him.

He circled around her. "Wait for you to miss, then go for the unprotected side." She was so fixated on teaching him that she couldn't learn from him, learn that she had to stop withholding information.

She swiped at him. "Don't focus on the weapon; look at the chest to detect the next move. Find structures to use as weapons. Draw me toward a wall."

At her next lunge, he chopped down on her forearm, and the knife fell.

He kicked it away. "I need every scrap of intelligence I can get—and you conveniently forget to mention the Gonds' habit of going over. Everyone knows. Even the godman knows."

She stopped, letting her hands fall to her sides. "So now I have lied to you?"

"Not lied, but neglected the truth."

Her face was hard and resentful. "My pattern, then? Neglecting the truth?"

A short distance away, the Hirrin watched from her perch, taking a new interest in their prolonged match.

"You tell me."

"Yes, I'll tell you, Dai Shen. I'll tell you how foolish it was for you to go down in the train cars and talk to godmen and then, even the Gond. Everyone within six train cars knows that you went, and that you sat with a godman. So you are extremely reckless, all for the sake of proving that I don't tell you all I should, though we have only been studying together for twenty days."

He took a calming breath. "I need to get information any place I can. And I will."

"Did you ever think that in taking extreme measures—for no reason—you jeopardize the young girl who is your daughter?"

A silence descended between them as he struggled with his temper.

Anzi went on: "If your death means nothing to you, then think of her."

He snapped. Lunging at her, he took her by surprise, and was able to yank her arm while delivering a punch to her shoulder. At the last moment he pulled back, so that he missed her, but he drove his fist into the half-wall of their coach. He left a dent the shape of his fist, and thought he might have broken a few fingers, but fortunately the material had given slightly. He cradled his hand for a moment, looking away from her.

He flexed his fingers as the adrenaline subsided. "I'm sorry I almost hurt you."

She gathered herself up. "You didn't hurt me."

"Still."

"I deserve to be hurt."

The Hirrin spectator turned away, as though embarrassed for his lapse. "No," Quinn said. "I don't think you do." The fist-dent in the wall was losing definition, flattening out.

He offered her a cup of water, and she drank with him.

"Dai Shen," she said. "I don't think you know me yet, though I believe I know you."

He sat down on the bench, using a towel to wipe down. Drained of tension, he looked at her for a long moment. A scrim of sweat covered her face, and her color was high. The effect was like a very subtle pink marble that now cooled again to white.

"I could tell you," she said, "that I will defend you with my life. But that's easy to say, isn't it? My uncle has told me to defend you, but I would in any case. You depend on me here. If I fail you, I don't want to live." She put a hand up to stop his protest. "But you don't trust me yet."

In the distance a smudge at the horizon registered the presence of the great storm wall, as they called the edges of the Entire. It would come to dominate the veldt in the days to come, he knew.

She sat next to him, watching the veldt dim. The sky, having lost its high glitter, now fell quickly into Last of Day. A lavender blush colored her face, the roof of the train, and the veldt. In the distance, the storm wall crouched dark and solid-looking, and to one side a wisp of the sky, an axis, fell to the plain like a dust devil. The train carried them onward, swaying and humming. They had been traveling for eight days, and in all that time they had not passed one other inhabited area. The Entire, Anzi had said, was mostly empty. This emptiness, combined with the vast distances, forced a calm on activities, as though there was time enough for all things.

"Tell me about yourself, Anzi," he said. "I want to know."

Her story came then, of her parents, who were both soldiers and had died at Ahnenhoon when she was very young. She was one of many nieces, children, and hangers-on in Yulin's court, where his general benevolence was not enough to fill the gap. Yulin had indulged her wish to be a scholar. He apprenticed her to Vingde, who thought her scholarship sloppy. She was looking at the Rose, but she pursued little more than personal histories. Vingde thought her prospects dim, but gave up trying to restrain her. She was, after all, Yulin's niece.

"Do you still wish to be a scholar of Earth?" Quinn asked.

"Once I thought so. But scholars pursue their endless facts. I wished to *really* know. The way you live, on the Earth."

"Why?"

She paused. "I am one of those who thinks the Rose is a lost place. A place lost to the Chalin, that we once had, in the sense that humans are the template for the Chalin people. And being a lost place, or a place denied to us, I feel its pull."

She went on: "Most sentients say the Tarig improved all Rose templates, and the Entire is superior in every way. But to many—to me—you are the revered ancestors, created from evolving matter. We are only pale copies."

He looked at her in the fading light. "It isn't better in the Rose, you know."

"I think that it is." She turned to him. "Don't you sometimes feel that the Entire is better? Because you are denied this place?"

He was stunned by her observation. Yes. He did feel that sometimes.

"I'm hungry to know about the Rose, Dai Shen. I always have been. All the glimpses I've ever seen through the veil, when I served Vingde my teacher—each one only increased my hunger."

The train hummed beneath them, and they were silent for a time. Then she said, "Tell me. About the Rose."

He had nearly forgotten his own world. It was far away, in all respects.

She prompted him: "Here is a thing we wonder about. The night. What is the night, Dai Shen? In your world, how does it seem?"

Such an obvious thing. But of course, to her, it was a bizarre occurrence. He tried to imagine nighttime from her perspective. "Everything changes," he said. "The world seems to sleep, and colors drain away. The sky is black except for the small spots that are stars."

"But still, is it dark half of the time?"

He nodded. And the thought came to him: The Tarig are afraid of the dark. So they created a world without it.

Anzi continued, "Do you stare at the traveling sun? When it disappears, are you amazed?"

"No. It seems as it should be. And the sun is too searing to look at."

"And do many go blind, doing so?"

"No one goes blind. No one looks." He thought this odd, but the truth. Looking up at the bright, he realized that here was the most profound difference between their worlds, this river of suns. Johanna could find no rest under its relentless light.

"I would look," Anzi was saying. "To see a star, it would be worth it. And mountains," Anzi went on. "You have mountains in a row."

"Yes, mountain ranges."

"I once saw this, through the veil. And never forgot such a sight."

In the next car, the Hirrin princess went down from her roof perch, bowing at them, a courtesy Anzi ignored this time, judging that she was too friendly and even friends could be an unwitting danger.

The train slowed, approaching a village that looked to be little more than a dozen rounded huts. Still, Quinn would have liked to debark and see what was there—as perhaps the Hirrin princess planned to do.

But he would debark in any case, in just a few hours. Tomorrow would bring them to the minoral, where they would leave the train and journey by pack beast to Bei's reach at the far tip of the minoral.

The minorals were small geographic features compared with the stupendous primacies. Like minor branches, they grew from one side of a primacy only, since the other side of the primacy was bounded by the River Nigh. At the ends of the minorals were the tips, or reaches, where scholars studied the Rose. From the minorals sprang still smaller branches: the nascences, with storm walls so close together they were unstable and could close up without warning. As bizarre and impossible as all this surely was, nevertheless he half remembered it and found it strangely normal.

The day fell into Shadow Ebb, when the sky simmered instead of boiled, and the wellings of the sky rose into brilliance and sank into folds of pewter. Although it was time for sleep, he and Anzi remained seated, neither one eager to end the day.

She asked, looking out, "Tell me what is love in your world, Dai Shen."

"It's the same as here, Anzi."

"No, not the same, I'm sure. Stronger, yes?"

"Doesn't Yulin have a favorite wife, and love her strongly?"

Anzi smiled. "He isn't consumed with love for Suzong." Looking out, she continued: "This strong affection is a thing I remember from my days of study. In your world, I saw people burn with desire for each other, and sacrifice everything." From somewhere underneath, someone laughed loudly, a jarring sound.

"Hasn't anyone sought you, Anzi? No one who wished to love you?" He thought that unlikely, despite her faults.

The soft purr of the train filled the silence. "No."

"You are young yet," he said.

She shrugged. "Nine thousand days."

Calculating, he came up with about twenty-five, in Earth years.

She regarded him a moment. "I know there is a price for how you live—

with intensity. I think, in the All, we can't live this way. We're too long on the Radiant Path, and in the end, we love as much as you, but in our many days, it's stretched thinner."

He thought about this remarkable summation, and for a moment he envied her that metered-out life. Stretched more thinly, both the good and evil of it. Perhaps if, like Caiji of a hundred thousand days, he lived long enough, Sydney's memory—and Johanna's—would grow more muted. Ci Dehai had urged him to look forward. So had Caitlin. *It's time.* Her words came back to him. *Time to find someone else.* There were moments when he had almost been ready; times when he desired Caitlin herself, the wife of his brother, mistaking her kindness for something else. Which was one good reason he kept apart from Rob's family.

Anzi was looking down onto the station platform, where the train had now halted.

Turning to look, Quinn saw four men carrying a burden—a hammock, in which reclined a Gond, just leaving the train. Bending over to speak to the Gond was the plump godman Quinn had met.

Anzi pushed Quinn back out of sight, but the godman had already seen him, and raised his hand in a wave, or in a gesture for the Gond to look up.

Quinn whispered, "What are they doing together?"

"Sharing information," Anzi whispered, her face frozen in a noncommittal blandness. "Did I not tell you that all godmen are rogues, and sell what they know?"

It was an hour before the Gond's load of live meat was unloaded from the train—a time during which Quinn and Anzi sat in dread of a knock on their door from the train magister. None came. Perhaps the godman—and the Gond—shared only gossip, not alarms. But when the train finally got under way again, neither he nor Anzi was inclined to sleep.

CHAPTER THIRTEEN

Saddle an Inyx and it will ride you.
—a saying

TWO THINGS SYDNEY GUARDED MOST CAREFULLY. The first was her journal, where she recorded her life; the second was the window in the stable beside which her bunk staked out a berth.

The journal was to record the wrongs that were done, for later reckoning. The window was for the pleasure of the light on her skin. Everyone wanted a window. But only a few, like Sydney, were willing to fight for them.

She sat hunched up by her window, punching the tiny holes in the paper, writing about Glovid's death and her new mount. Riod was a fine racer, but in accepting him, Sydney's status had fallen. Riod had a bad reputation. He had long refused war service, along with a few rogue mounts that he led on sorties to harass other Inyx herds, creating ill will and incurring Priov's displeasure. Making matters worse, he sniffed around Priov's mares, insulting the old chief. Given this poor match with Riod, she might draw trouble. In the stable, sometimes trouble was bloody.

She called her living quarters a stable, because she liked the irony of the riders living there. The mounts, of course, needed no shelter, preferring openness, always. So their riders slept and lived in a big, drafty barracks, created by the sweat of their own labor and poorly built, often leaking during a heavy dew.

"Click, click, Sydney. I hear you click click with the pin in the paper." From the next bunk came Akay-Wat's breathless voice.

Sydney gripped her needle and punched.

"Akay-Wat hears the clicks, yes. You tell your book about Akay-Wat, why don't you?" She chuckled, that wheezing strangle that seemed to close her windpipe.

"You're in here," Sydney said.

Akay-Wat gasped. "Oh yes?" She clapped her four limbs. "Pleased, then."

The rider wasn't the worst neighbor in the barracks by any means, though she talked too much. Akay-Wat was a Hirrin sentient, one of the best riders, despite looking like she could be ridden herself. She had a sturdy back and long legs with hoofed feet that could hug an Inyx's sides, holding fast. The mounts liked Hirrin, because they never wanted saddles. Her face was small compared to her body, a mere knob on the end of a long neck.

Akay-Wat was always trying to curry favor with Sydney, despite how mean Sydney had to be just to make her shut up so she could get some sleep at ebb-time. When Sydney wasn't around, Akay-Wat protected Sydney's things: her book, her bed, her blanket. So she was loyal. And stupid as spike grass.

"Click, click," Akay-Wat crooned.

You couldn't answer her or she would never shut up. Sydney punched with her needle, forming her ideograms that no one else could read because she had made them up. Particularly the Inyx couldn't read them, because they couldn't feel such subtle bumps. The diary was invisible to them, just like their world was to her. That was fair.

She ran her hands over the pages where she had recorded her days among the stinking beasts. Punched into the pages was the record of those grim days at the Ascendancy, when her world had collapsed. The blinding, the loss of Titus and Johanna. Time was when she had called them *Father*, *Mother*. After they abandoned her, after it was clear they would never come for her, they became only Titus, Johanna. Seldom thought of these days.

Now she punched in her account of her return ride after Glovid's fall, and the ripple of muscle under Riod's coat, his young body fairly exploding with energy. The bright overhead, the steppe beneath, and pressed between, only the ride.

Her right hand cramped at her task of punching words, but she continued to write.

Akay-Wat had grown used to the pricking noise. It came at all hours of the day and the ebb. Now that Sydney had secured a bunk with a nice warm window, Akay-Wat had become her neighbor, and her status had increased, yes, immeasurably. Akay-Wat's bunk was in a space between windows. When the bunk next to her emptied due to the Jout who went off to war—and, so sadly, never returned—Sydney laid claim to it and, by sheer ferocity, won it. This event, more than any other, taught Akay-Wat the value of violence. For herself, of course, physical violence was impossible. Because Akay-Wat, so regrettably, was a coward.

Akay-Wat was one of the few sentients actually born in Priov's barracks. At her majority, she could have chosen to go or stay, but if she stayed, she must be blind. Her mother, before she went to the Long War, had begged her daughter to leave for a better life, but Akay-Wat had been afraid to leave the life she knew. Then, shortly after Akay-Wat relinquished her sight, Sydney arrived: dirty, scrappy, and silent, unable to speak the Lucent tongue. Akay-Wat helped her to learn, but she knew she was not clever enough or brave enough to be chosen as a friend. Once, she had dared to join in one of Sydney's fights. An enormous Jout sentient had nearly taken her head off. Since then, Akay-Wat had resigned herself to the meekness that came so naturally. However, Sydney's contempt was hard to bear, and got no better despite the little services Akay-Wat performed for her. Someone should perform them, certainly, for Sydney was a personage, even if foul-tempered and disfavored by the mounts. She was a former denizen of the vast darkness, a creature of Earth—a human. Astonishing enough, but there was more: she had lived for a time in the Ascendancy, and been the special prisoner of the Lords Hadenth, Inweer, Nehoov, Chiron, and Ghinamid. Her father was the infamous barbarian Titus Quinn, criminal and fugitive.

None of Sydney's past history mattered to the Inyx nor singled her out for preference. The Inyx lived apart, in a sway far from the heartland, and in a manner remote from the cultures of the Entire. Lucent-speaking creatures feared and reviled them, oh very. The Inyx formed no ties except among themselves and their riders. Some even believed that the Inyx considered themselves above the bright lords. The Inyx despised all those who could not speak heart-to-heart. In other words, everyone else. The Tarig, for their part, tolerated the Inyx as little more than beasts who were too base to understand Tarig greatness. Truly the lords were gracious.

Akay-Wat heard a snuffling noise near Sydney's bunk. Someone was awake early, and came snooping. Bad. Sydney did not like to be interrupted when writing. Akay-Wat waited to see what the human would do at this provocation.

Sydney heard the noise too. Someone was shuffling next to her bunk. It was Puss, announcing his presence by a faint whiff of urine.

The catlike creature had long limbs for swinging in trees, of which there were none in this sway. For this reason, Puss's arms were always busy, gesturing and scratching and getting into trouble. Its long tail made it vulnerable at payback times.

"Got the book, I hear. Nice little book," he rasped, like he had a too-tight collar.

Puss was an Inyx spy, a smarmy Laroo, of a species that seemed born to be base. "Take a bath, Puss." He couldn't know the term, but he could guess it meant no good.

"What a sensitive little nose. I wonder how you can bear to ride. Our mounts are such animals."

She wouldn't be led into criticisms of the Inyx. Once, Priov had beaten her for an insulting remark about the state of the chief's broodmares. *Old, flabby, and barren*, Sydney had said. Some of the mares took exception, and Sydney had paid for it.

Puss rasped: "Tell what you write in that book, little rose."

"That you stink because you pee on yourself."

"Maybe you just pretend to write, but it's all nothing but pinpricks. That's what everyone thinks. The little rose thinks she's better than us, doesn't she?"

She was trying very hard to ignore the *rose* bit. However, after a certain point, her reputation was at stake. Once you showed weakness in the stables, you lost everything. Her knife hung in its sling on the bedstead beside her. It had drawn blood before.

"I try not to piss on myself. It's not a high standard."

Puss jumped onto her bunk, murmuring, with fetid breath, "I don't like you, and neither did Glovid, my good friend." She heard a stream of urine fall onto her mattress.

Sydney jumped off her bunk, yanking Puss with her by one furry leg. Puss screamed in pain as he hit the floor. Racing back for her knife, Sydney unsheathed it and advanced on the creature. "Lick it up, piss-face." She gestured at her soiled bed.

Riders were crowding around, always game for a good fight, the shouting equal for Sydney and Puss. Akay-Wat was clomping nearby, saying, "Oh dear, oh dear, bad fighting."

Puss leapt for Sydney, landing all four feet in her chest and bouncing off, leaving a claw mark on her neck. She froze in place to listen. A faint scraping sound preceded Puss's next jump, and she reached up to cut his stomach. By Tarig law, she mustn't kill him, but a nice cut was fair payback. She felt her knife slice through fur and heard a caterwauling as Puss raced for the barracks door.

Sydney charged after him, pushing past the gathered riders, who piled out of the barracks after her, into the gleaming bright. Some of Puss's fellow spies were in the melee, by the smell of them. They took turns darting in and out as she turned, slicing her knife to keep them cautious. Suddenly, one jumped onto her back, biting into her shoulder. She tossed him away, hardly feeling the wound, but ready now to murder them all.

The gang of Laroos grew silent. By the sound of a hoof slapping the dirt, she knew that a mount had come to see the fuss ended.

Unfortunately, it was Priov.

A breeze cooled the sweat on Sydney's body. She stood, knife in hand, as Puss whined for good effect.

Who is using bad knives? Priov directed at the group.

A hundred voices answered: Laroos accusing Sydney, Yslis accusing Hirrin, and, above it all, Akay-Wat saying, "Peed on the bed, did Laroo, to cause stinking."

As the voices quieted Priov sent, *Here is one with a bad knife.* She didn't need to guess whom he was looking at. She sheathed the knife in her belt, saying, "The Laroo have knives growing in their hands. Claws are just as bad as knives."

Now that a mount had arrived, sight trickled into Sydney's mind. She saw the ragged and dirty riders, a bad mix of the ugly and misshapen: the monkeylike Ysli with their sullen faces; the witless Hirrin, a cross between an ostrich and a donkey; and the Laroo, reddish fur glinting in the bright, standing stooped over like apes, with arms trailing at their sides. In their midst, a small human with matted black hair, as ugly as the rest of them.

Bring me the cuff, Priov demanded. A Laroo went to fetch the long-tailed whip that fit around the fetlock of the Inyx. *Sydney, go to the post*, he said.

She held fast, trying not to show her outrage, or even feel it. She wanted to give no emotional performance for the Inyx, but she couldn't help but remember the last whipping, when her nerves ran fire and she'd bitten through her lip without noticing. She thought of her book, and pin pricking this into the pages, the four hundredth wrong, unless it was the five hundredth. All could be borne, as long as there was a list.

Priov's mares, who stayed close by him, trickled into the scene, nervously gathering up their riders and tossing their heads, disliking the emotion-charged atmosphere. The Laroos climbed on, and several others, as Akay-Wat chanted, "Not fair, not fair."

Sydney walked to the post, keeping her walk steady, her head high.

Akay-Wat looked at Sydney with profound admiration. She felt more words gathering: her impassioned speech on behalf of her friend. But Priov's mood was irritable, and Akay-Wat feared he might whip her, too. Yes, let him whip me. She began to move forward. When she heard Priov stamp his foot, the impulse vanished. A whipping hurt badly, especially if Priov used the cuff with the knots. The shame of her cowardice cut deeply as she saw, through the eyes of many mounts, Sydney standing calmly in the center of the yard.

Akay-Wat's mount, Skofke, moved up beside her, bending down so that Akay-Wat could climb up. He caught the drift of his rider's thoughts, and reflected them back to her in a horrible reverberation: *coward, coward, coward.* She clung to Skofke's back in misery, watching her friend slowly turn to grip the post.

Priov approached, wearing the cuff.

The mounts kept arriving, gathering riders up, tossing nervously about, picking up a cacophony of emotions. Then a new emotion: foreboding and excitement. A mount was galloping down the gully near the barracks, black coat glistening.

It was Riod, his thoughts clear as a shout: *She is mine.*

Silence fell on the gathering as Riod came to Sydney's side. *Up*, he said.

No, Priov demanded. *First, the cuff.*

Her hand went out to Riod's strong face, making sure where he was. Sydney was thrilled but also wary. Riod risked much, especially in front of Priov's mares, all milling about, witness to whether Priov could control one renegade Inyx or not. But he had dared to side with her against another Inyx.

"I used a knife on the Laroo," she told him, to be fair.

Which Laroo?

"The one that pees on beds."

He sent an emotion of contempt, and then she felt his front legs dip for her to mount. She sprang up, and Riod charged out of the circle, Sydney holding tight.

They thundered down the gully by the camp, and then out onto the steppe.

Priov shall not hit you, Riod sent.

She liked hearing that. Even though it was in Riod's self-interest not to have an injured rider, she caught his emotion of loyalty. It was a fierce and lovely emotion, one that stirred her like no other.

Those who should be loyal often weren't. No one had stood by her in four thousand days here: not Johanna, not Titus, not the powers of the Rose who never came looking for the vanished family. Only one person in four thousand days: an old Chalin woman, the prefect of the Magisterium—and even she couldn't save Sydney from the cruel hands of the Tarig or the cruel hearts of the Inyx. Sydney nevertheless loved Cixi. Her messages came infrequently, whispered by couriers, Chalin legates bringing new slaves. Messages like, *Persevere, my strong girl. Remember the vows.* The vows she and Cixi had sworn to each other. *Someday soon we will be together again.*

Sydney rode on, letting all the bad things peel away on the wind. It was a good day to ride, and not be beaten. A good day to remember that the most powerful Chalin in the All was her foster mother—no, her true mother—who would come for her someday.

Twilight slipped into the Shadow time, and they slowed their pace. It seemed likely they would spend this ebb-time on the steppe.

Riod found a shallow ravine and a stand of spike grass, bending down so

Sydney could dismount. He walked away, hoofing the sand for a chance at water. Eventually a pool formed, and seeing it in his mind, Sydney came to cleanse herself.

Riod pranced closer, sniffing her.

"I'm all right," she said, feeling his curiosity about her wounds. Through his eyes she saw herself: ragged, short hair, and in the dirty face, eyes still blue but so blank.

It was easy to forget she was blind. Not so easy to forget the Tarig's embrace, as he held her, as the claw came closer. There was confinement, steel-locked arms, and the mantis lord whispering to her. . . .

Riod's warm breath wafted into her face. He licked at the deep scratch at her neck. When she loosened her collar, he cleansed her shoulder bite as well. Riod's warm tongue was probably full of germs, but it felt good. She didn't want to like this mount. She wanted to exploit him as he exploited her. It was disgusting that, to feel important, the mounts must have helpless riders. The Inyx claimed that blindness enhanced the ability of non-Inyx to pick up silent Inyx communication. Even if true, Sydney bristled at their domination. And at her growing affection for Riod.

I'm not your pet, she thought angrily, pushing him away.

What are you? Riod asked, rudely listening in.

"Stay out of my head!" she said aloud. She kicked the grass in frustration, stomping on patches of thread weed as Riod watched, feelings hurt, mixing his own feelings with hers.

Tomorrow she must face Priov again, and the thought sickened her. But she was weary now, needing sleep. She found a hollow in the ground and lay down, trusting Riod to watch over her because she was too weary to care whether that made her more dependent on him.

Standing guard, Riod faced out to the steppe. Through his eyes she saw the flat world stretched out, clean and empty, with a lavender blush dimming the land. As she drifted into sleep, she felt Riod's mind probing hers, looking for something. He hoped that, with her guard down, he might find a shred of reassurance.

Sydney fled into sleep, her only privacy.

As Quinn and Anzi debarked the train at the village of Na Jing, Anzi steered Quinn away from the Gond who had taken insult in their failure to purchase goods. The Gond urged her sling-bearers to hurry after Dai Shen, but this ploy failed when the Hirrin princess intercepted Anzi and Quinn and, striking up a conversation that Anzi now welcomed, offered transportation to Bei's reach. In this manner, Quinn found himself in the only mechanical air transport commonly available to travelers: a dirigible.

He called it a dirigible, and the princess, named Dolwa-Pan, called it a sky bulb. Dolwa-Pan was traveling to Bei's reach for scholarship, and thought nothing of the expense of a sky bulb for her sole use.

Now, the Hirrin princess stood next to Quinn gazing out the window of the dirigible, her small, round head perched like a flower on the long stalk of her neck. She had apologized a dozen times for reporting them to the train magister, and still she wasn't done. "I should never have thought you were a danger. So foolish, Dolwa-Pan." Her floral perfumes spiked into his senses almost painfully.

"One took no notice," he said, in the idiom.

A trip of ten days by beku was shortened to one day on this small airship that skimmed over the minoral valley at a height of two hundred feet. Nothing except the brightships soared higher here or anywhere that he had seen. No birds, no airplanes. The bright commanded the vertical space, and to approach it was to sicken. Flickers of memory suggested that Quinn had indeed flown there, and for a moment he was shaken by a keen sense of pleasure in that ride.

He was eager to ask Su Bei. Bei would know the truth, perhaps unlocking once and for all the memories that half intrigued, half haunted Quinn. So much depended on this scholar whom he had once known. Would Su Bei help him? Most immediately he needed the facial alterations—according to Anzi, not a difficult task or one, fortunately, that involved cutting. If Bei was willing to tell Quinn his past and alter his identity, then surely he would go the next step, of telling him where to find the correlates, since, Quinn reasoned, one treason led to another.

Su Bei was said to be in disgrace, partially blamed for Titus Quinn's escape so long ago. That could be both good and bad for Quinn. Bad, if Bei blamed him. Good, if he blamed the Tarig.

And who did Titus Quinn blame? Always, the Tarig. But they had intermediaries, and one of these had been Su Bei, his interrogator.

It wasn't at all clear that Bei would welcome him or even tolerate him. And if this gamble failed, he had only himself to blame, for insisting on Su Bei rather than on Anzi's choice for a surgeon. As well, there was the danger that Bei would see a chance to redeem himself, and betray Quinn to the lords.

He put his hand on the lump under his jacket, on the Going Over blade. He was no murderer. But if Bei tried to call Lord Hadenth down on him, he would kill Bei without hesitation.

Dolwa-Pan noted his absent gaze as he stared out the window. "What do you look for, Dai Shen?"

"Peace," he murmured. Stefan and Helice would never believe his goal to be so simple. But in the end, after Sydney, after *his own sway*, he wanted just that.

Dolwa-Pan said to him, "Surely all creatures may be at peace on the Radiant Path?" Her prehensile lip adjusted her necklace, a medallion on a blue cord.

Anzi was making her way toward them, putting a stop to his ill-advised conversation. She interrupted, exchanging bows with Dolwa-Pan. "A lovely ride, Princess. Allow me to reimburse you for your trouble."

Dolwa-Pan flattened her ears in a no, and they began a polite argument over sharing the cost of the sky bulb, with Dolwa-Pan finally persuading Anzi not to pay. Thus Anzi managed to deflect the conversation to safe topics. Quinn felt her reins on him, and chafed. Anzi had already assured him that Hirrin sentients could not be spies. They were afflicted—or blessed—with a profound inability to lie. If they expressed something they knew was untrue, they quite simply passed out. After learning this, he began to see in them a naïve sweetness. He was still on his guard though, Anzi should realize.

Through the window, Quinn watched the storm wall as it hovered blackly, a mere handspan tall at this distance. Along the top, it rippled where it conjoined the bright. It looked like a tidal wave of water, and had since the first time he'd spied it. That image was hard to shake since hour by hour the wall grew. The minoral narrowed toward its tip, where eventually the walls would converge.

Dolwa-Pan lipped at her medallion, bringing it up closer to one ear, as he had seen her do several times. This time he was close enough to hear a very faint chime.

Noting Quinn's gaze, the Hirrin said, "The tonals of regression. It is only a toy, a bauble." She gazed out the window and seemed to grow wistful. "It was my choice to journey to this sway, to pursue scholarship. But even in this far minoral, I know where the gracious lords dwell, in the heartland. The tonals sing very low. We are far away."

Anzi murmured, "Yet the vows keep us ever close."

The pious remark served as a reminder to Quinn that they were speaking to one devoted to the Tarig. Anzi had earlier noted the Hirrin's heartchime, and warned him to be wary. To some in the Entire, the Tarig were little less than gods, and not only because of their powers. The Radiant Path was the structure of justice and well-being.

Well-being for some, he thought. Not for a man of the Rose, or a human child.

Outside, a sight caught Dolwa-Pan's attention. The distant storm wall was pierced by a crack of blinding light, like a door through the wall, filled with fire.

"A nascence," Dolwa-Pan said. "It sputters from life to oblivion. Like us all, yes?" She gave a puff of air through her lips, a thing that passed for a sigh among her kind.

Quinn smiled. "You are a philosopher."

Her ears flattened. "I have no need for philosophy, as the bright guides me." With this lofty sentiment, she departed to tend to her Hirrin child, a tiny replica of his mother, who slept in the stern, lulled by the thrumming of the deck.

The wind blew the sky bulb, buffeting it, whipping its mooring lines as people ran to catch them.

The pilot worked his instruments as, outside, the world frowned gray with streaks of lightning. It was a storm, the perpetual storm here at the boundary of the Entire.

The young Hirrin screamed in terror, saying, "We will fall, we will fall down." Answering him, Dolwa-Pan clutched him under her body, saying, "No, sweet one, we will not fall." Then with a heavy thump she collapsed on the deck, her legs splayed out. Anzi went to her, and Quinn helped pull the princess off the terrified child.

"Fainted," Anzi said.

The sky bulb pitched and spun in the gusts. From outside, shouts came from those helping the sky bulb to dock. The pilot cursed and shouted instructions, although outside no one could hear him. Quinn felt a pang of contempt for a pilot who botched a landing. But at last, with a hard jolt, the craft was down.

"Now we are safe," Anzi told the small Hirrin, patting it on the front legs.

The pilot stood in the small opening to the control room. He scowled at the unconscious Hirrin lying on his deck. "Lied, did she?"

Anzi nodded. "She believed that she lied about falling. But because of your fine skills, we are safe."

He snorted and went to the egress door, throwing it wide and filling the ship with a sour wind.

A gaggle of scholars stood waiting to help. The pilot called for a litter to carry the Hirrin, and urged Quinn and Anzi to debark, anxious to be gone from this place.

Clutching his pack, Quinn stepped out, Anzi following, their hair whipping in the wind. On three sides towered the world walls, blue-black and undulating. The storm walls were stitched into deep folds, quilting space to time in a plaid of grooved lines. It was impossible to gauge how close the walls were. Sometimes they appeared to surge forward, and sometimes to recede, and then to do both at once. Craning his neck, Quinn could see the bright only as a narrow wedge, bravely holding a sliver of sky. The bright was irrelevant here, where the walls rose close and high, undulating and sparking with filaments of light. Ozone stained the air, along with an indefinable smell that made Quinn slightly nauseous.

It was easy to think of this gray and lightning-streaked sky as a storm, a weather front like those at home. But there was no rain or thunder, so the illusion wore thin. He knew very well it was an illusion. The reality was that surrounding him here in the minoral were the Entire's boundaries, the power-drenched skin of the world beyond which lay his own cosmos, a conjunction that might well be the branes of two universes, touching.

Not far away, perhaps a thousand yards, the storm walls converged to a vertical black scar, a seam that might rip apart at any moment.

The reach. The place scholars converged to view the Rose, and one of the places where exchanges between worlds occurred. A game of chance, with all the odds against you. Unless you knew your way.

A group of Chalin scholars herded Anzi and him away from the dirigible. Grit blew in Quinn's face. He let himself be led until he could just make out a low structure highlighted by an impressive streak of yellow lightning that ribboned through the air.

Once at the building, they ducked under an archway and through creaking doors. Out of the wind and chaos, they paused and faced their hosts. There were five ancient Chalin, black-haired and shrunken. Hearing Anzi's request to speak with Bei, they bowed, saying they must determine whether Master Bei could be disturbed. They disappeared through a door set in the far wall.

Alone now, Quinn and Anzi took in the unfurnished hall, its floor littered with sand oozing through chinks. The nearby tumult caused the air inside the hall to thrum. Then the doors flew open, announcing the arrival of Dolwa-Pan, carried on the litter. The young Hirrin cowered next to his mother, and the party disappeared behind the inner doors.

The building rattled in the wind. He noted its disrepair: the cracks along the foundation and a slump of stone in the corner.

Anzi pointed to the high, carved door where the assistants had gone. "That's the To and From the Veil Door. There's one such door in every reach where scholars work. It will take us down below."

Underground. He had wondered how scholars approached the tips of their world. He drew close, seeing that the door was etched with designs, now deeply pitted. He ran his fingers over the worn carvings. It was Lucent calligraphy, almost obliterated with time. He made out a portion: *withhold the knowledge . . . the reach of the Entire.*

Anzi came up next to him. "The Three Vows," she said. And it was: the Three Vows repeated over and over around the door.

"Anzi, does every minoral have a reach like this?" If so, there were potentially thousands of access points to the Entire.

She paused. "Like this? No. Every minoral has a tip, but not all are valued and occupied."

"Why not?"

"Not all are useful. Some yield nothing but darkness. But those that are productive, in those places the lords have provided the veils."

"But even these are sometimes unreliable."

She frowned. "Unreliable? They are all unreliable." Shrugging, she added, "Some more than others." She watched him closely, perhaps worried that she would be accused again of withholding information. "Scholars have great patience to wait at places like this."

"The Tarig don't wait, I'm sure." At her look of inquiry, he explained, "They'd know where to look, and when. Having the correlates."

She shook her head. "But the lords seldom come to the reaches."

"Maybe they want to hide the fact that correlates exist."

Anzi grew thoughtful. "Yes, they do deny it. But if they have such correlates, it makes a mockery of all the studies, all the years of waiting."

"Not very gracious of them."

She glanced sharply at him, noting his smile.

"No," she agreed. "It isn't."

A noise came from the inner door. Anzi murmured, "Now we'll see if Su Bei is a friend or not."

The door opened, and an assistant stood there. He had only a few strands of hair left, but these were carefully pulled up into a topknot. They followed him through the To and From the Veil Door and across a small anteroom into a box that, with much creaking and grinding, began to descend. And kept descending.

How deep was this world? And how could it be contained as it was? As the ozone-laden air infused his mouth and mind, it collected a memory: that he had once been captivated by that question, and that the answer had eluded him. Chalin legends said that the Entire was a natural place, enlivened eventually by the Tarig. Descending into this subterranean place, he felt a frisson of both awe and dread at this world's scale. It was said to be smaller than the Rose, but still profoundly vast, with land distances that normally could only occur in space. Nor was the Entire an extended ribbon of land: it was miles deep, perhaps infinitely deep. It came home to him once more that the bronze lords ruled more than the peoples of the Entire; they ruled nature.

With a small bump the elevator door opened. The assistant led them into a cavernous hall, where a domed ceiling arched over a center mound of instruments. Amid an impressive rack of stone well computing devices, only one was active, lighting the face of a lone scholar, an old woman bent over her screen. She craned her head to see who had interrupted her, then went back to her task.

They followed their guide into a corridor where the end was lost in darkness.

Without turning around the old man said, "If we had received warning of your visit, we could have enlivened a car. Now we must walk." He led the way down a smooth tube, rounded on top and sides but shattered here and there by intrusions of soil and rock. Light nodes budded from the walls, waxing and waning with a throbbing of the ground. Quinn heard the drumming and felt it in his boots, his skin. After a few minutes, Quinn noticed a harmonic underneath the general vibration. It was a repeated refrain of four notes, simple and annoying. As they continued walking, a deep hum surged and faded, like a bass string plucked once. Whatever the rock and soil was composed of, it sang under the vibrations of the storm walls.

They came to the end of the tunnel and found a small chamber, rounded and domed like the first. Instrumentation crowded the walls, sharing space with long roping ridges like buried cables.

A man waited for them. Standing in the chamber was a man whose face was as lined as a crumpled map. A heavy rope of redstones hung around his neck. His white hair was shot through with streaks of black and was gathered in a clasp behind his neck. He stood nearly Quinn's height, and erect, with the form of one who had been robust in youth. Instantly, Quinn recognized him. Su Bei. He dug for shreds of memory. None came.

Anzi bowed, but Bei's gaze was on Quinn.

Quinn said, "I think you know me."

Bei turned away, shaking his head. "A good day turned bad. Visitors, they said. By the bright . . ." He muttered something more, then turned back to them. "All that trouble getting you gone and what good did it do?" He nodded at the assistant, dismissing him back down the long tunnel.

Bei frowned at Quinn. "You've aged."

"Hazards of the Rose."

The old man snorted. "But they're your hazards, not mine. Why do you bring me your problems?"

"What makes you think I've got a problem?"

"If you're here," the old man said, "you have a problem." He glanced at Anzi. "Where was he found? Who knows about him?"

Anzi stepped forward. "I am Anzi, master."

"I know who you are."

She passed by this remark. "Wen An brought him from the Ti Jing reach, injured and stunned. She sent him to my uncle, and all who saw him are now silent, except Wen An, whom we must trust."

Bei moved to Quinn's side, studying him from that angle.

Now a gleaming section of wall came into view—a glistening and translucent membrane covering a cleft in the room. Here, the walls of the chamber converged at an acute angle, leaving the membrane to cover a gap of perhaps four feet wide by nine feet high. It was impossible that the transition between worlds was constrained by the thin veil, or was it. The walls receded past the membrane into a long and tapering crevice that appeared to be filled with a viscous solution that pulsed now and then, causing the veil to tremble. Its surface flickered with starscapes.

Noting his gaze, Bei said, "You remember one of these?" He peered closer at Quinn. "You remember me?" Then he answered his question himself: "No, you don't. Good."

"What are you afraid I'll remember?"

"Everything." He gazed at Quinn a long time, then said, "Why have you come, Titus?"

"For your help."

Bei grimaced. "No doubt. But why have you come back to the Entire?"

"For my wife and daughter." And revising, "For Sydney."

Bei closed his eyes a moment, and then shook his head. "The worst possible reason." He came closer, examining Quinn's face. "Are you sure it's you? Yellow eyes—I don't remember yellow eyes."

Anzi said, "Lenses, master."

"So," Bei said, "Yulin's helping him. Got himself an escort and fancy ideas about the daughter." He turned to Anzi. "Yulin sent him to me?"

She shook her head. "But my uncle knows he came here, master."

"So the old bear managed to avoid committing himself, eh? Doesn't surprise me."

The membrane darkened suddenly, to utter blackness. Bei noted Quinn's gaze. "If I had my way, I'd send you through here this moment. But as you see, there's only death on the other side right now. Someday the veil might be productive." He grimaced. "I'll have my grave flag by then. Meanwhile, the old and the infirm are welcome to it. And Hirrin royals with fancy ambitions."

Quinn held his gaze. "I don't want to go through. When I do, it'll be with my daughter."

"Daughter," Bei muttered. Turning to Anzi, he said, "He's been addled like this since he arrived?"

Anzi faced him squarely. "He thinks he can save his daughter. Might it be true, master?"

Bei looked at her like she had caught Quinn's madness. "Might it be true? Of course it isn't!" He turned to Quinn. "Your daughter is far away. Another primacy away. No one goes there; why should they? The Inyx are good for nothing but running and dying in the Long War. Do you think the Inyx would give up your daughter easily? Alarms would be raised, and before you had gone a day's journey, the lords would have you. In all that you have forgotten, have you forgotten that they travel on the bright? Have you forgotten how they hate you?" As though in answer, a thrum sounded under their feet, a profoundly bass note like a chthonic god saying *hmmmm.*

Bei waved a dismissive hand. "No, you don't remember, of course not. You can thank me for that. When I sent you home, I sent you with white hair and drowned memories. The drowned memories were so you would never come back." In a quieter voice he said, "The white hair was because I thought you might."

He reached up to pick at Quinn's silk hat. "Still white? Good. It worked, then. I'm not a magician, you know. I don't have the power to find your daughter or help you kill yourself. Yes, I once served the Tarig. I lived among them and had every power a Chalin could want. Then Titus Quinn fell into a rage and everything fell apart. You *struck* Lord Hadenth."

He peered at Quinn, waiting for a reaction. "Yes, struck him, with a lucky—or unlucky—blow that almost killed him. Then you fled Tarig justice, the first ever to do so. All this occurred under my tutelage, my responsibility." He turned from Quinn and stared into the grotto of light, flickering low. "They let me live, thinking me witless. But my scholarship was over. All my studies. Taken from me. All my scrolls . . ." His voice quavered. "I came here. There is nothing left but scraps. We paste them together. So I have nothing to give you."

He stood, looking old and defeated. "Go home, Titus. There's been enough ruin."

Quinn let that sit for a moment. "The memories you took. I need them." It was only part of what he needed from Bei, but the old man's mood was poor for asking favors.

Bei exclaimed, "What good would memories do you? They're all of the *Ascendancy*. It's all you knew, back then." After a moment, understanding dawned. "You're going *there?*" He looked in astonishment at Anzi, then back at Quinn. "You will lie at their feet. And as well, the girl who helped you, the girl who started the whole disaster. She'll join you." He peered at Anzi. "Yulin is allowing this?"

"My uncle says there is no stopping the people of the Rose. Now that Titus Quinn is here."

Bei turned to Quinn. "Is that right? No stopping the human hordes?"

Quinn said, "No stopping our use of the Entire to travel in the Rose, by a detour through the veils."

Bei looked from one to the other, running his hands through his hair. "And the daughter? She is relevant how?"

Quinn grew weary of the old man's hostility, but he kept his own impatience in check. He needed Bei's goodwill. "She's only relevant to me."

Bei sighed. "This will be easy. Snatch your daughter from the Inyx sway. Open the veils to human travel, trusting that they have no interest in staying to live forever." The old man paced, and as he did, his redstones clacked together, swinging on their strands. "I draw Titus Quinn to me like Paion to Ahnenhoon." He shook his head. "God has noticed me."

"You have no children, Su Bei." Quinn was guessing, but he thought that was right. If he'd had children, he'd know why Quinn couldn't give up.

"No, no children. But if I did, I wouldn't let myself be killed for them."

"I think you would."

Bei shook his head. "You haven't changed. You never learned that things pass. She's lost to you. Best to accept this."

"I can't do that."

Bei eyed him with disgust. "Human, you are human. I keep forgetting that. Even if I sent you home, you'd be back, chasing after life and all the lost things. Why did I ever think otherwise?" He looked at Anzi. "Yulin has set all this in motion. I blame him. And the red crone, who should know better." He raised an eyebrow at Anzi. "So they succumbed to the Titus Quinn spell, did they?" She didn't answer, and Bei turned back to Quinn. "You attract fierce attachments; you always did, Titus. Some you had cause to regret." He slowly shook his head. "You don't remember that part, do you?"

There was a long pause, filled only by the throbbing rock and its odd harmonics, endlessly repeating. Quinn thought that if he stayed here long, he would have to plug his ears against that music.

A long silence ensued as Bei twitched his mouth in thought. Then he said: "I'll give you what is yours. Your story. But you won't thank me for it."

"I will," Quinn said.

Bei snorted. "We shall see."

He walked to a side door and opened it, gesturing them through. As he did so, the veil's membrane flashed brighter, showing a streak of glowing, interstellar gas. A streak of white formed a finger of hot light, as though pointing the way into the abyss.

CHAPTER FOURTEEN

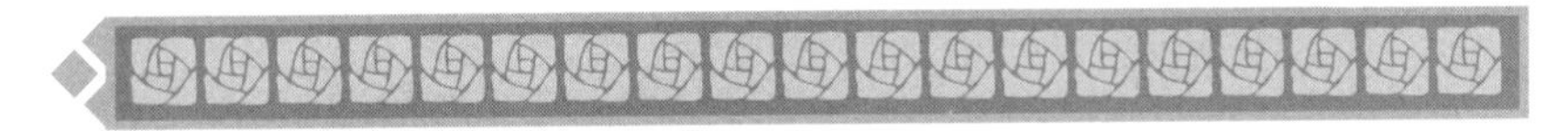

The student asks, Master, what is the other realm that we perceive through the veil?

The master answers, It is the cosmos of cold and fire and disruption; it is the place of delusion, thinking itself primary; it is the ancient sway of all templates, the core designs of all sentients, perfected in the Bright Realm; its worlds are spheres of war and misery; its worlds have scattered glories, among them a colorful sprouting called the rose; it is a domain of striving, and hopes lost to the decay of days; it is a zone where glorious day holds only half the sky; it is the kingdom of the evanescent.

It is what you see through the veil.

—from *The Veil of a Thousand Worlds*

THE THREE TOOK A MEAL IN BEI'S QUARTERS adjacent to the veil-of-worlds room. A tottering assistant brought a tray of dumplings and oba, and they ate in silence, chewing on the food and their next moves.

Shelves formed the walls, packed tight with scrolls and bristling with loose papers. Tables bore the familiar boxy stone wells, some of them disassembled. Amid this, Bei's rumpled bed squeezed into one corner.

Anzi told Bei of Master Yulin's scheme, that Dai Shen would go as a suppliant and a messenger to the bright city, to secure the blessing of the high prefect for a journey to the Inyx. Bei shook his head, over and over.

"She will remember you," he said. "She remembers everything." It presented an opening for them to admit they came for a surgeon's skills. Bei snorted, looking at Quinn's face as though it were hopeless.

A tapestry of medieval European design hung over Bei's bed nook. Noting Quinn's gaze, Bei said, "A particular interest of mine. That one is based on the Dutch, fourteenth century." His hawk eyes narrowed. "You don't remember our discussions of the Middle Ages, I suppose."

Quinn didn't.

The scholar rose from his chair and went to the tapestry, which depicted a bearded white unicorn surrounded by a fence. The unicorn wore an elaborate collar and was crouching as though considering a jump from its cage. Bei's gnarled hands touched the weaving. "You used to admire this tapestry. Saw yourself as the unicorn, no doubt."

Quinn did remember the tapestry, and for some reason, it filled him with a deep unease.

Bei had taken a scroll from a hook and laid it out on the table. Thumbing the nub at the top, Bei enlivened the surface, showing a written Lucent treatise. On closer inspection, Quinn saw references to rivers and lands of the Earth.

Bei's gnarled hand fluttered over the text. "The great discipline of geography. Each world has its mountains and valleys. Its face. Before you came, our knowledge of Earth geography was partial and misleading." He sighed, retracting the scroll and waving it at the stuffed bookcases. "With your help, we secured the missing pieces of your mathematics, history, political economy, chemistry. You were no scholar, but you knew things."

Quinn began to recall those discussions: long conversations threading deep into the ebb; Bei writing everything on a scroll.

"The Tarig wanted information on the Rose?"

Bei's eyebrows furrowed down. "What the Tarig wanted was to know why you came here." He turned to Anzi, who was paying strict attention on the sidelines. "Have you ever wondered why they failed to pursue you?" When Anzi nodded, he answered, "Because they were convinced the Rose *sent* Titus Quinn. They never guessed he was *retrieved* here. They always feared discovery by the Rose. The Tarig reasoned that it was intentional on the part of Rose warlords, to send a scout. It was my job to find out the details of the conspiracy."

From deep below, a tone vibrated, like a gong buried in wool.

"Even after thousands of days, they still wished me to follow that line of questioning, and this I did. You knew the game, and you answered as best you could, the details of the politics and the power structures. Thanks to you we know about Earth's hierarchies: the reigns of powerful commercial lords, and the magisterial lackeys that serve them. Minerva, that was one of the powers, wasn't it? In any case, the Rose seemed an unlikely threat. So the Tarig lords grew more satisfied with you, that there was no conspiracy. After that my questions were only a scholar's.

"That was when I began my great work. My book of cosmography, to lay out the structure of the Rose universe based upon the millions of views of the galaxies and clusters. There is no way to record a map of the Rose. It must be modeled mathematically based upon universal correlations and their relation to dimensionality." He shrugged. "It is an old man's fancy. When I am gone, no one will pursue the work."

Quinn said, "*Are* there universal correlations?"

Bei eyed him a long moment. "Some say yes. Others . . ."

"Tarig say no."

"And perhaps they're right. Mutability is the principle. Mutability of correlates. They change in ways no one knows how to predict. Sometimes the view is steady, and of an inhabited world. The veils are attracted to power sources, and by this accommodation, we sometimes can study a situation, a people, for a hundred days—giving us a data point. Then the membrane blinks, and we see someplace new and unrelated—another data point." He gestured in the direction of the veil-of-worlds. "Each point can be represented mathematically, even if it is black space. If you map such points, you have a geography of Rose space, a universal cosmography.

"That is my theory, and it has a strong following of one."

Quinn said, "So your cosmography—it isn't about correlating the Entire and the Rose."

"Against the vows," Bei muttered.

"But the knowledge must exist. The Gond. We've seen their kind, even on Earth."

Bei leaned in closer, lowering his voice. "Yes, Gond. Unstable, mentally. You have to be, to want to live *there* instead of *here*. A few of them have fled there to die, over the ages. They walk through the veil to vacuum space, and to the hearts of stars, and to frozen asteroids. And some, to worlds of Rose sentients. Your myths of monsters. Most of these are from the All. They were monstrous because they came to you in madness and despair, creating havoc. You killed them, employing your formidable arsenal of murder and mutilation. But they would have died anyway. To cross to the Rose is to become evanescent, just as to cross to the Entire is to be long-lived. That's why your people can never come here, Titus. They would overwhelm us." He pointed a gnarled finger at Quinn. "And war is no answer, for either of us. The Entire is fragile. Some of your weapons would collapse the storm walls. Our world was not built for war, not at the scales you practice it."

Quinn said, "All my people want is to use the correlates to travel in our own universe, through yours."

Bei's mouth curled into a sneer. "You're a fool if you believe that."

Quinn let that lie. Having just arrived, and finding Bei wary, if not hostile, now wasn't the time to push him.

The ancient assistant came back to collect their tray of cups and leftovers, shuffling out under his burden.

Watching him leave, Bei continued, "For those of us at this veil, the scholarship is mundane indeed. Most people have limited visions, after all. My dreams when I was called to the Ascendancy were vast and foolish. I would have a Rose sentient to question. I saw my ambitions of cosmography writ large. Now my dreams are small again."

Bei's voice lowered. "I'm not proud of what I did, Titus. But if I hadn't been your interrogator, it would have been someone else. I taught you how to navigate Ascendancy politics, both high and low, and in the end that might have saved your life. Everyone was vying for a piece of you, the Chalin legates more than anyone else, but also the lords. Everyone took an interest. No one had ever seen a Rose being before. And you had knowledge, in context. For the first time, our bits of knowledge found coherence—for as much as you knew. Not much, it's true, but a stupendous boon nonetheless." He paused, fingering his redstones. "You had power. And I taught you to use it."

Quinn felt a growing confusion. "Power?"

"Oh, not enough to bring back Johanna. She was long gone. A trophy for Lord Inweer, as recompense for his dismal posting at Ahnenhoon. They questioned her—that was the job of scholar Kang—but she told me your wife had few notions of politics and the scientific endeavors." He looked away, avoiding Quinn's expression. "As to your daughter, she knew little. They sent her away, to barbarians."

"Why?"

"They look for ways to woo the Inyx. The girl was a prize."

"And her being far away made it easier for them to compel me to speak," Quinn murmured.

"Yes, to compel you." He paused. "But eventually, you walked freely. You had few enemies and many friends."

That wasn't true. He had been a prisoner. Bei kept saying things that didn't square with how it was. How it had to have been. "I didn't walk freely."

Bei stroked his chin. "That was all long ago. You did what you could."

Quinn had forgotten to breathe.

The old scholar looked at Anzi, as though she should help him, as though it were her place to say what came next. But Anzi's eyes were as distressed as Quinn's.

Bei rose and paced away, as far as his little room allowed. He turned back, scowling. "This is why I took your memories. To keep you from all this. This urge to prove something."

"What do I need to prove?" The foreboding was now full on him.

"Nothing," Bei snapped. "Prove nothing. You are no better than other men, Titus Quinn."

But perhaps he was somewhat worse. To have had *friends*. To have had *power*. He sat down, staggered. "Give me my own memories," he whispered.

Bei shook his head. "I don't know how. I suppressed them, with as much knowledge as I had. It was incomplete knowledge. Now that you are back, I think they will come, gradually." His face fell into even deeper lines as his eyes darkened. "You think me your enemy, Titus. Perhaps I was. I told myself you were no worse off because of me, but it excuses nothing.

"The Tarig kept saying that if you relinquished information, your family might be returned to you. One day led to the next, and the information was never enough. Every day you asked. And every day the lords said, *Not yet.* The days passed. You had not seen your wife and daughter since the first day of your capture. You did all you could, Titus; content yourself with that. You never forgot them. You told and told." He gestured to his scrolls. "Everything you knew was written down, eventually. Because you persisted. But the Tarig would never have given them back. Why should they, when their absence was so productive?" He paused, looking away. "And then Johanna died. The daughter grew up. The past was over."

"Never over," Quinn whispered.

Bei shook his head, muttering. "No. I can see that."

The awful part was, there was more. Quinn could almost remember, but the memories were withdrawing just in advance of his questing mind.

"Tell the rest of what I did."

Returning to his seat, Bei fingered his redstones, collecting his thoughts. "You were part of the life of the court. You were close to the Lady Chiron." Here Bei paused. "You remember the Lady Chiron?"

Quinn shook his head.

Bei muttered, "Perhaps that is best." At Quinn's pointed look, Bei said, "The great Tarig lady. You liked each other. It was a dangerous friendship, but you could not be dissuaded."

"Liked each other?"

Bei pursed his lips. "So it was said."

When the old man had to glance away, Quinn took a stab at the truth: "I took a lover?"

"So it was said." After a pause Bei added, "Even the Tarig lady could not save you when you attacked Lord Hadenth, the day you learned that your daughter was sent blind into slavery." His voice lowered. "I had hoped that an exception had been made for the girl, and for all I knew, perhaps it had. But old Cixi knew the truth, and for some reason, after all those thousands of days, she told you. You appeared in the doorway of the great hall, looking half-crazed. You asked where Hadenth was. I didn't know. But you found him, eventually."

In the corner, Anzi shuddered. Quinn looked at his fists, big enough to break open a normal person's skull. But to a Tarig, just enough to addle a mind.

"You remember Cixi? She collects enemies like I do redstones." He sighed. "Your mistake was to expect restraint from a high lord. Your daughter was nothing to them. That is something to learn once and for all, Titus. They're not like us. In any way."

Bei continued, "I took you to a minoral, an abandoned reach where the veil had been destroyed. Long ago a maddened Gond crossed over to the Rose through that place. The Tarig obliterated it, but they didn't realize there were two access points at this reach. We waited there for many days, half-starved, while I waited for it to correlate with a life-bearing world. I used the time to change your body. You allowed this, thinking you would come back. I took the liberty of insuring you wouldn't want to, that you would forget everything. Then the veil became productive, and gave us our chance. We took it."

"Why?" Quinn asked. "Why did you risk helping me?"

Bei pursed his lips. "I've often wondered. You are impulsive, stubborn, and reckless." He shrugged. "Who knows? It's past, now."

"The past matters."

"That is only true if your future is short."

They faced off, each with his own view of the world. Of course it could not be the same view.

Bei drew himself up, resigned. "Listen then, Titus Quinn, Dai Shen, prisoner and friend of the Tarig. You will go, I can see, to the bright city. If you're lucky, the Tarig will take little notice and God will not regard you. There you will meet Cixi, the high prefect of the Chalin legates. If your subterfuge fools her, she'll send you to a far primacy from which you may never return. But that's beside the point. You'll rescue your child or die trying, the only thing that can satisfy you.

"Among the Chalin of the Ascendancy you may hear stories of a man of the Rose who once was among them. He began as a slave, and rose to influence, as eager to know the Tarig as they were to know him. It was, as you would say, many *years* in which you became accustomed to your prison, and in which it gradually became your palace. You found your happiness, because you had no choice. We, who began as interrogators and jailers, became your friends. How long can a man hold onto hate? You tried. I watched you try. Over years, mind you, the hate became despair, became numbness, became reborn as a new life." He sighed. "Time will do that. It's no shame.

"Now I've told you what you've been digging for. You knew, of course." Bei slumped into a deep chair, muttering, "I shouldn't have told you. But the memories—you were right—belong to you."

Quinn was standing next to the table, staring at the tapestry, at the several depictions of unicorns. He had been an oddity in the Entire. But a treasured oddity. A pampered one. Here, the hunters advanced on the caged unicorn. Looking pacified and well fed, the unicorn pranced up on its hind legs, its jeweled collar sparkling. It wasn't often you got a bird's-eye view of your soul.

"A palace," Quinn whispered. "A new life."

Bei's voice was gentle. "Let it go, Titus."

"I can't." The past for him was yesterday. Six months ago. Time was twisted out of recognition. If you betrayed your wife, you didn't move past it in a day. If you betrayed your daughter, perhaps you never did.

Quinn turned and left the room, passing through the veil-of-worlds room, walking like a blind man down the tunnel.

Bei snorted. "Such a waste of passion."

"I wonder if it is," Anzi said. Then she followed Quinn.

Bei watched them as their forms receded down the long tunnel. He trusted that old Zhou would be watching for them in the next chamber, and would lead them to quarters. Meanwhile Bei was left to decide whether to help Titus or not.

You old fool, he thought. You knew he'd be back. But to be caught so unawares, to be so staggered by the vision of Titus Quinn standing before you in this remote place!

Truly, he'd been living in a dream world, locked in his studies, thinking Titus Quinn gone for good. Now the man was back, with powerful allies. Yulin and Suzong. He could well imagine that old Suzong was behind this. She would have been whispering in Yulin's hairy ear: *Power, my husband.*

With more accuracy, she might have whispered, *Ruin.*

Titus's patrons knew the way in. Now indeed ruin waited behind a door, a door no longer locked, nor even latched. Humans would swarm through, and it would never be for travel and commerce. They would come with their hordes and their dark weapons, and the culture of Bei's world would become human culture, because their numbers were endless. There might be war.

Yes. A war that even the Tarig must fear. The storm walls. The bright. All so vulnerable. To prevail over the Rose, who knew what the fiends might do?

And now Bei had botched his one chance to discourage Titus. He could have sent him home with a shrewd and merciful lie, could have told him that Sydney was dead. That would have put an end to it. But, no, he had revealed the whole sordid story, unleashing the demon that would ride Titus's back until the bright burned out.

Bei swore under his breath. Never a good liar, that's my trouble.

I knew, he thought. I knew the man would hate what he'd been. To learn it all at once was different than experiencing it day by day: the relentless weight of days, days when the wife and daughter were gone, and never the slightest intimation of where they were. Titus would have gone mad unless he'd been willing to start a new life. But, God's beku, it was hard for the man to hear. And now he'll be out mucking about, proving his devotion. When you were short-lived, things like devotion to a wife, a child, seemed so crushingly important. But over seventy, eighty, ninety thousand days, you learned that there were always more children, more wives, more days, what did it matter?

Still. The man had a right to know his own history.

Bei had told most of it, including the worst things—things that a man of the Rose might think the worst—such as his bedding of the Lady Chiron.

He shuddered. Bei was no prude, but to bed a Tarig female, how was it even done? Well, there were many ways to pleasure one another, and not all of them required compatible anatomy. Besides, the lords had required that Titus stay among them. He had had few Chalin contacts, and no human ones. So when the lady took him, she might have seemed normal to him by then. He shook his head. Not the lad's fault—and who knows, she might have compelled him.

Bei had kept some details to himself, but soon enough Titus would remember them. It remained to be seen if he could rebound.

He sat down, worn out by pacing and the shock of the last few hours. When Titus had disappeared through the veil, Bei had hoped to banish thoughts of him and all that had transpired. But memories of Titus had haunted him. His role in Titus's captivity, of course; there was always that stain. But also, the friendship that they'd had—one that evolved from tolerance to admiration so gradually that Bei never noticed when it was that he had decided to help Titus escape. The distress Bei felt in seeing him again arose from knowing that the terrible longing and deprivation of his first sojourn here was now upon Titus again. And Bei would have to watch, and be as helpless as before.

To collude with him would only worsen, or delay, the man's fate. What, by the bright, did you do if a friend begged you for something that would destroy him?

Withhold. That's what you did.

Bei rose, feeling older than when he'd sat down. So, Titus was asking for surgeries. To hide among his enemies, the man wanted to alter his face.

Better if could alter his heart.

Bei paced the veil-of-worlds chamber, trying to fortify his decision to tell Titus no. As he paced, the veil lit up with a new view: a star surrounded by a huge shell of gas that glowed in a flood of ultraviolet radiation, its round shape looking like a fence around a lone prisoner. Bei stared at this view.

God's beku, but he knew what he would decide.

He'd aided and abetted in the confinement of Titus Quinn once. And that would never happen again. The older he got, the clearer it had become to him that shameful behavior was always on your own shoulders, no matter who ordered it. "God not looking at me," he muttered. His fate was entwined with Titus Quinn's. He'd known that from the day the Tarig first showed up at his door, saying that the lords required him to attend them and asking if his command of English was still perfect.

It was, by the vows, though he should have lied to them.

Learn to lie. That would be his advice to his children, if he'd had any.

Bei performed his transformations on Quinn's face, using needles that stimulated alterations in the cells. The bones in Quinn's face hurt with every vibration of the deep ground, but he refused the pain inhibitors, full of vicious secondary compounds. Perhaps ideal for a Chalin, the medicinals failed the test of his Jacobson's organ. They smelled bad.

During the days, Anzi sat at his side reading to him from Bei's scrolls. She had a thousand to choose from. He learned things that he had once known, and things that he had never known. He tried to pay attention, to learn, but awash in the pain of his facial bones re-forming, it was difficult to concentrate. Sometimes he took out the photos of Johanna and Sydney, to seek some comfort from them. But they were creased and faded, accusing him by their deterioration. *Prince of the Ascendancy*, they seemed to say.

He saw glimpses of the bright city—with its carved halls and wide, curving stairs—and the labyrinth underneath, where labored the legates, consuls, factors, and stewards. He saw himself threading into the city, into its fabulous byways, seeing wonders. He saw the Lady Chiron, almost human, yes, almost. . . . *Lady Chiron lay beside him on a platform of hot light. Her nakedness unnerved him. Some sexual acts were impossible. But one could be creative. She was without inhibition.* Forcing himself to attend to the memory, he recalled: *Hadenth appearing in the doorway. Jealous. Chiron driving him away.*

He hardly needed more details to know that what Bei had alluded to was true. He tried to imagine what kind of a man he had been. And then he was left to wonder what kind of a man he was now. His hands moved over his face, failing to find the old geography.

Seeing him touch his face, Anzi produced a mirror.

Even under the puffiness and bruises, Quinn could see that the face in the glass was narrow and strange. The blue of his eyes had become a burnished gold. Quinn didn't recognize himself. It was comforting.

He must have smiled, because Anzi said, "Good?"

"Yes." He pushed himself up to a sitting position, headache raging.

"Since you're better"—she glanced at him ironically, knowing he was still shaky—"there is a matter to discuss. You won't like it, though."

He was sick, dispirited, and confused. Now there was more? Best to have it over with. He sat up fully, giving her his attention. She offered him water, and he took it, while she gathered her thoughts.

"Master Yulin worries that you'll be captured when taking unwise actions at the Inyx sway." She looked at the floor. "I worry also."

Quinn's breathing grew shallow. So now Yulin was withdrawing from the venture? Without Yulin's help he couldn't go far—perhaps nowhere. He waited for her to go on.

"Yet he knows you have this great desire to bring your daughter home. Thus his proposition that he urges you to think about most carefully. . . ."

"A proposition you've waited so long to tell me?"

"Yes, forgive me. I thought it would anger you, when you were already displeased with me."

Quinn took a deep breath. When would she learn that it was best to tell him everything?

"My uncle says, yes, go to the land of the Inyx, but only to confirm that she's there, and alive. If possible, speak with her and tell her to be patient. Then, when humans come to bargain with the Tarig over routes through our land, demand Sydney's release. This preserves your disguise, and greatly improves the chances that both of you will survive."

"And greatly reduces Yulin's chances of being exposed."

She looked away. "That too."

He'd known that he had to free Sydney without anyone knowing it was Titus Quinn who had done it. Or that it was Dai Shen, son of Yulin, who had done it. Yulin was counting on remaining anonymous. Counting on it a little too hard. Yulin had hedged his bets by appearing to agree while planning to persuade him to more modest goals. The sudden arrival of the Tarig lord in the garden had cut short Yulin's maneuvering.

Quinn turned to Anzi, his nerves taut. "What about you, Anzi? What do you think?" He wanted her to dig herself in, reveal her true agenda, now before her agreeable facade took over.

She looked at him, and her bright amber eyes were unapologetic. "I think it likely you will die otherwise, Dai Shen."

So, she and her uncle were united. "Are my papers still in order? Or has Yulin voided the redstones he issued to me?"

"They're still valid. He can't change what you already have. And you do need to go the bright city, and must have his endorsements."

"Just a small change. He wants me to see Sydney, and leave her where I find her."

Anzi caught his bitter tone, and lowered her voice. "Yes, I'm sorry." Still, she maintained her serenity. He wanted to shake her. *Doesn't anything matter, Anzi?*

Quinn's mind was spinning with possible responses to all this. How much did he need Yulin's enthusiastic support? He staggered to his feet, needing to pace, but he faltered, and Anzi rushed to steady him. He shook her off. Yulin was a schemer, ready to ditch him at the first sign of trouble. No, ready to ditch him now, before trouble even began. Quinn shook with anger and moved away from Anzi, testing his sea legs.

"What if I refuse?" It was his first instinct, to tell Yulin to go to hell.

She responded, "Then you continue as before, Dai Shen."

"What?"

Anzi nodded. "We thought it likely you would refuse. Now you go on as before."

He doubted what he was hearing. "No strings?" At her confused expression, he amended: "Yulin was just making a suggestion?"

"Yes. A suggestion—a wise one."

He waited for her to say more, but it seemed that, for now, he still had Yulin's support, even if it was forced. Yulin wasn't abandoning him, only testing his resolve. The man didn't know him very well. "Does he expect I'll change later?"

"I don't know what my uncle expects. Perhaps he hopes, when you see how difficult it is, that you will remember there is a second way. But for myself, I know that you will never change." She bowed. "I have my answer. Thank you."

"What is my answer?" Quinn wasn't sure whether he had said anything or not.

"You said no, Dai Shen."

There was a moment of silence when Quinn let himself absorb her quiet summation. She was allowing him to decide.

Quinn murmured, "My daughter's waited long enough."

"Yes, I know." Anzi's look was one that a friend might have who'd heard that you were dying, and approved of your bravery.

Here she stood, knowing how he had betrayed his wife, knowing that he had given in to the lords. Here she was saying, *Yes, you have to go. Even if it kills you.* He would rather have her counting on his success than assuming he would fail, but she was giving him something else of equal importance: respect for his decision. He took a deep, cleansing breath. It wasn't all shame, then.

She poured him another drink of water, and he drank it, and another. Still, she remained quiet. The conversation was over; she was letting his decision stand. She was saying, *If you must die trying, I will still help you. If you are caught, I will go with you.* Anzi believed in his cause, not because she wanted the same thing, but because Quinn wanted it. He was profoundly grateful.

He looked around the small chamber. "A change of clothes, Anzi?"

She found a pile of folded, fresh clothes left by the servant Zhou. Quinn took them from her, and she helped him to change.

"I need to see Bei," he said.

"When you feel stronger, Dai Shen," she said, holding a new jacket for him.

"No, I need to see him now." He closed the fasteners. He'd waited too long in bed, laid flat more by emotional shock than the physical one. Suddenly he was eager to be back on track. "Would you tell him, please, that I need to talk to him right now?"

"Yes." She turned to go.

"And Anzi"—he had been meaning to say this to her for some time—"can't you call me by my given name when we're alone?"

Waiting by the door, she said, "Not Titus. That's too dangerous."

"I agree. But can't you call me Shen, at least in private, as I call you Anzi and not Ji Anzi?"

She smiled. "Yes, if you want."

"I want."

He bowed as she left. Then he went to the basin and splashed water over his throbbing face and head, having forgotten his headache.

Bei knelt in the soil beneath the subterranean grow lights, hands muddy and work tunic soaked in sweat from pruning gleve plants. He picked a rock from the soil and slung it with practiced accuracy into the pile of stones nearby. The physical labor eased his worries and calmed the storm of memories triggered by Titus's return.

Earlier in the day he had sent Zhou and the others out of the vegetable field so that he could work in silence, meditatively pulling tubers, checking leaves for mites, and harvesting grayals. But his serenity had been disrupted when Anzi came asking for a meeting with Titus, now apparently recovered enough to get out of bed.

And so Titus had come, looking hale except for swelling that must have felt like a Gond gnawing on his cheeks.

"I'm in your debt, Su Bei," he began.

Bei stood, brushing the soil from his knees. "Well, you haven't seen the result yet." And the *result* might well be a garroting from Lord Hadenth. But Bei pushed this worry aside. He was glad to see Titus. Oddly, after all they'd been through together, Titus considered him a stranger. No memories. It made for awkward interactions, with Bei keeping his distance and Titus still summing him up, weighing things like blame, resentment, and gratitude.

"The eyes shouldn't hurt you much," Bei said. "It's the facial bones that ache."

"Getting better."

The man had a high pain threshold; that was clear. He also seemed mentally improved. And had something on his mind.

Bei knelt to his task again, ripping out weeds and pruning. "Care to help? It's a big field." A little exercise wouldn't hurt the lad, or Anzi either.

Titus made no move, but said, "I'll leave soon."

Bei knew it. A few more days and Titus could leave by sky bulb, since Dolwa-Pan had instructed her pilot to wait for Dai Shen's departure. Bei tossed another stone into the pile. Good. Two stones, better than average.

"What's the rock pile for?" Titus asked.

"Without rocks the soil is easier to work. We've tilled this soil so long, there's hardly a stone left." Bei sat back on his heels, wiping the sweat from his eyes. "You've come to ask something. Then ask." He glanced away. "If you're sure you want to know."

Titus crouched down nearby, facing him. His yellow eyes had already vastly improved his face, although Bei had grown used to the blue, eyes that seemed to see farther than Chalin eyes. Not content to absorb things gradually, Titus always wanted to understand things right away. As now.

"The way to and from isn't random, is it?"

Bei sighed. "If I knew how it was organized, would I be a minor scholar?"

"I think you may know someone who does."

Bei glared up at Anzi. "Have you been putting these thoughts in his head?"

Anzi was watching with wide eyes. "No, Su Bei, your pardon. I didn't know."

How, by the vows, had the man found this out? Suzong, came the thought. Bei crept down the row of gleve, concentrating. He'd expected Titus to ask how he would get home once he had snatched the daughter from her jailers. But now, he demanded more, far more. Well, there were some things that even Titus Quinn couldn't have. He tossed another rock into the pile and crawled on.

Then Titus's hand was on his arm. "Bei."

They met, eye to eye. "Why would I know of such things?" Bei shook Quinn's hand off.

"Because you lived at the Ascendancy. The legates hoard information, and have been for a hundred thousand days. Someone there knows."

It was Suzong who told him, Bei was sure. She'd see the Rose as a great power, one worth cultivating. She hated the lords, but not for any noble reason, only for her personal revenge, having watched her mother die of asphyxiation at the feet of a lord so long ago that she should have forgotten by now. Damn the woman, anyway. If Titus's goal had been perilous before, this new meddling could sacrifice all.

He shook his head. "Titus, when you come back here, I'll try to think of how to help you get out. The veil may not release you—may never release you. But come back here, and we'll pray for luck. And that's the end of it. I've done what I can for you."

Titus was now on the other side of the row, pulling tiny stones out of the soil, making his way on hands and knees. He seized a decent-sized rock and flung it into the pile. "It's a big field," Titus said.

And I'm staying in it until you relent was the implication.

Titus didn't want just help; he wanted the secrets of the kingdom. He wanted everything, as he always did. Wanted the correlates, of course, so he could be the leader of the wave of immigration. Routes to the stars, indeed. No such thing. Humans wanted empire, not routes.

God's beku, why should he betray his own land? Bei didn't give a dumpling for the gracious lords and their paranoia. But wasn't it true that the universes had been separate from the very beginning? It was better to stay separate than risk mixing. Who, after all, could wish to live in the dark when the bright beckoned?

Now Anzi was down on hands and knees, sorting rocks from the next row over. They would stick to him like gnats on a beku's arse. Bei stood, slapping the dirt from his hands. His back ached, and his left wrist, where he'd been leaning on it, throbbed. Now he walked behind Titus as the man resolutely grubbed in the soil for rocks.

"Titus," Bei said, trying to make his voice more reasonable, "you can't use the correlates—even if someone had them in their possession—unless the lords permit it. You see that, don't you?" The man couldn't think that the Tarig would just stand by.

"I don't care if they're used. I just need to bring them home."

"Oh. A bonus is waiting?"

Another stone hit the rock pile. "My nephew is waiting. He's eleven years old."

Bei frowned at this irrelevancy. He trudged behind as Titus continued down the row. "That would be, let's see, Mateo? Your brother's son?" He'd thought the boy would be grown by now, but the time differences, yes, you could never forget *those*. . . .

"I have to get back. Or they'll put Mateo in a jar and never let him out. And I need to *have* something when I get there. I know that, eventually, the Rose will figure out the correlates. It could take hundreds of years, but they will." He looked up, his new yellow gaze as intense as the old one. "Let me be the one to find them."

Bei had to look away so as not to be snared by his passion, his intentions. "Who'll put Mateo in a jar?"

"My employers. Minerva." The venom in his voice was hard to mistake.

So, they had Titus Quinn in a harness. They were compelling him.

Titus went on. "They'll ruin the boy's future. That's why I want the correlates. Unless I have some power over them, they'll run me. I'll be their puppet, and so will my family."

Bei watched his altered friend. So Chalin-like, physically. So human. The man was still in a cage. Now Bei understood some of this passion that drove Titus. It wasn't all about love. Some of it was about hate. They compelled

Titus, threatening him. It was untenable. And even if Bei withheld what he knew, Titus would pursue it. Nothing would stop him.

By the vows, I'm going to tell him, Bei realized with a sinking heart.

"Stand up, Titus." The man did so, and Anzi with him, both of them looking expectant, trusting.

Don't trust me, boy. If you ask me which side I'm on, it's ever the Entire. And why not? It's my world. Imperfect, regulated by the lords, constrained by vows and laws and the arrogance that comes of immortality. But my world.

He sighed. "Titus. I'll help you. But with conditions."

Titus grew wary, and properly so.

"You must swear to me that you'll do everything in your power to keep humans from conquest. Pardon me if I don't trust that bunch of murderous, pillaging scoundrels. You may not be able to do much, but what's in your power, that you'll do. Swear to me."

Titus had the grace to think about what he was swearing. He looked down the long rows of gleve, and he came to his resolve. "I swear it, Su Bei."

"That your people won't come in numbers, staying. Swear it."

"I'll do what I can to prevent it. I swear."

Bei held up a hand, "Don't say on God."

"I wasn't going to."

Bei smiled. Titus was no believer. He knew the man well, and thought his plain word good enough.

"What I'll tell you is a capital offense, to know." He nodded in the direction of Anzi. "You want her to know?"

Titus raised an eyebrow at Anzi. She answered, "I already know enough to die a hundred times."

That was true. They all did.

Bei was conscious that his next words were potent. They might be a poison or a medicine, but they could change the Entire forever. "So, then." He fixed Titus with a gaze. "Here is a name to remember: Oventroe. Mark me, I don't know if he would reveal knowledge of the correlates." Titus watched him carefully. "But they're not all satisfied, you know. Some of them want converse with the Rose, of course. Some of them are against Hadenth and Inweer and the rest. Like Lord Oventroe."

The expression on Titus's face, though swollen and disfigured, registered his surprise. "*Lord* Oventroe?"

Heaven give us patience. The man thought the traitor was a Chalin. Or a Hirrin. Or a Gond. Didn't he know that such traitors would be powerless? The game was the Tarig, of course.

"Yes, *lord*. Lord Oventroe. He hopes to rise to influence as one of the five ruling lords. Perhaps he will see you as a potential ally. Or perhaps not. He has no reason to hurry his timetable in whatever he's planning to do—but you asked for a name. The next part is on your shoulders." Bei looked from Titus to Anzi and back again, at their incredulous faces. "Now you're in a bigger game than you thought, eh?" He closed his eyes. May god not look at me, now I'm in that game, too.

Bei thought of his scholarship and all that might be learned of the Rose, given free interactions between here and there. Free interactions . . . that consummation might be far in the future, and after unguessed-at turmoil. But the notion stirred him. Why not have converse? It was a question many sentients had asked over many thousands of days.

"You will hear," Bei continued, "when you get to the Ascendancy, that Oventroe is a fanatical enemy of the Rose. In fact, that is a pose. He's always believed that contact was inevitable. He's curious about the Rose, curious in a way that most Tarig aren't. He'd be interested in you, to say the least. But that would mean you'd have to tell him who you are." Seeing Quinn frown, Bei added, "A colossal risk, yes."

Quinn said, "But you believe him, that he wants Rose contact?"

"I believe it. Unless he's lying. In the end you'll have to make your own judgment.

One thing I can do for you. I have a token from Oventroe. It allowed me to see him from time to time, when I lived there. All at his whim. And we never discussed his plans; why would we? I was a scholar, not a partisan. At the time, because of you, I knew more about the Rose than anyone."

"Did he know me?"

"No. He kept well away from you, to preserve his disguise. Cixi watched him, always. But she watched everybody, as she'll watch you. The Magisterium is full of spies; remember that, and strive to pass unnoticed."

So, then. He'd uttered the forbidden name, uttered it to the Rose. Lord Oventroe might thank Bei for it, or kill him, but the words were spoken now, and could not be withdrawn. Bei didn't regret it. It felt like a completion—of what, he could not have said—but long in coming.

"The lord could kill you in an instant," Bei said, to cover a surge of emotion, "and no one would question him."

Titus still looked eager enough, or foolish enough, to take the risk. "But if I use the token, Bei, he'll know you sent me."

"Probably. But I'm not the only person who has one. Oventroe's spies are scattered through the Ascendancy and the sways. Don't trust anyone."

"Why did you trust *him*?"

That made Bei laugh, and he realized how naïve Titus was at this time, before his memories of the Tarig became complete. "I didn't, lad. But when a lord takes an interest in you, you submit to him." Bei rubbed his chin. "Or her."

Titus averted his eyes, not wanting to dwell on that.

They walked together out of the field, with Titus and Anzi helping to carry baskets of the harvested tubers.

Bei stopped for a moment, looking back over the tended beds. It had been a restful pastime, growing produce and working the soil. He thought that those endless and peaceful days were now at an end. What he had taken for serenity had been a suffocating peace, imposed by the vow of withholding the knowledge of the Entire. The reverse side of that coin had been to withhold knowledge of the Rose.

Well, he thought with resignation, the Rose and the Entire were about to get a rather strong dose of each other.

"Ji Anzi, wake up."

Bei shook her arm again, and Anzi woke in some alarm, her face wary in the light from the lantern Bei held. "What is it? What's wrong?" Anzi pulled her blanket around her, though she'd slept fully clothed. The chill in the deep ground affected newcomers that way.

"Nothing's wrong." Bei had spent the last hours thinking instead of sleeping. He'd been focused for so many thousands of days on cosmography that he had lost his once-acute sense of politics.

Tonight, it had come back to him: the balance of the Radiant Path was about to shift. Bei had always thought of Tarig hegemony as a monumental presence, as stable and unmovable as one of those stone pyramids erected by the pharaohs of Earth. What had kept sleep at bay this ebb was the notion that the pyramid was not stable if turned upside down. Then, its very breadth and weight could send it crashing with a nudge. A nudge from Titus Quinn.

"Ji Anzi," he said, keeping his voice low so as not to wake Quinn, sleeping next door. "I've been watching you. I think that you're loyal."

A woman of few words, she watched him. He looked at the girl, thinking that she was prettier than he'd thought at first. She held herself with dignity. She was what a young man might call fine-looking, although Bei had ceased wondering about such things since his last wife had left him a thousand days ago. A good woman, and one who deserved better than life in a minoral's reach.

Now Bei looked at Ji Anzi and wondered if she realized that she occupied a position of supreme importance: advisor and confidante of Titus Quinn. Bei had to know what their relationship was. Everything depended on it.

He couldn't order her to do what he had in mind. She'd have to see the wisdom of it herself. "Ji Anzi," he said, "the question for you—and for all of us—is, who are we loyal to?" When she didn't answer, he said, "Well, who do you serve, girl?"

"My uncle Yulin."

"Ah." Well, now that was out of the way; she had said what she had to. "Yes, yes. But beyond family obligations?" She watched him still. "Let me ask this, then: How do you find Dai Shen? Is he worthy—worthy of your efforts?"

"Yes."

The reserve was seeming less of a virtue. "And are you committed to him, then?"

"Yes."

"There! That's just my point. How far will you go for his sake? Surely you've thought of that? At some point you'll have to choose between the interests of the Rose and interests of"—here he spread his hands, indicating the world—"all this."

"Not if what he wants is his daughter."

He paused. "And the secret of going to and from?" He looked at her with compassion. She was fully committed to the man, but she had no idea where that might lead.

"As Dai Shen said, the Rose will discover it sometime anyway."

Ah, so guileless. He wished he could let her stay that way. But no. "Anzi, listen to me. Right now you only see a man on a quest to learn some things and take back something that belongs to him. As he should! But freedom to go to and from . . . that is a lever to move our world off its base. The correlates are the fulcrum." He sighed. She wasn't following—and she wasn't looking ahead.

"I don't know what the future will bring to the Entire, Anzi, but I know that the door is open now—open for many changes. Titus wants the correlates to bargain with his masters for the safety of his family. But the possibilities go far beyond that. They *could* go far beyond." He looked toward the wall separating her sleeping chamber from Titus's, and lowered his voice further. "If he is won to our side."

She frowned, and he plowed past her questions for the time being. "Listen to me. Titus doesn't love the Rose. The Rose has exploited him. He could be won over, Anzi, to the Entire."

"Won over?" She watched him with sober eyes, with that reserve she kept around her like a fence. "What more do you want of him?"

He paused, fingering his redstones. "I'm not sure yet. But it begins with his loyalty." Seeing the confusion on her face, he went on, "Anzi, pay attention. I'm telling you it matters where his heart lies. Even if we can't tell right now how it matters, it always matters what a great man thinks." He fixed her with a gaze. "Win him over. To the Entire. It always pulled on him—what he called *the peace of the Entire*. He was under its spell once. He loved it, Anzi. If he came to love it again, we'd have a chance to become a land beyond anything we've been before."

"Aren't we enough right now?"

Bei regarded her, wondering if she had a political bone in her body. "Perhaps we are. Or perhaps there's more that we could be. Who knows, now that we'll have converse with the Rose?"

"But . . ." She hesitated.

When nothing more came, he supplied: "You don't even know where *your* loyalties reside, much less his, eh?" He paused. "Because you hero-worship him. Even love him?"

She raised her chin. "No."

"Well. Even if not. Your duty is to this land, this people, this culture. You'll know that, eventually. Things aren't better in the Rose."

She looked up sharply at him. "That's what Dai Shen said, also."

"Well, yes, I'm not surprised."

They sat side by side, as the silence lengthened. He wished it hadn't come to this, that he must manipulate Titus. But Titus was the man who wanted everything, wanted power. All for a good cause, no doubt, in his own mind at least. And perhaps he would, in the end, be a boon to the Entire. But because Titus was only a representative of the Rose, and not typical of them, Bei must protect his people, his world.

He disliked this next part, but he had to be certain of Titus, and Anzi could help. "One thing might ensure his loyalty, Anzi. Physical intimacy. The man is robust. You could bind him to you."

She looked at him with contempt. Not the right timing for that suggestion, but when would he have another chance?

At last she murmured, "What else could the Entire be, Su Bei, than the All?"

He let the irony seep into his voice. "Well, it could be the Chalin All, for one thing, instead of the Tarig All." He saw that those considerations meant little to her. She was in love, and it blinded her. "Don't answer me now," Bei said. "Think about what I've said."

She shook her head. "How can you ask me to betray him twice?"

He paused, chagrined to be chastened by one so young. He found himself saying, in his own defense, "It's only betrayal if you *don't* love him."

Anzi sat there, her face knotted in thought.

He rose, bidding her a peaceful ebb. He'd probably destroyed her sleep, but for himself, he was finally ready for some.

The reach blew cold and dark, sprouting luminous dust devils, as though they carried specks of lightning inside of them. Bei watched as five of his least-feeble students released the ropes of the sky bulb, freeing it to rise from its moorings and bear Dai Shen and Anzi away.

He was both relieved and sad to see them go. Relieved because, since Titus's facial alterations, Bei had labored to keep Dolwa-Pan from seeing him again, fending off her requests to see Dai Shen, to whom she'd taken a liking. She'd have been surprised to find that he no longer looked familiar. But Bei was saddened too, because he feared that this might be the last time he ever saw Titus. He felt deep affection for him, and always had, even this new version: driven, haunted, and golden-eyed.

Now Bei had sent him into more danger than Titus had planned on getting into in the first place. Now there was Lord Oventroe, and the chance the whole façade would collapse right there.

He sighed, watching the dirigible wend down the minoral, shuddering from side to side in the wind and glowing from reflected auroras.

God not looking at you, my boy, he thought.

And Chiron not looking at you.

Titus believed that whole business had been a sexual relationship. As it had. But not only that, at least for Chiron. Because the Lady of the Entire had loved Titus Quinn.

Bei had watched with fascination as all this had played out before him. He had never believed that Tarig could love in the way of a man and a woman. But because of Chiron's possessiveness, he thought this had been the case.

It was best that Titus not know. His self-recriminations were poisonous enough, without wondering if *he* had loved *her*. Well, all in the past now, and best forgotten.

He tightened his jacket around him to keep the chill from settling into his bones. By heaven, Titus Quinn was heading to the one place that he should, at all costs, avoid. But it was his choice. Titus had chosen this path.

Free of the cage, yes, insofar as any man was.

Bei gathered his students, and they retreated from the storm to the quiet of their subterranean refuge.

The dirigible was a small bubble in the distance, receding quickly. Anzi and Quinn had bid their pilot farewell at the train station a few miles from the opening to the minoral. The hut on the train platform served double duty as a station office and living quarters for the train steward, a young man named Jang with a heavily pockmarked face and wisps of beard that failed to cover his scars. Despite his position in charge of the station, Jang couldn't predict the arrival time of the train, and doubted it would come soon.

But nothing could dampen Quinn's exhilaration. He had come away from the reach with everything he'd wanted. There had been a price to pay for it, as Bei said there would be: discovering the mistakes he'd made, the peace he'd made with his captors. Those mistakes made it even more urgent to get to Sydney. If she knew he'd risen high in the Ascendancy, she might think he'd forgotten about her, an almost unbearable notion. Therefore, he concentrated on his journey to find her.

His successes so far made him optimistic and impatient. Why go to the Ascendancy for an alibi that would explain his journey to the Inyx? This ruse that Yulin had devised, of offering commissions to Inyx sentients—would it draw unnecessary attention to him rather than provide cover? Would the high prefect Cixi believe this excuse to travel to the Inyx sway? Why walk into the den of vipers? He and Anzi had only to journey overland to the River Nigh, and from there to the Sea of Arising in the core of this world, from which central point they could pick up the River once more, to travel down the primacy where the Inyx dwelled. This long journey was best begun now, before rumors festered—those rumors that might start with gardeners, godmen, or Gond.

But he knew that he would not, despite the dangers, bypass the Ascendancy.

Because of what Suzong had told him of the correlates; what Bei had told him of Lord Oventroe. The pull of this great prize was a magnet drawing him in, though he believed without hesitation that the power he would gain was not for himself. It was for peace, for security, and to never be ridden again. Yes, he would go to the bright city.

Unfortunately, though, the train was late.

The steward Jang said that, on the one hand, it might arrive in the third hour of Heart of Day, unless it was delayed, and then perhaps it might arrive in the fourth hour of Last of Day, if it was not later.

By convention, days here were divided into eight phases with names such as Early Day, or Shadow Ebb, four of them considered "day" and four of them "ebb." The eighths were in turn divided into four hours—for a total of thirty-two hours. Each hour was comprised of thirty-two short intervals, like minutes. But the Entire contained no clocks or timepieces, because every sentient possessed an instinctive recognition of absolute time. It was one of the uncanny small things that reminded Quinn that the Chalin, though they looked human, were designed by the Tarig. That didn't make them inhuman, he reasoned. But he did wonder what other modifications the Tarig had made in the template of *Homo sapiens*. When he'd asked Anzi, she seemed offended to discuss differences. To her it was important to be human, and he didn't argue.

Now, at Prime of Day, they might have a long wait. The sky would brighten further into Heart of Day, and then begin its recessional into the ebb. The sky burned extravagantly, devouring its fuel—whatever that might be. The lords had at their command a vast power source. Yes, they commanded very much. But they didn't command Lord Oventroe, one of their own. Quinn made a point of collecting their weaknesses, but so far it was a short list.

To avoid unwanted conversation, Anzi decided they would wait outside rather than in the cramped station office. On the train platform, Anzi settled herself on a bench. All Quinn could do was pace and watch for a train that came now and then. It was maddening not to know how much time was passing in the Rose. He could hope that Helice Maki had not judged it too long a delay; had not taken out her frustrations on Mateo. He hoped that he had time.

The denizens of the Entire lived without rushing. If something was not accomplished today, there would be tomorrow. One might travel by beku. Or wait for a train. But where were the roads and vehicles that Chalin technology could easily provide? He asked Anzi this.

"But Dai Shen," she responded, "the Entire is too vast for transport."

"But you travel constantly. Why no roads?" He knew that air travel at most altitudes was not possible. The bright disrupted mechanisms, just as it precluded radio signals.

"Roads? But to where, Dai Shen? We have vast regions of emptiness. Cities are clustered along train paths." She shrugged. "Also, we are not in such a hurry."

But he thought it was convenient for the Tarig to limit travel as they saw fit. He said so, but Anzi countered: "We can go everywhere in the Entire. Eventually we get there, and the passage is safe."

"The River Nigh," he said. The other key to transport here, besides the veils. So far he had no satisfactory explanation for the river that was not a river. *Exotic matter*, Anzi had said. Like the bright, its science was beyond her.

The train steward brought them a meal on the small porch that sheltered them from the sky. As Quinn and Anzi ate, the steward lingered to talk. Had they heard, he asked, about the murders?

Anzi kept eating, but asked what murders, looking shocked that such things could happen.

The young man said four bodies had been found in shallow graves in the Shulen wielding. Now Quinn came fully alert. This was the region where Wen An had taken him that first day.

Anzi kept her tone even, inquiring about the incident, and the steward relayed the story that the four men who died had been seen in the company of a woman scholar and a stranger. Quinn felt certain that the murdered men must have been his captors, the ones who had put him in a jar and brought him to Yulin. By Yulin's way of thinking, they would have had to be silenced.

The steward's glance skimmed over Anzi and Quinn, in an artless assessment of this couple who traveled together and were possibly suspect.

A silence fell as the young man watched them eat. A veldt mouse came to beg food, and the steward shooed it away. It fled in bounding leaps, waving a fan-shaped wedge at the end of its tail that served to dump excess heat.

Jang turned back, looking hard at the man now eating his midday meal on the train platform. The fellow did indeed look a bit odd. For one thing, his hair was not the proper Chalin length. It was slicked back, but where there should have been a tail, it was short, with nothing protruding from under the hat. Furthermore, the few words the man had spoken to the lady were accented. Jang didn't know the man's sway, but it wasn't proper speech. So, he could easily be described as a stranger, yes.

His pulse raced at the sudden thought: What if, by incredible fortune of heaven, the very murderers of the corpses were now standing before him? He, Jang, would have the honor of apprehending vow-breakers. It could be a glorious thing, and raise him up in the estimation of his harping mother who always said he would come to nothing because of sloth. And if they indeed had killed not just once, but four times! An almost unheard-of massacre in a sway that seldom saw violent offense against persons. Yes, not only his frowning mother, but the magister of the village, and perhaps the legate of the city of Po would have to take note of Jang, the steward.

He tried not to stare. The girl was a beauty, with a slim body and fine, full lips that he could well imagine had pleasured the man she traveled with. Yes, though the man was her servant, he could sense their attraction for each other. Jang's instincts were honed in this matter, as he spent hundreds of days alone, hardly seeing a traveler, much less a female one as handsome as this one. Perhaps, to keep him silent, she would come with him into his quarters, and there perform for him the things he had imagined in his many days of boredom.

He could hardly believe his fortune, and to keep his excitement from overpowering him, he made a show of looking into the distance as though to spy the train.

He imagined himself standing before a lord and telling what he knew. That scene was less invigorating than the one he'd just conjured up. To speak in person to a lord—that would be a thrilling story to tell in the village. But he could feel himself shrivel at the prospect of that black Tarig gaze bearing down on him. And what if he were wrong? What was the penalty for false accusation? Oh, he'd seen the execution of a vow-breaker once, and though he was stimulated by the sight, in truth, the garroting had terrified him.

The woman was speaking to him, and he turned to face her.

She said sweetly, "What did the woman look like, the one traveling with the stranger? Did your sources say?"

He liked it that she had said *sources*, as though, at this juncture on the veldt, someone like him might hear many things from travelers of importance. He stood taller, strutting over to her. "Yes, there were descriptions." He glanced at the servant man. It was said his face was full, not narrow like this man's. When Jang looked back at the girl, he realized with confusion that she, in particular, could not be the one described. For didn't they say that the woman with the stranger was old and that she wore the redstones of a scholar?

"Perhaps," the girl said, "you could describe her for me, so that we can be watchful as we continue our journey."

"Oh," Jang said, his great fantasy collapsing, "she was old and ugly." He added, looking at her chest, where her woman's form was nestled against her silks: "Not like you."

She gave a charming smile. "Well, then, we shall be on guard against an ugly old woman and strange-looking man. You have been most helpful. I will tell my uncle—who is a man of influence—that this station is well tended."

He recognized that she was dismissing him, but in such nice terms. Perhaps she was suggesting that her gratitude might extend as he had hoped. But no. Jang, you worthless fool. Why would a great lady lie with such as you? He looked at the woman's companion, and hoped that the man didn't enjoy those favors, either.

He bowed low to the woman, and not as low to the man, and left to tend his tasks in the station hut, now eager to convey that he was too busy for further idle conversation.

Quinn turned to face Anzi. She shook her head, trying to silence him, but he crouched close to her.

"Master Yulin had them killed?"

She took a deep breath, as though weary of saying something he should already know. "They saw you. Who knows what they might have said to others about you?" Anzi looked at him squarely. "Dai Shen, I know this makes you unhappy. But now we have further problems, besides unfortunate deaths."

He nodded, having thought of that already. "Tarig justice. It will come into the sway." The Tarig conferred the penalty for murder, thus removing the chance for cycles of revenge among the diverse sentients who managed to live together. Killing was not just a community issue, but a threat to the whole Entire. That Yulin practiced it so freely gave Quinn a new sense of the master's desperation in regard to having housed him.

Anzi saw his agitation. She murmured, "Do you think that before all this is finished, you won't have to kill?"

The knife he wore inside his jacket was testimony to his willingness to kill. She was right, as she was about many things.

Anzi peered down the rut of the train's path. The yellow veldt was stunningly empty, its flatness making for a limitless horizon in three directions. In one direction, the storm wall bulked up like a distant mountain range, gray and brooding.

As the ebb came on, Quinn and Anzi decided they would sleep outside on the train platform. They sat side by side for a time, waiting for Shadow Ebb when the lavender cast of the sky made it easier to call it night, and sleep.

He took out his picture of Johanna and smoothed its wrinkles. Anzi looked over his shoulder. "Shen, your wife was beautiful."

Yes, she had been, especially to him. Hard to believe that she was gone. "You saw her once, Anzi. . . ."

She bit her lip. "Such dark hair—at first I thought she was very old, but then I saw that she was your partner, and very lovely."

He looked at Anzi's stark face and hair, thinking how opposite the two women were. He held her gaze for a moment. This woman of the Entire, against all odds, was his best ally. He knew her by now, and liked her greatly. Something flickered between them, catching him off guard. He could have reached for her, and almost did. Then Anzi moved away, her reserve back in place. They found their separate places to sleep there on the platform.

As they drifted off, she whispered, "Unwise to keep the pictures, Shen."

Her caution was a good thing, he supposed.

Late in the ebb Anzi awakened him, putting her finger to her lips. She led him to the other side of the station, and pointed.

In the distance was a blot on the sky. A crescent sped toward them, a black scythe, silhouetted against the bright. Under it, a curved shadow drove down the plains.

"Tarig," Anzi whispered.

Quinn fought the instinct to hide. There was no hiding here, after the station steward had seen them.

"We have our story," Anzi said, her voice husky, though she tried for calm.

Quinn could face them. He had been ready for weeks to face them, even if it was Hadenth, the enemy he could hardly remember. But the brightship filled him with dismay. It swooped down on them like a raptor, and a hungry one. There was something awful about those ships, not bright at all, but dark, dark, and he shivered involuntarily.

"The murders," Anzi said, frozen in place, watching the ship draw closer, a mile away and dropping altitude.

So, Tarig justice *was* coming.

But maybe not today. The ship suddenly curved away on a new path, rushing up the minoral toward Bei's reach. From behind, the brightship was just a crack in the sky, a black puncture revealing the black space that surrounded the cocoon of the Entire.

"Why are they going to Bei?" he asked.

"Asking questions, perhaps no more than that. . . ."

If so, then Bei was to admit having had visitors: Ji Anzi and Dai Shen. Anzi, he would say, was looking for scholarship, but she would not suit, and left disappointed. Bei would say she was accompanied by a Chalin warrior of Ahnenhoon, and when they left, they were bound for the Ascendancy on an errand from Yulin. Quinn hoped Bei was a good liar.

They watched the brightship until it disappeared.

When they could breathe again, Anzi rubbed her arms, suppressing a shudder.

Noticing her disquiet, Quinn murmured, "Like a bird of prey." Then a tendril of memory escaped the trap of his mind, and he thought, They are like birds. *And* prey.

For the rest of that ebb sleep eluded them. Then, as the bright waxed into Early Day, the train finally appeared out of the yellow dust of the plains.

CHAPTER FIFTEEN

IN THE CONTROL ROOM, Lamar and Helice stared at the wall screen. Titus Quinn had just evaporated from the lab module. The harness assembly suspended from the crossbar was empty and motionless, giving no hint that, moments before, it had held a 190-pound man. At the moment he crossed over, he had appeared to become two-dimensional. Then his whole body turned thirty degrees and moved backward, like a piece of paper being sucked into a copier.

"Did he make it?" Lamar breathed.

Helice pursed her lips, then said, "Let's be optimistic."

That sounded like a splendid idea, optimism. But Lamar was filled with a cool dread. Their instruments couldn't penetrate the other dimension at will. There was absolutely no way to know.

"How long do we wait?" Lamar asked. What, short of seeing Titus Quinn reappear, would constitute success? And when?

Helice turned to him. "You mean how long before we retaliate against his brother?"

Lamar was often startled by her pronouncements. She looked so clean-cut. She hadn't had time in her brief life to grow so bitter. Or had she?

Company gossip had it that her parents were both dreds. Or rather, to put it more politely, they'd opted out of their education, going instead for the dole. *Dred* was a word he never used publicly, denoting as it did those of average IQ: one hundred IQ points, give or take. *One hundreds* were the laborers of the world. Those who relied on muscle instead of neurons.

Helice had grown up smart despite her parentage. But no doubt the kids at school had thrown *dred* at her because of her folks, especially when she started to surpass her classmates. Jealousy. Kids could be cruel, often aiming for anyone who hadn't the decency to be average. The irony of it was that Helice was now jealous of Quinn, and was punishing him for excellence. Abrasive and lonely, Helice doted on her dogs and the damn parrot that went everywhere with her, the creatures that loved her in spite of herself.

Lamar got it in his head to contradict her. "If we sent him into vacuum space, there's no reason to take it out on Rob."

Helice frowned. "But that was the deal. A promise is a promise." She went on, "Plus, there's Mateo."

"Mateo?"

"Up for the Standard Test soon. I heard he might take it early."

She had *heard* no such thing. She was investigating the boy. "Mateo has nothing to do with this, Helice."

She turned on him. "He's our insurance that Quinn will come back." She popped open her water bottle and took a pull.

"If he can, he will. Why wouldn't he come back, for God's sake?"

With elaborate patience, Helice said, "Last time he stayed *ten years*. So I upped the ante. Even if the kid tests savvy, like his uncle and his grandfather did, his results are still going to look bad. Quinn knows this. It's our leash to bring him home."

Lamar muttered, "Even you can't subvert the Standard Test."

"But it's numbers, Lamar. I'm very good with numbers."

So *this* was why Quinn had made Lamar promise to protect the family, because Helice had threatened the youngster.

She noted the expression on his face. "Okay, be outraged, Lamar. Must feel good to be so pure. Just remember people are dying in those Kardashev tunnels—hundreds of people every year. And it's all we've got for transport. You think Rob and Mateo and their *careers* are worth more than that?"

"It's not as though shit-canning Mateo will save lives, Helice. Hurting the boy is just plain vicious. And he's practically kin to me. His grandfather—"

She interrupted. "Donnel, Quinn's father. Right. Well, he's been dead twenty years. All your contemporaries are dead, Lamar. I hate to point out that you are retired—and at the request of the board that no longer found your perspective helpful. You're out of the loop. Now that Quinn's in the other place, we really don't need your advice anymore. Don't interfere."

"You hate him, don't you?"

She stared at her water bottle.

"Because he got the assignment and you didn't?"

She turned to face him. "I hate him because he's going to scratch the assignment. He didn't go there for us, you know. He won't be on-task, not on *our* task."

"How do you live with yourself, Helice? How do your dogs stand you?"

Her face hardened. "How do you live with *your*self, Lamar? Look at you, pasty-faced, turkey neck, age spots. And that's only the beginning. Soon there's incontinence, impotence, and all the little transplants you can stand. I'm never going to be like you. Never."

Lamar was stunned. Where had all this come from? "Age comes to us all, my dear," he said with satisfaction.

"Perhaps." She paused, resetting her tone. "Sorry for the outburst. That was uncalled-for."

He nodded, not wanting to fight with her.

"Look," she said. "I hope as much as you do that Quinn will come back. If he doesn't, we'll have to send someone else, that's all."

A chime on the control board got Helice's attention, and she toggled the comm switch. "What?"

"Thought you'd want to see this," the tech's voice reported. On-screen, they saw what one of the cameras had captured Quinn from a low angle as he'd gone through the cleansing process before suiting up. The picture showed that his feet hadn't exactly been bare.

She squinted at the screen. The close-up view showed what looked like pieces of paper stuck to his soles. Helice swore under her breath.

Lamar suppressed a chuckle, but he couldn't help saying, "He never did mind." He imagined those were family pictures, taped to the soles of his feet—the pictures that Quinn had wanted to bring in the first place.

Helice stormed out to talk with the technicians, leaving Lamar wondering about her comment, *I'm never going to be like you.*

Did she just despise him that much . . . or did she hope for more out of life than most people got? He looked at the door where Helice had just exited. The woman had never learned to live with limits.

He caught his reflection in a darkened computer monitor and turned away, not liking mirrors and the story they told.

CHAPTER SIXTEEN

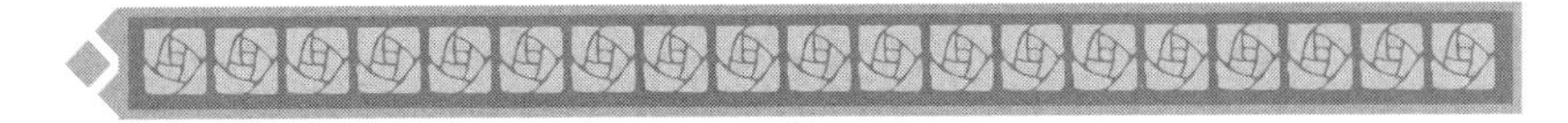

This is where the nascence leads: to the minoral;
This is where the minoral leads: to the primacy;
This is where the primacy leads: to the heartland;
This is where the heartland leads: to the Sea of Arising;
This is where the Sea of Arising leads: to the Ascendancy;
This is where the Ascendancy leads: to the heavens.

—a child's verse

SYDNEY WOKE TO A DRIP OF WATER IN HER FACE. The stables resounded with the patter of water falling from the roof.

Knowing that the fog must be heavy, Sydney drew on her padded jacket, cinching it tight around her waist. She slipped her knife into her belt, in anticipation of breakfast if she was lucky.

Akay-Wat stirred on her pallet. "The traps, yes?" came her voice.

"Go back to sleep, Akay-Wat." She wanted no freeloaders along.

"Your mount could bring you breakfast, but he is in mischief, oh yes?"

The whole stable knew of Riod and his pack of rogue Inyx. Again yesterday they had thundered off across the roamlands to test their courage against nearby hapless encampments, and better-behaved ones.

Ignoring Akay-Wat, Sydney slipped across the stables to the door, hoping to avoid the notice of the Laroo sleeping in a pile in the corner.

Outside, the fog met her face in a cool wool. It was early, the Between time. The fog might last until Early Day, by then filling their catchment system on the roof, supplementing the reservoir water that had retreated farther underground in recent days. Sydney snugged her jacket around her and made her way to her traps. She had high hopes for a steppe vole or two. The desert prey liked her traps in the heavy dew times, because they offered a roof—an innovation that other riders had copied from her. Technology in this sway was a receding dream. The mounts could use none, and liked independence from Ascendant things—the engineered food crops, their programmable adobe, their molecular computers.

Sydney liked that the Inyx shunned the mantis lords. Referring, in her former tongue, to the gracious lords as insects gave her a keen pleasure. Once a mantis lord had assaulted her, but that would never happen again, here in this far sway.

The stiletto claw flicked out. His voice, rasping: Now you will look out for the last time, small girl. But she had promised herself not to think about that. It was written down.

The things that could never be written down, nor barely thought of, concerned her friend, so far away, so close in her heart: Cixi. When, in her messages, Cixi urged her to remember the vows, they were not the vows of the mantis lords. Cixi had taught her new ones: *Oppose the lords. Forswear the Rose. Raise the kingdom.* The first two were easy, and she would have vowed them, anyway. *Raise the kingdom* was less clear to her, but Cixi had taught her that the kingdom yet to be was a worthy vow, and for love of her foster mother, Sydney had sworn to it.

Kneeling before her trap, she felt inside, finding several plump grubbies massed around her bait. She clipped them to the chain at her belt to carry them back to the roasting pits.

A noise pierced the fog, the high scream of an Inyx in the distance. She stood, listening, attending. Riod was home. She worried when he was gone, worried that he would stumble, as Glovid had, or that Priov would punish him, or that one of the herds he set upon would teach him a lesson.

Inyx hooves pounded in her direction. By the mount's sendings, it wasn't Riod, but Skofke, the battle-worn mount of Akay-Wat.

Drawing close, Akay-Wat announced: "They come with a stranger and large!" Her mount was eager to be gone, and stomped impatiently. Sydney picked up Skofke's excitement that Riod's band had captured a monster.

"Bring me with you."

Akay-Wat extended a leg to help Sydney swing up behind her. On Skofke's back, they pounded toward the pasture.

"What monster, Akay-Wat?" Sydney asked as they galloped.

"Big as a mount! Dumb as a rock!"

Well, the monster must be dumb indeed, if Akay-Wat thought so. They approached the pasture, along with a throng of Inyx and their riders. Through many Inyx viewpoints, she was aware of the hulking mounts, horned and broad, and their unkempt alien riders. But of course, they were not alien here, only herself. Their smells clotted the air, a familiar stench that had long ago ceased to offend.

Through Skofke's eyes, Sydney saw Riod, his black hide darker and more lustrous than the others. Also, among the mounts, a troll moved, dark and lumbering.

More Inyx pounded in from across the encampment, massing into a dense herd. Not a good thing. It would have been better if Riod had sneaked in with less notice, since Priov disapproved of the forays. Riod tossed his head and snorted at Sydney, for now staying by his fellow rogue Distanir, an enormous dun-colored beast with one of his neck horns missing.

Riod sent, *Riod is back, best rider.*

Priov nosed into the center of the crowd, along with his rider, the detestable Feng. Cruel and big-boned, the Chalin hag still rode despite a withered leg, the result of a crushing fall under Priov. She nursed a particular hatred of Sydney for no good reason except that Sydney equally despised her, and once had beat her in an Inyx race when others would have let Feng win.

Feng spat at the stranger's feet. "Ya. Ugly as a turd." The Chalin man—for he was Chalin, surely, despite his lumpish and gigantic form—glared at her with blind eyes. A nice trick, one that Sydney would like to learn.

From a hundred pairs of eyes, Sydney saw a fractured image of the man. The top of his head came nearly to Distanir's ears, if you counted his prodigious white topknot, gathered up in the military style. His arms were as big around as one of Sydney's thighs, his chest like a rain barrel. Even on such a large body, his face was oversized, from crumpled forehead to wide chin. In the stony face, the only expression was in his eyes, small and mean.

Priov's mares capered around this newcomer, sniffing rudely. But none of them looked big enough to be his mount. Besides, Distanir was sending a clear message, that he had already chosen the giant. The story came out in fits and starts, of how they had come upon the distant encampment of the band led by Ulrud the Lame, and the monster, this Chalin giant, had grabbed Distanir by the forehorn and nearly brought him to his knees by sheer power of his arms. Not expecting to steal anything other than honor, Riod and his fellows nevertheless charged away with their prize, and Ulrud's herd pursued them until the fog set in, covering Riod's retreat.

Riod came to Sydney's side, urging her to trade mounts. She sprang over to join him, and their delight in each other was instant. "Back, Riod, yes," Sydney said, caressing his strong neck, realizing that without her planning it, and almost against her volition, Riod had found a place in her affection.

My rider, he sent to her, with overtones of exhaustion and pride.

Priov's hoof crashed down, shattering the mood of reunion. The old chief's displeasure radiated out to the assembled riders and their mounts. This raiding of Ulrud's roamlands would not do. They had brought an ugly prize, not even worth it. The mares screamed and pranced, defecating in agreement.

Goaded to action by this display, several mounts nipped at the giant, pulling on his clothes. He turned to glare at the harassment, but his beefy hands hung at his sides, passive. His attackers cantered away, and seeing that he would not retaliate, others darted in to yank at him.

Oddly, as the charging and nipping continued, not a single thought came from this man. To his credit, he seemed unafraid. But there was something insensible about him, as though he did not quite rise to the level of sentient.

Then Priov stepped close to the giant, and from her perch Feng reached down and pinched the man's bulbous nose. At this, the Laroo decided he was fair game, and left their mounts behind, clawing at his legs. Puss stood near the giant's boots, doing his usual: peeing.

Asserting his right of property, Distanir chased the Laroos off, leaving the Chalin man looking down at his wet feet. Being blind, he could easily smell what he could not see.

Sydney urged Riod to approach the giant. She looked down at the man. "You can fight back, you know. It's permitted." She waited, seeing no reaction. Perhaps, being stupid, he couldn't talk. "Can you speak?"

The man stared into the fog, his mind as empty.

"It'll go better for you if you speak. It'll go better for you if you fight." The man was becoming a fine target for cruelty, but he was causing it himself. "Most sentients have a name. Do you?"

Then the giant spoke, but it startled her, and everyone. His voice was soft, even effeminate. "Mo Ti," he said.

The riders laughed. *Mo Ti*, they mimicked in lisping tones. Feng cried out, "Balls the size of marbles! Take off his pants and have a look!"

A Laroo jumped from his mare and approached Mo Ti, but warily.

Catching Sydney's displeasure, Riod surged forward and sent the Laroo sprawling.

Riod spun in a circle, looking for more fights, but this tussle was not about Mo Ti, Sydney realized, too late.

Puss, who had slipped away from the crowd, was now back, scampering up to Priov, handing something up to Feng. With a jolt of dismay, Sydney saw what it was. Her book of pinpricks.

Feng held up the book for all to see, while Akay-Wat took up a ululating cry: "Unfair, unfair."

Priov sent: *Thirteen days ago Riod's rider ran from her beating. Now she will lose her book.*

As Akay-Wat's chant of "unfair" grew louder, Feng swung around to growl, "Keep your face shut, or I'll tie your ugly neck in a knot." At this, Akay-Wat's cry halted as she cringed from Feng's threat.

Satisfied that she had the camp's attention, and sitting high on Priov's back, Feng opened the book and pretended to read. "I am a little princess of the Rose. Akay-Wat is very stupid, and should worship me."

With a brief kick Sydney tried to nudge Riod forward, but he held fast to his position. Meanwhile Akay-Wat threw her distress into the minds of all, as though she had any reason to care.

Sydney turned in Akay-Wat's direction, giving vent to her disgust: "You spineless Hirrin. Your own mother a soldier! I would sooner look like this monster than a creature like you."

Then, propelled by frustration, she recklessly jumped off Riod's back and stalked toward Feng, who was still pretending to read: "A princess like me should have a decent mount, not a scabby, mareless—"

Sydney reached for the book, but it was far out of reach, and Priov danced in a circle, keeping Sydney at bay.

Then, overcome with fury, and ignoring Riod's sent warnings, Sydney yanked as hard as she could on Feng's withered leg. The woman toppled from Priov, landing on her back in a thud. From the ground, she managed to toss the book to Puss, who bolted away. Sydney fell on the woman, landing a punch in the big woman's eye. Or somewhere that hurt badly, since it was all conveyed secondhand and the visual disappeared in a bewildering array of perspectives. All that was left was Feng's hatred flowing back from a hundred Inyx.

Riod stepped between them, a great wall of disapproval.

Sydney moved back, shamed that the crippled Feng was having difficulty rising from the ground. At Riod's command, Sydney mounted him, her misery now compounded by her own despicable behavior.

Akay-Wat was making an absurd whining sound that only someone with such a long neck could make.

Sydney hissed at her, "Just shut up, can't you?"

The shouts of the riders abated as a few of Feng's cronies helped her back into the saddle. In this comparative quiet, Sydney strained to find any sign of Puss, but the thief had fled with the book.

The only image that came strongly into her mind was that of Akay-Wat dismounting from Skofke and hobbling away, ears flattened and a slump in her neck.

With Puss's escape, Sydney's pinpricks of memory were lost. Gone was her record of those first days in the stable, when the old lord Flodistog had broken her spirit and commanded her to groom his ticks and clean his hooves; when she had learned to bunk with criminals who took her silk clothes and her scrolls and every other thing she had acquired in the mantis realm; when it first came to her that she would never go home, nor did her mother wish to go home, nor did her father remember her. When she had first learned what it was to be blind. And then to see the world in shattered glass.

Tears gathered, and though hidden in the fog, every mount knew her sorrow, and conveyed it to every rider. Her humiliation was complete.

"Wants her mommy," Feng crowed. "Ya, we'd all like to have her mommy!"

Sydney urged her mount out of the camp. Riod, his mind filled with dismay, shoved his way out of the crowd and bounded away, seeking the privacy of the steppe. As he ran, the tumult of the camp with its chaotic sendings gradually diminished.

In a nearby gully, Sydney dismounted, leaning against Riod's solid neck. More tears might have come then, but she remembered her advice to Mo Ti: It will be better if you fight.

She would live like this no longer. She could endure fights, the camp's hatred, even whippings. But she must have honor, even if it only came from Riod. As the sky waxed into a stronger fire, the fog tore apart, clearing her mind.

"You know what I want," she said to Riod.

To kill Feng? To ride Priov? Best rider has many wants.

That was true. Except about Priov, who was old and slow. "I want . . ." She struggled for words. "I want you to think of me as a free rider."

Into Riod's mind came an image of the steppe, and a swift ride. This was what freedom meant to an Inyx. She would have to teach him what it meant to a human. "A free bond," she said.

You accepted Riod.

"Not freely."

What is a free bond?

"That I take you as my equal."

You are small. Not Inyx.

"It doesn't matter."

On the ridge Distanir appeared, and on his back, the giant Mo Ti, almost the same size as his mount. Sydney didn't want them near her. The giant had no true thoughts; he was an animal.

As they watched, Distanir and Mo Ti joined them. Through Riod, she saw the glower in the giant's little eyes, and knew one day he would strike out, and any sentient in his way would be dead. Maybe she would provoke him, and end her life. Sensing this, Riod's distress flooded her.

Sydney whispered to him, "I'd rather die than live this way." She raised her face to feel the day's warmth, and its power came into her. "But if you make me free, I will raise you high, Riod. As my equal."

Then Riod bent down, persuading her to mount again. As she did so, he sent: *Yes. Equal. Free bond.* By the flood of his mind, he gave her all that she asked for.

She leaned across his curved horns, rubbing her face against his neck. "Yes," she answered. "Beloved Riod." He didn't want her as a prisoner, but as herself. And trusted that her heart would still be bound to his. *Yes, always, Riod.*

Standing nearby observing all this were Distanir and his new rider. Sydney resented having to share these intimate thoughts with them, much less hear the giant intrude, saying, in his soft voice, "And Mo Ti, free bond, too."

A surge of emotion came from him, hitting Sydney with unexpected force. The man had opened a window, and out had come a gust of desire.

Distanir bristled under the man's weight. He sent, *You must prove yourself among us before such a gift.*

It was a reasonable judgment, but Sydney was now considering Mo Ti in a different manner. He wanted free bond. This Chalin beast had heard her ask, and it had awakened his own desires. Wouldn't all riders desire it?

"Distanir," she said. "Let Mo Ti be free. It's a better way to ride, yes?"

Distanir pawed the ground, remaining quiescent, holding his thoughts. But Mo Ti's eyes were alight, looking at Sydney with a new intelligence, with an assessing look, if her clouded view could be trusted.

A thought tugged at her, from under a pile of resentments, wrongs, and pinpricks: Wouldn't they all desire free bond? She let go of this thought in order to consider it further in private.

Her business with Riod was not finished. There was one thing more she must have, for honor's sake. Addressing Riod, she said, "My thoughts, beloved. Those are mine alone. Teach me to hide them."

This drew agitation from Riod. *Riod can't. Why hide what is plain to all, speaking heart to heart?*

"Your thoughts aren't plain. You must send thoughts. But mine can be stolen. Some thoughts I don't want to share." Thoughts of Cixi, for example, whom she must avoid thinking about for fear of exposing her. "Teach me to keep my thoughts, beloved."

Riod can't. But Riod can create storms around your thoughts. Others will hear only confusion.

His pronouncement thrilled her. If what he said was true, no longer would Feng or Puss read the thoughts she so desperately wished to contain. "What if we're separated, Riod, when you're alone with your rogues? Can they steal my thoughts then?"

Riod creates a storm even from a distance. Others will not like it.

"Oh, but I'll like it, Riod. I'll like it very much."

Her response flooded him with gratification. She laid her cheek against his horns and thought that already their free bond was a better bond than before. When she straightened, she sensed that Mo Ti had urged Distanir closer to her, until their knees almost touched.

Then Mo Ti brought forth something from his jacket. In his large square hand Mo Ti gripped the book of pinpricks, slightly charred, but intact. He handed it to her.

The book's leather cover was burned. Sydney felt pieces of it flaking away. But the rest had survived.

Distanir sent, *Mo Ti put his hand in the fire. No one dared approach him. Feng is angry.* An overtone of amusement threaded into the comment.

Sydney felt a grin spread across her face. She liked this Chalin monster, no matter how ugly he was. Unlike Akay-Wat, he was a worthy companion. She tucked the book in her jacket. It would never leave her side again.

"Perhaps, Distanir," she said, "Mo Ti has proven himself?" Leaving Distanir to chew on that notion, she gripped Riod's rear horn. "A race?" she proposed.

Before the terms were even decided, Riod and Distanir charged out of the gully, onto the tundra. Sydney leaned forward, gripping the horns, whooping in joy.

It was a magnificent race, and one that she long remembered, even though she and Riod lost. Because against all odds, Mo Ti was a better rider.

"Don't look at them," Anzi hissed as they rode in the open pedi cab.

Quinn tried not to stare. But in the crowds of the teeming city of Po, many Tarig roamed, their height making them stand out among lesser beings.

"Ignore them, Dai Shen. The murder has attracted them to the wielding, especially this axis point where a criminal might flee. If they stop us, I'll answer them." She didn't look as though she was eager to do so. They had no idea how the Tarig questioning of Su Bei had gone; if badly, then Quinn's disguise might not hide him any longer.

Anzi kept her voice low, so as not to be overheard by the cab owner, who pedaled them toward the landing field. There they would take passage on another sort of blimp for their trip to the Nigh.

They wound through the pedestrian streets crowded with food stands, vendors, and hostels—most catering, Anzi said, to sentients needing to send communications. Quinn spied dozens of Tarig, often merely standing and watching, at other times towering over those they spoke to, their gazes neutral yet disturbing. He couldn't distinguish male from female, but he knew both went abroad with equal power. Their sculpted faces drew his gaze. It unnerved him that he'd chosen their image for the door knocker on his house. It was a cry from his subconscious to remember. But when he got home, he'd strip it off.

Anzi kept her hand on Quinn's forearm, in a gentle reminder to be inconspicuous. She didn't often touch him, and he wondered if she thought him so unpredictable that he'd do something to attract attention. Lately her worry was at the prospect of his contacting Lord Oventroe at the Ascendancy. He intended to pursue this matter of the correlates, although to induce Oventroe to deal with him, he might have to reveal who he was. Anzi argued against that, but in the last few days, seeing his resolve, she'd given up.

Pedaling furiously, the driver turned to look at them. He was an old Jout sentient, with massive shoulders and almost no neck, making turning around no mean feat. "Taking which road, mistress?" He pointed to an intersection where thousands of pedi cabs converged with people on foot.

"The quickest way, Steward," she said.

"I'm no steward, by the bright." The Jout's skin, rough with the overlapping armors of his hide, tightened in peevishness. Apparently the flattery hadn't been welcome.

"Then, Factor, pedal us the fastest way, and there'll be extra for you." They were in a hurry to be out of this public setting; although Quinn, after five days on the train, was eager for a change.

An hour previously, they had arrived at this axis city, situated at one of the great sky pillars. On the outskirts of the city they had passed endless fields of gleve, the staple plant in this region. Engineered to produce edibles, gleve plants hung heavy with many staples, colorful vegetables and pods of quasi-meats. But by far the most arresting new view was the axis looming over the city. It was a massive and shining rope, connecting ground to sky, falling from a height of perhaps thirty thousand feet. Unlike the bright itself, the axis didn't buckle and fold like boiling porridge. Instead, it fell straight downward like a laser, where a domed structure accepted the beam into its roof. This pillar was the communication stream. Was the bright limited to sublight speeds? Quinn couldn't remember. But there was no other way to send messages, with radio impossible.

Now, coming to the end of the long ride through the city, their pedi cab arrived in a region of low hills covered with a fuzz of blue ground cover. There, hovering over the land, was their conveyance, an Adda, a floating being filled with a buoyant gas. Many days ago, when Quinn had been a prisoner in the jar, he'd looked over the plains and seen these beings dotting the sky. The creature was a true symbiont, one that had developed a relationship with travelers in exchange for food. The Adda who took passengers were all female, since the great cavity of the belly was used to transport young, and the males were too small to be useful.

"The Adda is sentient?" Quinn asked. Anzi had said so, but the beast did not look a likely winner in the intelligence race.

"In a way. There are more varieties of sentience here than on Earth. Her sentience is for electromagnetism and vanes of bright radiation."

This symbiont would be their conveyance, if they could arrange passage. However, the lone Adda floating overhead was in high demand, beset by hundreds of Chalin and other sentients hoping to travel in the direction of the River Nigh, a direction called in the Chalin vernacular *to the Nigh*, as traveling away from the river was *against the Nigh*.

"How many can she carry?" Quinn asked.

"Oh, many, Dai Shen. Twenty or twenty-five individuals, if small."

"We'll have a long wait, then." They were far back in the line for passage.

She motioned him to follow, and they climbed up the slope of the hill where people were gathered. At the top, Quinn found that below them lay a deep crater.

In this depression floated a congregation of many Adda. To stabilize themselves they gripped guy wires in their mouths.

"The Adda assemble here out of the winds," Anzi explained. "This valley is a subsidence, where an aquifer collapsed long ago, from overuse." There were ways that a geography of sorts could form, but most uplift, of hills, for example, happened near the storm walls where the land bent from the forces of the dark boundaries. Still, this was a dramatic valley, in Entire terms.

Anzi plunged down the side of the hill, pushing through the crowds where people were climbing ladders and handing up satchels and bags of the fare: the seed food that motivated the Adda to take on passengers.

"That one," she said, pointing to a smaller-sized behemoth that had lowered a membranous ladder but had not attracted riders thus far. "No one wants that one, so we may be able to journey alone."

They purchased four bags of seed from a vendor, and Quinn hoisted three of them on his back, Anzi taking one. He followed her as she approached the symbiont. "Passage, grain for passage," Anzi shouted to the Adda.

The great beast's side eyes shifted to examine the seed bags. The thick eyelids descended in a ponderous blink. Then the Adda lowered, signaling permission to enter.

Anzi climbed the ladder, then took the bags one by one from Quinn. As the last bag went on board, a flurry of activity drew Quinn's attention.

A personage was approaching, pushed in a decorated cart by three large Jout. Although the person's body was obscured by the sides of the cart, its head identified it instantly. A Gond.

The Jout pushed the cart toward Quinn as the Gond looked up at the Adda, shouting, "Passage for the godwoman, Nigh bound!"

The Gond's great horned head stared up at the Adda, exposing the Gond's aging neck, deeply hung with flabby flesh. She wore a white vest and sash, marking her as a follower of the Miserable God.

The cart came alongside Quinn, and the Gond, although sitting in the cart, came nearly eye to eye with him. The red gums of her mouth hung down, exposing the roots of her carnivore teeth. In the back of the cart were the sacks of grain that would be the godwoman's passage.

Quinn put up his hand. "We're full."

The godwoman grinned, taking the comment amiss. "Not at all full. Plenty of room."

"The Chalin woman travels alone."

"The Chalin woman travels with you, my friend."

"She likes not godmen."

"Neither do I." The Gond waved to her Jout helpers to take the sacks of grain on board. One of the Jout hoisted a sack and headed for the ladder, but Quinn blocked his way.

"Find another berth. You're not wanted here."

The Jout stood shorter than Quinn but bigger around, and there were two more where that one came from. The Jout said without expression, "Give way."

Anzi's face appeared in the orifice of the symbiont's belly, but Quinn was already dealing with the Jout, pushing him backward.

As the Jout surged by him and set a foot on the ladder, Quinn brought out his knife and thrust it into one of the sacks. Brown kernels spilled out, raising a cloud of dust. In her bass voice, the Gond barked, "Foul. The grain paid for!"

Several coins sprayed down from above as Anzi threw payment on the ground in front of the godwoman. The Jout paused, looking at Quinn's knife, still drawn. Then, sourly, he descended. "Foul," the Jout repeated, but without conviction. He set the sacks down and motioned his cohorts to abandon the cart. They wouldn't fight for a godder, as the clergy were sometimes called.

In the ensuing quiet, Quinn sprinted up the ladder. When he started to draw it into the pouch, Anzi said, "No, the ladder stays down."

As Quinn backed away from the opening, he heard the creature growl, "May God bless your journey."

Hearing this, Anzi thrust her hand into her purse and threw many more coins out of the pouch opening. "Take back the prayer," she shouted as the Adda let go of the ropes tethering her to the ground.

The godwoman laughed out loud, rumbling, "And may God keep you in His gaze all your days!"

As Anzi fumbled for more coins, Quinn stopped her. "It's only words."

She looked doubtful as she crouched at the orifice, but ceased throwing money down.

The Gond sat in her cart with a wide circle of emptiness around her. Her wings glistened, wings that could never hope to raise her off the ground. A fallen angel came to mind, as the creature conjured visions of heaven and hell combined.

"I didn't know Gond could be priests," Quinn murmured.

Anzi recited, "No sentient being is beyond hope." She eyed Quinn. "But you, Dai Shen, should not have drawn a knife."

He knew he shouldn't have, but sharing quarters with a godwoman could have been disastrous. Anzi bit her lip, but said nothing.

The Adda had risen into the sky to a height of about a hundred feet. Nearby, other of the blimplike creatures were letting go of their guy wires and starting a slow movement away.

They watched as the gathering in the valley receded.

He looked around him at the Adda's travel pouch. It was perhaps two-thirds of the creature's size, and was surrounded by pink, fleshy walls smelling of warm yeast. The balloon in which they rode swayed gently as the prevailing winds pulled it into the great migration path toward the River Nigh. As long as the seeds lasted, the Adda would not be tempted to descend and forage.

From high in the fleshy cavity came a whooshing sound.

"The wind in the Adda's sinuses," Anzi said. She opened a bag and propped it against the Adda's side.

In a few moments, from the roof of the cavity, feeding tubes descended. They plunged into the first bag, producing a snuffling sound that clearly signified a boisterous feeding.

Quinn glanced at the orifice that served as the door of the passenger cavity. Once again he had drawn notice to himself, despite his resolve not to. But it was unthinkable to travel with a godwoman, much less a Gond. Godmen and godwomen were lonely souls, eager for converse and gossip. Some might well be in the employ of the Tarig. He took out the Going Over blade and began cleaning it.

Anzi sat next to him. "It was well done, Shen. To prevent the Gond from boarding. You had no choice."

"No help for it now."

"No," she agreed, looking out through the orifice as though scanning for pursuers.

As the Adda drifted toward the Nigh, they began the longest duration of any leg of their journey.

Even though the primacies were narrow—perhaps four thousand miles wide—it was a slow journey to the Nigh from the populated centers on the other side of the primacy. But once a traveler arrived on the riverbanks the journey was almost over. So the heartland was near in a sense, as was Quinn's destination: the Ascendancy in the center of the heartland. From this hub radiated all the lobelike primacies, each with its own great river. He would travel another of those rivers to reach the primacy where Sydney lived.

Would she remember him? *How* would she remember him?

Since his meeting with Bei, he knew it was not a settled question.

In the valley of the Adda, the godwoman BeSheb looked around her, noting that her Jouts had fled and no one would approach her now to offer assistance.

She brushed her jacket, wiping away the grain particles that soiled the sacred white of her vestments. Foul, foul. A waste of grain, and now the coins lying where any miscreant could pick them up. She watched as the vile Adda set out on its journey, one that she prayed would be plagued by river spiders.

BeSheb shifted her weight in the conveyance and prayed to calm her spiking emotions. "Oh, Miserable God look at me; oh, counter of sins, observer of sorrows, creator of evil, craftsman of the poxy Chalin! Look at me. I am not afraid, I am not debased to attend thee, I freely give obeisance. . . ."

A passing Hirrin looked with alarm in BeSheb's direction and ambled away, flattening her ears so as not to hear the prayer. The circle around the Gond grew wider, but no one dared touch the coins that sparkled in the bright like the yellow eyes of a buried god.

BeSheb threw her head back and voiced her prayers, and as she did so, her distress eased, and finally she grew silent and began to count the coins. Twelve of them, two of them primals. Well. That was ten times the price of the grain, and rightly compensated for her humiliation. So then, paying for one more sack plus the muscles of some hapless sentient to carry it, there should be plenty left to—

A shadow bent over one of the primals.

A Tarig crouched to pick it off the ground. He turned to BeSheb. "Your coin, ah?"

The Gond drew her wings around her, to settle her appearance and prepare to deal with the fiend. The Tarig were not believers, and God hated them even more than He hated most. Such was the teaching of the seer Hoptat, who set down the Ways of God the Miserable archons ago, before the days of radiance.

"Yes, Bright Lord, my life in your service," BeSheb whispered, knowing that her voice was more subservient when gentle.

The lord approached her, holding the primal in his long fingers.

"Someone pays very handsomely for your prayers."

BeSheb lifted her head to better see the fiend. "As to that, pardon me, it is not the case. The miscreants paid for damage to my sack of grain, which they inflicted by means of a sword, improperly drawn and threatening my Jout helpers."

"We see no Jout helpers."

The Gond licked her lips in irritation. "Certainly you do not. They fled." She was still waiting for the fiend to give her the coin.

The lord fixed her with a most unpleasant gaze as the circle of emptiness around her widened and even the Adda moved off farther.

The Gond added, "One is sorry to contradict the lord, but truth is not always pleasant." If he wanted to take offense, so he would. But the miscreants had insulted her, BeSheb of Ord, and she'd sooner end her days than keep quiet about it.

The Tarig's voice came melodious and calm. "Who has a sword and is using such?"

The Gond pointed skyward. "There, the Chalin man goes, riding alone, because he did not wish the Miserable God to accompany him."

"Hnnn. Wished to be alone." The Tarig seemed to smile. "Many wish to shun the God of Misery. We give permission to shun God, ah?" He fingered the gold primal, moving it among his four fingers like a filthy conjurer.

BeSheb scowled. "And permission also to wield knives?"

"You are bold, BeSheb, to speak so."

He knew her name. Not just a lord stumbling upon a situation, then. Perhaps she had let her irritation show improperly.

The lord went on. "We like you. Speaking directly and fearlessly. Not often the case, BeSheb. One welcomes such diversion."

BeSheb smirked. "They are all groveling toadies. A Gond speaks her thoughts."

The coin fell, and BeSheb caught it. The Tarig turned, summoning with a gesture a Chalin boy who watched them from a distance. "Pick up the coins for this personage, young Chalin," the lord commanded. "Then do the god-woman's bidding until the ebb, not requesting payment. Ah?"

The boy stammered his agreement.

As the lord stalked off, BeSheb settled her bulk more comfortably into the cart, smiling to herself. The God of Misery sometimes came through generously. She fingered the coins as her new helper brought them to her. He was a good Chalin boy, nice of feature, though grubby. She put her mind to the task of planning how the boy could further serve her, in private, until the ebb.

As the Adda floated onward, Quinn and Anzi sat cross-legged on the fleshy floor, just close enough to the orifice to watch the land slide by.

As they sat side by side, Anzi took something from her pocket. On a long blue cord was a circular medallion. It looked familiar. She put it to Quinn's ear, and the heartchime struck a tone, clear and soothing.

"Dolwa-Pan's heartchime," he said.

"To listen to the approach of the heartland," Anzi said, handing him the necklace.

Quinn couldn't reprimand her. She never kept anything for herself. He wondered if the Hirrin princess would make a decent scholar, like Bei, or a failed one, like Anzi. He said, "The princess liked to keep track of how close she was to the Ascendancy."

"Yes," Anzi said thoughtfully. "She should get over it."

Quinn held the heartchime in his hand, wondering how it measured distance and translated it into music. "You're not devoted to them," he said to Anzi, thinking how there must be many in the Entire besides Suzong and Bei and Lord Oventroe who didn't serve the gracious lords.

"They know all the knowledge—all the things I wonder about." She smiled. "But no, Shen—would I be here if I served them?"

He had to remind himself how Anzi jeopardized herself, being with him. But he didn't think that she thought of herself as a dissident. Or that any Chalin did.

"The Chalin haven't ever rebelled. No one has, right?"

She blinked. "Rebelled? As in war?" The thought was clearly beyond her. "Why would you ask such a thing?"

Clearly, his question had disturbed her. Perhaps she saw the people of the Rose as prone to war, and feared a confrontation. He'd promised Su Bei that he'd protect the Entire, should the correlates ever become known. To do what he could. Thinking of the predations of Minerva, that might not be much.

"It may come to war, between our people," he said to be as honest as he could.

She sat with that thought for a time. Then she murmured, "Whose side would you be on, Shen?"

He started to say the Rose. Because he was of that place. But something blocked the saying of it. He remained silent.

They sat without speaking a long while then, and Anzi let the subject pass.

The hills gathered closer, into a rumpled plain that would have defied a train's path. Toward Last of Day, they passed over a forest of stubby golden trees. In its depths he spied a floating chain of winged insects, linked together, sweeping clouds of gnats into the airy basket. They watched the ground give way to corrugated valleys. He felt a peace descend, a familiar thing, something that came from the Entire, or the bright, or the singular vastness of the place with its unknowable horizon.

Hours later they tired of the views and, making what beds they could on the grain sacks, slept.

He woke to the waxing bright, greeted by the sour smell of grain and the innards of the Adda. They had left the forest behind and were skimming very slowly over a lake.

"It's very shallow," Anzi said, having wakened and come to the edge of the opening to sit with Quinn. "Water doesn't generally collect on the surface. The bright burns it off." She stopped short. Then she shoved him in the chest, with a sharp whack of her hand. "Back," she hissed.

Just beyond the shore of the lake, a figure stood on the ground, hailing them. Beside the figure, a brightship sat on the plains. The Adda had slowed.

"Tarig . . . ," Anzi whispered. "He comes."

"Maybe the Adda won't stop."

"By bond law, the Adda has to stop. That's why the ladder is always down."

She hauled him across the floor, pointing up. "Climb, climb."

"Why? We have our cover story."

"But you drew a knife; they might question you too closely. Go!" She pushed him toward the wall. "Use the ridges as footholds; go into the sinuses. Hurry!"

"What about you?" He struggled with her as she kept pushing, and as the Adda kept lowering.

"I can pass! You can't!" She started slapping at him. He began to climb, then looked down at her. "Go," she repeated, waving her arms at him.

He climbed where she'd pointed, finding that the skin was ridged enough for a handhold. Near the top of the wall, the air grew hotter, alive with a yeasty smell. He saw a curve. It led into a small tunnel that required him to go on hands and knees. The yeasty smell grew deep and sickening.

He felt the blimplike body shake as it became clear that the Tarig had grabbed hold of the ladder and was coming aboard.

Quinn entered a bony, scalloped structure that spiraled wildly, with depressions and tubes branching out and dead-ending. This must be the sinuses Anzi referred to. A breeze wafted through, and Quinn hoped that the Tarig didn't smell keenly.

He folded himself into a ball to keep from falling in this slick place. But hiding wouldn't help much if the Tarig had reason to search. Had the godwoman raised suspicions about them?

He huddled and listened.

"Ah, the Chalin girl," a melodious voice said.

"Lord, my life in your service," came Anzi's small voice.

"We do not know you." The Tarig's voice was deeply rich, and resonant, but the Adda amplified it hugely, and made it the voice of the beast herself.

Anzi said, "I am Lo May, of the Chingdu wielding, Bright Lord."

God, she was lying. Quinn closed his eyes, listening hard.

"Going where?" the Tarig asked.

"Lord, by the Nigh, to visit my parents' graves, both brave fallen of Ahnenhoon."

"The Chalin girl is dutiful in grave-duty, to travel the Nigh."

"Lo May would see a grand sight, of the Nigh."

"Less dutiful, seeing sights."

"Oh, please pardon such a girl, Bright Lord."

A long spell of quiet. Quinn's skin prickled with sweat and consternation. What was the Tarig doing?

"Do you see, Lo May, four sacks of grain?"

"Yes, Lord."

"Passage for a lone Chalin girl?"

A pause. Then: "No, Lord, there was one other here."

"Where is this other? Hnnn?"

"Lord, he wished to lie with me and was insistent. By my rights of bonds, I used force to compel him down the ladder."

"Ah. A Chalin man? And now he may die because you left him untended in the wilds. This can be murder, of the bond law."

"Heaven give me mercy, I meant no harm, Lord."

A long pause. Quinn's mouth was dry. Murder? How could the conversation veer so sharply? Quinn thought it better to descend and kill this individual before he killed Anzi. He rose.

"A pretty Chalin girl," the Tarig said.

Quinn didn't like the tone. Silence again. Quinn was imagining things. Anzi, he thought, give me an indication of what is happening.

"Yet we saw no stragglers," the Tarig continued.

"Perhaps, Lord, he was already rescued. Many Adda set out from the axis yesterday."

"Hnnn. A pretty Chalin girl. Are we to think you are strong enough to compel a grown man down a ladder?"

"Yes, Lord. Lo May is."

The Tarig's voice came: "Ah, and keeps the bonds."

"As the bright guides me, and as God takes little notice of one such as Lo May."

And the Tarig again, more ominously: "We take notice."

"Yes, Lord," Anzi whispered.

"Do you know, Chalin girl, one named Wen An?"

A pause. "No. Is this a personage I should know?"

Quinn crept forward to listen more intently. Wen An—the scholar who had sent him to Yulin. This was a bad trend for the conversation. He put his hand on the Going Over blade, wondering how many Tarig were in that brightship, and if right now they stood outside holding guy wires while their fellow lord made inquiries.

"The Chalin scholar Wen An, her life is forfeit, and we seek her. Thus, if you know her, you will tell us, ah?"

"By the vows, I do not know Wen An."

"Shaking?"

There was a silence as Quinn strained to hear words said more softly. Was Anzi shaking in fear? What was the lord doing? And he wondered if they carried their garrotes with them.

The silvery voice of the Tarig came: "We have frightened you."

Again, Quinn couldn't hear Anzi answer. He was beside himself with anxiety, and so crept to the very edge of the sinus cavity, where he could just see the sleeve of Anzi's arm as she backed away from her inquisitor.

"There is no need for fear, Lo May. How long have you been traveling, and from where?"

"Lord, a sequent or more from the wielding, from Chingdu."

She'd said five days, a *sequent*.

"In that journey, Lo May, you beheld the bright realm laid out before you, ah?"

Quinn could now see Anzi leaning against the wall. Anzi nodded.

"The bright realm lives in peace, the peace of the Entire. And Wen An has broken that peace, and sentients lie murdered. So then, do you fear our justice?"

"No, Bright Lord. It is the radiant path, heaven give me mercy."

"Just so, Lo May. A good Chalin girl." A bronze hand came forward and wiped a wisp of hair back from Anzi's face.

If he touched her again, Quinn would use his knife.

"We like you, Chalin girl," the lord said.

Quinn couldn't see the Tarig, only Anzi standing like an animal frozen in a carnivore's gaze.

"And now we leave you in peace."

Anzi didn't move, but watched the lord as he apparently moved away, toward the orifice.

As the lord climbed down the ladder, he said to those who waited below, "Only one Chalin girl, of no consequence."

"Swords?" a voice asked from farther away.

"No swords," the lord answered, his voice fading.

A long pause. Quinn wiped the sweat of his hands against his tunic, waiting and listening. The Adda lurched with the jump of the Tarig from the ladder, and then again with the release of the rope or ropes that secured the Adda in place. He felt the symbiont rising again, and the breath came back into him. By its motion, the Adda was under way again.

A whisper from below. "Dai Shen. Come down now."

He climbed down the wall to meet her where she stood in the middle of the floor, very still.

"Gone," she said, but her voice broke.

"Anzi." He stepped closer, seeing that she looked whiter than usual.

She nodded at him, smiling. "Gone."

"Are you all right?"

"Of course." She looked around her. "Four bags."

Yes, that almost did them in. Each person brought two bags. He should have brought two bags up the wall with him. It had almost gotten them killed. She had lied to the Tarig. The lord would have killed her. And then Quinn.

"It's all right now," he said.

"Yes, fine," she said, trembling hard.

Quinn beckoned to her. "Come here."

She went to him and buried her face in his tunic. His arms came around her, holding her to comfort her, to comfort himself. He felt a wash of tenderness drive through him. After a moment he said, "Lo May is a fast thinker."

She laughed, leaning against him. "Lo May had to be. The other girl's mind had fled."

CHAPTER SEVENTEEN

On the eternal River Nigh, the navitar guides the ships. Did you think the Bright Realm flat? Not so, for it is curled. Nested within the river are the binds, the nexus points. Only the navitar can guide the ship into the binds, and across the twisting domain. The navitars take no payment. The price is theirs to pay: their lives. They travel the terrible high-sentience path, and count it happiness. They know the exotic laws that lie beyond the Radiant Path, but when asked, they are dumb before you.

—from *The Book of the Thousand Gifts*

SLOW AND STEADY, the Adda floated across the endless topography. In their haphazard drift, they had long since parted company with the other Adda that had launched at the same time, though now and again they spied one floating far away, its ladder hanging like the tail of a kite.

After the immense prairies, they crossed regions of stone up-crops, and abysmal chasms where the ground had split. Although no tectonic forces shaped this world, Anzi said that the nearer to the storm walls, the more that shocks split and shaped the land. It made her uncomfortable to talk of the walls—the bulwarks that sheltered this world in a necessary but violent embrace.

Bags of feed gradually disappeared up the Adda's feeding tubes. At times Quinn rode on the ladder, inhaling the clove-scented air. He missed seeing the horizon and the sky, where the Entire's soothing aspect was more profound. Huddled inside the Adda's pouch, his thoughts drifted to his betrayal of Johanna. He wondered, not for the first time, if the peace of the Entire so overtook him the last time that he'd lost himself, and if that peace might again rob him of his will. But no. This time, he was going into the thick of it.

The Adda bore them onward through a heavy fog. In the Entire, fog was the usual form of precipitation, sometimes so thick the condensation rained from the ladder. The Adda absorbed the humidity, and her tissues temporarily swelled throughout the cavity. Among the other things Quinn learned about the Adda were her riders' innovations in relieving themselves: the ladder partially folded up into a reasonable seat to cover the entrance orifice. It became the privy when sitting was called for.

Quinn had come to the end of his scrolls, and to pass the time, Anzi told tales and histories—of the five ages of the Entire, including the First Age when the lords lived in their original realm of the Heart, and the subsequent ages of building lands and creating sentients. There were stories of the manifesting of animal life from many different Rose templates—true stories of when and how such things occurred. She also recounted mythological tales of creatures like dragons—a tale from Earth, she conceded—and stories from other worlds, such as the myth of the river walkers that crept along, hanging upside down from the surface of the Nigh.

She also told stories of the Long War, and the warrior traditions of the Chalin. Anzi was an expert fighter because she expected to go as a soldier someday, when Yulin decided she should bolster the ranks of conscripts from his sway. The Entire military traditions were as old as the famous Paion Incursion, happening at a period that Quinn thought of as six thousand years ago, but expressed by Anzi as seven archons ago, each archon a span of three hundred thousand days. A thousand years later the Long War began in earnest.

Except for the Incursion, which occurred in the Long Gaze of Fire, the primacy where the Inyx dwelled, Paion attacked only one primacy, the one they were now in, and in only one place, at Ahnenhoon. If, as Anzi believed, they were not from the Entire, then their accuracy in returning to Ahnenhoon was worth noting. Here were beings who might know at least something of the correlates. But Anzi thought not.

"They aren't of the Rose. They're from elsewhere."

"Where else is there?" It was a startling question. Where indeed?

"Between," Anzi said. "Realms between."

"What lies between?"

But she gave the standard response: "No one ever knows."

It left him musing about other regions beyond his cosmos and hers. No reason that there should be only two . . .

In the direction of the Nigh, a black tidal wave grew. They were approaching the other side of the Entire, with its storm wall. Here there were no minorals or nascences—all chased away, as Anzi put it, by the great river that was not a river. The heartchime throbbed against his chest. Drawing it out, he put it to his ear, wondering at the evolving tone that proclaimed the proximity of the bright city. He prayed to be there only a short while, to pass Cixi's scrutiny and have her endorsement of his Inyx mission. With this in hand, his disguise would be perfect, only to be shed once Sydney's escape raised an alarm. He had already planned how they would camouflage themselves then: as godmen. Who would take note of two castaways of the Miserable God?

So he would come home with two prizes of inestimable value: the correlates if he was fortunate, and Sydney.

Wait for me, he sent to her, as if thoughts could journey and arrive intact.

The time came when the bags of seed were depleted and they had arrived on the banks of the Nigh. The Adda went to ground, allowing them to climb down the ladder. The creature was quick to depart, having failed to attract a seed-bearing rider here, and disliking to linger near the perpetual storm of the wall.

The height of the storm wall was sickening. It looked like it couldn't stand, that it was already falling. It seemed wrong that the Entire was contained and defended by such chaos. In the distance, at the foot of the wall, the River Nigh streamed in a coarse blaze. Between him and the river's edge was a transitional marsh, with pools of reflective river matter.

The smell of ozone flooded across Quinn's mouth. The blue-black undulations of the wall were very close, and air turbulence rippled clothes and tents. A small crowd of travelers—some sentients he hadn't seen before—

were scattered at the edge of the marsh waiting for a boat. They kept their gazes averted from the wall, tending cook fires with flames that flowed unnaturally, in greasy slicks. Between tide pools, tendrils spread out like dendrites.

Anzi warned against stepping in the pools. "Suzong told me that a small girl of the court traveling here with her parents fell in the river. She lived, but she never talked again."

Since Anzi had never traveled on the Nigh, all that she could tell Quinn about the river was what she had been told. She was no physicist, to talk of space-time or temporal and spatial turbulence. Nor was he, for that matter. But one thing Bei had told him: Travel on the Nigh was not faster than light; there would be no time-dilation effects. In creating the Nigh, the Tarig used a technology far beyond what humans knew.

The river made it possible to traverse the primacy from end reach to heartland. Along the lengths of the primacy were the Empty Lands that corresponded, Quinn felt, to interstellar space. These lands were solid ground only in a conceptual sense, and not according to everyday logic. Sometimes everyday logic didn't apply, as with Einstein's explanations of gravity and relativity. Long ago a mathematician had said, "In mathematics you don't understand things, you just get used to them." Quinn—the new Quinn—was getting used to the Entire.

They had just kindled a fire to cook supper when the crowds stirred. The travelers pointed out toward the Nigh.

A boat was coming. It was no more than a small blot skimming across the marshlands until it stopped some hundred yards off, hovering slightly above the ground. It looked very much like a small ship, except that it had a funnel in front that Anzi said served to collect river matter for fuel. In the center of a surrounding deck was a passenger cabin crowned by a smaller upper deck. Even as he and Anzi hurried in its direction, they saw a person on the prow, standing and waiting.

"The navitar?" Quinn asked Anzi as they hurried.

"No, Dai Shen, that's an Ysli, the servant of the navitar."

Quinn hadn't yet seen this manner of sentient, and watched with interest as the boat approached.

The Ysli was short and apelike, with a bare snout, and eyes peering from shaggy hair. It was difficult to think of it as sentient because it wore no clothes, but in fact the Ysli's eyes were alight with intelligence as it surveyed the crowd now massing before the ship. The navitars were utterly dependent on the hired servants, since they were incapable of mundane tasks. The individuals that gave themselves over to navigating the Nigh had abandoned extraneous capacities for the sake of a Tarig enhancement: to guide ships by sensing the fundamental forces underlying the Entire. *The navitars do not know what we know*, Anzi had said. *They know different things.*

Suddenly Anzi was pulling on his sleeve. "Don't take notice," she warned. "Tarig."

"Where?" He turned, spying a tall figure in his peripheral vision. And more: he smelled the Tarig. He had been close to a Tarig in the Adda, but the yeasty smells of the sinuses had cloaked other scents. Now, the smell came strongly, like burned sugar; not unpleasant by itself, but overlain with old emotions.

The Tarig was making its way toward the ship. The crowd parted amid bowing and murmurs of *Gracious One*. Anzi tensed and pushed Quinn ahead of her. She was nervous that she had lied to the Tarig earlier, nervous that they were searching for Wen An, that they knew the name of the person who'd first helped Quinn.

Now the Tarig stood next to them looking at the Ysli, who bowed but seemed unimpressed amid his other concerns of who should board and who should not. The Tarig wore a sleeveless tunic that revealed glistening arm muscles. Quinn was acutely aware of the creature, but avoided looking, most of all, into her eyes. It was a her. He could smell this. He could also smell Anzi's sweat, her fear.

The Tarig turned to Quinn. "We do not know you."

Quinn turned to her, gazing into her black eyes. "Dai Shen of Master Yulin's household, Bright One," he said, in his best unaccented Lucent tongue.

"Ah. Inyx matters," the rich voice murmured.

It chilled him that the Tarig knew this, although it was their prepared story. That she had called attention to *Inyx*, the very heart of the matter, worried him.

"Yes, Lady."

At that moment the Ysli screeched to the crowd, "Where bound?"

Shouts of destinations greeted this question, and among them, Anzi's cry of "The Ascendancy!"

The Tarig looked over Quinn's head, scanning the crowds, alert. It was unnerving that the creature *could* look over his head. Then she said: "Ascendancy bound, then. Good." She fixed her gaze on a nearby Chalin man. "And you, going where?"

The Tarig brushed past Quinn, trailing her scent, like sugar gone wrong. Anzi was pulling on Quinn's arm, dragging him to the ship.

Spying her, the Ysli asked, "Number traveling?"

"Two."

The Ysli beckoned, releasing a movable stairway that spanned a pool of river matter.

Anzi and Quinn pushed through the remaining crowd and boarded. Anzi murmured at him, "The Tarig dismissed us because the guilty do not travel to the Ascendancy." Quinn couldn't resist looking behind him, toward the Tarig. She was watching him. He cursed himself for looking. Then, glancing at the upper deck, Quinn saw a reddish blur where something moved inside darkened windows.

Behind Quinn and Anzi came a Chalin, weighed down by boxes roped to his back. The Ysli directed him and his luggage into the cabin, where, perspiring and panting, he accepted Quinn's help in lowering them onto the deck.

"Careful!" he said. "Meant for the legate, you oaf." He waved at the baggage. "It's all written down, for the eyes of the legate Min Fe and the consul Shi Zu." He eyed his fellow travelers to reinforce the importance of these names.

Through the window Anzi watched the Tarig as the man went on: "Min Fe must have everything in a hurry so it can sit in piles while he does not read it." He shook his head, looking at the central cabin that they must all share. "I don't know where you intend to sleep, but not on my trunks, thank you."

The Ysli frowned. "Talks too much," he chittered. Then he went aft, ambling past the companionway that led to the upper deck. He disappeared into the small aft cabin, and soon the vessel was under way, purring as it gathered speed over the marsh.

Despite his concern for his trunks, the man sat on one and wiped his brow with a silken cloth. He was slight of build and of that maddening middle and indeterminate age of the Chalin, who seemed to be thirty for most of their lives. "I am Cho, steward of the high clarities." He seemed unperturbed by the recent presence of the Tarig, a being he must have grown accustomed to in his duties. "And who might you be?"

Quinn and Anzi introduced themselves.

When Cho heard *Dai Shen of the Long War* and *Master Yulin's household*, he stood up in alarm. "Of the household of Master Yulin? Of the Long War?" He bowed. "Pardon. You must pardon. Born in a minoral. Inexcusable ignorance." He bowed again. "You are great personages, then. I am only a steward. You may sleep on my trunks. Pick as you like." He bowed again.

Quinn said, "Only distantly of the master's household. A minor soldier of Ahnenhoon. I take no notice."

Cho shook his head. "I am honored, even so. Allow me to serve you, of course." He seemed unable to decide to sit down again.

Anzi intervened: "It would be agreeable if you would consider us simply fellow travelers, until we arrive in the Ascendancy. There we must wear our distinctions. Not here."

Cho nodded gratefully. "Just so. In the bright city you will speak to the legates directly, even to the high prefect herself?" He snaked a look at them. "But fellow travelers, yes. I would be honored, naturally." He shook his head, murmuring, "A simple steward with great personages."

From the upper deck, a warbling voice cried out: "Ahh, Ascendancy ways can be opened. Bind the travelers to me. Scatter the lines. Scatter. . . ."

Cho looked at the ceiling. "The navitar. It's all nonsense, pay no attention." But he looked nervously at the stairs to the upper deck. "Her name is Ghoris. I have traveled with that one before. Very good pilot, I assure you."

From the aft cabin, amid slamming of cookware, glorious smells of cooking began filling the cabin. Despite having just seen a Tarig an arm's length away, Quinn was settling down enough to be hungry. But soon the Ysli climbed up the companionway carrying platters laden with soups and dumplings and baskets of unguessed-at delicacies. Soon the Ysli was cleaning the galley. It seemed that, for the others, supper was not in the offing.

Cho sat back, deflated. "We must feed Ghoris, or she won't last through the binds."

They were on the river. Through the windows on one side was sheer dark, where the junction of storm wall and river boiled. On the other side of the boat, the river lay thick and flat like mercury, sucking into eddies here and there, but otherwise smooth and empty of other craft. Quinn felt a heaviness grow in his stomach, and his mind dulled.

At last the Ysli brought down the platters with their remnants and set them out on Cho's crates, where the Chalin steward tucked in with relish. But Quinn had lost his appetite, as had Anzi.

Finishing his meal, Cho looked at his traveling companions. "Sleep is the only thing now. I have been on the Nigh a dozen times, and each time I am sicker than the last." He made a bed among his boxes and lay down.

As they sailed closer to the storm wall, a bluish light infused the ship, and the nausea that Quinn had first experienced at the minoral returned. Anzi leaned against the bulkhead, closing her eyes. "Rest, Dai Shen," she said. Her skin had taken on a bluish cast. "When the navitar goes through the knots, it's best to sleep."

He'd already resolved he wouldn't sleep through this experience.

The ship shuddered. In the Ysli's galley, implements rattled. Looking down at his hands, Quinn thought they were not occupying just one space, but several. He watched them, intrigued. An undercurrent tried to sweep his thoughts away and pull him under. He fought it.

Beside him, Anzi and Cho were already asleep.

He looked outside. The river came halfway up the cabin windows. They were descending into the binds, an alarming sight. Just outside, he could see a strange creature. Walking along the river, but hanging upside down from the surface, was an animal with a number of legs, almost like a spider. River walker, he thought. But he couldn't be seeing it, because it was a mythological beast of the Entire. If you followed a river walker, it would lead you to oblivion in the binds. He turned his face away, muddy-headed.

The lights in the cabin blinked out.

Quinn walked, tottering, to the galley, peering in. He was going to ask the Ysli if he could fix the lights. In the corner was a hammock where the creature hung in a lump. From the galley windows Quinn saw that they were now fathoms deep in the Nigh. It was not water out there, but a more vital medium, exuding its own dull light and pierced by icicles of lightning. Turning to the other side of the galley, Quinn saw a similar view. The vessel shook again, rattling the galley wares.

Quinn caught a glimpse of light outside the galley door. He saw that the companionway was lit, spilling light from above. His mind was crawling.

The door narrowed and then bulged out. Belly churning, Quinn steadied himself against the galley counters and walked toward the light from the companionway. As he came to the first step, it moved farther away, but when he took a step up, he had gone halfway up.

At the top, he faced an oblong room with a dais at one end. The ceiling was of a membranous material like the veil-of-worlds. On the dais sat Ghoris the navitar, her head quite close to the ceiling.

Dressed in a red caftan, her body was of an indeterminate shape and size. Her white hair hung loose, flowing around her chest. She pointed at him, the end of her finger coming closer than he thought possible. Then he saw that she was moving her hands in front of her, without reference to him. She was conducting. She opened and closed her mouth, over and over again

"See the twist, there," she said in a shredded voice. Her wrist turned, and she smiled beatifically. "See, traveler, do you see?"

"The lights went out," he found himself saying, wondering if it made any sense.

The navitar's hands were pudgy, as though her muscles had all gone to skin and gristle. She looked down at them, her face doughy and rounded.

"It is not light; it is the fundament. Yesss." Her eyes closed, but her hands played in front of her. "There are thirty-six, and some are paired. Then eight fields and all the generations. Coming in now. To my hands." She picked one out of the air, bringing it to one side.

She continued, her voice a gargle: "To make them a family. Combining them, creating a structure, from which we know what we know. Yesss, the symmetry of it. Gone are the anomalies. Coming to my hands, the complete set of symmetries, yes." She opened her eyes, sweeping her gaze over him, never quite focusing. "You cannot see them. Light is what you see. It is not light. That is the surface of one thing. Being what you are, it is your mistake. You have all agreed on the world, to keep from going mad."

Madness was more a term he would have applied to *her*. That, or savant.

"Traveler, what holds it all together?" she said, as though teaching a pupil.

"Holds what, Navitar?"

She gestured around her. "All. What keeps it from collapsing? Think of the—ahh, the cosmos. What keeps it from succumbing to its own weight? Because it is flying apart, do you perceive? But the Entire does not move, in your plane of life. Think on this, most carefully. In your ignorance, you answer that the storm walls resist collapse. But what powers the great storm? What is its energy? That is something even you can know."

In his plodding logic he said, "The Tarig power it."

Ghoris sighed. "Poor under-sentient." Her attention moved to a point just over his head. "The lines," she whispered. Opening her mouth, she stared as though she was trying to smell the lines. Quinn opened his own mouth, letting the air move over his Jacobson's organ. He thought *he* could smell them.

"What—," he began.

"No speaking! It frays, frays."

She was looking directly over his head. "Traveler, you are the knot. Things converge in you. It will make our journey much harder."

She began to move her hands more quickly, as though dealing with a tangle of invisible yarn. "All the lines converge. You are looking, looking. Yes. Finding things you never looked for, losing all that you sought. I see. I see her, too. She is at your side. A tangle of lines also. Ah yessss."

"Who?" Quinn whispered. "Who do you see?" He believed her. That she saw things in the lines.

The navitar's heavy face fell slack for a moment. She shook her head. "Her knot is at the center of things. You are there, but her lines are, yes, strong."

He fumbled in his pocket for the pictures. Grabbing the picture of Sydney, he thrust it toward the navitar. "Is this who you see? Tell me."

She glanced at the picture, then stood abruptly. Pulling a fastener at her neck, she stood up, and her caftan fell around her waist. She stood tall, pushing into the membrane, distorting it, and then puncturing it with her head, standing as though decapitated. She brought her hands up through the membrane.

He looked at her fleshy body, her breasts like deflated balloons on her chest.

Poor creature. Fire, oh fire. He heard her voice inside his head now. *Lost. Her strings are cut. In all the worlds.* After a moment she sat down as, over her head, the membrane closed up. Her hair hung in ropes, curling and wet. Closing her eyes, she whispered, "Gone to fire."

Quinn was stricken by her words. "My Sydney," he murmured.

The navitar's eyes blinked open. She growled, "That is not her name."

From her sitting position the navitar began conducting the lines again. She reached out her hands in his direction, grabbing the air, curling her fingers, and drawing the lines close to her chest, forcibly pulling him in her direction. He staggered to the foot of the dais, where he fell to his knees.

Pointing up with a finger, she said, "Look up!"

He did so. The sky was stitched with needles, stabbing down, retreating up, like an aurora borealis made of knives.

She moaned, "You have many lives. I have many lives; all are up there." She shook her head, flapping her heavy jowls. "But you cannot see."

"No," he admitted, devastated. He was both very emotional and fending off sleep with all his strength.

She rose up again, plunging through the membrane. She swayed, as though buffeted by exotic winds. He heard in the back of his mind: *I see your lives, your knotted lives. It twists, oh twists. But which world is it?* He could see her blurred image above him as she waved her hands above her, where knives of light slashed down and gathered in her fists, making her look like a goddess of lightning. *I see the world collapsing, the fire descending. I see a burning rose. Oh so beautiful, so dead. They do not combine; they do not have symmetry. One excludes the other; both cannot be true. The rose burns, and the All flies apart. Choose, Titus, choose.*

He whispered, "What must I choose?"

The navitar suddenly crouched down and squatted over him, her face slimed with mercury. Her thoughts came to him: *Your heart.*

She was silent for a long while, hanging her head in exhaustion. Then she picked up eight or nine threads—this time Quinn could see them, spiraling filaments that came from thin air into her fingers—and, tugging on them, she thrust her upper body and hands into the sky. As she did so, the ship's prow fell into a long well, and Quinn fell forward, onto the soft and puffy wood deck.

Sleep sucked him down.

Quinn opened his eyes a crack, just wide enough to see the Ysli's pinched face scowling down at him.

Someone was saying, "We're here, after all. And Dai Shen is the only sick one, when I thought it would be me." Cho's voice.

Quinn came fully awake in a room filled with an eye-stinging light.

Anzi hovered anxiously. "You went up, but why Dai Shen?"

The Ysli chittered. "Sleeping. You should all have been."

Sitting up, Quinn said, "The lights went out. I went looking for light."

The Ysli's face crumpled into a deep frown. "No light in the binds." Then he brought forward a crumpled photo, thrusting it into Quinn's hand. Without another word, he left them, retreating to his galley.

"Are you all right?" Anzi asked.

Quinn nodded. His stomach felt grease-laden and his head ached, but he was in one piece. He flattened the photo out. It was a pale wash of film, now so faded that he could hardly see the image. But, unmistakably, it wasn't Sydney.

Not his daughter. It was his wife. The photo he had inadvertently shown to the navitar was Johanna. Ghoris had been talking about Johanna. *Poor creature. Her strings are cut in all the worlds.* On the upper deck he had understood what that meant, but now it was not so clear. He must have one more interview with the pilot.

As Cho, struggling with his trunks, left the cabin, Quinn whispered to Anzi, "The navitar—she said that—"

"Said what?"

"Things will burn. Fly apart."

"Her type is half-mad," Anzi said. But she looked alarmed.

"She said the lines—the lines she sees as events, that they converge in me. In Johanna." He jerked to his feet and confronted the Ysli. "I would bid farewell to the pilot."

"Leave," the Ysli squawked, standing in front of the companionway.

A noise drew Quinn's attention. Looking up, he saw that the closed door at the top of the stairs shook in its frame.

"Let me speak to her," Quinn said. From the upper deck came a whimpering noise.

The Ysli's face contorted. "The navitar is unwell."

In proof of these words, the foul smell of excrement came from behind the doorway, hitting Quinn's sense organs in a wave of revulsion.

The navitar was paying the price for seeing things. No wonder she was mad; if the river played with space-time, perhaps she sometimes observed effects before the cause. He wondered how the madness and suffering could be worth it. But then, he didn't know what she saw, and thought that, quite possibly, it was everything.

He took a last glance at the companionway and nodded to the Ysli. He'd never let Quinn upstairs now, and quite possibly Ghoris was rendered helpless at the moment. Quinn picked up his satchel and followed Anzi onto the deck.

As he stepped out and looked around him, the world fell away.

With his focus on the navitar, Quinn hadn't registered the fact that they were *here*.

At the Ascendancy.

It was a view to stagger the mind. The boat was tied to a floating dock amid a mercurial sea, vast in all directions. Pillars of exotic matter extended from the sea to a distant structure overhead, tiny at this distance of some thirty thousand feet. However, it was, Quinn knew, an enormous habitat containing the impregnable mansions of the Tarig.

Of course, the pillars didn't hold up the city. Rather, they supported the Entire by replenishing the exotic matter of the sea and the great rivers of the primacies. On either side of him and far away, Quinn saw the storm walls of the primacy converging on the great sea. Closer, the great Rim City stretched out, hugging the shore and forming a profoundly long and narrow metropolis connected by the instant transport of the navitars.

Amid a small crowd, he and Anzi were shuffling toward the center of the dock, where a gatekeeper metered the flow of travelers. As they had planned, they would give their names, which had been sent ahead by Yulin from an axis communication node. The Chalin sway was not forbiddingly distant from the heartland, and, for this reason, timely communication to and from the Ascendancy was possible, although limited to the speed of light.

Quinn lifted the end of Cho's trunk from the man's back, to help him.

"Many thanks, Excellency!" Cho huffed. "I could have brought all this in redstones, but Min Fe will have his paper." He lowered the trunk to the dock with Quinn's help as they waited for a Chalin legate to check them through.

Anzi was staring at the view above her.

"Born in a minoral?" Quinn asked, grinning.

Her cheeks flushed. "I . . . I was," she said, giving up on pride. "I never saw such a sight."

Nor had he. The last time he'd come here, it was by the bright. But he knew there was only one other sight to match this one in all the worlds. And that was at the top.

It was time to leave his photos behind. He had agreed that they were too dangerous to take to the bright city, but now that it was time to discard them in the sea, he hesitated. They had been his traveling companions as much as Anzi had. And although the photos were bleached to ghosts, his heart had supplied what was missing. At last he knelt on the dock and let them fall. When they lit on the water's surface, the images seemed to come back. As they floated a moment, he saw Sydney in acute detail, and for a moment it seemed that she was a young woman grown, with blighted eyes. . . .

Anzi was at his side, gently pulling him away. They stood in line. He wished he'd put the pictures in the water one at a time so he could have seen Johanna, and what the lens of the sea would have shown him, or the lens of his imagination.

The line inched forward. Anzi was giving her name to the legate. Ahead, shimmering in the streaming pillar and meant to ascend in it, was a spacious elevator capsule with its door open. Quinn tried to shake the uneasiness of being in close contact with a material as dangerous as river matter; but others seemed unconcerned. The capsule created a region of safety.

Something was amiss. Anzi was saying, "A mistake, surely. I have been sent by the master of the great sway."

The Chalin legate was shaking his head. He looked at Quinn, scowling. "You are Dai Shen, to see the high prefect?" Quinn nodded. "Then you have leave," the legate said, "and no one further, of Master Yulin's sway."

The legate tried unsuccessfully to wave Quinn past. Anzi went on, "We have a clarity of great importance, and I will help present it to the high prefect, for the sake of the realm."

The legate turned a stark gaze on her. "No, you will not. One named Dai Shen has leave to ascend." He turned to Anzi. "Wait here for him if you wish, and if you don't mind sleeping on the dock."

Cho was watching this exchange with consternation. He had already passed through the checkpoint and was ready to board the elevator, but now he came back. "I can vouch for the woman," he said. "A very high personage, and so forth. Charming, with important connections to the Yulin household, I assure you."

The legate turned a withering glance on him. "Do I need help from a *steward?*"

Cho backed away, murmuring, "No, no, pardon."

"I don't ascend without her," Quinn said, stepping closer to the legate.

"None of my concern," the man answered. "Who is next, with approvals in order?"

People pressed in from behind. Quinn stepped out of line, going to Anzi.

"No, Shen," she said. "You know all that you need to know. You are all that you need to be. Without me."

"I need you with me, Anzi."

Her mouth formed the word *no.* He had the sinking feeling that she was going to leave him.

She pulled him toward the edge of the dock, where the mercurial sea lapped up against immortal pilings. "Shen, you will succeed without me. You have the redstones; you have your story."

"We've been together all this way, Anzi. I'm not sure I can do this without you."

Now her face had grown stubborn. "Yes you can. Despite what my uncle thinks, I believe you can succeed at the Inyx sway. You can earn back this daughter."

Unexpectedly, and at the mention of his daughter, he found he couldn't speak.

Anzi nodded. "You'll love your daughter finally, and enough."

They stood looking at each other. The dock seemed bleak indeed, and its views more daunting than before. "You know what I was," Quinn said in a low voice. "All that I did and didn't do—before."

"Yes. But you remember Ci Dehai's wisdom? The river runs forward. We are what we will be. I have to believe this. So I can be good in my own view."

"Anzi, come with me. We'll make this legate listen." The legate might be mistaken, it might be cleared up—his mind cast about for ways around the gatekeeper.

"No." She put a hand on his arm and tightened her grip. "You're like that gatekeeper, Shen. You stand at the place where our worlds will cross, will mix. You'll have to choose how it will happen—who will win and who will suffer."

"I don't have that kind of power. If you only knew how little—"

She waved the response away. "Titus," she whispered, "the navitar is right."

She had used his true name. It gave him a shiver.

"Things converge in you. Because of who you are, because of Johanna, I don't know why. But you're a great man. Bei told me. The navitar says so. I believe. I've always believed."

He turned away, looking at the sea, blindingly reflective. What Anzi said was true. Maybe he wouldn't control the gate. But it would come down to the question of where his loyalties lay: with this land that held his daughter, or the one where she used to reside. Rather than straddling the worlds, he would have to put both feet in one place. And he had no idea which place that would be. Even though he couldn't say exactly why—and when—he must choose; he knew that if he didn't, he would never stand on firm ground again.

The line of travelers was moving forward. Now and then the legate frowned at Quinn and Anzi. Cho waved from the elevator capsule, urging him to hurry.

There was no more time for conversation.

Anzi looked as though she wished to say more. As though she wanted to confess that she had feelings for him. He wanted that from her, but he had no right to hear it.

In a rush, he said, "Anzi, why are you so aloof? You say that you admire Rose passion, but you're composed, even now."

She looked away. "Bei asked me to bind you to me—by intimate means. To win your loyalty to our world. So it became part of my honor not to."

He looked at her, those features that had become so familiar to him: ivory and white. Once so cold. "Anzi, I . . ."

She put her hand on his mouth. "Say nothing. Go."

"You can't wait here," he said.

"I'll take lodging in the Rim City. The first place I come to. You can find me when you're done, above. Make no more trouble here. Pass through, like the common thing that it is." She gave him a small push, tense and urgent.

Quinn picked up his satchel, still thinking how to persuade the legate. But in the end, he knew that Anzi was right: making a scene would draw the kind of attention that they must, at all costs, avoid.

Quinn walked to the elevator, his stomach clenched, still casting about for a solution, but finding none. He turned around just as the doors began closing. He saw Anzi standing, the silver sea behind her, a smile on her face that he was ashamed to find he could not return. He lifted his hand in farewell.

The door closed.

At his side, he heard Cho exclaim, "Oh dear. That was ill luck. I wouldn't be surprised if Min Fe was behind it, may God look at him." He sighed. "Politics."

People found seats on benches. "Make way," Cho spat at someone. "A personage must sit here." Quinn was so stunned by the turn of events that he hardly registered the launch of the elevator. He sat next to Chalin officials who no doubt had made the trip many times.

There was no view in the cabin as they shot upward. Someone turned a spindle, pulling a filament from a spinning basket.

It would be a long ride.

PART III

DARK AS ROSE NIGHT

CHAPTER EIGHTEEN

THE PREACHER ON THE CORNER proclaimed that the end was near. He kept his post despite the relentless drizzle, waving tracts at people on lunch break. He managed to thrust one into the hands of Stefan Polich.

Stefan was surprised. It had been a long time since he'd gone on foot at street level. He'd assumed that the city was more presentable, that people, with their basic needs met, were less inspired to deal religion and drugs. But he'd forgotten that some folks had runaway minds. The ones who thought they'd spoken to Jesus, and the ones who thought they *were* Jesus.

"Jesus got room for you, too," the preacher said—a vagrant dispensing grace to a billionaire.

The tract was a pulpy wad in Stefan's fist. He hurried onward, putting distance between himself and the thoughts of the kingdom to come. He was trying to clear his thoughts, not complicate them.

But Titus Quinn kept coming to mind. Like this street preacher, and the losers who congregated out of the rain under awnings, Quinn was a mental runaway.

Stefan had thought so from the day they'd found the man in a mining camp on Lyra, where no out-of-system freighter had come in years. Aside from being on a planet where he couldn't be, Quinn had done little to inspire confidence in his exotic claims. Even after hospitalization and rehab, the man was a wreck: a loner, a misfit, and a dropout.

Now, Stefan depended on that same man to save him. He needed Titus Quinn a damn sight more than he needed Jesus.

Especially since a Kardashev tunnel had devoured another shipload of colonists.

At the residential tower where Caitlin and Rob Quinn lived, he entered the lobby, shaking the rain from his umbrella. He bypassed the elevators and took the stairs to give his quads a workout.

There came a time, Stefan mused, when a man had to decide what he believed—about death, about what it all means. At forty-three, Stefan Polich thought it might be time to nail that down. Once the newsTides got word about the evaporation of the starship *Appolonia*—and that would be about twenty minutes ago—he'd be hounded for an interview, explaining, justifying, apologizing. He'd done it before. But there were those on the Minerva board who might challenge him after two such failures in as many years. Suzene Gninenko, for example, always watched for an opening. If he started replacing ships, it would be an admission that they weren't seaworthy. No one would book passage on the older ships. At 900 million a pop, the fleet replacement would drive profits into a gopher hole.

Thus his crisis of faith.

Floor two. He removed his wool coat, tucking it over his arm and continuing the climb. By floor six he ought to have the meaning of life figured out. As a savvy, he was always good at the big picture. But the ultimate big picture? Stefan shook his head, trudging up the terrafab stairs.

Floor ten. His legs felt like molten ingots. Giving up on his quads, he pushed through the door to the elevator stack, no closer to his epiphany.

Minerva controlled nineteen Kardashev tunnels, domesticating them and creating a transport system that linked the thirty extrasolar colonized planets. It was a kingdom dependent upon cataclysmic forces. An empire based on blindingly violent past events: the supernovae of stars of more than five solar masses.

So when these handy space-time tunnels ripped apart a ship or two, it wasn't as though anyone should be surprised. All passengers signed papers that openly disclosed the dangers in excruciating detail.

In his pocket, he fingered the damp religious tract. He wondered if the passengers on the ill-fated *Appolonia* went straight to heaven—or made a stop in Titus Quinn's *adjoining region*. As the man himself had once done, when all this began.

He stood in front of the Quinns' apartment door, flashed his silvered hand in front of the smart surface, and waited. Caitlin Quinn had little reason to open the door to the likes of him. She knew that Minerva had threatened Rob's job to get her brother-in-law to go. What she didn't know was that Helice had thrown fuel on that fire, putting Mateo's future on the line, too. He was glad Lamar had blown the whistle on her. Helice was an amoral zealot, with ambitions to succeed her betters . . . thinking she'd go along with Quinn, threatening their man without consulting him. She was walking the edge, and at the first chance Stefan would give her a little push. So Caitlin Quinn owed him a little payback, and he was here to get it.

She did open the door. It took her a moment to recognize him. She couldn't help knowing his face from the company newsTides.

A shadow fell on her face. "Titus . . ."

"No, it's not about Titus. There's no word yet." He looked beyond her shoulder, into the apartment, but he knew that Rob was at work. "May I come in for a moment?"

Caitlin crumpled her lips. "I'm not sure. I don't know if I want to hear some things."

"I swear. Nothing like that."

After a moment she stepped back, and he entered the apartment.

He avoided looking around. It was ugly and cramped. The walls had little divots where new data structures had been replaced. He observed this with his peripheral vision, taking care not to embarrass her. This residential cube had its share of virtual enhancements, and when they were live, the walls must look considerably better. Her husband could afford it. Minerva paid top prices even for talent like his.

She closed the door. "So Rob still has his position?"

He nodded. The forty-year-old savant tender should be retired to the dole. But wouldn't be, because his brother was protecting him. Caitlin Quinn no doubt considered this Rob's due. Entitlement was the game, and every dred and middie knew exactly how to play it.

"In that case," she said, "you can sit down."

They faced off. Caitlin was stocky and healthy looking. Nice features for her age; might once have been pretty. Probably no aesthetic enhancements, unlike his own wife, who frankly made Caitlin look like a wet dog.

Now that he was here it was hard to make a beginning. He made a stab at it: "I know you despise me."

She looked as though she was weighing this idea.

Stefan continued, "Quinn and I had our differences when he lost his ship." After a pause: "I made mistakes."

Caitlin wasn't giving him much. She just sat there, looking at him without any trace of fear or toadyism. He didn't much care for the judgmental gaze. He went on: "I didn't believe his story. I couldn't entrust another starship to someone with ideas like his. No ship would have fully booked under his command. He ruined himself. I know you don't believe that."

"Nope. I don't."

"I take some of the blame. I was wrong about what happened. But if I'd championed him, the board would have dumped me in an instant. With Titus no better off."

"All right. But you went beyond just sacking him. You said things that made sure he'd never work again."

He stared at the floor. "Mistakes." Stefan had never liked Titus Quinn. When the man had come home raving, it was just that much worse.

"Do you expect me to forgive you, Mr. Polich? Is that why you're here?"

"No." He looked into her eyes. She had a quality that the poor often had, of what might be called integrity. And he wanted some of that, even if only for a moment, so that he could stand himself. "Up to Titus, isn't it?"

"Damn right."

The warm room began drying his wet collar and shoes, making him feel little pinpricks at his neck and ankles. He shouldn't have come. There was too much past. Ugly past. But he was here now, so he blurted, "You and Titus are close. Even closer than he and his brother."

A movement distracted him. He looked up to find that her son was standing in the doorway to a bedroom.

Caitlin turned to him. "Honey, school's still in session."

"I heard voices."

"This is Stefan Polich, Mateo."

The boy looked at him a long beat. By the cool gaze, Stefan was afraid his name had been taken in vain a few times around this household.

"Are you a savvy?" Mateo asked. "You look like one."

The question startled Stefan. "I . . . am. Yes."

Mateo smiled. "Me, too. I'm studying."

Stefan felt an awful half-smile paste up on his face. You either tested or you didn't. Studying made no difference. And sometimes, even if you did test well, things happened to your score records. Confronted with the boy's brown eyes, Stefan cemented his resolve to protect this boy. Stefan might be a sinner, but he wasn't a ghoul.

Caitlin escorted Mateo back to his virtual tie-in. She closed the door, eyeing Stefan.

"Sweet, isn't it? He actually thinks there's room for self-improvement."

The room was growing hotter. He should never have come. He couldn't fix the world. He couldn't change the fact that there was a natural divide in ability for the human race. That the world had become so detailed and complex that it surpassed the Caitlins and Robs of the world.

He was desperate to be gone, but he plodded on, wanting the thing that Caitlin could give him: hope.

"You're close to Quinn," he said. "That's why I came. To ask you."

"Ask then, Mr. Polich. I'm a busy woman."

He paused. "Do you believe him?"

A small smile came into her face. She knew exactly what he meant. But she turned away, looking out the sliding-glass door that led out onto a lanai. She stared into the city. "That he went somewhere? Do I believe he went to the other place and lived?"

"Yes," he whispered. He wanted to believe. He wanted to know if she believed, and why. He knew she wasn't dumb. She was average-smart, a right-down-the-middle engineering graduate. But in some ways she had a wisdom about her. An ability to sit with the CEO of the fourth-largest company in the world and tell him with all grace, *I'm a busy woman.*

"Why does it matter what I think?"

Because you're the goddamn cheerleader for Titus Quinn, he thought. Because you actually like the man, and have some reason to think that he's not a mental runaway. Because you still hope to see him come home from high adventures.

He said, "Because I'm losing ships, Caitlin. If Quinn doesn't help us, we won't have any other options."

"You mean *you* won't," she said, an edge coming into her voice. "Some of us don't care about interstellar travel, Mr. Polich. Some of us are trying real hard just to deal with the world we've got."

That stung. She was on *his* dole. Implying it wasn't enough.

"But I'm still asking you. I'm asking for your frank opinion." She knew Quinn at a level no one else did. If she could believe, maybe he could, too. Maybe he could sleep at night.

She rose from her chair and went to the window. Her voice came small and lost. "I don't know."

He felt the weight of those words, few and soft as they were.

Caitlin faced him across the living room. "I want to believe him. I've chosen to believe him."

"Chosen?"

"Yes."

He saw what she was driving at: that faith was something you decided on. But she hadn't soothed his troubled brow. She hadn't given him the answer he wanted. He'd expected that Caitlin Quinn would have that simple middie susceptibility to faith. And that some of it might rub off on him.

"You don't get to, though," she added, and her voice had turned hard, along with her eyes.

"I don't?" He didn't get to choose?

"I believe him because of how much we all love him."

Love. Well, if *that* was the prerequisite . . . "Not a very objective position," he said, with some bitterness.

She shook her head, looking as though she actually pitied him. Here she was in her crappy little apartment, standing like the Statue of Liberty, Miss Holier-than-thou. Like a lot of people, she thought love solved everything: just smear it over the problem, and it'll all work out. Then they had the arrogance to pity you if you saw things more rationally. He wished he hadn't come; wished he hadn't exposed himself like this to her. He was at the top of the food chain, and she was a bottom feeder; and now she stood there on her high moral ground. . . . He had an urge to put her in her place.

"Caitlin," he said, rising to leave. "If Quinn does come back, there's something you can do for me. He'll give us a full report; we'll make sure of that. But if he holds anything back—any little side deals he's made over there—we want to know about it." They should have sent Booth Waller along, damn Titus's conniving heart, anyway.

She looked at him with incredulous eyes. "Why on Earth should I tell you?"

"The Standard Test is coming up soon, isn't it?" He flicked a glance at the closed bedroom door.

She followed his glance. "What about it?"

Stefan was now stomping in Helice's realm. The youngest member of the board had started the whole idea, and now Stefan would finish it. He let his voice convey how little Caitlin knew: "Did you think the Standard Test was really standard?"

Now the statuelike quality of her hardened. She couldn't move, couldn't speak.

"Just keep us in mind," he said. "In case you hear things. Things he'd only tell you. You will have my gratitude, I assure you."

"Get out of here."

Stefan didn't move, and for a moment Caitlin wondered if there was more. If he had more bodies in the closet. If he was going to throw acid in her face, repossess the furniture, put up on the newsTides pictures of her in her underwear. . . . She was furious, and afraid. But she also was flying high above this conversation, seeing something clearly from that birds-eye view: that Stefan Polich would never let them go. He'd never be satisfied with what her family could give him. Like a man on a drug, once he ruled the Quinn family, he'd control them to their graves. It came like an awful and freeing truth: she was doomed no matter what she did. So she might as well stop the whole thing right here and now.

"Think about it, Caitlin. Don't make up your mind right now." He handed her his card. "Call me. Anytime."

"No," she said, making no move to take it. "I won't be calling."

"That's a mistake."

She nodded. "I know." Of course it was a mistake. He'd have to prove that he was serious; a man like that couldn't be crossed and not retaliate. But everything she could do would be a mistake. So goddamn it, let him come at me. Oh, Titus, she thought. We all should have gone with you. That's where your heart is, anyway. Maybe we'd find ours, too. Maybe Rob and I could start over. Maybe Mateo . . .

She fought tears, and won. Not in front of *him*.

She led the way to the door and opened it, standing aside for him.

There, he turned to say good-bye, and seemed to soften for a moment. "If he doesn't come back, there's twenty million for you—for the family."

"He's coming back," she said.

The door closed. She had dismissed him.

Stefan took the elevator down. The chill of the lobby air was welcome, but couldn't match the chill in his gut. She'd turned him out without giving him even a crumb of hope.

He opened his umbrella and pushed back into the rainy city. In her eyes, he didn't deserve to believe. But though she despised him, she was wrong if she thought it was all about money and empire. People were dying. The *Appolonia* had sunk, all hands on board.

Jesus could have saved them. If he'd chosen to.

Stefan guessed he didn't get to believe *that*, either.

He found the crumpled tract in his pocket and tossed it away.

CHAPTER NINETEEN

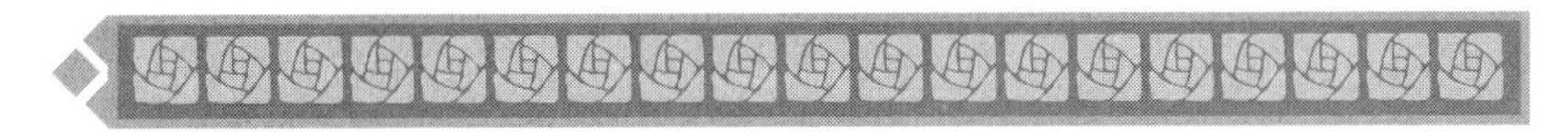

As one being my mount and I went to war.
As half a being, I came home.
I turn my face upward. Does the bright still shine?
—lament of an Inyx rider

TO THE SURPRISE OF THE ENCAMPMENT—and the fury of her enemies—Sydney had acquired a bodyguard: the giant Mo Ti. Although he spoke little, and made no threats, her fellow riders feared the man. He had a reputation as a fighter of Ahnenhoon, and several days ago had effortlessly tossed a Laroo half the length of the barracks for scratching Sydney. Even the camp's sole Jout—the only sentient Mo Ti's size—kept a distance from the man.

Sydney didn't know why the man attached himself to her, but he now had a free bond with his mount, so he had already prospered from her friendship. So far, the concept of free bond had a loyal following of two riders.

Feng considered free bond a heresy, relentlessly agitating against Sydney. But with Mo Ti near, Sydney could brazenly promote her idea, countering the arguments from the riders that free bond—a term she'd made up—would make the herd weak. On the contrary, she and Riod had developed a strangely fierce devotion, one that knitted rider to mount, opening the gates of emotion and loyalty until it was a clean, swift river passing between them, one that at times overtook its banks and spread to the herd.

Most often, though, Sydney and Mo Ti rode out alone, keeping apart from others. She enjoyed his quiet presence, and took from him the lesson that strength could be gentle. He never blustered or picked fights, and in stark contrast to the obsequious Akay-Wat, gave Sydney subdued respect. In imitation, Sydney began to modify her behavior, carrying herself with more dignity, a change that Mo Ti seemed to approve. Even so, in nearly two arcs of days together, Sydney had never felt one reflected emotion from him.

Thus the days passed, and Sydney knew a measure of happiness that surprised her. Riod, too, was less apt to go off raiding, and day by day grew more certain of free bond.

Lurking in the background, and now so cowed that she seldom spoke, was Akay-Wat, watching with limpid brown eyes as Sydney transferred her interest to Mo Ti, allowing him to serve her and utterly supplant the duties that Akay-Wat had enjoyed, such as keeping Puss from soiling Sydney's bed and watching over her book of pinpricks—moot in any case, because now Sydney carried it with her in a pack wherever she went.

Sydney had developed a habit of signaling Riod with a tap on his neck when she wished him to convey her thoughts to others. Such as when she passed Akay-Wat, thinking, *Miserable coward.* Or when she passed Feng, thinking, *Slave. Afraid of free bond.* In this way she and Riod kept the appearance of her thoughts leaking out, a necessary precaution lest they tackle too many taboos at once.

However, these peaceful days were at an end, as they were soon to learn.

The four of them rode back to the encampment after a long ride, with Riod shedding restive thoughts, and then alarming ones. Instinctively, Sydney and Mo Ti hunkered down for a fast ride, and at last thundered into a strangely quiet yard.

Silent riders stood in clumps in the yard, watching them approach.

Riod was picking up the news that someone in the camp had died.

"Who?" Sydney asked.

In the barracks, Riod sent. *Akay-Wat.*

They dismounted, and the group parted for Sydney and Mo Ti as they approached the barracks. Riod broke custom and entered the rider quarters with Sydney. Two sentients occupied the room, one of them unconscious.

Adikar, the Ysli healer, turned at their approach. "Akay-Wat," he said. "Her mount has killed her."

Through Riod's sending, Sydney saw the Hirrin lying in a mass of bloody bandages. Eyes closed, Akay-Wat softly bleated.

"Dies," the Ysli said. "Her foreleg. A pulp."

Sydney caught a glimpse through Riod's eyes of Akay-Wat's grievous injury, her shattered right foreleg. "Skofke did this?" Sydney asked, stunned to think that a mount would maim his own rider.

Adikar said, "Free bond, she wanted. This was the answer."

A clumping sound announced that Feng was approaching the bunk. Her tone was grim. "We got to remove the leg, and we would if any of us had the eyes for it." She paused. "Ever seen somebody die pus-filled and raving? Put her down, I say."

The Ysli healer muttered, "Against the vows, a kill like that."

We do not tell the lords, Riod sent.

Feng offered, "We could send for a Tarig surgeon."

"Won't last till then," the Ysli muttered.

Put the Hirrin down, came Riod's command.

Sydney turned to him, putting her hand on his broad face, "My friend, not yours."

It shamed her to call Akay-Wat a friend now, as the Hirrin lay dying, when Sydney had given her hardly a thought before. Akay-Wat had pleaded for scraps of friendship, scraps that Sydney withheld out of annoyance—and worse, a kind of involuntary dislike. Her careless words of insult had driven the Hirrin to a rash demonstration of bravery, and now she would die for it.

Sydney was thinking hard. "Maybe we could take the leg using Riod's sight to guide us."

Feng snorted. "Ya. And a beku can pilot the Nigh." She thunked her cane on the floor. "Take the creature to my cabin. No one wants to hear her screaming."

Mo Ti bent down and gathered up the Hirrin. He carried her easily, as though she was made of straw.

In the yard, Priov cantered forward, his emotions cold. *She angered her mount*, he sent. *But he did not kill her.*

"Go to hell," Sydney said, in English.

The bright dimmed, and Akay-Wat ceased her bleating. Her wound, though washed, was putrefying. Sydney crouched by the cot, holding the unconscious Akay-Wat's other foreleg, stroking it, while Mo Ti stood watch nearby. The vigil wouldn't last long.

The Ysli healer brought candles to the room, lighting them for good luck. But Akay-Wat needed more than luck. She needed an amputation.

With the fragrance of candles burning, the smells of Akay-Wat's wound subsided a little. But nothing could ease Sydney's dismay at her part in all this. Worse, she was aware that wanting Akay-Wat to survive was partially to forestall the self-recrimination she would go through after the Hirrin's death. It was hypocritical to hope for Akay-Wat's life. But it was not all selfish. The Hirrin had indeed been a friend, or had tried to be.

When Adikar left, Mo Ti drank from a water jar. His throat opened, and down went a jarful of water. Sydney heard him wipe his mouth against his sleeve.

Then he crouched down to Sydney's level. "I fought the Long War," he said.

She knew he had been a soldier, but since coming to the encampment he had said nothing further about himself. Sydney was surprised he did now, in these circumstances.

"How did you end up here? You must have made enemies."

"Mo Ti killed a man in a fight. A fellow soldier."

She hoped her silence would encourage him to elaborate, and he did.

"They let me live, because of good service. They said I would come here. Five soldiers took me aside for my blinding. All had fought with me. They shackled me and sent me on the long journey. There was the great forest, the veldt, the storm wall, and the River Nigh. Then I came to a new primacy. I had no friends. Most sentients were afraid of me, all except you."

Akay-Wat twisted on her pallet, but remained silent.

"On my journey," Mo Ti said in his soft voice, "I saw all the wonders." After a pause, he continued, "I am not blind."

Sydney considered this stunning pronouncement. "But you have to be. Everyone would know."

His voice went to a whisper. "Mo Ti hides thoughts."

"Touch my hand." Sydney stretched her arm out to the side. She felt his large hand grasp hers with assurance. Then she believed him, partly from this demonstration, and partly from a conviction that he wouldn't lie to her. "Your fellow soldiers never carried out the blinding."

"They did not. So I learned to pretend."

"How?" she asked. But Mo Ti didn't answer. Perhaps by his very bulk he could shield his true self. Clearly Mo Ti was smarter than he acted, perhaps smarter than them all.

As Sydney struggled to absorb this news, Mo Ti's singsong voice came to her: "I can take this Hirrin's leg," he said. "I did many surgeries in the Long War."

This was an even more alarming thought. "If you fix her leg, they'll know you can see." Then they would perform the blinding that should have been done long ago.

"Mo Ti must remove her leg, or she'll die, and badly."

He was asking her advice, and maybe her permission. Sydney wrestled with how to answer. It was Akay-Wat's life. But it was Mo Ti's sight at stake—and she'd be complicit in his lies.

Mo Ti said, "We could say that Riod was present, and we did it through his sight."

"Would they believe it?" she asked.

"Friends would believe. Not enemies."

She had spent little time making friends, and she would have one fewer if Akay-Wat died. "What shall we do, Mo Ti?"

After a long pause he answered, "How much does Riod love you?"

He had just told her he would risk it, if Riod agreed. She was startled by his courage. Needing a moment to think, she walked outside, inhaling the fresh air, her thoughts crowded with Mo Ti's revelation.

Mo Ti watched her go. Next to him, Akay-Wat rolled her head from side to side as she fought the infection. The smell of putrefaction filled the room.

So then, young mistress, Mo Ti thought. Now we'll see what stuff you're made of.

He rose to stretch his legs, knowing that a long period of crouching and bending lay ahead of him if he was to save the leg below the knee. If he could, then the Hirrin might walk again. Otherwise, best to use the knife on her neck, not her leg.

Akay-Wat, he thought, you stupid beku. The old dragon wouldn't want me taking risks for a witless Hirrin. And yet. Akay-Wat showed courage confronting her mount, and no act of courage deserves a death as bad as this one.

Cixi, you have to trust me now. Who else do you have who will do your bidding here, in the Long Gaze of Fire? How many times did you try to plant one of your own among the Inyx? How many times did your spies fail to achieve banishment to the Inyx, or fail to reach this encampment? Only Mo Ti found a way to Priov's herd. Mo Ti, who waited a thousand days in Ulrud's encampment, and seeing a chance with Riod's renegade attack, seized it. Yes, and now that Mo Ti is here, Mo Ti must decide whether to be blind or not.

Watching the Hirrin toss in her delirium, he considered how the problem with her surgery could be turned to advantage. It would be dangerous, and must have Riod's support. Much depended on Riod, who would one day lead the camp. Also, much depended on the young mistress, and whether she was ready for acts of courage. If she wasn't ready now, maybe she never would be. Soldiers of her same age died at Ahnenhoon every day. She was old enough to prove her worth.

He'd proven his to Cixi at an early age, when the legates brought him before her at the Ascendancy, accused of a treasonous remark. He'd been nothing but a clerk, and an ugly one, reviled and goaded, bitter with the All of his life, and hating the Tarig since birth. He expected a death sentence, standing before Cixi's throne. Then she had sent her attendants from the room.

"Tell me your heart," she said. She was so small, she came up to his belt. But he was afraid of her nevertheless. "If you tell me all the truth, you shall live," she said. "I swear by the bright."

That high pledge convinced him to say what his heart held. All dark things. How he had cringed at his father's devotion to the lords; how he was embittered by his father's lack of advancement despite many thousand days of service; and how he had grieved when his mother, seeing how Mo Ti grew uglier every day, had jumped to her death from the rim of the city. Thereafter his enemies had called him Son of the Falling Stone, and he learned to hate the legates and the fiends they served.

Cixi gave him a new chance. Eventually he learned that he and the old dragon were bound by a hatred of the lords, and that the young girl who languished among the Inyx could be counted on to share this treason. "But hate," Cixi had told him, "is not enough. There must be a worthy desire. That, Mo Ti, is the kingdom raised."

The kingdom the young mistress would raise, if she could be brought to see it.

And now Mo Ti was here to help her. Perhaps because of Akay-Wat, raising the kingdom must come sooner rather than later.

The Hirrin's surgery would cause an uproar. It would shake down the encampment, forcing all to take sides. Then they would know friends from enemies, and the weak from the strong.

Priov was an old beast, and must yield to Riod soon, before mating season. Then they would be set for greater things, once the mistress rode at the front of the herd. Mo Ti had considered hamstringing the old chief himself, but it would be better for Riod to overcome him, if Riod could be inspired to move on Priov before mating season made fighting look fine. The season was still six hundred days off, too long to wait, for Cixi's purposes.

He took his whetstone from his jacket and began sharpening his small knife. It would need to have a good edge for the small work. For the large, the mistress must find him a saw.

Outside, the yard was empty except for Riod. In the sky, the evening's deep pewter folds coiled overhead. Riod trotted up to Sydney, eager for comfort as Akay-Wat neared death. Sydney hugged his neck and let her thoughts pour into him.

As Riod absorbed Mo Ti's secret, his distress flooded back to his rider, completing a loop of shared emotion.

"Beloved," she whispered to him. "Why should Mo Ti be blind? To be blind makes us need you. So it isn't a free bond, after all."

You are free, Riod asserted. *Choose another mount. Then know, you are free.*

He couldn't help it. He wanted to see the world for her, to strengthen the emotional ties between them. What was the custom, she wondered, for the species the Inyx were copied from? In that other world, who rode the Inyx? She liked to think that they were not blind.

At this moment she didn't want to challenge Riod's ideas, but the decision about Akay-Wat couldn't wait.

"I'll help Mo Ti save Akay-Wat's leg," she told Riod. "And then I'll fight to protect Mo Ti."

He paced away, distraught. Sydney let him consider. Riod had to think who he was, and what he was willing to die for. She had never guessed free bond would come to violence and choosing sides. But since it had, she needed Riod with her.

When at last he trotted back to her, she leaned against his flank, feeling his warmth and the beat of his strong heart. He whispered into her mind: *I will fight for Sydney, who fights for Mo Ti.*

It was settled, then. Perhaps it had been settled from the day she and Riod pledged a free bond. Hadn't she said, *I'd rather die than live like this?*

"Send for Distanir," she told Riod. "Ask him if he'll stand with us, or if we need a new mount for Mo Ti." Riod hesitated, nervous. But finally he acquiesced, moving off to find Distanir.

Late into the ebb, with Sydney assisting, Mo Ti performed the surgery that removed Akay-Wat's leg. Adikar had left medicinals behind, but refused to be further associated with the whole affair.

Now, the surgery over, Akay-Wat lay sleeping under heavy sedation. By her side sat Sydney and Mo Ti. The door lay wide open, clearing the sick room of vapors and closeted heat. The Hirrin would live, Mo Ti predicted. But Sydney wasn't sure how a Hirrin could walk or ride with a false leg.

They sat in silence for a time. Sydney felt a little self-conscious that Mo Ti could see her, and she raked her hair back with her hands, trying to arrange it.

At this, Mo Ti laughed, but it was a warm sound, not mocking. He was relaxed, and his assured manner calmed her.

"You aren't worried, Mo Ti?"

"No, mistress. Only decisions are hard. Now we see what comes to us." Akay-Wat bleated softly and her eyes fluttered open, but without consciousness. He continued, "It's good to stand for something, Mo Ti thinks."

He was right. It did feel good. "We can never be free if we're blind," she said.

But Mo Ti's next words disturbed her: in his deceptively soft voice, he said, "You think too small."

She sat up, stung by the criticism. "You think it's small, to defy Inyx custom?"

He turned to the water bucket and ladled a large dipper full to his lips, gulping it down. "Yes, vastly small."

"Then why," she blurted in irritation, "are we doing this?"

She heard him shift positions, leaning across Akay-Wat's prone form. "Who is your enemy, mistress?"

"Priov," she answered. Then added: "Feng. The Laroos." When silence greeted these answers, she murmured, "The mantis lords."

"Yes, the lords," Mo Ti said in that voice that was no match for either his bulk or his brains. "Because of their cruel hands."

Sydney paused. She'd never told anyone about how Hadenth had personally taken her sight. "How do you know about cruel hands?"

"That's a common story. Every grunt has heard it."

It stung to think her humiliation was a common story. If it *was* common. "Did someone send you here, Mo Ti?"

For a moment she hoped that he might be a messenger from Cixi . . . but now Mo Ti crushed that hope: "Mo Ti is alone," he said, "but I will help you to overcome your enemy."

Overcome? That was not a word that made sense, when it came to the mantis lords. But here in this tiny cabin, she strained forward to hear more. She was drawn to Mo Ti, his steady heart and mind, and his vision. It was as though she stood on his broad shoulders, and could see across a far-flung land.

"Tell me how, Mo Ti."

"Ah, mistress. It begins with the Inyx, and depends on the Inyx."

"Tell me how," she whispered, her nerves on fire.

And that ebb they watched over Akay-Wat, and talked, as Mo Ti's voice droned on, soft and thrilling.

CHAPTER TWENTY

The icons of service are the sole privilege of the officers of the great Magisterium. Only these high servants may invest their garments and offices with the emblematic devices. This iconography is a study in itself, with meanings rooted in the million days. Just as a clerk wears the icon of the beku, the subprefect wears the river walker, and the wise will know why. Just as the steward adorns herself with the golden carp, the legate must have the great spinner, nor is this a mystery to the iconographer, or the perceptive.

—from *The Book of Ascendant Joys*

MIN FE GLANCED THROUGH HIS SCROLL, muttering, "Inyx, Inyx." He shook his bald head, turning pages. "The sway is barely noted in the codex." He slurped from his cup of oba, not having offered his guest similar refreshment.

After five days of waiting for an interview with Cixi, Quinn had progressed only to the level of Sublegate Min Fe. Perhaps he should feel lucky; the suppliant in the cell next to him had been waiting *five hundred days* for her matter to be heard by a legate.

Quinn breathed deeply and kept his face passive. He was enveloped in an alien maze of bureaucracy. Though it surpassed even Minerva's corporate tangle, he had to conform. He was, astonishingly, on the threshold of his old prison. He had come so far—across the veil, as Bei had said. Now every move might trigger disaster: if someone recognized him, if the Tarig named Oventroe turned on him.

Even Min Fe, though a minor legate, could thwart him. Cho had told him when they first arrived that if Dai Shen was assigned to Min Fe, as seemed likely, his mission could falter. "One might wish that you could go directly to Shi Zu," Cho had said. "Of course, it isn't possible to bypass Min Fe. No one bypasses anything." He nodded with a bleak wisdom. "It keeps the order of things."

Quinn hadn't seen Cho since that first day, when he'd helped carry the man's trunks to his office, in the close warren of stewards. Here, it came out that Cho was not a full steward, but an understeward, a post he'd held for most of his life.

Now, Quinn stood before Min Fe, and his annoyance must have been obvious, for the legate said, "You are impatient, I see." He removed his spectacles—the first that Quinn had seen in this world—and rubbed his eyes. "You are a warrior of the Long War, the Battle of Ahnenhoon, and so forth. Used to impetuous decisions. A minor son of the great Yulin, a man with many sons, perhaps some of them spoiled?" He waved away the response that Quinn was about to make. "Be that as it might be, you have been waiting, as you say, *five days*, and now wish to see the high prefect."

"Yes."

"No doubt. But do you know how many people wish to see the high prefect?" He raised his eyebrow, or, rather, the ridge where one of his brows would have been if he'd had any. "Do you know how many suppliants bide their time in the Magisterium with just your same goal? How many, like you, have clarities to propose for the refinement of the Radiant Path? The answer to this interesting question is two thousand one hundred and thirty-one. At last count. You can therefore imagine that it is necessary to prepare briefs and commentaries so that the prefect's most valuable time is preserved." He pointed to a spot on the scroll. "Now here is a context for chain of command. However, it is not for armed combat, but for the inspection of vegetable products transported across sways. So it will not suit."

Quinn summoned the most reasonable comment he could manage. "I have confidence that the sublegate is skilled in overcoming technical obstacles."

"Technical obstacles," Min Fe repeated, his face tightening.

"Yes."

"Not to diminish their importance?"

"Not to let them defeat you." Quinn felt the room pressing close around him, the lines of power swooping in from all sides, like a spider's web. The words of Ghoris the navitar haunted him.

Min Fe squinted at him as though trying to decide whether Quinn was impertinent or not. "Still," he began, "there are approvals needed at each stage, not the least of which is the consent of Consul Shi Zu, which will not be in order until I have fully considered your matter and, if I find it worthy, have passed it along to the full legate himself, in a form of my choosing." The channels of power were precise: above Min Fe's position of sublegate were full legates, preconsuls, consuls, and subprefects, before reaching the position of high prefect. Min Fe licked his lips, still poring over the codex on vegetables.

Through the myriad vows, bonds, and clarities, the legates controlled all matters of law and civil function. Those who chose the life of the Magisterium made themselves indispensable to the Tarig. Through this means they participated in the Tarig's power—a pale copy of that power, Quinn thought, recalling Anzi's summation of her people. He missed her at his side, and had become more cautious without her to provide cover for him. But she'd said that he was ready. He thought so, too. He had to be.

As Min Fe inspected his document, Quinn looked around the cell. Despite Min Fe's minor function, he did have a window office. The shaft leading to the outside edge of the Magisterium was some fifteen hundred feet long, but if one stood in front of it, one had a postage-stamp view of the city, a perpetual scene of a stained cascade of roofs.

The city was the spacious realm of the Tarig, and beneath it clustered the warrens of the bureaucracy: the Magisterium. The Magisterium was shaped like a bowl, one filled with labyrinthine levels and corridors. The center of the bowl was cut away, so that views from the Magisterium could provide glimpses of the great city. Evidently, the Tarig liked their handiwork to be admired. But other views from the Magisterium were just as fine, displaying the circular heartland, the Sea of Arising, and, far in the distance, the storm walls on every side.

Min Fe's voice broke into his thoughts. "That will do for today." Min Fe rose to his feet in dismissal.

"Do?" Quinn was being dismissed. "But what progress, sublegate?"

Min Fe answered with clipped precision: "Progress will be made when we discern where in pandect the proposal might fit. If we simply attach it like a bauble on an offering tray, nothing is in order in the body of the law. Progress will be made when we translate your clarity into the language of the law, which is a rhetoric without ambiguity, that flows with the rhythms of systematic referential language." His voice had risen through this recitation, and his eyes looked large and angry in the watery lenses of his glasses. "I don't expect that you can grasp this, being a man of weapons."

Quinn said, "Know that I must account to Master Yulin, and soon."

Min Fe's voice grew eerily soft. "Soon? Do you say that I am lagging?"

Quinn knew he should defer, but it went against the grain. "Not lagging. But not hurrying, either."

A smile poked at one side of the sublegate's mouth. "It will be necessary to take your suggestion under close consideration. As to *hurrying*."

Min Fe closed the computational scroll, and he held it like a wand until the redstone budded out at the bottom. Then he placed the redstone on a tray behind him, in one of a thousand tiny dimples. As he turned to do this, Quinn saw, embroidered on the back of the sublegate's vest, the image of a spinner, the legless spider bred to produce the great silks of the Chalin. From the squat creature's mouth came a rainbow of metallic threads.

Min Fe turned back to him, saying, "Dismissed, Dai Shen, minor son of Master Yulin."

Quinn bowed and left, shutting the legate's door behind him, crumpling his paper summons in his hand. Here was a man who'd made a career out of making sure that little happened at all, much less quickly.

Standing before him in the corridor was the sentient who bunked next door to him. Braharíar was a Jout, and a large one, with a thickset body and stubby legs. The overlapping petals of her hide rippled in pleasure at seeing him. Noting the crumpled summons, the Jout said, "What was the legate's humor?"

"Poor."

The Jout sighed. "I have no summons, but I hoped—"

"To drop in on him?"

Braharíar looked deflated. "Futile?"

"Perhaps today. I think I ruined his mood."

"Ah."

Quinn needed to walk, to release tension. At his side the Jout shuffled as Quinn paced down the corridor. They turned into a main corridor, their boots thudding on a floor with the look of hammered copper. The ceiling threw a perpetual light on the Magisterium, a pale bronze fire. Sometimes the floors blurred as an unknown process cleaned specks of dirt. Although this edifice was thousands of years old, it appeared newly minted.

"This tertiary level is nicer than the level of our quarters," the Jout said, referring to the third level where they walked. "The legates have much luxury." Each level was wider and more gracious than the one under it. Quinn was eager to see the upper levels—to see Cixi and Lord Oventroe. Oventroe hadn't responded to him yet. Thus, more waiting.

Walking in silence, Quinn and Brahariar finally entered a great hall. Here, tall windows cut the bright into rectangles that fell on the floor like molten ingots. A staircase led to a mezzanine where legates and lesser functionaries talked in clumps or viewed the city. He and Brahariar leaned on the deep reveal of a window, gazing on the bright city. A habitation of bronze and silver, it glinted under the bright. Light and shadow sculpted the Tarig city as spires flushed in the day's glare and threw down deep shadows at their roots.

They were looking up at the city from its basement, as it were. Most of the views in the Magisterium faced outward into the sky from the bottom of the bowl-like construct. But in some places the Magisterium plucked a better view, where the metropolis's wells and terraces plunged down in the center, opening views to the city's interior.

Quinn had found that this view was familiar: the superstructure, the great hill containing the five palaces of the high lords. Clinging like encrusted jewels to the palatine hill were the habitations of lesser Tarig. On wide verandas minor lords could be seen, their skin glinting bronze. Among themselves the Tarig were solitary, not often gathering socially, yet desiring social contact with other sentients. Sentients like Quinn, for example. And had he desired that contact too?

Quinn stretched out his hand, placing it against the invisible barrier that served for window glazing. He wanted to walk in that city, and knew he couldn't. He had listened to Anzi's cautions for so long that she seemed with him still. *Do not put yourself in their path.* Except one Tarig whom he would see in secret. He had that hope, as remote as it might be. In pursuit of that hope, he had sat several days in a row at a small pool in a remote outdoor garden of the Magisterium. Into this pool he had placed Bei's redstone, while he pretended to feed the carp that swam the interconnected canals. After a few days, a silver carp with an orange back took the redstone in its mouth. He'd watched it as it swam away, thrilled to have given the proper signal. *Not all carp are carp*, Bei had said.

Brahariar turned her luminous green eyes on Quinn. "You have a mission of importance, to see Min Fe so quickly."

Quinn couldn't tell whether she was resentful, but the Jout seemed more wistful than anything. "It's a matter my master thought important. Political things that I hardly understand. And you, Brahariar?"

The Jout's eyes clouded. "A matter of grief, not politics." She turned away, stopping the conversation for a long while as she stared at the view of the city. A commotion nearby signaled the approach of a personage. Stewards and legates began bowing as, presently, four large Chalin clerks appeared bearing a sling. Reclining in it was a Gond wearing a bright jacket. Her horns were painted silver.

Brahariar bowed deeply, murmuring to Quinn, "Preconsul GolMard."

Rising from his own bow, Quinn said, "I never knew Gonds rose so high." He had the distinct impression that most Chalin, at least, hated Gonds.

Brahariar looked startled, intoning, "No sentient being is beyond hope."

Ah yes, Quinn thought, the Radiant Path of the colossal meritocracy. But he prayed that his petition would never require approval from a Gond. He had enough trouble from the likes of Min Fe.

"How does one get to the second level?" Quinn asked.

The Jout shot him a sideways glance. "The long way or the quick way?"

"The quick way."

"I have been here so long I know the back ways. But they are not as nice."

Nor were they. It seemed that the glories of the Magisterium fell short when the Chalin remodeled the walls for their own purposes. Between walls threaded a passageway just large enough for a Jout to walk through.

"For spying," the Jout said, as though disappointed that such things went on.

"Tarig spying or legate spying?" Quinn asked as he followed her.

The Jout's voice came in a whisper as she led the way. "Why would the Tarig need such? No, it is the legates that contend with each other, vying for advantage."

They climbed a ladder and emerged into a room full of humming machinery of unknown purpose.

"Do the Tarig know of these spy routes?"

Brahariar's skin fluttered in a manner that Quinn recalled signified amusement. "Certainly. If the legates wish to play this game, the Tarig are pleased to allow it. Chalin are pampered, you see." *And not Jout*, was left unsaid. "I will go back now. Perhaps my summons will be waiting for me." She returned by the same route, a being in need of shortcuts, but doomed to follow the rules.

The second level was by far more ornate than below. Quinn passed through arching galleries and narrow wings burning with light on both sides. Eventually, by asking again and again, he came to the domain of the consul Shi Zu. The great door was unlocked.

Entering the empty quarters, he approached the carved desk of the consul. Finding an empty scroll, he activated it and wrote: "Here is a matter Min Fe could not bear for you to see." Next to the scroll, he placed a redstone, one of several copies of the Inyx clarity.

Just as he turned away, he caught sight of an activated scroll left open on an ornate side table. A face stared out at him, and for a moment he thought it might be Shi Zu. But the face, when he looked again, was his own. He approached the scroll, and as he did so, it began streaming a segment that showed him and Anzi on the pier below. He saw himself bend down to place something in the water. Then Anzi was pulling him away to the line of travelers, where she argued with the gatekeeper. Then the segment began again.

To his dismay, he had already attracted their attention.

CHAPTER TWENTY-ONE

Among the gracious lords of the Bright Realm are the high lords over all, masters of heaven:

The Exalted Lord Nehoov.
The Sheltering Lord Hadenth.
The Supreme Lady Chiron.
The Noble Lord Inweer.
The Masterful Lord (the Sleeping One) Lord Ghinamid.

—from *The Book of Ascendant Joys*

CIXI ALLOWED HERSELF TO BE TAKEN to a *place of interest* by the legate Zai Gan. It was an endless source of amusement, watching her legates strive with each other. The high prefect indulged Zai Gan because she wished to give him the impression that she favored him, which she did not.

Interrupting their preparations for an outing into the city, Zai Gan had persuaded her to come on a minor detour. She fought to hide her anxiety, to give no hint to Zai Gan that she would far rather be on her way into the city, where her fate might be decided.

Zai Gan towered over her. Well, most Chalin did, despite her habit of wearing stacked shoes. The legate also possessed an ample circumference, but unlike his brother Yulin, whose girth was all muscle, Zai Gan was soft. She didn't make the mistake of thinking him soft of purpose. His purpose had ever been to supplant Master Yulin, and Cixi had been playing off this ambition for so many days it began to bore her.

They exited the second level of the Magisterium onto a small deck, where her view of the sea was far and clear. She bowed for a moment, acknowledging the vast empire of the lords. May they fry in the bright, she thought.

She and Zai Gan stood on a balcony, one of hundreds of viewing platforms, ramps, and balconies hugging the city's underbelly. Since the underside of the city was shaped like a bowl, most sentients thought that when they stood outside on the lower levels, they were not observable from above, but this wasn't so. At Zai Gan's command, the floor realigned itself, and Cixi could see through to the level underneath.

Below her stood a well-built Chalin man, looking over the edge. Was he going to jump? She hoped Zai Gan hadn't brought her here to observe a forbidden suicide.

"It is Dai Shen, Your Brilliance. He comes here, day after day."

"And?" He should come to the point. There had better be a point.

"It's not normal to stare at the sea. What is he looking for?"

"That, Legate, would be your job to discover." Dai Shen, Dai Shen—she was tired of Zai Gan's entreaties about this messenger. Yes, he had suddenly appeared as Yulin's long-absent son. Yes, he had suddenly been sent on an important mission to the city. Many things happened suddenly. All that *sudden* meant was that your intelligence outlets had failed you.

Zai Gan said, "He stares. Suspiciously stares."

"Like one with a head injury?"

Zai Gan puffed out his lower lip. "Then why was he not in the garden when Lord Echnon sought him? And why has my gardener disappeared?"

Cixi snorted. Yulin had had the spy killed, of course. She could accuse the fat master of the sway, but best not to accuse without proof. And she had some sympathy for Yulin's execution of a member of his very own household who would tell tales. Even so, Cixi would have made an issue of this murder if the tales the gardener had told had been worth hearing. Unfortunately, they weren't.

Desperately wishing to be on her way, she fixed Zai Gan with a look that said, *One's invaluable time has been wasted by this stinking beku.* Cixi had made an art form of facial expressions, and her minions had composed treatises on the subject.

But Zai Gan would not be hurried. "Dai Shen's petition, Your Brilliance. Deny it. If he succeeds with this Inyx matter, it strengthens Yulin and delays my inheritance." The man was desperate for Dai Shen's mission to fail. A few days ago he had barred Dai Shen's companion, Ji Anzi, from ascending.

He spoke presumptuously. But she forced herself to indulge him, for the sake of her larger plans—oh, far larger than Zai Gan could hope to grasp. "But," she said, "if Yulin's proposal is carried out and fails, you can set up your throne in his sway. Indeed, Yulin's idea might fail in a spectacular manner. Inyx beasts as officers of battle! Absurd."

The legate's eyes peered out at her like an animal trapped in a fleshy cage. "Such a failure could take a thousand days to manifest."

"Mmm," Cixi murmured, a sound she quite liked as it could be interpreted by the listener as favorable or not, and sometimes, as now, she chose to be ambiguous.

She looked down at the young man standing at the edge of the rim. Indeed, he looked oddly fixated. And something else about him: his stature, the way he stood, reminded her of someone.

Meanwhile, standing below the two observers, Quinn was counting the days he'd been here. A total of eight. Three days since his unsatisfactory encounter with Min Fe, and one day since he had succeeded in meeting the consul Shi Zu. The very fact that they had met and no Tarig had swooped down on him led Quinn to believe that surveillance was customary, that he had not been singled out. Still, he had not escaped notice, as Bei had strongly advised him to do.

Yet his strategy to go over Min Fe's head direct to his superior had worked. To Quinn's great good fortune, Shi Zu despised Min Fe. With one exception, the meeting had gone well, and Quinn needed to think hard about that exception. But for the moment, he was distracted by the view of the sea far below.

Thirty thousand feet below, the Sea of Arising lay in a glittering platinum sheet. Although he could see only a wedge of the ocean at the moment, Quinn knew it was circular, and a million miles in circumference.

He had been coming here over the last few days because the sight had been steadily restoring his memory.

A field barrier stilled the winds, replacing the need for a railing. The unobstructed view fell away, drawing his eyes to the hammered sea, crawling with wisps of exotic clouds. The walkway was only a yard wide. It was possible to fall, but it would take a push. One could fall for five minutes. With a 360-degree view, it would be the supreme free fall. However, rather than being struck by the height, Quinn was keenly aware—as he had always been—of the feeling of centrality. Of being in the center of a radial universe: the center of the bright, the heartland, and the power. This was the memory that had visited him again and again in the Rose. As he sank into these memories, he thought of how, in some sways, even thinking was dangerous. He wondered if, for Sydney, the Inyx ability to decode thoughts was a particular misery. It would be for him, and he thought her very much like her father.

In the far distance, the squat storm walls surrounded the sea like a hurricane circling the eye of the storm. Overhead, the bright looked like a hammered plate of light resting on distant blue legs. The storm walls were broken in his view by two small gaps where the visible primacies plunged outward from their source. Though he knew that he should not be able to see all the way to the storm walls, a miragelike bending of light brought the walls closer.

He remembered this. Quinn had lived there, as he had been told, as he now recalled. He remembered Bei pouring steaming oba from a pot and discussing medieval Earth history. Quinn's suite of rooms looked onto a courtyard. A remarkable tapestry adorned one wall of his room. There were no locks on the doors.

He remembered the Lady Chiron's kindness when his sorrow had been a million miles in circumference. When Hadenth goaded Quinn, she stood nearby, forbidding the lord. And that protection—for no one could protect against a high lord other than another—brought Quinn's gratitude, and later, that retreat into physical solace, an act that now repulsed him.

They lay on a shining bed, lit from above. Lit from a sky window, releasing the bright over their naked bodies. As he moved, she matched him, angle for angle, curve for curve, keeping contact along the lengths of their bodies, although she was taller than he. She was supple, curious, inexhaustible. He had vowed to stay away from her, and had succeeded for a long while. But eventually, he went to her suite. *She rushed to meet him. She could not fully accept him into her, because the divide between her legs was small. Over time this became irrelevant.*

He understood why it had happened. There was the loneliness, the years of separation from Johanna. But he would give anything for it not to have happened while Johanna languished at Ahnenhoon.

It gnawed at him. To so completely succumb to the Tarig. Was it the power that he had relished? He couldn't see himself as that man. Remembering the navitar's prophecies, he wondered if his betrayals had set in motion some profound wheel of retribution.

He turned from the maze of these thoughts. Tomorrow he would come back and confront them again. Until Shi Zu arranged a summons from Cixi.

Shi Zu was pleasant but dangerous. He affected elaborate dress, including brocaded trousers and a golden jacket. The symbol embroidered on the back of his garment was that of a sky chain, bright insects linked and floating in the sky, a configuration he had seen before. This foppish consul was amused by Quinn's bypass of Min Fe. Then it occurred to the consul that, given the importance of a matter altering military protocol, perhaps a person of high standing should present Yulin's clarity to the Inyx sway. Quite possibly that functionary should be Shi Zu himself. Quinn hoped his arguments against this were persuasive.

He looked around him, thinking that he might even now be observed. If so, it wouldn't hurt to show his heartchime—that bauble of the devoted, that told the wearer how close they were to the beloved Ascendancy. He brought forth the heartchime and held it to his ear, listening to the high tone that was the Ascendancy's pitch. He wondered where Anzi was, and hoped she was safe.

Heading down the ramp to return to the inner Magisterium, deep in thought, he made his way into the third level. A familiar voice caught him off guard.

"Your Excellency," Cho said, bowing before him in the junction of a small corridor with a wide one.

"Steward Cho," Quinn replied, matching the bow.

This brought a look of consternation and a yet lower bow. "Please, Excellency, I'm an understeward." Rising, he said, "Seeing the sights, are you? Everyone sees the sights on their first visit." He looked past Quinn to a doorway to an outer deck. "There are better views. Seating areas, and so forth."

"You must know them all, my friend. Did you deliver your trunks to the legate Min Fe?"

Cho's face fell only a little. "A pressing weight of duty has not allowed him to view the documents. So far." Sidling closer and lowering his voice, Cho said, "We've heard that Min Fe has suffered a rebuke from the consul Shi Zu."

Quinn stifled a smile. "Has he? Perhaps it's long overdue."

Cho looked startled. "An alarming thought, Excellency."

"Please, Cho, Dai Shen will do."

Cho bobbed, agreeing, and they began to walk together. Hearing of Shi Zu's notion to usurp Dai Shen's mission and travel to the Inyx sway himself, Cho looked worried. Then, hearing that Quinn had tried to talk Shi Zu out of such a notion, Cho said, "Forgive me, Excellency—Dai Shen—but you may be in jeopardy of a small misstep in protocol."

"Or a rather large stumble?" Quinn could not quite recall the Chalin equivalent of *bull in a china shop*, though he was sure there was one.

"No, no stumbling, none whatsoever, but if I may suggest . . ." He waited for a nod from His Excellency. Receiving it, he went on, "You must let him win, of course."

They came upon a great atrium. Arising from one end was a narrow but ornate staircase that twisted at intervals to disappear into the second level. Leading the way upward, Cho continued, "If I may offer a small idea, let him have the mission without protest."

That wasn't damn likely. "My father would think me a failure to give my duty to another."

A rustle from above them signaled that someone was descending the stairs. Quinn looked up. Just turning onto the next landing came a grandly dressed Chalin woman attended by ladies wearing heavily embroidered silks. Quinn and Cho bowed deeply as the entourage passed, Cho murmuring, "Subprefect Mei Ing, and glorious consuls." Switching quickly from unctuous to practical, he returned to his subject: "By letting him win, you will win, Dai Shen, do you see?"

Quinn turned to watch the ladies descend, especially the one with the river walker emblazoned on her tunic. Perhaps if the high prefect wouldn't see him, the plain prefect might.

Cho continued, "Permit me; it wouldn't be seemly to disagree with the consul that he is the most fit to handle the matter. But once you agree with his superior judgment, he will abandon the plan. He would never leave the Ascendancy, Dai Shen. He'd lose his place in line."

Quinn glanced at the steward, thinking that Cho the hapless might in fact be quite the master at navigating the bureaucracy.

"I haven't presumed too far?" Cho asked, cutting his eyes at Quinn.

"No, it's very valuable advice. I'm not a subtle man." He shrugged. "A soldier."

Cho stuttered. "But I'm subtle, you think?"

"Yes, Understeward Cho should advise all newcomers here. It could be a side business. There's a Jout I know who could use some help."

Cho hardly knew how to respond to this half-jest, but his steps came more lively, and he pointed out the sights, most of them actually new to Quinn, although not all.

They had come to the highest level of the Magisterium by means of the asymmetrical staircase, into a narrow passage with a vaulted ceiling. As they started down this hall, Quinn thought he knew where Cho was leading him. It was to the chamber of Lord Ghinamid.

"Most newcomers want to see the Sleeping Lord," Cho said.

They passed through tall galleries lit by windows and crowded with prosperous-looking legates, including a few Hirrin sentients. Then, crossing out of the Magisterium, they came under the sky for a moment into a sunken garden, then climbed curved stairs and came into the city above. They were in the city, where he should not be seen. Not planned—but not unwelcome, either.

At the head of the stairs and through an outdoor gallery, they came at last to the open doors of the Sleeping Lord's chamber.

The cavernous room was filled with an orange light from burnished walls that looked to be quilted in giant squares of etched metal. The chamber was empty except for two features: on three sides of the room a raised gallery was supported by columns; below the gallery and in the center of the room was a raised platform. From the gallery, a scattering of sentients viewed the Sleeping Lord's resting place.

As he had lain for two million days, Lord Ghinamid rested on the raised platform on a black bed of exotic matter, never aging. Quinn didn't expect that the Masterful Lord would look any different than he had the last time Quinn had seen him, nor did he.

Approaching the platform, they bowed, then gazed up at the Tarig lord. The face, long and narrow like all the Tarig, looked carved but alive, and harder than most. There was that quality to Tarig skin that was both metallic and supple. Ghinamid's form was clothed in a black chitinous-looking robe. The eyes were covered by two black, oblong stones that looked like they might topple off if the lord came into REM sleep.

"Asleep," Cho said. "What must he dream of?"

"Home," Quinn replied, remembering that he had once fled into sleep himself from sheer homesickness.

They had lowered their voices, as though not to disturb the sleeper. Cho asked, "You know the stories, then?"

"Some." He well remembered the tale of Lord Ghinamid, who couldn't bear his separation from his original home in the Heart. He had been among the first great lords to rule the Entire, and therefore was impossibly old.

"Of course, your pardon. You are of Yulin's household, an educated man, naturally."

Quinn looked around the hall. It was now deserted. Both the mezzanine and the hall were empty except for the two of them.

And a lord, on the perimeter.

A Tarig stood at a doorway, watching them. Cho was now as still as a mouse in an owl's gaze.

Quinn turned to leave, and Cho fell in step with him. From behind, he heard the clicking of the Tarig's feet approaching.

A voice, wasted, deep, and familiar said, "He dreams, do you say?"

It was a mistake to pretend the lord hadn't spoken to them. Even before he turned to face the Tarig, Quinn remembered the main way to tell one Tarig from another. By voice.

He turned to face Lord Hadenth, and in that moment it seemed that time looped back, and that he had never left this place.

He had forgotten what the lord had said.

"Dreams?" Lord Hadenth repeated.

Recovering his wits, Quinn answered, "We wonder if the great one dreams. We are ignorant, Bright Lord."

Cho was bowing so low Quinn thought he might topple.

In a terrible moment, Quinn declined to bow. He knew what he should do, and couldn't.

Lord Hadenth had reached the dais and stood there, resting a bare muscled arm on what Quinn had always considered *the bier*. Hadenth wore a sleeveless long tunic over a straight skirt, slit to the knees for easy movement. Over the tunic was a vest of woven platinum thread. At his neck he wore a collar of twisted metal. Quinn had always thought of it as a dog collar. He had learned how to hate at the feet of this creature. Fearing that it showed, he breathed deeply to quiet himself.

Hadenth looked at Cho. "We do not know you."

Cho bowed. "Bright Lord, Steward Cho of the fourth level, of the Hanwin wielding of the house of Lu. Bright Lord."

"Ah, the understeward." Hadenth flicked his gaze at Quinn. "You, we know."

The three words cut at him, stopped his breath. He would not be captured; he had set his mind to that, a million miles ago.

"Bright Lord?"

The Tarig hadn't moved, and said casually enough, "Watching, watching." He reached up to touch Lord Ghinamid's feet. "For eight days, watching, on the rim. And for what? What approaches, hnnn?"

So the legates were not the only ones who spied—but to have Hadenth take notice, that cooled his heart.

"The view, High Lord. A fearful view, and beautiful."

Hadenth had now turned his full attention to Ghinamid's feet, which were at eye level for him. He petted the feet, as though meditating with what was left of his mind. The smell of overbearing sweetness came to Quinn's sensitive mouth.

From beside Quinn, Cho made a sound like a strangled whistle. But he was only attempting to swallow. No doubt Cho was used to Tarig; but he may never have been in the presence of one of the five high lords.

Hadenth's voice, although deep like all Tarig voices, had a shredded quality, as though he had been shouting too long. "Who watches from the rim?"

"Bright Lord, by your sufferance, Dai Shen, soldier of Ahnenhoon and smallest son of Master Yulin of the great sway."

Quinn looked closely at Hadenth for scars. The blow he had delivered was crushing, almost killing him. But why should any Tarig keep scars? He felt a keen disappointment.

Hadenth said, "From Ahnenhoon to the heartland. Such a long way. And not getting lost, either. Hnnn. Without companions all the while, wearing a chime?" He approached swiftly, but Quinn held his place, and then found himself an arm's length from Hadenth, the lord who had blinded Sydney. And told her father about it in excruciating detail.

Extruding a three-inch nail, Hadenth reached toward Quinn and lifted the chain from around his throat. He drew forth the heartchime. In the Tarig's hand a remarkable sound erupted from the pendant, like a distant scream.

Quinn's eyes met Hadenth's. Now, at this range, would be the test of Bei's surgeries. It seemed impossible that this creature would not remember him, would not see him for who he was. But the Tarig did not attend to faces.

The lord dropped the chime and pointed to Cho. "Is this not a companion, and traveler?"

Cho visibly flinched, and opened his mouth to answer. Then, thinking better of it, closed his mouth.

The lord shouted at him, "Speak, Steward!"

Cho gargled something. Then, beginning again, he said, "Traveled. Yes. Bright Lord. On the River Nigh, by your leave and gracious permission for the legate Min Fe, the lowliest matters, of course. A mere understeward."

Lowering his voice, Hadenth said, "Enough speaking." He turned and walked slowly back to the bier. Suddenly he spun around and, flicking his hand, indicated that they were to follow him.

Quinn did so, putting a hand in the small of Cho's back to steady him.

At the bier, Hadenth once more took up a rhythmic stroking of Ghinamid's shod feet as his black gaze lit on Quinn again. "Fighter of Ahnenhoon, a pleasant little title. Wounds? Any?"

"Small wounds, Lord." But lasting ones, he thought. And in the next thought, Anzi's words came to him: *Do not, do not risk . . .*

Anzi wanted him to put the past behind. But for Quinn the hope still lingered: father, mother, and daughter together once more. Being in this city, it still seemed possible. But seeing Hadenth reminded him that it would never come again.

"Wounds," Hadenth whispered. Perhaps he remembered his own. Those received. Those given.

The lord was weaving from one subject to the next. Perhaps he roamed these halls like an elder with dementia: respected but ignored. With no mechanism of retirement or abdication, the Tarig didn't know how to remove a high lord from power if one became unfit for duty.

"Son of the great sway," Hadenth murmured, gazing at Quinn. "Does Yulin know where the leaks are? Hnnn? How the invaders travel into the realm?"

Invaders. Did the lord sense something amiss? He answered: "Yulin confides little in one such as me, Bright Lord."

"But you are son of Yulin, so you said? Did we mis-hear?"

"No, Lord. I said so."

"Ah, son of Yulin knows what Yulin knows. So, again, does Yulin know how the aggressors slide into the All?"

Aggressors. With relief, Quinn realized that Hadenth was talking about the Paion. He answered, "No, Lord. He does not know. Nor do I."

The lord's gaze was unnaturally steady. The Tarig had no need to blink, a thing Quinn had always hated.

"You speak bravely. Too bravely, for one who stares at views. We do not favor you," Hadenth said.

No, and never had. "Bright Lord, my life in your service."

Hadenth waved this away. "Yes, yes." He picked at the shoe of Ghinamid, muttering to himself. Then he turned to Quinn. "You think yourself brave, to face the Paion?"

"No more than any soldier, Bright Lord."

"Braver still, to face your Lord Hadenth, ah?"

Quinn remained silent, not liking this turn of conversation.

At the lord's next action, Cho gasped. The Tarig sprang up on Ghinamid's platform, crouching like a gargoyle at the foot of the sleeping form. "Hnnn?" His voice had risen higher, louder. Cho was now shaking hard. Hadenth's voice echoed in the room. "You think I cannot kill the invaders at will? You think this lord a coward?"

Quinn guessed that the lord was beyond conversation. He glanced at the Sleeping Lord, half expecting him to wake up in all the commotion, but he slept on.

"Well? Well?" Hadenth rasped.

In a whisper, Cho pleaded, "Answer him, Dai Shen."

"A simple soldier does not presume to judge a high lord."

Hadenth beckoned to Quinn, and Quinn walked closer to the bier.

Still crouching, the lord bent close, his scent coming strong to Quinn's senses. "You do not tremble like the steward." Hadenth flicked a gaze at Cho. "Such poise, for a common son of Yulin."

Quinn needed to mollify him, and was able to bring himself to say: "Bright Lord, I have not the grace to know Ascendancy ways. Being a common son of Yulin."

A line formed on Hadenth's cheek, less a frown than a ceramic crack. "And being common, you gape at our high views. Hnn. The heights alarm you? Yes, admit that the fighter of Ahnenhoon fears the long fall."

Quinn could barely bring himself to speak to Hadenth. His stomach clenched with the effort of it. "It would take a long time to hit the ground. A fearful thing." He thought of pushing the lord. Of seeing the fear on Hadenth's face.

Cho softly cleared his throat, eyes pleading with Quinn.

Hadenth jumped down, landing lightly on his feet. Whatever mental damage he might have suffered, he was still agile. "Perhaps we will have you stand on the rim for our amusement, ah?"

From behind, Cho whispered, "Supreme Lord, we are called to duties, below, in your service, by your leave."

Hadenth swung around to face the steward. "No, not so. We are called to duties. You are not called." He squinted at Cho. "Ah?"

"Yes, pardon, Bright Lord," Cho managed to say.

With that, Lord Hadenth turned and walked away, boots clicking on the floor, striding like an upright insect. He passed through the small door from which he'd first entered. After a few steps, he stopped and turned around.

Returning to the doorway, the Tarig reached out and pushed the door closed.

Quinn watched the door for several moments, unsure whether Hadenth was gone for good. But the door remained shut.

"He's gone," Cho whispered.

"Yes." Quinn wasn't sure if he was glad or disappointed. Hadenth had deteriorated from the old days. Reduced to muttering paranoia and intimidating stewards, he was still capable of higher viciousness, Quinn was certain.

Cho led the way from the chamber. Silently, they emerged onto the steps outside, which led to a plaza where a view of the city spread in one direction and the innards of the Magisterium spread in the other. Still intent on controlling his emotions, Quinn descended and walked across a small courtyard toward the fountain he'd visited before.

The steps sank directly into the pool. He sat on the steps and pulled out a small brick of food, a compressed bar that was his food allowance for the day, and shared it with the carp. The bits of food floated, attracting a pod of fish, but not the orange-backed one.

Cho stood at the head of the stairs mopping his brow with his scarf. His jacket bore the understeward emblem of the lowly white carp. Cho took a step forward, startled. "Dai Shen," he said, "here is a sight."

As Quinn joined him, Cho said, "This is a day of wonders. There is the high prefect herself."

Quinn joined Cho at the head of the stairs and looked where he pointed. Here was the very woman he'd come to see. On so short a woman, her hair looked impossibly tall, and glinted as though lacquered. She held a parasol, and was dressed in bright green edged with orange. At her side was an enormous Chalin man, richly dressed.

"The preconsul Zai Gan," Cho said. "You had known Master Yulin's brother in the great sway?"

"No. I was banished from court."

Cho cut a glance at him. "Indeed? Shocking, Excellency." He frowned, considering something. "That must be why he knows so little of you, and is reduced to asking questions of a steward such as myself."

Quinn covered his alarm. "What sorts of questions?"

"Oh, as to your business here." He looked offended. "I told him nothing, I assure you. As though I know the business of personages!"

Bei had spoken truly when he'd said that the Magisterium was full of spies. Far from passing unnoticed, Quinn's every movement seemed to draw interest. Truly, his best chance was to leave as soon as possible. But, so far, he could not leave.

Cixi hated to be under the bright. She once had had a reputation for never leaving the Magisterium, but she had gradually changed her habits in order to allow just such an outing as this. Once every few days she took a walk, and often, it *was* only walking.

Unaccustomed to walking, Zai Gan was already puffing at her side. But he wouldn't have turned down an offer to be seen with the high prefect. Many eyes were following them, Cixi was sure, though no one dared to approach them without a summons. Around the promenade near the canals her presence was becoming noted, as functionaries bowed, even from a great distance away. She was the center of attention. Given this inescapable fact, it became essential to do her treasons in a most public manner.

Zai Gan did not often accompany her on these little forays. She bestowed the honor of her company on a different functionary each time. Once, to shock her sycophants, she had walked with a clerk. But it was all for one purpose, that out of her many forays, she would hear the thing she longed for in the tower of Ghinamid, in the alcove where she could lose her life.

Her hands felt slick with perspiration, but she didn't dare wipe them on her jacket, lest a hundred pairs of eyes take note. God's beku, but she hated going abroad!

Zai Gan whipped out a fan from his belt. "Are you warm, Your Brilliance?" He fluttered the thing at her face.

She cut him a look: *One more evil exhalation from your mouth, and I will have it stuffed with offal.*

Zai Gan snapped the fan shut and they strolled on.

"Such lovely swimming creatures," Cixi said in her sweetest tone. She had cultivated the impression over these thousands of days that she was fascinated by the fish, though there was not a nonsentient in the All that she could abide. Of course, as the saying went, not all carp were carp.

Zai Gan grunted. "It's not natural to breathe water."

"Whatever the lords decree is natural," Cixi snapped.

He slid a glance at her, always watchful for how far her loyalties went. He knew she spied incessantly, and perhaps he wondered what her purposes were. No. Zai Gan didn't wonder. He could see no farther than master-of-the-sway. He no doubt believed that her machinations were all for who should be promoted in the Magisterium, and who merited advancement in the sways. Someone like Zai Gan could not imagine that Cixi's vision reached farther than his own.

She made a turn toward the great tower. She meant for it to be a natural meander in that direction. On some outings she stopped at the tower, and some outings she didn't. All to make the real visit appear trivial.

Leaving Zai Gan outside the entrance, Cixi entered the tower. Ahead of her were the three hundred stairs. She had only a few moments to do what she must. Once finished, she must climb to the top and appear to be taking in the view from the ramparts. Sentients all over the city—those who had noted that she visited the tower—would expect to see her there.

Cixi took off her elevated shoes, leaving them at the first bend in the stairs, and raced upward.

They were stairs made for giants, and already her thigh muscles ached. The Tarig could ascend them easily; the length of their stride was unnerving. They could cross a room in an instant just by standing and taking a huge stride forward. She shuddered.

Coming to the alcove, she placed her hands inside and pressed the nub that gave her access to the bright. Or that might give access. Here, in the tallest structure on the palatine hill, one was very close indeed to the river of fire. The fiends shaded the city from its fierceness, somehow. And also, somehow, they passed messages through the bright, and not at speeds they allowed their subjects, but *at bright speeds*. Cixi's spies had discovered this long ago. Nor was she surprised to find this so. Of course the bright lords communicated at a distance. Would they have created the Entire any other way?

And where could they send messages or receive messages from? Her investigations had revealed three additional places: the brightships, any axis city, and the River Nigh. Only Tarig commanded the ships; and only Tarig knew how to empower messages at bright speed at the axis cities. But all navitars knew how to send messages from the binds. And whether navitars were loyal or not, now that was a question of great complexity. For one thing, they were deranged.

After a thousand days of subterfuge, Cixi had found a navitar who might send a message. The navitar was one who plied the river in the Long Gaze of Fire. Cixi had both ends covered.

Once all this had been well ordered, Cixi began looking for the message. But so far, her envoys had failed to signify that they had reached her beloved girl. For four thousand days, there had been no word, but she kept faith, returning again and again to the tower.

Oh my dear girl, Cixi thought. Her devotion to the child was an always-burning coal, and the girl had a matching ember in her own heart. So Cixi's messengers had told her. *She loves you still, mistress.* Cixi believed them, because her own heart was that steadfast, and because she had told them that, should they lie, she would pull out their intestines through their navels. Slowly.

Now, kneeling in the alcove, she placed the redstone in the cup, and it disappeared. Nothing, nothing. But these things took time.

There were days in which Cixi felt that Mo Ti was her last hope. Mo Ti was the most intelligent, able, and fearless servant she'd ever had. If he couldn't succeed, she might never in this life have another chance to bring a mentor to the dear girl's side. Had Mo Ti escaped blinding? Even if he hadn't, had he managed to infiltrate Priov's encampment? And if so, had the girl come to trust him?

And then, miraculously, words formed on the wall, a section of stone that for a moment became a screen. Her answer. She stared at the letters forming: *Always to last.*

Always to last . . . Cixi's face flushed hot with shock. Mo Ti had arrived.

There was no further message, nor was there need. Had he failed irrevocably, Mo Ti would have sent, *Dark as rose night.* And if he had not yet surmounted barriers, *Hold up the bright.*

Without completely absorbing this joyful news, Cixi rushed up the stairs, raising her knees high under her robes, straining against the demands of another hundred stairs. Her legs stung with pain, but she yanked her old body up the risers. Up, up, and may God look upon all fiends. Up, up . . .

At the top she leaned against the stones of the rampart, her chest near exploding, her legs melting. Below, Zai Gan kept guard, ready to create a diversion should someone try to enter before he saw her at the top.

By his demeanor below she knew that he'd seen her. No doubt the fat fool must wonder what she was doing all this while. How astounded he would be to know the truth.

Turning to leave, she found a Tarig standing before her.

"Lord, my life," she said.

But it was not a fiend. It was the image of a fiend, captured in the stone walls of the tower. His features looked pockmarked and rumpled in the imperfect screen of the rough wall.

"Ah, Cixi," he said.

By his voice, it was . . . But he must speak again.

"Is that you, Bright Lord? Your likeness in the stone?" She wished she were not barefooted. Perhaps he wouldn't notice.

"Yes, it is our likeness, not our self. Unless we have become ugly in one day?"

Lord Oventroe. Cixi almost collapsed with relief. It was a disaster if he knew what she'd done. But he was the best fiend to encounter here.

"Lord, my life," she repeated, skipping the rest of the benediction, as she dared to do as high prefect.

"Yes. Your life." He watched her with stony eyes, stony face. "Have you ever thought how you would choose to die if a lord uncovered repugnance for you?"

Her heart sank like a stone in a pool. He was going to kill her.

"Yes."

"Now we shall guess. You would die by poison rather than by the slow death." He held up a long-fingered hand. "No, not true. We think this would not be your way. Ah, we have it." He pointed to the rampart, where it was cut low enough to create a viewing port. "Stand near there, Prefect."

"Shall I climb up?"

"Don't be dramatic. What if you please us, and you go down again, down the long stairs? Then there would be scandal from the prefect having stood on the lip of the tower as though despondent." He looked behind him, giving the impression that he was actually there. "Everyone is watching you, ah?"

"Surely they do watch. But cannot see you, Lord."

"No. We must be secret." He turned and paced, walking around the circular summit, walking in the walls.

Lord Oventroe was the only lord she knew of who paced. He'd often claimed that it was the only useful thing that humans had ever taught him. It was peculiar in the extreme, that after all they knew of the Rose, he picked this senseless thing to mimic. This minor thought came unbidden into her mind as she considered throwing herself from the tower. She thought of her dear girl, and her throat constricted.

"Secrets," Lord Oventroe was saying. "We both of us have secrets, Prefect."

She tried to think which one he knew, besides that she used the bright like a lord.

He went on: "My secret is well kept by you, Cixi of Chendu wielding."

It was almost a term of endearment, his use of her childhood name. She held her breath.

His face came to rest on a flat piece of stone, bringing his features into better resolution. He was fuller of face than most fiends, and it softened him. The ladies of the city—Tarig ladies, of course—found him handsome. "Yes," Lord Oventroe went on, "you have known that we have a personal alcove. Other lords know not of it. This is the secret you have kept, Prefect."

She *had* kept it secret. All secrets were coins to be hoarded, and praise be to Heaven, she had hoarded this one.

A change in Lord Oventroe's expression signaled pleasure. "We would thank you, but it's not our style, is it?"

"Unthinkable, Lord."

"You should have been a Tarig, Cixi of Chendu." No doubt he meant it as an extraordinary compliment.

"Sometimes I feel that I am." She cut a glance down the stairs, thinking of the alcove.

He said, "There are legates who know what you know?"

"No."

"We hope this is true, Cixi. We also hope that your messaging is for minor villainy and doesn't cross this lord's interests."

And what were his interests? Cixi would give much to know. Lord Oventroe had a fanatical hatred of the Rose, as all sentients knew. Also, and as few sentients knew, he had hopes to replace Hadenth as a high lord, because Hadenth had failed in security in the past. But no high lord ever stepped down, so this was not a reasonable goal. One could assume it was not.

"Dragons are content with their caves and their treasures, my lord."

His face flickered with amusement. Cixi thought that pacing was not the only thing that Oventroe had copied from the Rose. In all his fanatical observations of the enemy, he had unwittingly become more like them.

"The day you are *content*, Prefect, we will open the doors to the Rose."

She bowed very low, acknowledging this truth. She was not content. But let him believe that she possessed common ambitions. Let no one guess—and never the lords—that she meant to raise the kingdom. The Chalin kingdom.

When she rose from her bow, Lord Oventroe had disappeared.

A slight breeze wicked sweat from her face. "By my grave flag," she whispered, shivering.

She was safe, for the time being. But he knew that she partook of forbidden things. How had he discovered her, and who else might know? From now on she was under his scrutiny. Where else did he lurk, and in what guise? Did he really see her today, or was it only an image? It was sickening to think that the lords might spy so easily. . . .

She began descending the three hundred stairs. Why had the lord spared her life? Only one reason: she might have told someone else what she knew. And now he needed her to keep them silent, who otherwise might divulge his secret. Oh, the power of secrets. By their leverage one could topple a high tower, or an empire.

Partway down the stairs she slipped into her shoes again.

At the bottom, Zai Gan met her, noting her distress. "A hard climb, Your Brilliance?"

"No, Preconsul," she managed to say in a neutral tone. "But sometimes the way down is harder than going up." And when he looked at her inquiringly, she gave him the face that said, *Shut up and let me think.*

Then she concentrated on making it back to her quarters without collapsing.

That night in his cell, Quinn stared at the luminescent ceiling, dimmed for ebb-time. In its cool light he saw Hadenth's face, heard his shredded voice. The creature had been watching him. *Eight days on the rim . . .*

The Chalin rumor wasn't true, that Quinn's beating had addled the lord's mind. Hadenth was the same as he'd always been. Predatory and unpredictable. Why had Hadenth been watching him, or did the Tarig watch everything?

He felt cooped up, and restless. Nine days in the Magisterium, and still no contact with the traitor Tarig. If he was a traitor. And no word from the high prefect. . . . Abandoning sleep, he rose and took his clothes off the pegs on the wall. The cleaning fabbers had done their work, and he dressed in his silk garments, now spotless.

Out in the corridor, he noted that the Jout's door was open. Brahariar had also given up on sleep, and sat on her bed weeping. He knew that the Jout's petition, whatever it was, languished. Pitying her, earlier Quinn had asked Cho to help her, if he could.

Quinn walked. Was Hadenth watching him even now? If they thought their city so vulnerable that they spied incessantly, why have the Magisterium here at all? Why not install it at the base of the pillars instead?

The halls at ebb-time were as active as during the day. The great bureaucracy needed every hour of every long Entire day to govern the universe, the only universe worth having. The All they sometimes called it, their way of assuring themselves that they were superior.

He descended the ramp to the fourth level, which housed the archive, where scholars and functionaries pursued their arcane studies, and where all knowledge gathered by scholars eventually found a home.

There were several subjects he longed to pursue there. But it would draw attention if he pursued Johanna's records, from the time she was interrogated here. A minor son of Yulin shouldn't be looking up information about Johanna Quinn and her interrogator, Kang. Even though Kang's record would only be a fragment of Johanna, fragments might be important, if, as the navitar had said, Johanna was at the center of things.

This level was crowded with clerks. They wore the wide and backward-sloping hats that housed their computational boards, a type of stone well. From the back, the clerks' hats were alive with readouts as the stones made their way from top to bottom, spitting into a long sock that hung like a kite's tail down the clerks' backs. Making his way through twisting corridors, past the cells of factors and stewards, he came at last to the archive, which he wanted to enter, and shouldn't. He stood at the open door to the great hall. Here, giant pillars held the computational wells, and stairwells corkscrewed around the columns, accessing the wells.

He would have liked to see what information the library held on the Inyx sway, so that he could bolster his plan to free Sydney, the one that Yulin was so sure would fail. Certainly if the Inyx could probe his mind, then he was deprived of his strongest tactic: stealth. As well, he hungered to delve into the question of the correlates, if the lords by some lapse had left clues here.

But none of these paths of inquiry were open to him. He didn't know how to use the library. He didn't know how data was stored, how to access it, how to conduct searches. His very ineptness might draw attention.

He stood at the archive door undecided. Once, he had known the ways of the archive. Once, he had come here looking for the correlations between here and there. But he was not that same man. This version of Titus Quinn was stone well illiterate.

He turned away from the archive door. Min Fe was standing in the corridor.

The legate blinked at him, his eyes magnified in his glasses. "A soldier who studies? A wonder."

"I was curious about the great library. Very impressive." He tried to pass, but Min Fe blocked him.

"The man of weapons offends us."

"Was there an offense? If so, my pardon."

Min Fe hissed, "Pardon, is it? I grant no pardon for your insults." Two clerks emerged from the archive, bowing deeply as they passed. Min Fe watched them retreat down the corridor.

"Cho's promotion is an outrage, of course. He is without merit, without distinction. A pedantic, visionless underling who has contributed no new scrolls to the pandect in five thousand days. . . ." Min Fe noted Quinn's look of surprise. "Certainly you've heard that Shi Zu, taking revenge against me for imagined faults, raised the worthless menial to full steward?"

So the consul had promoted Cho at long last.

He went on, "Shi Zu credits Cho with guiding you in your assaults on protocol. Don't think it a victory, Dai Shen of Yulin's household. You've made an enemy here. A not-inconsiderable one, I assure you."

Quinn looked the sublegate squarely in the face. "I'm in a hurry, for Master Yulin's sake. Lest I suffer a beating." He tried to let Min Fe win, but it was no use. The man hated him.

Min Fe said, "May a beating be the least of your rewards."

"Many days to you, Sublegate." Quinn walked away. Min Fe did not follow him as he headed back to his quarters.

Quinn knew what Anzi would have advised: to placate the man, win him over. Well, it was too late for that now, and he didn't regret it. He wouldn't yield to Min Fe, as before he had yielded to the Tarig . . . for ten years. He was not the same man.

Before he left, he meant to prove that.

CHAPTER TWENTY-TWO

HELICE MAKI, DRESSED AS A VALKYRIE, adjusted her helmet and breastplate, and looked up at the night sky. Lately, the stars made her uneasy. Only a week ago she'd thought that missing her chance to enter the adjoining region was a crushing setback. Now, it seemed, the threats were on a far larger scale. But she was at a costume party, with party duties, and the stars must wait.

Minerva had chosen the zoo for the site of their annual equinox party. The roars of beasts mixed with the laughter of the guests, and torches lit the darkness among the animal cages. Zoos were dreadful places, filled with suffering, demented animals. She'd spoken against it at the board, to no avail. As the newest member of the company, she couldn't expect to win every time. But she'd like to win once.

Helice stalked the grounds, on the lookout for board members to chat up, and for staffers to charm. Over there was Lamar Gelde in a ten-gallon hat, conducting an earnest conversation with Marie Antoinette. She'd find him later, when he'd had too much champagne; maybe that would soften him a little. She'd handled Lamar badly so far. Charm. Work on the charm. She'd been born with little, she knew, and hadn't yet learned to make up the deficit.

As a servant in a galley slave outfit passed her, she scooped a champagne flute from the tray and roamed the crowd, stopping at a fountain to ditch the alcohol and replace it with water. Brain cells. Be needing them all, soon.

Near the seal pond sat a bemused bear with a studded collar, looking at the sleek sausages frolicking in the water. The bear was almost stupid from drugs, a cruelty she would have prevented if they'd consulted her.

She sat for a moment on a bench, and looked skyward once more. The stars. Because of the startling and inexplicable events of the past week, they could never look the same.

Stars were dying—dying early, dying wrongly. Near the horizon and rising steadily was Orion, with its belt of stars. She almost expected to see them wink out, one by one—as had happened on Tuesday to a few stars in the Orion Trapezium Cluster. Astronomers said four of them—young, hot stars—had vanished, and without last gasps, fluorescing gases, or outbursts of stellar material, without the slightest trace. Vanished.

She tried to see the situation as Stefan Polich did. The stars could be obscured behind Bok globules, clouds of cold gas and dust. Theories abounded of how stars like these could disappear from view, not only here, but at monitoring arrays at every one of the space platforms. A similar fate had befallen the star Beta Pictoris, far removed from the Trapezium group. Gone. The problem with the dust cocoon theory was that the events had been nearly instantaneous, and in essence defied every known physical law.

Helice looked around her at the costumed revelers. Despite fleeting mentions of the cosmic events in the newsTides, no one here looked up at the sky, or took note.

Stefan found it coincidental that it was happening now, just as they were probing the adjoining region. *But it's a new phenomenon*, she'd argued. And his answer: *No, it's new to* us. *Just because we've never seen it before doesn't mean it's really new.*

Perhaps, she thought. But the coincidence made her uneasy. Minerva was tinkering with higher-dimensional space-time. Sending probes, sending people, across a brane, a barrier that might exist for a *reason*. So, as much of a stretch as it might seem, suppose there was a connection between piercing the adjoining region and the deaths of stars?

She hoped that the star catastrophes were not due to some kind of retaliation. Retaliation on the part of the inhabitants on the other side who might have such capabilities. No, that truly was too fanciful.

However, it wasn't a very great leap to imagine that the cosmos contained beings more advanced than humans. Cosmologists had long thought that the age of the universe suggested that highly advanced civilizations must exist somewhere. If the universe over there was as old as this one, perhaps an advanced civilization had asserted itself.

And an even more astonishing thought: If their powers were such that they could darken stars, could they also see into this universe? Could they know Minerva plans? Could they, for instance, see Helice herself at this moment?

Fanciful, perhaps. But leaps of understanding often began with outrageous conjecture.

And this was exactly the kind of thinking that Stefan Polich was incapable of. Instead, when she had hinted at these conjectures, he had dismissed them as too far-fetched, treating her like a dred or a precocious child.

It galled, and it hurt.

The man would never give her credit, would never mentor her or give her the opportunity to enter the region she longed to see. Thus her need for allies, the need to attend parties. Her forays, however, must be tentative and inconspicuous. Such as her conversation with Booth Waller a few days ago, when she'd let him glimpse, for a moment, her heart.

"Did you want to go?" she'd asked him. To catch him off guard, she'd stated it baldly, without preamble.

Booth had paused, then figured out that she was referring to Quinn's mission. He decided, evidently, to be frank. "No."

"*I* wanted to go." She had let that sink in while Booth waited for some bitter comment or threat. But she couldn't threaten him. He was Stefan's handpicked man, and a favored senior staff member. He'd make a fine ally. She wondered then if Booth Waller saw the future as being with forty-three-year-old Stefan Polich or twenty-year-old Helice Maki.

A voice came from behind her: "Counting stars?

Stefan Polich approached her, a rather gawky Captain Hook. In his wake trailed Booth Waller himself, dressed as a Royal Canadian Mountie.

"Yes. Eight are missing." If *he* wasn't counting, *she* surely was.

She greeted Booth, who looked guilty. He was the favored one, and she wasn't, and he had the grace to feel bad about it.

"Eight stars," Stefan repeated as though they were far from his daily concerns. He took a gulp of champagne. "Don't you ever let your hair down?"

As Helice looked more carefully at him, he seemed oddly vulnerable, and a little drunk. "Valkyries don't."

He looked wistful. "No, I suppose not."

Gamely, she tried to be playful. "They've got important work on the battlefield—selecting the warriors destined for death."

As the three of them wandered toward a small arched bridge overlooking a stream, Stefan asked, "What about me? Am I headed for Valhalla?" He looked down on her from a height emphasized by his enormous pirate boots.

She said, dangerously, "No." Then, to throw him off balance, she smiled.

"And me?" Booth asked. He hitched up his gun belt with its wooden pistol.

If you were inclined to be pudgy, you shouldn't wear a glorious red uniform like that. It emphasized his inadequacies. "I haven't decided yet," Helice answered, fixing him with a sweet but pointed look.

Stefan pressed his drooping mustache to fix it more firmly on his upper lip. As they watched the carp swimming below, Helice murmured, "Those stars—I still wonder if there's a connection."

Captain Hook snorted. "Our man next door, crapping around, burning up stars?"

She felt a surge of annoyance. "We should at least *think* about these things."

"Helice, Helice. He's only been there a week. Surely he hasn't had time to destroy the fabric of the universe."

She shot back: "But we have no idea, actually, how much time has passed there. If last time was any indication, he might now have been there for *months*."

The three of them watched as a mottled gold-and-white carp circled in the slow-moving stream.

Stefan spoke softly. "On the other hand, he might not be there at all. He could be floating in space, charred and burned out, himself."

These days Stefan looked increasingly like a worried man. The company needed Titus Quinn. Even if the adjoining region wasn't a superhighway to the universe, it might be—at the very least—prime real estate. No, Stefan didn't want to give up on his man on the other side.

But on that score, Helice was confident. "He's there all right. Call it feminine intuition."

Stefan held up his hands in mock earnestness. "I wouldn't call it *feminine intuition* to save my soul."

"That's only because you don't *have* a soul, Stefan." And smiled. Charm, she reminded herself.

On the banks of the stream four partygoers were staggering in the water. One, dressed like Robin Hood, took aim with his bow and arrow and struck the golden carp dead center. It continued to swim for a few moments, a bit lopsided.

Helice growled, "Whoever did that, fire them."

Stefan waved the comment away. "It's only a fish, Helice." He lurched from the railing to intercept a galley slave bearing drinks.

As Stefan turned away, Booth closed the gap with Helice. He tilted his head toward the drunks splashing away upstream, saying in a low voice, "I believe those four are marginal performers. They'll be gone on Monday."

Helice let the words hang in the air while she savored them. She hadn't realized until that moment how dark her mood had been. Now, she brightened. Booth was still holding her gaze.

"Let's drink to that," she said, sincerely.

Booth signaled to the galley slave, and retrieved two glasses.

The three of them clinked glasses, but it was only Helice and Booth who were sealing a bargain.

Stefan was past noticing, way past his alcohol limit. He slurred, "We've got to stick together, Helice."

She smiled a consoling smile. "Of course we do."

"Troubled times," Stefan murmured. He sipped his champagne. "Ships sinking."

"Mmm," Helice said, watching the fish-killers vanish into the darkness.

CHAPTER TWENTY-THREE

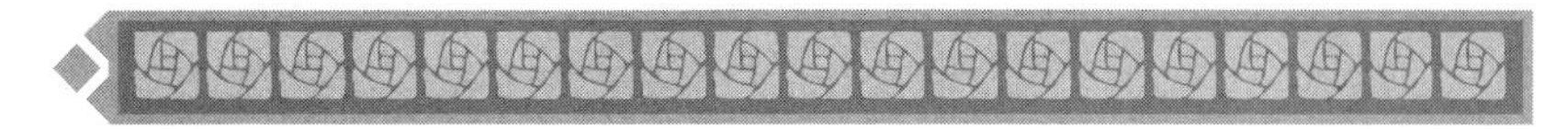

Birds fly, in the Rose,
Flowers bloom, in the Rose,
The sky is dark, in the Rose,
Kings die young, in the Rose.
—a child's verse

STANDING OUTSIDE HIS CELL on a dazzlingly clear morning, Quinn held the summons in his hand.

At last, Cixi had sent for him.

The summons, on a fine rolled parchment, was written in elaborate Lucent calligraphy. The appointment with the high prefect, arranged by Shi Zu and delivered by a full steward, would be tomorrow at the first hour of Shadow Ebb. Quinn was both eager to see her and uneasy. Here was a person who once knew him, and it would be a supreme test of his facial reconstruction. Threads of memory warned him that he and this woman had not been friends.

Turning to the window and its view of the city, Quinn fingered the scroll. Thanks to Cho, barriers were falling away. The steward had been right about Shi Zu. The legate had quickly dropped the idea of heading the Inyx mission once Quinn pretended indifference.

Now, he had a day to wait.

The city called him. And pushed him away. He must not meet, much less engage, the Tarig lords, who, despite his altered face, might recognize him. However, the city was large, and he would likely pass unnoticed in its byways. Hadenth hadn't recognized him, after all. He marshaled his arguments in favor of going. Since he *was* going.

From the moment he'd come back to the Entire, he'd been haunted by who he'd once been in this place. His memories were still imperfect—just vivid enough to torment him.

So Quinn found himself walking toward the doorway into the city, where, if he walked, perhaps he could know if he was different this time.

He climbed the winding staircase to the second level of the Magisterium. He went down the passage with the vaulted ceiling, and through the gallery where columns divided the view of the city with their vertical bars. The voices of his two selves accompanied him, saying, *Go.* And, *Do not.* Clerks, factors, stewards, and legates bowed as protocols dictated. He moved past them in a dream, past the Hall of the Sleeping Lord and down the broad staircase into the city. Nearby, carp swam in the pool, and he stopped long enough to observe that the orange-backed fish, the one he had fed Bei's redstone to, was not among them.

It was a relief to be out of doors. The bright fell over the towers and plazas of the city like the silver wings of an invisible god. He was not entirely oriented, but wandered, glimpsing new views of the city with each twist in his path. Water coursed through the canals. Along the pathways and in bazaars and plazas, non-Tarig sentients roamed freely, feeding fish or walking the promenade. Occasionally Quinn glimpsed a lord striding along an intersecting canal, but never close enough to cause concern.

So Titus Quinn walked through the city, marveling that he was here—that he had returned at all, that he was walking freely among his enemies. That, on the verge of leaving the Ascendancy, he had gone into its heart.

The bright streamed overhead—very close. Its buckling folds looked more than ever like porridge at a boil, a sight he now took for granted. Along the skyline of the city he saw the familiar spires that served no function that the Tarig would ever admit, except an aesthetic one. Like those godder temples, God's Needles, but taller by far, they looked ready to spear prey infringing on the bright. In the heart of the palatine hill was the tallest spire, Ghinamid's Tower, said to be the vacant habitation of the Masterful Lord, waiting for the time when he would awaken from his sleep. Bridges looped over the canals, feeding into meandering pathways that widened into plazas and plunged into shaded alleys overhung with black and purple vines.

He had asked Chiron once why the Entire had no flowers. She had pointed to black, glistening vines—beautiful, to her alien eyes. But not to human eyes.

They're not like us. Not in any way, Bei had said. The old scholar's words came winding back to him: *The Tarig kept saying that if you relinquished information, your family might be returned to you. One day led to the next, and the information was never enough. Every day you asked. And every day the lords said, not yet. You persisted, Titus. You never forgot them.*

He gazed up at the palatine hill. He knew which mansion was Hadenth's, and which Chiron's. He walked toward the deserted home of Lord Inweer, long absent, long the keeper of Ahnenhoon—and Johanna. Here he was unlikely to meet a Tarig of consequence.

Closer to the palatine hill, the lesser mansions filled his view. The reflective metal walls tired his eyes, and he glanced instead through the deep windows, into the interiors where the Tarig lived their private lives. With their needs met by their technologies, they had no household servants. Nor were there commoners among the Tarig. In their supreme arrogance, all Tarig were nobles of the Entire.

Quinn found a narrow passage of stairs leading upward, and climbed it through circuitous twists colored by purple shadows.

He continued his climb, and the paths narrowed until he found himself on a private walk, opening onto a sunken garden. Around the entrance arch a vine looped, heavy with obsidian berries. He walked inside. Trees and shrubs stood at attention in regular lines, trimmed and precise. Unmistakably, it was a Tarig garden. In the center of the garden was a small pool.

He sat on a low wall at the pond's edge. Eddies and currents disturbed the water, rumpling the reflections of the surrounding palace walls. This was the dwelling of the lord who once had custody of Johanna, and still led the armies at Ahnenhoon. It was the one lord he'd never met. But the grounds did not look abandoned.

His thoughts turning to Johanna, Quinn hardly noticed that a small boat approached. It tilted past a vortex and nudged up against the side of the pool near him. The boat was an excellent likeness of a navitar's vessel. On the upper deck, in the navitar's spot, was a doll.

"Push it back," came a voice.

Quinn looked up. On the opposite side of the pond, where dark vines cascaded from the bank into the water, a branch trembled. He gave the boat a shove in that direction, but misjudged the current, and the craft circled aimlessly in the center.

"Hnnn," came the voice, high-pitched and soft.

Could this be a Tarig child? In his past life Quinn had not met that many Tarig children, as they were always closely watched by an adult. Tarig children were as rare—perhaps rarer—than youngsters of other sentients.

The branch shook again. "Push it in to us," came the command.

"Hard to know where to push it when I can't see you."

"We are hiding."

"I know you are. It's a pretty good hiding spot."

The boat slipped out of the eddy and, propelled by the centrifugal force, drifted across the pond, thumping against the side.

The voice in the bushes said, "The ship hit the storm wall. Everyone has become dead." With that, a young Tarig stepped out of the hiding spot and went to retrieve the boat. To Quinn, to human eyes, she looked to be about six years old, except that her face was an exact miniature of an adult's. By the heavy bracelets, she was a girl. She wore a black jumpsuit and a long, sleeveless coat. Leaning over the edge, she fished the toy from the pond. Her black hair was cropped short and heavily greased. As she picked up the boat, water dripped onto her lavender coat, creating dark spots.

Looking into Quinn's face, she said, "The Chalin man."

"Dai Shen, soldier of Ahnenhoon, young mistress."

She took the doll out of the boat and peered at it closely before stuffing it back inside the toy. "You call us Small Girl."

She gazed at him for a long while, not attending to her boat. It was a child's gaze: open and frank. "Small Girl has a boat of the Nigh," she said at last, speaking with childlike gravity.

"Yes, you do. Show me how it sails."

Just as she was about to oblige him, she sat back on her heels and glanced at him. "You do not tell us what to do, though."

"No. Only sail the boat if you like to."

"We like to." She leaned in and set the boat into a current. "But this boat went into the storm wall and got all knotted up and died." She watched the boat as it drifted under the overhanging bushes.

"Maybe you can fix it," he suggested.

"Hnnn. But what is fixing?"

"Repairing." He tried another synonym, but still she looked confused. "When you give attention to something that is broken."

She sat on the low wall next to him, swinging her legs. He noticed her shoes were the most elaborate thing she wore: colorfully beaded, and the toes, pointed and curled. A poor choice for a child's adornment. They sat in comfortable silence for a time, in the way he remembered sitting with Sydney. He thought this Tarig child had never run at play or climbed a tree. Her dress was too elaborate. It was no way to raise a child, not even one destined to grow tall and cruel.

She looked at him with large, black eyes. "Tell Small Girl what is fixing."

He should leave. The child's parents might not like her talking to a stranger. Sitting next to one, in a private garden.

"Fixing," he began. "If my clothes are dirty, I clean them. If my knife is dull, I sharpen it. So I can use these things again."

"Some things cannot be fixed?" She swung her feet, and the beaded shoes sparkled under the fiery sky.

"Sometimes you can't, if something is badly broken."

The girl craned her neck around and gazed up at the high windows of the courtyard walls. Her guardians would not leave her alone for long. He rose.

She glanced up at him. "The Chalin man sits down."

"I have business elsewhere, Small Girl."

"Ah. Business. But not right now."

He looked down on her. She sat primly swinging her feet. She was nothing like Sydney, but his heart caught at the sight of a child of the Entire.

"Fixing," she said again. "Badly broken, and then things must be abandoned?"

"Yes," Quinn replied. "Sometimes I will buy a new thing to replace the old."

"But sometimes the old one was better?"

He looked more closely at her, wondering at how much she understood of things being broken and the fondness for what was.

"Yes," was all he could say.

"If Small Girl's shoes get dirty, we throw them away." She seemed wistful, gazing at her sparkling shoes.

Something prompted him to challenge her thinking. He said, "Or you could ask your mother to fix them."

Her dark eyes flashed at him, as if to say, *You do not tell me what to do. . . .* Then she stood, placing her feet carefully on the clipped lavender grass. She returned to the bushes where her boat had drifted, kneeling carefully by the water to avoid soiling her coat.

Now was a good time to leave, before she could command him to stay. He bowed, saying, "Small Girl."

She reached into the pond where her boat had caught in the branches. Pulling the toy from the water, she reached into her coat pocket and took something out, placing it on the boat. Then she launched the boat in his direction.

As it sailed toward him, a flash of light spit from the top, and a flame quickly caught the upper deck on fire.

On the upper deck, the doll's hair was on fire, while the deck below added fuel to the burn. Finally, fully engulfed, the boat floundered. An acrid smoke threaded through the air. The smell hit him hard, a revolting smell of burning hair and poisonous compounds.

As the boat sank, Small Girl watched gravely. "Everyone has become dead." She looked up at him. "Tomorrow, you will fix it?"

She had ruined her toy in the expectation that a Chalin man could fix things. It was pathetic and bizarre—it was time for him to go before her caretakers smelled fire and found a stranger among them. "Small Girl," he said. "I can't come back tomorrow."

Her voice quavered. "You cannot come back?" She looked at the eddy where the boat lay submerged.

"No, I can't." he said. He shouldn't have come. And he must not come back.

She looked stricken. Tarig didn't cry, but their faces were exquisitely expressive, once you learned to read them. He walked away.

After a few paces he turned back to find her standing by the garden entrance, watching him. She would live out her life in Tarig restraints, never learning what normal beings knew, never stubbing her jeweled toes.

He descended the stairs from the palatine hill, seeing no one on the paths. High above him, a few Tarig stirred on the balconies.

He walked, putting distance between himself and the child in the garden. Small Girl, as she called herself, was in a prison. Like a unicorn in a corral, they had her on display, cut off from whatever true childhood she might have had. It was the same with the brightships. They were a dreadful cage, full of pain. Somehow he knew this from the time before. Confinement was all the Tarig knew, for all their power and knowledge. It was a piece he'd missed the first time; he'd caught up, now.

The city revolted him. Its sterile palaces and bleak gardens . . . it was nothing he could ever have loved. The smell of fire and burning hair lingered in his nostrils.

He rushed down the steps, eager to be done with the bright city, eager to reunite with his daughter. His throat tightened with emotion. My little girl, he thought. No longer little. Grown up now. He tried to imagine her mature face, but saw only Johanna's.

Hurrying down the promenade, he nearly collided with Cho.

The steward bowed deeply. "Sightseeing in the city after all?"

Quinn managed to say, "Yes, Cho, sightseeing."

The steward nodded, looking worried. He fell into step beside Quinn, and together they made their way toward the Magisterium, with Cho uncharacteristically silent.

An Ysli sentient passed them, looking cross and preoccupied, and then several Chalin clerks busily chatting. The city, in all its pursuits, was normal. But not for Cho.

Cho hardly knew how to begin this conversation with Dai Shen, son of Yulin.

From the moment he'd met this most interesting personage, he had greatly liked him. Dai Shen was a man of importance, yet behaved without pretenses, despite Cho's offensive behavior at their first meeting, an event he still cringed to remember. *Don't sleep on my trunks, if you please. . . .* But now he had disturbing questions about this personage.

Truth to tell, doubts had been building each time he'd seen Dai Shen. There were little things: something about his accent; the occasional mangling of an idiom; his skin tones marking him as from someplace far away, yet his history suggesting that he was of the great city Xi. By themselves the things were trivial, but someone with a talent for details might just wonder about the man. And Cho was a man of details, a functionary who prided himself on accuracy.

Now there was the matter of Johanna Quinn, and Cho was disquieted.

Walking next to Dai Shen, he at last forced himself to say, "You asked me to look into a matter."

Dai Shen said, "Yes, the woman of the Rose. The woman called Johanna."

The way he said the odd name, *Johanna*. Almost a perfect pronunciation. But not quite. Cho's stomach churned with unhappy doubts. Looking firmly ahead as they walked, Cho murmured low, "I have found the scholar Kang's records, of course."

Dai Shen didn't respond, forcing Cho to add: "Anyone might have found them. *You* might have found them."

"Thank you, Cho," the soldier of Ahnenhoon said. "A service to me, thank you." Dai Shen kept walking, but slowed his pace as they approached the banks of a canal.

Cho responded, "I owe you more than such a simple thing, Dai Shen. A matter any clerk could accomplish."

"You don't owe me favors. You earned that promotion, probably long ago."

Cho could leave this topic now, could abandon his suspicions and give the man the information he'd requested. But he would not. He had been a functionary in the Ascendancy for seven thousand days. He had served the Magisterium, the Great Within, since his childhood, and loved it as his home. It had not always been kind to him, but the thought of living in the Great Without filled him with dread. Could he lose everything? What, after all, did he really owe to this stranger?

His resolve stiffened. "You didn't want to research the woman of the Rose yourself."

After a pause came the response. "No."

Cho stopped and looked directly up into Dai Shen's face. "Are you loyal on the Radiant Path, Dai Shen?" As he asked the question, the man's eyes slid away, and he grew very still, and then Cho knew with a sinking heart that something terrible was unfolding.

Dai Shen said in a low voice, "I have a mission beyond the one I told you. It's one that other Chalin share with me. Some might be against me."

"Some."

Dai Shen glanced at the palatine hill. "Yes."

Cho felt his chest constricting, his stomach turning sour. Then he asked with more boldness than he could believe, "Are you the son of Yulin?"

"Sent by Yulin, I promise you."

Cho turned his gaze to the waters rippling by in the canal. He could leave now, report to Min Fe, and be excused from further complicity. But something drove him to help Dai Shen, to give him a chance to vindicate himself. He thought he knew why he was doing this. It was because of Brahariar.

Dai Shen was now looking at him, his gaze firm and yet vulnerable. This was a man you didn't easily cast aside.

Cho began in a soft voice, low enough not to be overheard on the crowded pathway. "I am troubled, Dai Shen, by doubts. I did owe you this favor, and much more. I liked you from the time when I met you and your companion on the Nigh. You didn't flaunt your status. And then you told the consul Shi Zu that I had helped you with protocols of the Magisterium, to avoid needless stumbling. That was a kindness. Still, you might have done it in order to put me in your debt, in order, pardon me, to ask for this favor of finding records of the woman of the Rose."

Dai Shen was still looking at him with an impassive face. Not arguing, not fearful.

Cho leaped to his decision. It was the most impulsive action of his whole life. His skin began to zing with the tension as the implications cascaded into his mind.

He turned back to Dai Shen, searching the taller man's face. "I have come to a conclusion. My judgment is that you are a personage of good intent. And the reason? Because you asked me to help the Jout, Brahariar, a sentient whose petitions—whatever they may be—have now found a decent hearing. A lesser man wouldn't have noticed her troubles."

He saw Dai Shen's relief as the man murmured, "Thank you."

They resumed their stroll in the direction of the great plaza in front of the Hall of the Sleeping Lord. Cho asked, "Have I shown good discrimination?"

What else could Dai Shen—or whoever he really was—say, except yes? But Cho needed reassurance, now that it had come to treason—treason of some sort, he couldn't imagine what kind.

"I think my cause is worthy," Dai Shen said. "But I can't tell you what it is." He added: "I don't think you want to know."

Cho glanced up at the Hall of the Sleeping Lord. "No. I don't."

With that, Cho held out his hand, revealing a small redstone. With this action, he had become part of the assault on protocols. That was what Cho preferred to think was going on. "There is no visual likeness of the personage here, nor any auditory, and so forth. But it's Kang's account of the interrogation of the woman Johanna."

"My gratitude, Cho," Dai Shen said, taking the stone. He smiled at Cho, and Cho managed one in return. Then, bowing, Dai Shen parted company with him.

Cho was upset, but not as agitated as he might have predicted. What was the use of spending all your days amid scrolls and clarities and the fear of mistakes? And when you met a personage such as Dai Shen, might your life have been touched by the glance of greatness? He could be wrong. And then he would pay dearly. *Heaven give us few surprises*, he thought fervently.

Quinn took a detour past the pond, checking for his carp, but it was not among those congregating there. Quickly, he moved into the interior of the Magisterium, putting distance between himself and Cho.

The steward had seen through him, and knew that he was an imposter. Cho had been friendly, but by God, he was a lifelong servant of the Magisterium, keeper of rules, follower of rules. Quinn stopped for a moment, ordering his thoughts, calming his nerves. He leaned against the adobe stone of an archway. Cho had implied he would be quiet, but for how long?

Hastening down to the third level, he held the stone tight in his fist.

Johanna was here, a sliver of her at least. It had been risky, even stupid, to ask Cho for this. Amid all his lies and plots he was grasping for a subtle thread that converged with all others in his heart. The knot. The lines the navitar saw. He was caught in their web. Instead of passing directly to his goal, he had fatally paused. Impulses were pushing to get out.

Still, Cho had that aspect about him that spoke of integrity. What would he gain by calling attention to Dai Shen? After having been so friendly to the imposter, Cho might even draw suspicion himself. Quinn had to count on Cho now.

When he arrived at his cell, a familiar but unexpected smell came to him. Someone was in the room. Kneeling down, he looked under the bed. In the shadows, bright golden eyes met his.

"Anzi," he whispered.

CHAPTER TWENTY-FOUR

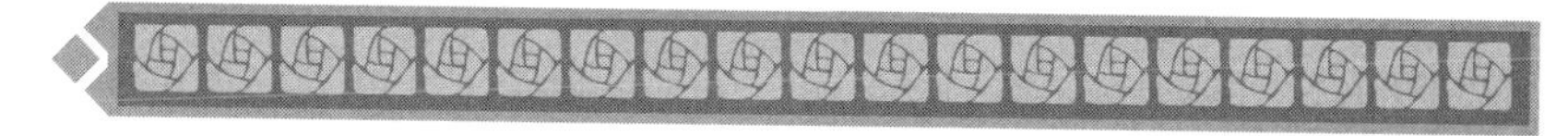

I went to the heartland, and what could I see,
But the five lands branching far from me.
The Radiant Arch said come here and look;
I went and wrote its wonders in my book.
Bright River Primacy was great to behold,
But it was not home, and I grew cold.
The Arm of Heaven went long and long,
My heartchime played its dulcet song.
The Sheltering Path went to the end of All;
I walked the whole way, so strong was its call.
But the Long Gaze of Fire is ever my place;
It holds my heart, it knows my face.

—"Song of the Five Primacies"

SYDNEY STOOD AT THE BASE OF THE CLIFF, hearing Mo Ti's footfalls above her as he climbed.

"What do you see?" she called.

"Nothing yet." Small rocks skittered down as he climbed, unafraid, now, to show that he was sighted.

Riod restively paced nearby, occasionally charging at a steppe vole or an insect. Practice charging for the coming fight. Her mount's thoughts came to her in emotional gusts: the urge to gore Priov, and the uncertainty of fighting him out of season.

Sydney silently prayed: Careful, beloved. Don't let Priov choose the battleground.

They could wait. In 520 days, mating season would course through the herd's blood. Riod would be in full powers, then. And before that season, there would be time to win support for the heresies: free bond, Mo Ti's sightedness, and—someday soon—her own sightedness.

At present the encampment was in turmoil. Akay-Wat was hobbling on her false leg, learning to walk again, hoping for a new mount. The scandal had stirred brawls among the riders and among the Inyx. But no one dared take a knife to Mo Ti's eyes.

Mo Ti had done a superb job with the Hirrin's leg, carefully taking apart the complex muscles of her knee joint and stanching the bleeding while knitting up the stump. Sydney had helped him, guided by Riod's sight as her mount stayed through the surgery, binding himself to the crime and its aftermath.

Afterward, she and Riod had listened with amazement as Mo Ti spun out a forbidden dream: the ruin of the mantis lords.

Sydney had listened, moved yet doubtful. She had just begun to find peace in her captivity—since Riod, since Mo Ti. Mo Ti was becoming a champion and a friend. As for Riod, she had come to love her mount with a complex devotion, returning his loyalty with fervor, trusting him with her life, and far beyond that now—trusting him with her heart. They each held vastly different ideas of freedom, but he had given her freedom as she defined it: freedom to stay with him or go, to share in decisions, to be someday sighted again.

Now Mo Ti had told her she was thinking too small.

"The lords," he had murmured to her that ebb-time by Akay-Wat's side: "Are they a knife in your heart?"

As he spoke, she had felt that old wound burning with her every breath.

Next to her Riod had sent, *We have our lives. Far from them.* And then, much later in the ebb, *It is a dream.*

"A dream?" Mo Ti had left the Hirrin's side and drawn closer to Riod, looking at him eye to eye. "A dream?"

A dream without hope. Riod's view of Mo Ti's gnarled face came to Sydney. Mo Ti's eyes were shining, watching the mount as he said, *A thousand thousand days of dreams. To never again fear the lords, never to fall to them. As the Chalin have fallen. As all have fallen everywhere, except the Inyx. But it is a dream, too old, too weak.*

In pictures more than words, Sydney saw the generations of mounts living and riding, roaming and dying, fearing the lords who wanted to subjugate them. The lords who subjugated with persuasion, through the Radiant Path, receiving as their due gratitude and awe—things the Inyx would never grant. Sydney saw the hundreds, the thousands of Inyx gone to the Long War. She felt the carnage and the anguish of war from the minds of herdmates who shared every pain, every horror.

A dream too old and weak, Riod said again.

"No," Mo Ti said. "The dream is alive." He added: "But it needs legs."

And then, through the ebb, he had laid out a plan, audacious and breathtaking, of a great change to come, beginning in secrecy and gaining in power, no matter how long it took. To raise the kingdom, a sentient kingdom with no lords.

Who shall be chief, then? Riod sent.

Mo Ti's glance slid sideways, as though to snag a thought not yet in his grasp. "We will see. But no fiends." Then he looked at Sydney. "Perhaps there is one who we would all gladly serve."

Sydney shook her head. "They would smash us. They have the bright. Their ships. Their hands. They have—"

"—it all, yes," Mo Ti finished for her.

A silence fell. Outside, the distant snort of an Inyx came from the pasture where the herd slept standing, sending their dreams to their riders.

Mo Ti began again. "The weak place," he said. "Everyone has a weak place. Even them."

Sydney thought of the lords and tried to imagine a weak place.

Mo Ti's voice came soft, high, and calm. "The Inyx must find the weak place."

She took a wonder-filled breath. The Inyx are the key, she thought.

Riod sent negation. *We hate them. We choose never to touch their minds.*

"That must change," Mo Ti murmured.

And they had watched over Akay-Wat in silence then, each with their own thoughts.

Now, at the base of the cliff, Sydney looked up at Mo Ti's high perch. "What do you see?"

Mo Ti answered, "Priov comes."

"How close?"

"Close now, mistress. And he has many mounts with him."

To fight, then. It was all very well to dream of fighting the lords, but here came a more immediate foe.

Mo Ti's sure, muscular movements soon brought him down from his perch on the rock wall, and he mounted Distanir.

Riod approached Sydney, dipping front legs for her to mount.

"Who's coming with Priov?" Sydney asked.

Riod sent, *The mares.*

"Don't fight," she said. They were outnumbered, and Priov had blood on his mind. He would stamp out free bond and Riod all at once. But Riod didn't answer. Ahead of them was a canyon with no exit. Riod set off at a gallop toward it.

"Turn back," Sydney pleaded. Riod's only answer was a dark resolve.

Mo Ti urged his mount close to her, saying, "Let him prove himself, mistress. It begins here."

They thundered into the canyon. Riod's thoughts were strangely hidden from Sydney as they came to the snub-nosed end of the canyon. Around them soared columns of rocks, casting a reflected yellow light. Riod circled to face the oncoming group.

Mo Ti rested a hand on Sydney's arm to steady her. "Come over to me."

She clambered behind him onto Distanir's back, holding tight while he carried her to the canyon wall. There, they dismounted. Hooves echoed in the ravine as Priov's band came around a bend in the cliffs.

Through Distanir's eyes, Sydney saw Riod standing alone, his black coat glistening.

Distress and excitement colored Distanir's perceptions: Priov thundered into the arena formed by the stone walls. Feng slipped off Priov's back as the mares bunched around Priov, cantering and snorting. Separating himself from them, Priov pranced for their benefit. The canyon echoed with the shrill screams of the mares as they lifted their tails, spraying feces.

This should not be happening. It should wait for mating season, when the mares were at issue. Today, though, it wasn't about mares, as everyone knew.

Riod stood unmoving, conserving energy under the molten bright.

Beloved, Sydney murmured.

Mo Ti admonished her: "Do not weaken his concentration, mistress."

Well then, Sydney thought. Let it begin. She calmed her mind to better receive the images sent by Mo Ti's mount. The mares quieted, retreating behind Priov.

Then, posturing done, Priov charged.

As he raced in, Riod's head lowered, bringing his horns to the fore. Priov feinted toward Riod and raced away. Circling around, he charged again, this time with his head lowered, veering to the side to swipe at Riod, who evaded, taking a defensive stance.

Across the expanse of spike grass, Feng stood like a queen, her hand on the hilt of her sheathed knife. Sydney felt for her own knife, patting it. Beside her, Mo Ti stood quietly with his mount.

Again Priov charged, this time clanking horn to horn with Riod. Hide ripped and separated. Blood flowed. It was Riod's blood. His flank. Mo Ti rested a hand on her arm, giving her his strength.

Out of season, Riod wasn't fighting well. Priov, on the other hand, had been stoking his own resolve all across the steppe.

Priov raced in again, making sickening contact in a crack of locked horns. Digging in his front legs for leverage and twisting violently, he yanked Riod down to his foreleg knees.

Disengaging, Priov pranced for his mares. For his arrogance, he took a wrenching kick in his ribs as Riod rolled on his side to bring his own legs in the air.

Enraged, Priov turned on his rival again, dashing in to slash Riod's foreleg.

Blood spattered as Riod scrambled to an upright position, and both mounts breathed fitfully, near exhaustion.

Then one of the mares came forward. With a burst of speed, she ran toward Riod, swiping his flank with her own body and dashing away. Then another mare dashed in to attack.

By Sydney's side, Mo Ti stirred.

He climbed onto Distanir. Of one mind, he and his mount plunged into the fray.

The mares pounded to and fro, in a confusing tumult of viewpoints and emotions. But Sydney could just discern Mo Ti's strategy: he didn't strike at the mares, but herded them. Expertly, he led Distanir in herding patterns that cut off the mares, and left Riod to recover his wind.

Seeing that Riod would only get stronger, Priov charged once more. The older mount's head was down, coming at Riod, forehorns aimed low. Their skulls crashed together; then, as they separated, Riod turned his head to the side and gored Priov's mouth. Priov roared in pain.

Sydney heard something behind her. She spun, drawing her knife at the same time. Someone was there.

"Little rose," Feng's voice growled.

Sydney now had her own fight. She held out her knife, turning in one direction and then the next, listening for Feng.

The whoosh of air came—the path of a knife.

And again Feng's weapon flashed by. Having a fix on Feng's position, Sydney dove for the big woman's legs, bringing her down with a thump. They thrashed, but Feng was bigger, and gave Sydney a punch that knocked the wind out of her. For a moment she was helpless before a bigger, better fighter.

But then Feng paused, hearing, as Sydney did, the outcry of the mares.

Feng sobbed, "Priov." And then she pounded away, leaving Sydney to pick herself up. Quiet surrounded her.

Amid a new and dreadful silence, Sydney staggered in the direction of the bloody arena. As she pushed her way among the now-quiet mares, she began picking up images: Two mounts, gushing blood. One mount on the ground, one standing.

Sydney made her way, grasping for sight, at last seeing through dozens of viewpoints: Priov was on the ground, horribly torn. His lip fell away in a slab of meat. He tried to stand, but Feng urged him to lie still. Beside Priov, Riod stood, with wounds on his flank and foreleg welling blood. But he could still move, and now he paced closer to Priov. Feng was on her hands and knees next to her mount. She looked up with loathing as she sheltered Priov's head with her body.

Riod had won.

The mares stood quietly, absorbing the meaning of all this. Riod ducked his head at two mares, and, instead of shying, they came to sniff him, breaking the tension. Riod pranced into the middle of the crowd of mares—he managed what might be called a prance—and nuzzled a few of them, which they allowed. Sydney would have run to him, but this was not a time for her to interfere, she knew. Riod must take the mares, take their loyalty.

Then, with a trumpeting sound, Riod signaled for the mares. They slowly sorted themselves out—the eager, the tentative—but all came to him. Gathering them together, Riod galloped down the canyon, leaving behind the former leader. A dying one.

Mo Ti reached down for Sydney's hand and, clasping it, pulled her up to ride behind him. Now Feng had a duty she must perform—a duty Sydney had once carried out for Glovid, but with less anguish.

Mo Ti turned Distanir away, leaving Feng to her task.

"He won," Sydney murmured to Mo Ti, leaning exhausted against his back.

"Yes, my lady."

She leaned against Mo Ti's back as they trotted down the valley, with the bright beating hard on her head and each stride bruising her anew.

"Why did you call me *lady*?" Sydney said into Mo Ti's strong back.

"Because that's what you are now. If Riod is our master."

"We have no lords and ladies," Sydney said.

"That will change."

He had his large ambitions. Too large, she thought, while still thrilled that he would think them. That *anyone* would think them. Where had Mo Ti learned such high ideas? He had only told her that many people thought thus.

"Take me home, Mo Ti." She was too weary to think. And taking command of the herd was enough for one day.

Out on the flats, Riod's commanding presence came to her. He had not forgotten her, but he was bringing the mares to his side.

She urged him on, fierce with pride.

Later that day back in the encampment, Sydney went searching for Akay-Wat.

Feng's special quarters were now hers, along with a new deference from the riders. Even Puss, whose real name was Takko, gave her a nod, almost a bow.

Wordlessly, Sydney passed through the yard, unaccustomed to esteem, or even courtesy. But evidently, Priov and Feng would not be missed.

She found Akay-Wat resting behind the barracks. Her right foreleg, with its molded prosthesis, lay stretched out before her. Sydney sat next to her on the hard-packed clay.

The Hirrin blurted out, "Now, free bond comes to us, oh yes? We will have it at last, my lady?"

Sydney rested her arms on her knees, preoccupied. Softly, she asked, "When will you be strong enough to ride?"

Akay-Wat flattened her ears, worrying about her answer. "Oh dear. No riding yet, for Akay-Wat."

"When you can, I want you to leave."

Akay-Wat gasped.

Sydney didn't have time or leisure to argue with the Hirrin. Akay-Wat was either up to the task or not. Sydney was getting tough under Mo Ti's tutelage, so she had decided to pass it along.

"We'll find you a mount who wants free bond, Akay-Wat. When we do, you'll go to Ulrud's herd."

Akay-Wat was as silent as the steppe around them.

"Live there and teach them of free bond," Sydney said.

Akay-Wat made a mourning noise deep in her long throat. "My lady . . ." Then she breathed, "Don't send me away. I will serve you, I will be brave, I will do anything you say, will Akay-Wat. Please, mistress."

Sydney couldn't bear this pleading. Yes, it was hard. Yes, Akay-Wat was afraid and wounded. Get tough, my Hirrin, she thought.

"Akay-Wat, listen now. I need those around me I can trust."

"You can trust me, you can!"

Sydney interrupted. "Prove it."

Then, slowly, Akay-Wat staggered to her feet. Her voice warbled in a plaintive ululation.

Sydney rose, too. Remembering Mo Ti's steady hand, she placed her own on Akay-Wat's back, pressing down firmly. They stood together for a few moments, and she felt the Hirrin's warm hide tremble under her hand. Then she walked away, leaving Akay-Wat to cry in privacy.

And make up her mind.

CHAPTER TWENTY-FIVE

May the dragon you find be well fed.
—a blessing

ANZI WALKED BESIDE QUINN to his meeting with the high prefect. He'd confessed to her that he'd gone walking in the city, and now she refused to stay behind in his cell. Here at his side, she was determined to prevent similar lapses in judgment. So it was just as well he hadn't told her about Small Girl.

Although she was dressed in stolen clerk's attire with sloping hat, she made an unlikely bureaucrat. She strode tall, lacking the hunched back and squinting eyes. The garb had served double duty so far, since they'd used the hat to read Cho's redstone. The uniform wasn't all that she'd taken. In order to ascend one of the other pillars of the Ascendancy, she'd assumed another visitor's identity. She delighted him with her audacity, and he was surprised by how glad he was to see her—even as dangerous as her presence was.

He'd kidded her, "So I wasn't ready to do this on my own, after all."

She had pursed her lips, but the smile came through. "I'm selfish, Dai Shen. My uncle would have me whipped for leaving you." She'd let him save face, but he knew he was better off with her near.

And he'd been glad of her company last night as they pored over the document Cho had provided: Kang's account of the interrogations of Johanna. It was a dry summary, but Johanna shone through because of the lies she'd told. She had lied about Earth politics and company politics. Lied about Minerva, about technology, and about small personal matters. How many children did she have? *Eight*. How long had she lived? *Fifty years*. It was as though she was determined to thwart them even if it did no good. She had fought them with all her wits, and enjoyed it. No wonder he loved her.

Here, close to the salon of the high prefect, legates packed the halls, clutching scrolls or pausing to gossip, while clerks mingled with downcast eyes to avoid continuous bowing. Fluted columns framed the views of the heartland, now fallen into a dusty lavender time. Since Cixi preferred to meet in the ebb of day, it had become the fashion on this level of the Magisterium to work all ebb and sleep all day.

A wide staircase marked the boundary of the high prefect's salon doors. Legates stood in knots on the stairs, glancing at times to the gilded doors, hoping for a glimpse of Cixi.

Barely hiding a growing elation, Quinn walked to his interview. Drawing closer, he drew looks from legates who must have wondered how someone dressed in plain silks could hope to find a place in line. He bowed to the closest few. He was ready for his greatest challenge: securing the old woman's endorsement of his journey to the Inyx.

Pausing before the steps, Anzi whispered, "I will wait for you here, Dai Shen."

"No, Anzi. Too conspicuous."

"I will wait, I think."

The legates on the stairs were watching him; it was time to go. He looked at her. Faithful Anzi. In danger because of him. He would send her on a harmless errand. "Find me a toy boat," he said.

Anzi looked doubtful.

He lowered his voice. "One about this big," he said, gesturing. "A boat that can be put in the water."

He glanced up at the legate guarding the salon doors. The practice matches with Min Fe and Shi Zu were over. "To the dragon," he said.

Anzi whispered, "Remember not to step on the dragon."

He started up the stairs, threading his way through legates and preconsuls, the finely plumed birds of Cixi's aviary, whether Chalin, Ysli, or Hirrin. They turned to watch him as he made straight for the door, clutching his summons. This he presented to the Chalin gatekeeper, who perused the scroll and, finding it in order, reached to open the door. At that moment Quinn caught a glimpse of a familiar legate standing off to the side. Min Fe bowed in his direction, a jackal on the fringe of the lions.

Quinn stepped into Cixi's domain, into a foyer. A spike of worry hit him, that the old woman would remember him. Unlike the Tarig, Chalin were good at faces.

A Hirrin servant stood guard at yet another door. On the floor at the Hirrin's feet coiled an inlaid design in the likeness of a snake that appeared to slither under the door.

As Quinn approached, the servant opened the door, ushering him into an expansive colonnaded room with a sweeping view out to the city. Amid a dozen Hirrin attendants, Cixi sat on a raised chair. Dwarfed by the elaborate chair, the old woman perched there, her feet supported by a footstool. A Hirrin knelt at her side applying a lacquer to the prefect's fingernails. The fumes of the lacquer swept over Quinn's Jacobson's organ, along with smells of Hirrin perfumes.

The prefect's stiff gown and hair created an imposing façade, but the woman herself, as he'd noted before, was as small as a child. Her startlingly black hair was sculpted into a high bonnet framing a lined and crumpled face. Her fingernails were three inches long, curling in at the ends. She hadn't changed a bit.

Next to the dais, but standing somewhat back, was a huge man clad in a tentlike embroidered jacket and pants. This, he guessed from his glimpse of the man the other day, was Zai Gan. The man's scowl cut into the folds of his face. He looked like his rotund brother, but a crueler version.

Quinn bowed, noting that beneath his feet was the rest of the snake that he'd seen in the foyer. However, now he saw that it was no snake, but a dragon, scaled and whiskered. Jeweled teeth glowed in the grinning mouth.

When he rose from his bow, Cixi was glaring at him. The Hirrin at her side had stopped her ministrations and also stared at him.

Cixi looked at Zai Gan. Her deep voice had lost none of its authority: "Stands on Breathing Fire, Preconsul. You saw?"

"Shocking, High Prefect," Zai Gan said.

Quinn had shocked her before he had even opened his mouth. She'd said *stands.* . . . He looked down, seeing that he stood on the dragon. Moving to the side, he stepped off it. The Hirrin attendants on the sidelines moved their heads in unison to note this.

Cixi smirked at him. "Born in a minoral?"

"My noble father despaired of me, Your Brilliance."

She regarded him for a moment. "Are you of my acquaintance, petitioner?" Her face was all squinting eyes and wariness.

"It has never been my honor, High Prefect."

"Yet you sound familiar."

A pause stretched long enough to shred his stomach lining.

The Hirrin attendant blew too strongly on her nails, and Cixi jerked her hand away, frowning and readjusting the drape of her robes. "Minor son of Yulin. No, I suppose not. Does your father still pretend to service ten wives?"

"Nine, these days, Your Brilliance." He'd seen Caiji's funeral procession.

A hiccup emerged from the prefect, an eruption that passed for a laugh. "Even so." The Hirrin spectators fluttered their lips in amusement, and in an instant the suspicion on her face had passed.

"Which wife must claim you?" she asked.

"I am nothing so grand, High Prefect. No wife claims me." With Yulin's brother standing close by, Quinn hoped to avoid speaking of things Zai Gan would know intimately. But Cixi, of course, controlled the conversation.

Cixi examined her glowing purple nails. "Well then, bastard son of the One Who Shines, is it an insult to send such a messenger to the high prefect?"

"It's true that the sublegate Min Fe found me unworthy. He would have sent me home before I could shock the great Cixi." He glanced at the dragon on the floor.

"Perhaps that would have been well." The attendants stood like a row of pawns on a chessboard, waiting for the queen's next move.

It was a hall of power. Quinn thought of Ghoris the navitar reaching out and gathering the lines of choice, of fate. Crisscrossing this room were invisible wires, the burning shadows of things that must be, or should be. All he had to do was grasp them and pull them toward him.

Cixi's voice came to him like a vibration almost beyond hearing: "Perhaps it takes more than that to shock the high prefect."

"I'm relieved. It wasn't the image I had of your personage."

"And what image did you have of this *personage*, bastard messenger?"

He took a chance at flattery: "A woman who wears the dragon, the only one who dares to wear it."

"Ha." Cixi pointed a blue-nailed finger at him. "This one is either very stupid or very smart." She turned slightly to inquire of Zai Gan, "Which, Preconsul?"

Zai Gan muttered, "Stupid, it would seem."

Cixi closed her eyes for a moment, revealing eyelids crusted with silver. "I am surrounded by stupidity. Why do I prefer Hirrin attendants, messenger?"

"Because Hirrin can't lie," Quinn said.

She turned a virulent gaze on the preconsul. "But Chalin can, is that not correct?"

Zai Gan moved closer to the dais. "Yes, Your Brilliance."

"Stop calling me that ridiculous name."

Quinn made a mental note to do likewise, while Zai Gan squirmed under her gaze. Then Cixi turned once more to Quinn, beckoning him with a long finger. "Approach me, messenger."

As Quinn did so, the Hirrin vacated the footstool where she had been seated, and bid him take her place. Sitting, Quinn met Cixi's gaze and managed, he thought, to look relaxed. Her hair wax smelled rancid, barely covered by her perfumed body powder. She looked like a gnome-queen presiding over a grotesque court. But she didn't suspect that the one in front of her was the most peculiar of them all.

Speaking more intimately now, Cixi asked, "Why should the Inyx be leaders of battle, when they cannot utter commands?"

"Madam, they can speak silently among themselves to coordinate."

She held up a lacquered nail to make her point. "But silently. We do not trust those who whisper."

Quinn nodded. "Wise, if whisperers have a choice. But the Inyx have no choice. All their speech is silent."

Zai Gan snorted in response, and Cixi cut a glance at this impertinence. She resumed, "Then how, son of Yulin, do we know if they are loyal, when they never affirm that it is so? When we see no evidence of respect for the gracious lords? These creatures have no writing, no music, nothing to celebrate their Tarig creators. Is this natural, is this loyal?"

"It is loyal to fight for the high lords. This is worth more than bowing and writing."

She allowed herself a small, awful smile, showing an even row of yellow teeth like kernels of corn. "Fighting worth more than bowing? You insult my legates, perhaps?"

Quinn murmured, half apology, half irony, "Born in a minoral."

Cixi's face warred over whether to be amused or annoyed. By her tone, annoyance won. "But sent on high matters to the dragon's court. Strange."

"My father gives me a chance to make up for past indiscretions, madam. If I succeed, I am redeemed."

Her face twitched as though assaulted by a gnat. "No concern of mine."

"No, High Prefect, your pardon." But he'd told her the personal stakes. If she had a heart, it might affect her. Even a woman like this loves something, he thought.

She nodded at Zai Gan and he sidled forward, his bulk now looming next to Quinn. "How can the Inyx lead a battle, being silent?" he demanded.

"Your Excellency, they send their thoughts into the minds of others, and communicate perfectly. But not to lead a battle, merely to lead their own contingent. The battle strategy remains with its Chalin generals."

Cixi examined her index finger, which shone more than her other nails. A tiny pattern of calligraphy appeared there, and Cixi scanned it. She went on: "Why should Yulin care what the Inyx do? The sublegate Min Fe has opined that Yulin has no loyal reason to plead for the Inyx."

Words continued to scroll over Cixi's nail, and Quinn wondered if Min Fe was privy to the conversation, and dipping in. "Min Fe has spent too long with his papers. He knows nothing of Yulin now, if he ever did."

Cixi was very still. "And the high prefect? Is her knowledge, too, a thing of paper?"

"Your pardon, madam. Min Fe and I have stooped to common brawling. We forget ourselves."

The nail scrolled with protest. Cixi devoured every word, her eyes hungry for gossip and dispute.

Quinn pushed on: "Master Yulin's motives are simple, madam."

Zai Gan could restrain himself no longer. "The bastard, banished son of Yulin knows him better than his closest brother?"

Quinn took a chance that Zai Gan was not as favored as the man supposed. "The preconsul has been absent from the sway a few days, and has not renewed ties. Thus, a worthless bastard son may indeed know more about some things in Xi."

Cixi looked up from her nail, watching the two of them with something like glee.

Zai Gan's eyes shed pure loathing. "You presume much," he murmured. Then louder, "So then, expert of Xi, tell us Yulin's secret reason for this enterprise."

Quinn had his answer to this one ready. "It was never hidden, Excellency. The Inyx fight well, but their conscripts are declining. This clarity will inspire enlistment."

Cixi muttered, "Such *inspiration* might have come ten thousand days ago."

Quinn said, and immediately regretted it, "Perhaps Master Yulin should learn hurrying from Min Fe."

Cixi's face darkened. "Do you instruct me on efficiency, messenger? Do you presume to speak as my equal?"

She made a motion as if to rise, and the Hirrin removed the footstool where her feet rested. Lifting her heavy robes, she stepped down, and Quinn stood also, moving out of her way. As she swept past Zai Gan and moved toward the windows, Quinn saw the woven icon on her back: an astonishing dragon in intricate detail, stitched in silver thread with red, green, and blue embellishments for scales, fins, and teeth.

Zai Gan followed her, bending down to whisper in her ear.

Turning back to Quinn, she stood on dramatically elevated shoes, but her height still fell short of four and a half feet. "Why, we ask again, is this clarity here now rather than before? What has changed? Why has Yulin changed? This fat old man who was more content to service wives than the war?"

"I do not know." He watched as Cixi stood with the huge preconsul, dwarfed beside him. But it was obvious where the power lay. It fairly burst from the dragon magistrate.

Cixi stalked closer to him. "Now, suddenly you are stupid? You decide when to be clever, and when to know nothing?"

"I am no legate to play at court games, madam."

"Court games," Cixi hissed, looking up at him. "Is that what my questions are?"

He had pushed too far. She both despised the bureaucracy and reveled in it. He didn't know which end to play. He bowed, hoping to look tongue-tied.

Cixi's voice lowered as she flicked her gaze over the Hirrin attendants straining to hear. "I never liked Yulin, and he always despised me. Our antipathy goes back so long that we are both quite fond of it." She glanced at him, her eyes like hardened amber. "It may be the only thing in your favor." She turned to Zai Gan. "Leave us, Preconsul."

He protested, "I have more questions, Your Brilliance."

"Well, Her Brilliance does not. I am done with this interview."

Quinn forgot to breathe. Done?

Slowly, Zai Gan bowed and swept from the room with surprising grace. But Cixi hadn't dismissed Quinn.

She approached him. Then she said, her voice taking on a formal tone. "After due consideration, and against the advice of my functionaries, I have decided to see Yulin's concept put to the test. This matter of Inyx officers of battle. It may please the Inyx to be so nominated."

Quinn looked at her, stunned.

"In other words, I will enact your clarity and send you on your way." She smirked. "No thanks, no bows?"

"Madam, my thanks indeed." He bowed low, and meant it, heart soaring. He had read her correctly: that proud and brittle, she still craved a man who didn't fawn.

"Of course," she murmured, "if this change in custom fails, your sire may blame you instead of himself. That would be like the old bear."

Quinn said, trying to restrain his elation, "Perhaps my father would credit me for trying."

Cixi sucked on her teeth, causing her face to collapse into its many lines. "Then he would be soft as well as fat." She waved him away.

As he turned to leave, she said, "You were poorly prepared for this meeting. No petitioner has ever stood on the dragon."

Quinn turned back to her. "Consul Shi Zu gave me instructions. But they were lengthy, and I fell asleep before finishing them."

She smirked. "Shi Zu is a long-winded Adda with too many clothes." Her eyes held him in place. Then she said, pleasantly enough, "Are you a schemer, Dai Shen?"

"I am what I am, High Prefect."

"Oh, I doubt that. No one is what they are. Except the Hirrin." She leaned forward. "I do not trust you, messenger. You are too smart to be a minor son of Yulin. Whatever you are, you have lost something today that you might value."

"What have I lost, madam?" The lines in the room grew sticky, and sagged. He hoped it was Cixi who got caught in them, and not he.

"Your anonymity," she answered. "Consider yourself under my close gaze from now on."

"I risked much to be under your gaze, madam." It was the truest thing he had said to her.

She regarded him, murmuring, "You are good with words. Perhaps you have a future as a legate, after all."

Quinn bowed. "May God not look on me."

"Mmm," he heard her utter, a sound like a dragon purring.

CHAPTER TWENTY-SIX

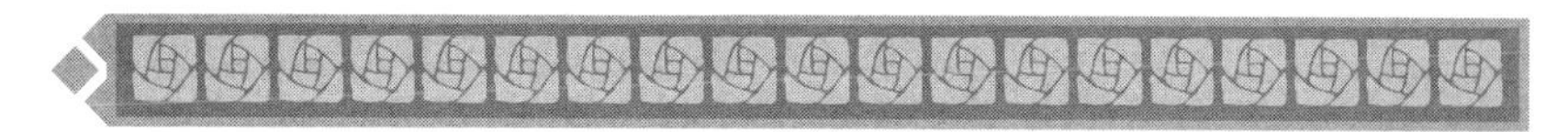

Three things are lowly: the godman, the beku, the clerk. But only one is buried in the sky.

—a saying of the Magisterium

THE FUNCTIONARIES WATCHED QUINN as he descended the stairs. Min Fe was not among them, nor Anzi. Quinn felt their gaze drill into his back as he passed them, but his relief made him immune. Despite Cixi's doubts, he had won this piece. She didn't trust him, but she didn't trust anyone. She knew that Yulin was lazy, and in this new enterprise of his, she smelled a whiff of rot. Her nose was good.

As he headed for his cell, he saw Brahariar coming toward him down the corridor, bowing to all as she came. He caught the Jout's eye, but she ignored him. Passing close to his elbow, she murmured, "Cho in the catacombs. Now." She continued past him.

The catacombs. That would be a good place for whispering, if Cho needed privacy. Quinn descended the stairs and ramps to the level of his cell and then headed for the perimeter of the Magisterium, to throw off anyone following him. Let it appear, then, that he was going to his favorite balcony. There, he sat in his accustomed spot—one he hadn't visited since his meeting with Hadenth three days ago. He gazed out at the glinting sea, pockmarked with mercurial clouds, wondering which of the distant primacies was the Long Gaze of Fire, the name of the one where Sydney was.

After a time he rose, and instead of his usual route back, he climbed a short ramp to enter the Magisterium by another level. He hoped Cho's secretiveness didn't imply inauspicious news. He ducked into the interwall area that Braharìar had shown him. It didn't lead all the way down, but by the time he was on the fifth level, and moving as quickly as looked normal, he thought he'd shaken any pursuer.

The cleric level was the smallest and most crowded level of the city's underbelly. In their white silks the clerks looked like altered angels . . . a notion dispelled by the homely icon embroidered on their backs: the beku. Hundreds of stone well columns formed a tight forest of pillars. Avoiding the ceremonial entrance to the catacombs, Quinn threaded his way among the columns toward a minor access point. He knew the way. His knowledge of the city's underbelly was emerging like a picture being stripped of sand in the wind. He felt that if he stayed here many more days he would have all his memories at last. But he would not stay. He would leave as soon as Cixi's approval was recorded in the pandect, and his papers in order. The hope for the Entire's great secret, the correlates—that hope must be deferred. He would come back for them, though. Even now he was casting about for some way to send Sydney back home, leaving him on this side of the veil.

Standing before the door to the catacombs, Quinn saw that the surface of the door was covered with writing. The Three Vows: *Withhold the knowledge of the Entire from the non-Entire, Impose the peace of the Entire, Extend the reach of the Entire. . . .* Entering, he descended the narrow stairs, coming at last to the bottom of the floating city.

A wall of cold air met him. Passing through the climate-control barrier, he found himself in a dark hall, filled, he knew, with banners for the cremated dead. He recalled that a supreme inducement to life at the Ascendancy was to plant one's burial flag in the bright city catacombs. There had been a time when he assumed his own bones would reside here. As he walked, the floor lit up, then dimmed behind him, surrounding him with a soft halo. On either side of him the flags thrust out of funereal ovoids snugged up like the combs in a beehive. So far, by the vast darkness around him, he was alone.

Even in death the hierarchy remained. Here was the clerk section, with earnest flags: *Clerk of Humble Tasks, Glorious Masters. Servant trusted by Consul Jin Se. Thirty Thousand Joyful Days.* The flags sparkled now and then with molecular fabbers scrubbing the dust away.

A noise stopped him. Ahead of him, a figure in white stepped out from a side aisle. As the figure came closer, he recognized Anzi.

She tapped her heel on the ground and they were in darkness.

"Anzi," he whispered. "I came to meet Cho. Do you know why Cho called me here?"

"I didn't know he had. I followed you," she said. "I was afraid to contact you. There's a legate watching me."

"Min Fe." After a beat he said, "She approved the mission, Anzi."

"Oh, Shen! Approved?" He couldn't see her face in the utter blackness, but her voice conveyed her happiness.

"I'll tell you later, but yes, approved."

They listened in the dark for a while, watching for lights, but only the dead kept them company.

Taking Quinn's hand, Anzi placed an object in it. She had been successful in her assignment. It was a toy boat.

By the feel, it was crude, and not a proper replacement for Small Girl's fine boat, but it might do.

Anzi said, "This is not for your daughter, certainly."

"No." He hadn't had time to tell her everything. Now he did so, glad he couldn't see her expression in the dark.

At last she asked, "Because you love your daughter, now the Tarig young are included?"

"I don't know." Nor did he.

"Truly, Dai Shen, it's time to leave this place."

"Soon."

She put her hand on the toy, trying to take it, but he held on. "Anzi. There's more." She waited. "It's about Cho. I did more than ask him to look up Kang's reports."

Again, she waited.

"The navitar said Johanna was at the center of things—of things relating to me." He murmured, "She always was."

Anzi's voice grew dusky. "Yes, I know."

They stood in silence for a long time, and around them the flags were still as alabaster. He whispered, "I asked Cho to look up a term. Arlis."

"Arlis?"

"Johanna's maiden name. There might be other code words she could hide under. I gave them all to Cho."

Her voice was barely audible. "Heaven give us not looking. Now Cho will know it's more than curiosity. It's an obsession. An obsession on the part of a man that you cannot be."

"Perhaps," he said. It brought them all into danger. But he intended to get them out again. There was always a door out.

But just now he was looking for a door in. There were secrets here, in this Magisterium. Secrets that Johanna had. This is what he had gleaned from the navitar, though she hadn't said so, not directly. Truthfully, it hadn't taken much to push him toward Johanna, or what was left of her.

A scratching noise came from one side. Someone was on the aisle next to theirs. The shuffling noise continued until a loud pop occurred. Anzi tapped her foot, and the floor lit under her. By this wan light they saw that a compartment was empty, and something was snaking through from the other side. It was a hand.

The hand opened up. In the center was a small redstone. Quinn took it, and the hand disappeared. Then a funeral oval was jammed back into place. They listened for footsteps then, but the person had melted away.

Quinn held the stone in his fist.

"Read it later," Anzi urged, looking around in alarm.

He stared her down. "We need a corner where you can stand guard for me."

He led her to the rounded outer wall of the catacomb, where he borrowed her clerk's hat. She stood guard some distance away.

In the dark and the silence, Quinn paused, hands sweating. Then he inserted the stone in the computational well of the hat. He waited while the stone dissolved and locked onto its bits of data.

And then Johanna was with him. It was only her voice, but it was as though she was sitting at his side. He struggled for control, trying to listen to the sense of what she was saying while feeling her absence like an empty realm within him. She was talking to him, telling him how her interrogator, the scholar Kang, had grown fond of her, and after many years had placed this redstone in the archives, and would be telling Titus where to find it. She had begged Kang for this favor, and had prayed that Kang would convey the redstone to Titus.

Kang never had. Or perhaps Titus had already fled the Entire by then.

He sat with his back to the wall, and cradled the hat in his arms.

Johanna said that if she was discovered, Lord Inweer would kill her. That after listening to the recording, Titus should destroy it. That above all, he must never keep a redstone copy, because she would die of it, if discovered.

Then she said that she still wanted her life, and that he should want his.

"No," he whispered.

As though she'd heard him, she laughed. "Yes," she said. "It's all that's left now. Our separate lives. Take yours back, Titus. Because I'm taking mine. I don't despair, and neither should you. Even after they sent Sydney away, I still believe somewhere she'll salvage a life. If I didn't believe that, I wouldn't want to live."

Perhaps she had heard to the contrary, and that was why she died. Of grief. But there was no time to speculate. She went on.

"Sydney has been sent to the Inyx sway. You know that, I'm sure. They say they are all slaves there—but I thank God she isn't in Hadenth's reach. She's gone from us, Titus. I pray for her. I know you don't pray. But you have to live. You have to find a way home. You have to tell them what this place is, this terrible world. A place so dreadful they hate God. I know you don't think that's much of an indictment.

"It doesn't matter about God." She sighed. "About us, Titus—what can I say? I expect you've found someone else by now. It's all right; it really is. I've made a life, as much I can. You do the same. Lord Inweer has me here; if you ever saw this place, you would never hope for me again. I'm not sad, Titus. Life is a gift, even here, and even for you, whatever you may suffer.

"All right then, here's what I've come to say. Even Kang doesn't know. No one knows except the lords. And me." She paused. "You've heard that this place has a great engine that protects Ahnenhoon from invasion. That's a lie. The fortress isn't built to fend off the Paion. The armies do that well enough.

"The engine is worse, so much worse than that. It's the secret to the storm walls and the bright. I never thought about what powers things here—those storm walls and their sky—did you? We should have. The energy it takes is beyond imagining. Whatever power source the lords had in the Heart, where they came from, is running out. Now they're going to feed off the Rose. I don't know how it can be done, but the lords can do this. You've seen their power.

"I think that they've already started. The Entire is feeding slowly now, but soon the lords will collapse the Rose into the form that suits them, into a furnace, a gigantic star, is how I think of it. It's the best sort of fuel for this place. The Rose has maybe a hundred years left—and then it will be a sudden collapse. These things are impossible to conceive of. Just remember what you know of the Tarig, and then you won't doubt it can happen. Titus, I know that you must wonder how I know these things. All right, I'll tell you. I've said I've made my peace here, and I have. Sometimes I'm close enough to the creatures that they tell me things. They could have lied, but why would they? Perhaps you'll have to take what I say on faith. Hard for you, I know."

She made a small sound in her throat. "No time, no time. Oh Titus, there's so much I want to say. But none of it makes any difference now. Listen, then: Disable Ahnenhoon, destroy it if you can. I'll gladly die with the place. Go home to the Rose and warn them." She paused again. "He's coming. You'd think they'd learn to wear soft-soled shoes so their footsteps didn't echo so. I'm glad they make mistakes. Good-bye Titus. May God guide you."

She added, "You know which God I mean."

He walked down the rows of the mausoleum, his hand drifting along the ovoids so that he could pace in the dark. Anzi was listening to the recording now, and afterward they would destroy the redstone, so that no one could find it.

As he paced down the darkened aisles, the flags slapped at his hand.

She had said, *Take back your life, Titus. Because I'm taking mine.* The words cut a swath.

She had said, *They're going to feed off the Rose.*

He heard Anzi approaching. "I ground it into dust, Dai Shen," she whispered.

She embraced him, and he held her in the dark. Anzi whispered into his shoulder, "If I had never lived to hear such things . . ." She didn't finish the thought. He couldn't finish his own thoughts about the Rose. Soon to die. To power the All. To the Tarig, the Rose was only fuel.

Amid the large shocks, the small: *It's all that's left now. Our separate lives.* She had released him. It left him with an unsteady feeling, like walking on a beach where the tide ran up and stole the sand from under your feet. A separate life. Did he have one, then?

Anzi asked, "What will we do?"

The dark chamber filled with this thought. There seemed to be lines falling from the ceiling, filaments from a spider's mouth. He felt paralyzed by a web more complex than he could fathom.

"I'll find Sydney. Then I'll go home with her—and tell what's happened here."

Anzi's voice came so soft and small, he thought it might be the words of a spirit: "If you die or are captured, Shen, who will bring the warning to the Rose?"

The darkness was so thick, he thought he might suffocate.

"I have time to do both," he whispered, because he prayed with all his heart that this was true.

Anzi's silence was terrible. If he didn't rescue Sydney, if he ran back to the Rose, was he betraying this Chalin woman who thought things of greatness converged in him? Was he betraying Bei? Because what came next could condemn the Entire.

"When I come back—when my people hear this—we'll be at war."

"Yes."

In confusion, he exclaimed, "Whose side are you on, then?"

"That's not the right question."

"But it is. Why not put it off for as long as you can? You've seen war in my universe. We're good at it. The lords may win, but it might not matter after we're done with the Entire."

"Not the right question," she repeated.

"What *is* the right question?" He was confused and ragged, and she wasn't. He was glad of her steadiness, but he also wanted her allegiance back. The woman who was going to the Inyx sway with him, the woman who had said he could start over.

Her voice came softly. "The question is, Whose side are *you* on?"

The Rose was his place; how could it not be? But that didn't mean he wanted war. "Tell me not to do this, Anzi. Not to bring war to the Entire. Can't you tell me that?"

"No, I can't." Her voice sounded small, but certain. "You know why, I think."

He knew. She was on the side of the Rose. "I need time to think." He began backing off. "I can't think right now."

"You can think. You just don't like your conclusion."

He shot back at her: "What's it like being so certain, Anzi?"

"Like burning up inside."

He tried to say something, but failed. He turned and enlivened the light under his feet. It lit him all the way to the door.

He walked through the Magisterium, half-blind, not knowing which level, which corridor. Returning no bows, he got sideways looks. Not good, not good to draw attention. He turned to see if Anzi was following him; but no, he was alone.

At last he found himself sitting outdoors by the pool, by the Sleeping Lord's monument, where he was half-hidden from view but could still snatch narrow views of the city. On the promenade a few Tarig strolled, as well as all the other motley and wearying variety of thinking beings, walking and strolling and hurrying. Among them all, he alone was human. For the first time, he was lonely. He sat staring dully at the pool. Johanna's voice came to him: *They will collapse the Rose into a form that suits them.* To power the storm walls of the Entire. This, then, was the end in fire that the navitar Ghoris had foretold. This was why Johanna was at the center of it all. Because she was going to tell him.

And here, too, was the true meaning of the Third Vow: *Extend the reach of the Entire.* It was so obvious now. The Entire must reach outside itself to survive; it must devour the Rose. Despite the long lives of its denizens, the Entire itself was short-lived. It was obvious—and he had thought it before—that its energy requirements could not be sustained without extraordinary measures. Extraordinary, indeed.

He must have sat for a full hour or more. Above him, the bright blasted into

Prime of Day. He was weary of the bright, profoundly weary, with his mind buried under everything. The Entire had finally managed to overwhelm him.

The carp had been swimming in place for a long time. The carp with the orange back. Quinn was staring right at it, not seeing it. Until he did see it.

Its scales humped in ridges, looking wrong. Then the mottled marking looked like Lucent script. A word formed: *Follow*.

Then the carp swam away toward the canal.

Quinn followed.

He fought to keep his agitation under control, thinking he must look like a man who'd just seen a plane crash. He felt stunned and horrified, sick and galvanized. He didn't know what he felt, but he was sure he looked odd. Kneeling beside the canal, he stooped to gather water in his hands. He washed his face. It was all he could think of to brace himself, and it helped. Lord Oventroe had sent for him. Sent for him now, at the worst time, when his thinking had slowed and his body was indescribably weary.

Ahead, the carp was waiting for him, swimming in a little eddy. Then, seeing him, it swam slowly away, upstream. He strolled, trying not to stare at the carp. The fish was easy to spot, waiting for him and then swimming on. Quinn forced himself to look away from the canal, as any ordinary person would; to look at the spires of the city, to gaze now and then at the palatine hill. Once or twice he stopped to sit on the canal walls, looking like he had no place to go. Whereas he had the most important places in the world to go. And all at once.

He followed the carp in this dazed state, recalling his plan for that moment when he might talk to this lord. The plan now seemed very ill advised. It was always going to be a risky thing, to see this lord. But from great risks, great rewards. That logic had held until Johanna changed everything. Now he must get home no matter what—Anzi said so, and she might be right. And, if it came to that, then he had to go home without the correlates. Without Sydney. He pushed that thought aside. No, not without Sydney.

A shadow fell on him. He was standing there, gazing at the water, and astonishingly, a Tarig had come to stand beside him. He'd heard no boots, no sound at all.

Quinn turned and bowed, to gain time, to gather his wits. Had he been discovered, now of all times?

"We do not know you," the Tarig said.

This Tarig was only a half foot taller than Quinn. The lord's voice was deep, and Quinn did not recognize him.

Quinn answered, "Dai Shen of the house of Yulin, my life in your service."

"Ah, Yulin. We know of that Chalin man. A famous personage, indeed." The lord regarded him with a calm assurance that was far from Quinn's own state. "Su Bei is not so famous, though some remember him well. We gave him a token once."

Quinn's breathing became very shallow. It was Oventroe, then. The redstone he'd fed the carp was Su Bei's. And now, after thirteen days, here was Oventroe come to see him out in the open, and not hiding. Quinn felt his scalp prickle. Were other Tarig coming toward them even now, and was it over? But no one was nearby. No Tarig. Other sentients passed, bowing low, looking relieved that they had not been singled out for conversation by the lord.

"Su Bei is of my acquaintance," Quinn said carefully.

The lord did not look at him, but gazed at the canal, as though idly watching carp. "Bei, by his redstone, begged this lord to see you, Chalin warrior of Ahnenhoon. You have ten words. Give them up."

He had only ten words to convey what he wished. That settled it, then. There were to be no games of *how can I trust you*. The lord demanded everything, immediately.

"I am Titus Quinn."

A small breeze wicked the sweat from his face and neck. He felt ill to say it in the outdoors next to the mansions of the Tarig. To a Tarig.

"Prove that you are he."

"Do you speak the dark languages?" Quinn asked. He'd been ready for this moment. "Such as that language that Titus Quinn spoke when he was first here?"

The lord turned to look down on Quinn. His face was somewhat rounded, his black hair knotted into rows and gathered at his neck with a glittering metal clasp. The eyes: black, merciless. Oventroe said, "Conceived in liberty and dedicated to the proposition . . ."

He was speaking in English.

"That all men are created equal," Quinn whispered, finishing the sentence in his turn.

Quinn was shaking. Speaking the words, speaking in English. It was all exposed now. He commanded himself to get a grip.

"We favor the Lincoln speech," Lord Oventroe said. "We select it as one to memorize." His face seemed to soften for a moment, if it was not Quinn's imagination. One had to be careful not to impute human feelings where none existed. But Tarig had *some* feelings, and sometimes they appeared understandable, as Quinn knew to his profound regret. The lord continued, "You are not favored here."

The understatement was staggering. Perhaps a joke?

"Yet you return," Oventroe continued.

"To open the Entire to converse with the Rose, Bright Lord. Help me."

"You believe that this lord would do so?"

"Yes. But I can keep your secrets." Now Quinn had revealed that he knew Oventroe to be a traitor. So it was all on the line now, or most of it.

"Converse, ah?" The lord had been staring at him, and now looked back to the carp, which seemed uneasy to be the focus of his attention, and darted away. "An interesting proposition. But breaking the First Vow, and breaking is to die." They had reverted to Lucent, perhaps not to severely test the lord's capabilities. And to avoid having a dark language overheard.

Quinn was conscious that his interview could be cut off at any moment, and so he plunged on: "The correlates, Bright Lord. Let's by God open this door. Allow us to bargain for passage through the All to distant points in the Rose. Once humans come, there'll be an exchange between our races, between our worlds. If that's what you want, help me."

"An open door, ah?" Oventroe's look became haunted. The lord had a great passion, and its intensity was palpable. Quinn felt it clearly.

Oventroe was saying, "All beings know this lord as one who hates the Rose."

Quinn nodded. "But it's not true, is it?"

"You do not question a lord."

Quinn had thought that they might be beyond the usual deference games. But even in bed with Chiron, he had given her deference. It never changed, never.

Now that it was all out, Quinn felt calmer. They could take him, or kill him. Eventually, there was nothing worse they could do. He saw the carp and the city through jaded eyes. It was just a place. It was just a life. In the end, you did what you had to do. He looked into Oventroe's face, waiting for an answer.

It came, and struck hard. "No," Oventroe said. "Why would we give you such powers?"

"Because I am the messenger from the Rose."

Oventroe looked at him with something like yearning. "Yes. Aren't you. Their messenger." He took a step closer, forcing Quinn to look up at him at a steeper angle. The lord's eyes darted over his face, like a scanner, devouring what he was seeing.

Quinn had time to think whether to plead with the lord about the engine at Ahnenhoon, but if he told that astonishing secret, if Quinn revealed that *he* knew, would he die right now at this lord's feet? Did Oventroe know this secret himself? Yes, of course he must. Would he fear that Quinn would come with an army to defeat the Tarig? Even a dissenter among the Tarig might well fear that outcome.

"Messenger of the Rose," Oventroe mused. "But you have nothing to give one such as this lord." He paused. "The Rose is sweet, but without powers. All power is with the five."

The five high lords, whose company Oventroe needed to join.

"Thus," the lord continued, "as to the door, no, it is too much to give. For no advantage."

The Tarig turned away again, and Quinn rushed to drive home his plea. "But how will the Rose ever touch the Entire? Help me, Lord Oventroe."

The voice came stabbing at him, removing hope, setting barriers: "They do not touch. The Rose never touches us."

"Help me to change that." Quinn waited for the answer on which everything depended.

Then the lord said, "Perhaps, in time. In time we may be moved to help you."

But I'm leaving, Quinn wanted to shout. "There isn't time," he said. "Decide now." Oventroe wanted a piece of him, but Quinn couldn't stay.

"There is always enough time, Titus Quinn. You should have learned that by now."

"How will I find you? I'll be in a far primacy—or farther."

"On the Nigh, seek the navitar Jesid. Petition him to find us."

"What river?" Each primacy had its river, Quinn knew.

"They are all one," Oventroe said, and then he walked away.

CHAPTER TWENTY-SEVEN

Heaven gave me three husbands, and twenty beku. But of names, only one.
—from *The Twelve Wisdoms*

VERY LATE INTO THE EBB, QUINN STILL HAD NOT SLEPT. He wished that Anzi were here. Her best disguise was to lose herself among the clerks for now, but he would be glad to see her, to mend whatever had come between them, and to tell her of his meeting with Oventroe. There was hope, he wanted to tell her . . . about opening a door between their worlds. Perhaps that door itself might forestall annihilation in some way, if the two cultures could talk to each other. But no, the Entire *must* burn the Rose.

They're going to feed off the Rose, Johanna had said. *The energy the storm walls take is beyond imagining.* But what if Johanna was wrong? She wasn't wrong; an end in fire had been predicted by the navitar. Johanna was at the center of things, Ghoris had said. Only one world could live. So now Quinn would make sure it was the Rose. Johanna had pleaded, *You have to tell them what this place is, this terrible world.* And was it terrible? There were Anzi and Bei and Ci Dehai and Cho—people who had helped him and cared what he became.

He remembered his promise to Bei: that humans wouldn't come to settle. No, first they would come with arms, he thought bitterly. But hadn't they the right to defend themselves from Tarig aggression?

To delay bringing the warning home was unthinkable, and yet he was thinking of it. Having left Sydney behind once before, how could he do so again? He lay there, forming plans and abandoning them.

A knock at his door startled him. Opening it, he found Brahariar standing before him. She bowed. "Forgive the ebb intrusion, Excellency."

Glancing at a satchel at her feet, she said, "I am leaving. My mission is complete, thanks to Steward Cho."

"A worthy man. I hope your petition was successful, then."

"It was." Her skin fluttered, the petals closing and opening in pleasure. "The shining consul Shi Zu ruled in my favor."

"Well done, Brahariar. Your waiting is over."

"Excellency," she said, "you took pains on my behalf. I hope it did no harm to your own mission, but I fear that it did." Looking up and down the corridor and finding it empty, she said, "The great legate Min Fe came looking here, while you were gone."

"The great legate has disliked me since I met him. Not your fault."

"I am relieved," Brahariar said. She picked up her satchel. "I wish to thank you, but have nothing to give you."

"Nothing is needed. Many days to you, Brahariar."

As the Jout still made no immediate move to depart, Quinn said, and then wished that he hadn't: "What was your mission, if it pleases you to say?"

Her mouth elongated in a Jout smile. "Oh, yes it does please me, Excellency. I pleaded for the strangulation death of one who might have saved my father from falling from a God's Needle."

Quinn waited, confused.

"He was the last person to see my father alive. He should have prevented it."

"He pushed your father?"

"No. Still, someone must be responsible. It is good that Shi Zu agreed with me. I will watch the strangulation with satisfaction. Then I can be at peace." She bowed again, and departed.

Quinn watched her bulky form recede down the corridor. He remembered what he had once known about the Jout: that they carried a grudge longer than a beku could go without water. The conversation left him feeling uneasy and complicit.

He sat on his bed, staring at the opposite wall, his mind skittering from one thought to another. Anzi's voice echoed: *If you die or are captured . . . who will bring the warning to the Rose?*

Not that it was dangerous for him to enter the Inyx sway. He had his endorsements, his identity. But escaping with her was the difficulty . . . the alarms raised, and the sudden disclosure of who he was—because who else but Titus Quinn would come for Sydney Quinn?

He put his head in his hands and felt a blackness descend. In his whole life he had never come to such despair. Sitting on his bed and staring at the wall, he let go of thinking and gave himself up to dark thoughts. After a long while he slept.

And dreamed.

Ghoris the navitar stood on the dais, her head and torso protruding through the membrane above her chair. She wrestled with the lightning bolts of the binds, grabbing them and throwing them at the storm wall, trying to pierce those dark folds. But the storm wall only absorbed the lightning, growing stronger and darker. Quinn stood on the roof of the navitar's cabin, watching as Ghoris struggled. But now it was not with lightning that she wrestled, but with Johanna.

Fire, oh fire, Ghoris thundered, giving Johanna a dreadful blow that took away half her face. Her face is ruined, Quinn thought in deep remorse, and as the two women grappled he thought that Johanna looked like Ci Dehai, and fought as well. Finally, with a strong shove at Johanna, Ghoris cried out, *Choose, choose!* Regaining her footing, Johanna stood very still, saying with reproach, "I already have." Then Johanna turned to look at Quinn. He'd thought himself invisible, but she saw him. And kept gazing at him, her robes fluttering in the storm of the walls. A knocking sound came from below. Someone trying to tell him to get off the roof.

He jerked awake. Someone was knocking on his door. Stumbling to answer it, he found Shi Zu standing before him, flanked by legates.

"Ah. Here you are," the consul said. In his finery, Shi Zu looked like a male peacock amid a flock of plain females. He brought out a scroll from his tunic. By its golden spindle, Quinn knew that it was from Cixi.

"Your approvals, and official clarity to be presented to the Inyx," he said. "By heaven, a fine accomplishment, Dai Shen of Xi."

Quinn accepted the spindle, holding it in numb silence.

Shi Zu said, "It would have been a suitable undertaking for my retinue and me, but many duties hinder such an indulgence. Do it justice then, soldier of Ahnenhoon." Nodding at Quinn's mumbled thanks, the consul left, accompanied by his clerks.

Quinn read the calligraphy, confirming its essence. A redstone rattled inside the spindle cap, a data stone the Inyx didn't know how to use. He stared at the scroll. But now it was useless to him. He must go home. Without her. It wasn't about Sydney's life anymore; it was about everyone's life. *Everything we love*, Johanna had said, *all to burn.*

He would rather have died than chosen. But he chose. He felt his heart cooling into something more steady and basic than before: a logical, mechanical engine. He could keep going; he must—and all the reasons why were clear and stone cold.

A vision of Sydney came to mind—his grown daughter. How long was it, he wondered, before she gave up hoping I would come for her? Probably long ago. And now, in the event, she was right. He wasn't coming for her. He had to turn away from the look on her face.

Now he and Anzi would leave this place. A few loose ends to wrap up, and then they would leave.

He tucked the scroll into his satchel lying near the bed. Then he took out the toy boat and walked out of the Magisterium into the city.

With few sentients abroad, the Tarig city was eerily quiet as Early Day renewed the cycle of the bright. Looking at the sky, Quinn thought how profligate, how wanton, was that fire. He didn't know what kind of fire it was, except a devouring one. The beauties that he'd seen in its waxing and waning moods had now grown somber. He couldn't help but mourn its loss, and the loss of his attraction to it. What was the Entire, but an inverted flower that sucked dry the real world? And, unwilling to think that thought for long, he let himself believe there was yet a way to resolve all problems. He was tired; he knew that. He would sleep soon, and then depart.

A flock of ground birds sped about the plazas, pecking at specks of food. He couldn't remember if they were real animals or merely vacuums. Crossing a canal, he walked across a nearly deserted plaza, toward the palatine hill. The city stretched out on all sides, this circular city in the heart of a circular ocean, in the center of the great arms of the primacies—the whole of it shaped like a starfish. And he, at its center. The wires holding it all together plunged to their destinies here.

Perhaps, to avoid his awful decision, he should have told Oventroe about the engine at Ahnenhoon. The lord might have been an ally, if he loved the Rose, or was fascinated by it. But if Oventroe already knew, then he was as bad as the rest of them, and no friend to the Rose. And no friend to Titus Quinn, to withhold the correlates—although who would give an enemy the key to such a door? Now that the Rose was an enemy of the Entire.

So finding the correlates was another reason to come back. He would come back, of course. That thought kept him going.

He stood in front of the walled garden, with its arched entrance, and cool interior beckoning. It looked the same as before, but empty of children and toys.

He entered the garden, brushing past the lush climbing vine. No one was in sight. Just as well. At the pond, he set the boat in the water. It rocked in the gentle current of the pond. Not as fine a boat as the child had burned, but his parting gift.

Turning to go, he saw Small Girl standing at the garden entrance.

She showed no surprise at finding him here. "The Chalin man," she said.

He bowed. She was up early, and dressed formally, as before.

"Fixing," she pronounced, looking at the pond. She ran to the water's edge and stretched out her hand for the boat, but it had drifted too far.

Quinn snagged the boat from the water and gave it to her. She smiled, and it lifted his spirits. There remained small pleasures. He was grateful for them.

The bright was warm on his head and hands. Sitting next to Small Girl, he felt exhausted and spent. He could almost have lain down next to the wall and slept. They sat together as she examined the boat, turning it over and over. Finally she said, "Thank you."

He nodded. "Yes. Of course. A small thing."

"A fixed thing."

"Yes, Sydney, fixed."

She continued to gaze at the boat.

But Quinn's heart had stopped. What had he said? Dreamlike, he looked around him. He had said his daughter's name. Slowly, he stood up. Time to leave.

"The Chalin man sits down."

He was frozen, watching her. She wouldn't remember the word, that name, to repeat it to her parents.

But her eyes commanded him to sit, and now he was afraid not to. He sat next to her, trying to stay calm.

"What name did you say?" She still gazed at the boat.

He was sick, his heart beating erratically. "Nothing," he said.

The bright was growing hot, monstrous.

"Something," she said. "It is something."

What could she possibly know? He was rattled for nothing. He would brazen it through, get her mind on something else. "But Small Girl likes the boat?"

"Yes."

"Good."

"But Sydney doesn't."

She was not going to leave it. He looked at her, and she returned his gaze, putting the toy aside on the ledge. "You are not the Chalin man."

He swallowed. She knew.

"I am," he said.

"You do not go against what we say, though."

"And what do you say, Small Girl?"

Her black eyes looked into his. "Your small girl is Sydney. We know who you are." She stood, at eye level to him, as he sat. "Hnnn?" The expression was predatory.

She knew. It was all coming down. The false names, the grand plans.

He shook his head. He looked at the Tarig child. He had to go home. Because they were burning the Rose.

Small Girl put her hand under his chin, and peered at his face. "Titus, then," she said.

"No," he whispered.

"Come back. Ah?"

"No," he said again.

It was all on his shoulders, the terrible plans of the Tarig. If Small Girl betrayed him, everyone would die. All the worlds. All the Earth.

He would knock her out; it had to be done.

Small Girl caught the intention in his eyes, and turned to run. He caught her tunic, dragging her backward. She clawed at him, a hot downstroke that gashed his cheek but missed his eyes. She cried out.

Then he struck her, trying to stun her, so it could be the end of their struggle. But she wouldn't give up, and she shrieked, her cry reverberating in the garden. He covered her mouth, lest she call to her Tarig parents, and holding her in an iron grasp, he immobilized her. As she thrashed with ferocious strength, his grip began to slip.

Renewing his hold, he cast about for what to do. There must be something. He could take her to an empty room—the mansions were full of empty rooms—and tie her up while he escaped.

An arm came free of his hold and smashed against his temple, knocking him backward for a moment. She bolted from his arms, screeching, "Titus Quinn, Titus Quinn." Diving for her, he pinned her to the ground; placing his hand on the back of her head, he forced her face into the ground to stop her screams.

Any moment now the Tarig would come.

The Rose. He must go back and tell them. That the Earth would die. They would kill it, and every other Earth. . . . And he knew then, with awful clarity, that Small Girl had to die, before she raised the alarm and prevented him from leaving.

He pulled Small Girl into the pond, keeping his hand over her mouth. Oh God, he prayed. Oh, Johanna, how can there be a God? A good one, a just one? No, it was a Miserable God.

Small Girl twisted in his arms like a steel coil, but he managed to push her down in the waist-high water. He sobbed for this small creature, even as he submerged her head. She came up once, shrieking, "Titus!" But pushing her down again, he held her there. He looked down on himself from some mental vantage point, seeing a monster drowning a child.

Then, to his horror, from deep inside the palace, he thought he heard shouts. He thought he heard someone shout his name.

Small Girl had ceased struggling. He lurched away from her body. She floated, facedown, her tunic turning purple as it became saturated.

He crawled from the pond, backing away. Then he turned and ran from the garden.

On the other side of the gate, he nearly collided with Anzi. She looked like a person from another life. The one where he had not murdered a child.

"Anzi," he breathed. "Run."

Anzi looked over his shoulder, toward the pond, where the child floated.

He looked too, hoping that it was some terrible vision, not an irrevocable event. But the Tarig child floated there in the water. "I killed her," he whispered.

Anzi was dragging him down the narrow path. How had she come here, and where could they go? Quinn pulled her into a side street, deserted for now. They stopped, looking wildly around for pursuit.

Anzi murmured, "I tried to stop you from coming here. Too late."

"I killed her," Quinn said. He looked at Anzi, hardly seeing her. "She knew me." Her voice came back to him: *Titus, then.*

"I killed her."

"Yes," Anzi said. "You did. And now we're going to leave."

"Leave?" He heard the words, but not the sense.

"The pillars," she said. "Hurry." She tugged at him, trying to drag him down the pathway.

Instead, he pulled her down the side street. "This way, Anzi."

Her face was frantic. "To where?"

The pillars were too obvious. He ran for the mansion he knew well: Lady Chiron's. He knew the way, although his mind was nearly empty with shock. He had murdered Small Girl. Part of his mind kept saying that it couldn't have happened, couldn't . . .

They climbed a long, winding staircase higher into the palatine hill.

In the distance, he heard voices. Looking back, he saw, on a high terrace, several Tarig. They ran across, and disappeared.

"Running," Quinn said, his voice low. Anzi followed his gaze, and became very still. Tarig didn't run. With their long legs, they were superbly equipped for it, but he had never seen a Tarig run.

The fourth level of the Magisterium was in chaos. Cho heard from every side: *Titus Quinn, Quinn, Quinn. Small Girl, dead in the pond.* Functionaries scattered from their posts, running, as though they had duties of a martial nature. They didn't, no more than did Cho, who sat at his stone well, bewildered, sweating.

The Chalin man sent by Master Yulin. Oh, by the everlasting bright, it had been Titus Quinn. He had never imagined it. All knew the famous face, but the man must have undergone surgeries.

He bent over his computational well, sick in his gut. His nose hit a nub on the stone well and the screen flashed at him, and it made him sit upright and gather himself with more dignity.

Dai Shen had never claimed to be on the Radiant Path. He had said his goal was worthy. Was that goal to connect the worlds, to convey the knowledge of the Entire to the Rose? Surely, if Titus Quinn had gone home that first time, he had already conveyed that knowledge. Ah, but if he hadn't, then he was escaping to do so now.

Cho wondered: Was this forbidden converse between worlds forbidden for a good reason? Cho had never questioned the Three Vows. *Which breaking is to die. . . .*

Well, he thought, I have already broken the First Vow, by helping Dai Shen.

Filled with anxiety, he stumbled to his feet and fled the warren of stewards. He made his way upward toward the city, pushing past crowds of frantic clerks, stewards, and legates. He knew that he would help Dai Shen one more time, if he could. But how?

And why? Indeed why? His life would be forfeit if he did. But when he thought of his life, he knew that he had hardly lived at all. Not compared to Dai Shen, nor even compared to Ji Anzi, or any of those beings who lived in the Great Without. Possibly each one of them had lived more fully than any steward of the Great Within.

Today that would change.

He hurried to the nearest pillar, the third pillar. There, a capsule had left a short time ago for the sea. He nubbed the screen to find who had been aboard, and added Dai Shen to the list.

He stood back from his work, startled and a little saddened. He had altered a record, inserting an inaccuracy. The great pandect of the Magisterium had been defiled. Good.

Backing away, he turned and gazed at the palatine hill, thinking of Small Girl, wondering why such a personage would have killed a child. Surely he hadn't. There were so few Tarig children, surely they must mourn every lost one.

He put some distance between himself and the pillar. Perhaps he had created enough confusion that Dai Shen might have a chance to leave the city.

It was such a slim chance. About as slim as a steward of ten thousand days suddenly wearing the icon of the golden carp; about as slim as a career steward finally taking a stand on something.

He thought of his new icon, the golden carp. Let me be worthy of such a glorious symbol, he prayed. And may God not look at me.

Cixi gripped the railing of her open porch, her eyes darting over the cityscape.

Behind her, Zai Gan stood, breathing hard, having come to her salon on a dead run.

Titus Quinn, she thought. By the bright, he stood in front of my very face. The perfidious father and betrayer.

She swirled on Zai Gan, spitting at him, "Run to the fourth pillar, that is closest to Inweer's mansion. Find him. Stop him."

Zai Gan bowed and dashed for the doors.

"Preconsul," she barked at him before he could disappear. When he stopped to await her, she said, "If you fail to apprehend him, you will wear the emblem of a beku."

"Yes, Lady." He rushed from the room, a great engine of a man. Titus Quinn mustn't escape to brag that he'd fooled them all. He must not escape to bring back to the withered Rose whatever prize he had snatched from them. She was sure there *was* a prize. If he thought it would be Sydney, he was addled indeed.

Something had gone wrong with his plans. And she meant to complete his ruin.

Quinn continued to haul Anzi up the winding staircase into the heart of the palatine hill. She protested, begging him to run for the pillars. Ignoring her protests, he pulled her up the stairs. "They'll be looking for us down there," he said, panting by now. "No one will think we'd go into the mansions."

"Because it is without merit!"

They came to a widening in the staircase, one that looked out over the city. Below, the plazas and pedestrian ways were still deserted. But something was odd about it. The ground was moving.

As a ripple moved through one of the plazas, Quinn said, "Birds." He pivoted away, resuming his rush up the stairs.

Anzi allowed herself to be led, complaining, "The longer we delay leaving, the worse our chances."

"We don't have a chance anymore. The birds, Anzi. They aren't birds. They're drones, used for cleaning."

It came to him, this knowledge. As though his memories were a deck of cards that up to now had been randomly shuffled, but in his extremity, were dealing him a playable hand. The one he would need to survive.

The flutter of wings thrummed in the distance. "The Tarig have brought them all out at once. Millions of them."

Anzi looked wild with alarm. She began murmuring a prayer: "Do not look at me, do not see me, do not note my small life. Do not look at me, do not see me . . ."

They had come to a palace where all the side doors and accesses were well known to him. "In here," he said. They ducked through a carved door tucked under an arching gate.

They stood in a semidark, narrow passageway. On either side were panes of glass bulging out to form curved sides. The floor was translucent, but unlit. It was good that this hall was dark. Since the Tarig hated the dark, it meant the palace was empty just now.

At his side Anzi whispered, "What is this place?"

"Lady Chiron's dwelling."

"She will not help you against her own people!"

He started down the passageway, but she grabbed his arm to make him listen. "Do not give up, Dai Shen. There is always a chance. Even when I thought I would take my own life in despair, I thought there was a chance you might survive Tarig captivity. And you did. You must never give up."

"I haven't. There's a way, Anzi—a way out. The brightships. We'll steal one." A spike of elation carved through him. He would oppose them in a way they could not have imagined. He told her, "It will be your crowning theft, Anzi."

She repeated flatly, "A brightship . . ."

At the end of the glass tunnel, they came to a round, open doorway, and stepped into a hall cluttered with statues, tall vases, and elaborate chairs. The bright streamed in from a ceiling peppered with skylights.

He chose a path, snaking through Chiron's collections of things copied from other worlds. This whole dwelling—and all the others—were tasteless museums, stuffed with other worlds' cultural and domestic items. The lady was wealthy beyond imagining. But she had no taste. The Tarig, for all their knowledge, created no crafts of their own, no art. Perhaps that is why they had never known what to make of Johanna.

Behind, he heard the outside door open, then shut. Footsteps clicked along the glass floor of the tube. Quinn took Anzi's arm and sprinted with her toward a door, one of several. They ducked through it, into a small chamber with translucent walls. A moment of disorientation caused him to stagger. It had been a long time since he'd taken this shortcut that would instantly deliver them to the second story of the mansion.

Passing through the elevator chamber door, they ran down a winding corridor, deserted. Quinn tried to get his bearings. Chiron liked to reprogram the layout of her dwelling, and he felt lost now, as the corridor became a ramp heading steeply up. Rooms glimpsed on either side of the corridor seemed oversized, as though they were potential rooms, not all of which could fit in the twisting spaces defined by the hall.

"What is this place?" Anzi whispered.

"They live like this," he answered. *Experimentally*, he wanted to say. But it was no time for discussions. He led her quickly onward, but thought they had lost their pursuer for the moment.

All he needed were a few unchanged features and he would know his way to the brightship, the back way, where he had played at changes of his own.

Down a side ramp he glimpsed a door he recognized, an elaborate door that once had closed upon his trysts with the lady.

Entering, they found themselves in an expansive room with a ceiling so high it seemed to place them in a well. In the center of the room was a platform gilded by a shaft of light falling from above. Quinn walked over to it, to Chiron's bed. Putting his hand into the shaft of light, he felt nothing of the high pleasure that the stream of light seemed to bestow on those who embraced here. He pitied the man who had wanted it. Even pleasure was a cage, if there was too much of it.

Anzi tugged at him. "Hurry."

He took her hand and they rushed to the open veranda, revealing the bright city.

Just before Quinn could step outside, Anzi yanked him back.

A bird strutted outside on the balustrade. Its head swiveled completely around, looking. Then it jumped from its perch, gliding away—not programmed to fly, but able to soar from a height.

"Now," Quinn said, guiding Anzi outdoors and pointing to a ledge. Climbing up, he led the way along it, flattening his back against the wall. Joining him, Anzi made the mistake of looking down. The view fell away ten stories. "Just a short way now, Anzi. Steady."

She sidled along the ledge, finally jumping onto a connecting roof where Quinn waited.

Glancing down, he saw another roof filled with thousands of birds. Strutting, swiveling. Reporting. Anzi and Quinn backed up from this view and turned to climb through the window just behind them. A movement caught their attention.

Someone was standing outside Chiron's bedchamber. It was Min Fe.

The legate made a shallow bow across the small space that separated them. "Titus Quinn," he said.

So, they all *did* know his name.

The sublegate craned his neck, trying to see Anzi. "Who is that with you?"

Anzi shrank back into the shadows. "No one," Quinn said.

"She is a clerk, but not a clerk. Perhaps the full steward Cho knows her name?" Min Fe was assessing the ledge, judging whether to use it.

"Cho knows nothing."

"We shall see. As I have just discovered, he has pursued the story of your wife, so he knows some things. This will be of great interest to Cixi."

Min Fe moved toward the ledge. "Of course, if I accomplished the capture of Titus Quinn, perhaps I would consider Cho unimportant. I could hide Cho. In return for your surrender to me."

"An attractive proposal, Sublegate." Quinn watched Min Fe sidle onto the ledge. He'd have to go out on the ledge after this fellow. "But who else knows about Cho? Certainly not just you."

Sweat beaded on the sublegate's face, causing his spectacles to slip down his nose. "Oh yes, just me. I am Cixi's eyes in this matter."

"Are your eyes fine enough to see all the way down?"

Min Fe frowned. Then he looked down, seeing the unexpected dramatic drop. He swayed, then flattened himself against the wall, staring outward.

He was afraid. An easy lunge from Quinn could topple him from his perch.

Behind Quinn, Anzi hissed, "Birds." A flock of them were turning to watch Min Fe. Anzi whispered to him from her hiding place, "The birds have seen us."

Quinn saw that they had, and abandoning Min Fe where he stood paralyzed with fear, Quinn plunged through the window opening.

They were in a very long hallway lined on one side with stone carvings. One sculpture was of a being like a Tarig, carved with pronounced insectoid features. The figure held in its four-fingered grasp a sharp golden pole like a lance.

On one side of the hall, windows let in a flood of light. Glimpsed through the windows, specks of black streaked downward. Birds gliding. He and Anzi raced for the end of the hall, where they came to an open porch. Two sets of stairs led in different directions.

At a noise from behind them, he turned to see Min Fe rushing down the hallway they'd just come down. And behind him, a Tarig appeared.

Anzi drew her knife to take a stand, but Quinn urged her down the nearest stairs instead. They fled into a park of yellow trees, down paths bordered by espaliered vines.

In a few moments they entered a place that Quinn knew well. His former garden. He led Anzi in a dead run across it. His old room was open to the garden, through arched openings framed by columns.

He and Anzi entered the place where he had once lived.

The room was as he'd left it. His bed covers lay smooth, topped with brocaded pillows. Scrolls lay scattered as he had left them. He rushed to the Flemish tapestry hanging on the wall, tearing it down. The wall was smooth, but it housed his great work.

He had spent years experimenting, learning how to program the adobe. He had stolen the needles that, thrust into the surface of the organic stone, could direct its shape, creating vacuoles, pipes. A tunnel, eventually, after thousands of days.

The room had once been his bright cage. But, with a rush of understanding, he knew he had always hated it.

Kneeling by the tapestry, he found the place where, thousands of days ago, he had hidden his working needles in the cloth. He pulled a group of them out of the weave and scrambled to the wall. He inserted them at the correct angle, forming a circle. Immediately, a tiny hole appeared, widening like the outward ripples of a stone thrown in a pond.

Anzi was frantic. "In the garden!" A crashing sound came from that direction.

A Tarig swept into view. The figure stopped in the middle of the grass sward, searching.

Time had shriveled into a wad. He had hoped it might be the Lady Chiron who was coming down that hall, a person in whose eyes he might have found some mercy.

But Quinn turned to face Lord Hadenth.

Hadenth saw him. A stone's throw away from each other, they paused, eyeing each other.

Quinn drew his knife. "Anzi," he whispered, "Go through the hole."

"No."

"Tell Bei what you know. Tell someone. Go now."

"The hole is too small," she whispered.

"It will widen. Don't touch the left side of the wall, do you hear?"

From the garden, Hadenth said, his voice shredding, as though full of static, "Come to us."

Anzi needed only a moment or two more before the door to his tunnel grew large enough for her. "Go," he whispered to her. Then he advanced toward the lord.

The next things happened so fast, he could hardly afterward remember their sequence. From one side of the garden came a scream. Someone ran at him. A sparkling shaft pointed at Quinn's chest.

Hadenth pivoted, flicking out a talon from his hand, and lunging, ripped open the belly of Min Fe, who had been aiming the golden pole from the art gallery at Quinn's middle.

Min Fe fell heavily on the Tarig, and the golden rod fell over Hadenth's ankles, stopping his leap up from the ground where he'd staggered.

Quinn backed up, then fled into the room and dove for the opening in his wall, scrambling into the tunnel, the one he'd spent ten years shaping. Crawling just behind Anzi, he let himself hope that Hadenth couldn't fit in the tunnel.

Zai Gan bent his efforts to recalling the elevator capsule to the top. Such a thing had never been done before, but he knew his city and its mechanisms.

Below him, at his command, the capsule stopped in its swift descent. Then, slowly, it began ascending.

The fool had listed his name on the passenger manifest. But of course, he would have had to. There must be a record of all goings and comings. It was all recorded.

Exultation flooded over Zai Gan. He had secured the fugitive on Cixi's behalf. And not just any fugitive, but Titus Quinn himself. Zai Gan called for reinforcements, and a stout team of Jouts came thudding across the plaza.

Watching all this from the other side of the plaza, Cho watched Zai Gan.

Cho felt safely anonymous, hidden there among the many stewards, clerks, and legates who were gathering outside, hoping for a view of whatever came next.

Soon, a contingent of Tarig were swarming in that direction. Overhead, flocks of birds clumped and dispersed, on the watch for the fugitive.

A flurry of activity on the edge of the plaza signaled the return of the capsule to its slot. Presently the door slid aside. Cho watched as Zai Gan plunged through the door.

There were a few moments of quiet as Jouts and Tarig fanned out around the capsule.

Then Zai Gan came out, standing with his hands at his side. If Cho could discern his features the least bit at this distance, he would have said the man's expression was halfway between terror and rage.

Then the preconsul shouted something, and the flock of them raced to the next pillar.

Cho had saved Dai Shen . . . Titus . . . only a few intervals of time.

It was so little, it could hardly be an advantage. But as Cho looked around him at the hidebound officials milling in the plaza, he was filled with a quite unaccustomed pride.

Quinn and Anzi scrambled on hands and knees through the smooth pipe. He heard the Tarig's breathing. Quinn judged that he was at the tunnel entrance, pausing, perhaps daunted by the darkness.

They hurried on, toward the only place the tunnel could go, and matter. The brightship platform.

"Do not touch the left side," Quinn whispered as they hurried, crablike, through the stone passageway.

He might die here in this tunnel, but his heart was strangely lifted. Here was his tunnel, his proof that he'd tried to escape. The agonizingly slow process of manipulating the walls—walls that were old and sluggish, and he without proper knowledge, and unable to ask.

Yes, Johanna, he thought. I fought them too.

The tunnel was not entirely dark because of the light from the opening. It must have been this thin light that emboldened Hadenth to crawl in, sending scuttling noises to Quinn's ears, and the scent of Tarig to his nostrils.

Hadenth could fit.

As Anzi scooted forward, Quinn followed, keeping his shoulder against the right-hand wall, the passage dimming as they moved farther from the entrance.

The lord whispered to him from down-tunnel: "We are inclined to mercy, Titus Quinn. No retributions. Only come to us."

Quinn was in total darkness now, and the lord hated to enter it, perhaps hated the confines of the tunnel as well. But Quinn had little doubt that Hadenth would pursue him through the blackness. When he did, the first retribution would be for making him come into the dark.

Quinn still clutched one of the needles. The programming stylus was small, made for delicate work, not tunneling. But once, he had had all the time he needed. He had had nothing but time. Now, crouching in the tunnel, he inserted the needle into the stone, twirling it to find the correct vector in the dark.

Hadenth's breathing became more labored. He might be breathing harder, or approaching closer. Working quickly, Quinn's own breath came heavily in the suffocating warmth and confines of the tube.

Up ahead, Anzi had found the exit, and called to him. Working furiously, Quinn at last finished his manipulations. Then, a faint buzz zoomed down the left-hand wall where a jet of high-temperature plasma streamed, a weapon he'd planned long ago, in case of pursuit.

Behind him, Hadenth, whose body must have touched the left wall, let out a reverberating bellow. The smell of seared flesh wafted over Quinn, nearly doubling him over with its strength. Stunned for a moment, Quinn remained plastered against the right-hand wall.

"Titus . . ." Hadenth's pain-racked voice came to him. "Titus. The girl was in our arms when we blinded her. We told her what was going to transpire, so she could watch it approach."

Quinn had stopped. Listening.

"Her cringing only tightened this lord's grip. The more she shuddered, the harder we confined her. So easy, so small a girl."

It was too bad Hadenth had opened his mouth. Quinn had intended to let him live, but now the creature would be better off dead. Quinn began the tough maneuver of turning around in the tunnel without touching the live side.

Hadenth's ragged voice continued. "The girl squealed when one's talon entered her eye. If she hadn't squirmed so, we could have done the thing without maiming her. It was exquisite to see her suffer, feel her very breath on one's face. But Titus Quinn knows the glory of such a moment, having killed Small Girl. Ah?"

Quinn forcibly calmed his breathing, making himself speak to the creature. "Hadenth. It's time for lights out." To the Tarig, the dark was an intolerable environment, a psychological horror. "I'm going to shut off the tunnel's end now. You will be in total darkness."

Hadenth whispered, "Do not."

Quinn inserted a needle into the skin of the tunnel. First, he deadened the plasma stream, quenching the light. A faint glow still came from the exit hole, up ahead. Then he directed his needlework to close the opening in his room, to prevent Hadenth's escape in that direction. This took a while, since it was so far removed from Quinn's location.

Hadenth had time to plead. His words sounded like gongs in a minor key. "We did not kill her. She lives, by our grace."

"May God know all your sins, Hadenth. Even in the dark." It was a curse he thought Johanna would appreciate.

"We will forgive you," Hadenth said. "Forgive all."

The Tarig had trouble staying clear on who needed forgiving.

The light dimmed as one end of the tube closed off. He heard Hadenth's heavy, labored panting, like a wounded lion.

Emerging from the tunnel, Quinn applied his needles, closing the wall. As he did so, for a moment he heard a high scream. And then another.

Anzi was crouching by the wall, covering her ears.

The bellow came again and again, each time muffled by further layers of wall as Quinn coaxed the stone closed.

They stood in the hangar at last. Wedge shaped, the enormous launch platform lay between the mansions of Chiron and Nehoov, its lip jutting out of the circular city. Overhead, a wavering field of light provided a shield from wind. Five wedge-shaped bays spread to the perimeter.

On each rested a brightship. Shaped like crescents, their shining forms sat upon numerous black struts, creating a look of crustaceans about to scuttle.

And scuttle they must—all the ships would leave at once. So no one could follow.

They hurried to the nearest ship, feeling the heat of the sky glaring through the shield overhead.

"No one can fly near the bright," Anzi said. "We will sicken. Only the Tarig can fly the great boats."

Quinn took her by the arm. "If I believed those things, I would have knelt down to Hadenth in the garden." By now he had a rough plan. A reckless one, but better than no plan. "We're taking them all," he said.

Underneath the ship, he looked up at the access door. It was too high for a human to jump. For their excursions, Chiron had held her long arm down, and he had grasped it, and she pulled him up.

He'd never been sick; and now he remembered why: protecting their travel powers, the Tarig perpetuated the notion that bright made air travelers sick. Slow and difficult travel was one more control they exerted on the Entire's population. They also protected their monopoly of the ships.

The ship creatures that were always trying to escape.

Chiron had told him that the ships were sentient. In some forms that they took, the ships were sentient. But in the form that the Tarig imposed on them, they were not.

Reaching up to the underbelly of the ship, Quinn thumbed a nub in the hull of the ship. From the smooth sides, a circle of material softened, became a membrane. Anzi gave him a boost up, and he crawled in, pulling her after him. They passed through a membrane as thin as soap film.

As they entered the ship, Quinn's nostrils detected a complex array of scents: metallic spikes, and the heavy scents of fuels; underneath, a stew of organic chemicals, so subtle that only his Jacobson's organs could detect them. He hurried to the forward compartment that served as a cockpit. Although there were no conventional viewing ports, a transparent bulkhead curved around the nose of the ship. He checked for movement in the hangar. But all was still. The ships, sleek and low, lay frozen in place like a taxidermist's handiwork. Remembering how Chiron had activated the ships, Titus placed his hand along the bulkhead. Under his hand, a display grid brightened. The navigation commands could be issued by touch, anywhere.

Anzi stood next to him, her knife in her hand, watching through that clear portion of the bulkhead that provided a forward view. From time to time she glanced down at Quinn's manipulations of the instrument panel.

"What course?" she asked.

"Bei's reach."

They exchanged a glance, no more. He wasn't going to the Inyx sway, but home.

Working as fast as he could, Quinn hunched over the instrument panel now glowing under his hand, trying to remember how Chiron had navigated. Many times he'd been at her side as she flew the ships, and each time he had been watching carefully. But she hid her movements well. It had been a game of cat and mouse with her. If he had grabbed a ship, she would have grabbed *him*. Her arms could be soft or strong.

He concentrated hard, sweat greasing his skin. Hadenth had prevented Min Fe from killing him. Hadenth wanted him alive. It was a great inducement to haste.

But even as he worked, he knew the limits of his knowledge. The truth was, he had very little idea of how to operate these ships. The systems were alien; a compromise between preferred Tarig interfaces and those possible with the alien beings known as *fragmentals*. Quinn knew how to launch the ships, he hoped. Beyond that . . . *Beyond that* would have to wait, because there was no time to think of anything except the launch sequence.

He could hear Anzi's breath. It was the only indication that she was afraid. He was glad she didn't know the rest of it; that she was entrusting herself to a pilot who couldn't fly.

Finishing there, they ran through the hangar to the next ship. Overhead, above the shield, clouds of birds loomed and receded like an infestation of locusts. Like God taking revenge, sending trials. *Taking notice.* He and Anzi scrambled into the next brightship.

Quinn's hands sweated as he pressed against the bulkhead, calling up the display, coaxing another ship into a ready state. The colored grids of the display fluoresced his fingertips as he pressed the commands. He could do no more than direct the ships outward. Ultimately, they would fall into the storm walls. His great hope was that, once launched, the Tarig had no mechanism to call them back. Or that, even if the Tarig could, that the ships wouldn't *want* to come back.

The reality of what he was doing began to catch up with him. He turned to Anzi, to set her choices before her. "I can't fly these ships very far," he told her. "I don't know how to navigate. Or how to land, except here at the hangar." He let that sink in. Then he said, "You can still hide in the city. Try to get out. They don't know who you are."

Anzi took that news in. He could almost see her thinking, analyzing. Then she said, "We go together. Keep moving."

He wasn't surprised at her answer, just at how relieved he was.

In the last ship he set the course, and motioned for Anzi to strap in. In the most complex maneuver he had yet done, he remotely activated the other ships. Then he thumbed the grid, releasing the fields that defined the edge of the hangar.

Outside, a motion on the ship's nose caused him to flinch. A bronze hand swiped at his face. Outside, a long arm swept down from the top of the ship, scraping a hand along the viewing port. Then, a Tarig slid down the pane, holding on somehow, and peering in.

It was Hadenth. The lord was clinging to the front of the ship. He stared into Quinn's face, a curdled phlegm dripping from his mouth, the eyes large and fixed as though they'd been staring at something too long. Maddened by the darkness of the tunnel, he shrieked at them with short, panting cries, more animal than sentient.

Quinn released the ships from their tethers. They all began a slow, melting movement toward the edge of the platform.

Anzi brought up her foot, slamming the bulkhead with her heavy boot heel. But Hadenth didn't flinch or release his grip. In fact, he had begun drilling his talon into the viewing port. Meanwhile, the ship crawled toward the perimeter.

Twenty yards away from launch point, the talon popped through and began sawing down the pane. Anzi hacked at the claw with her knife, but the blade bounced off again and again. At last she whipped off her belt and hooked the cloth under the talon, temporarily cushioning its downward slice. The lord frowned at this tactic, a cleft forming in his brow as he squinted at what Anzi had done. Looking behind him, he saw that the edge was almost upon him. Then, too late, he tried to yank his talon free.

The brightship launched from the platform, ripping Hadenth from the ship's prow. Instantly, the city receded below them. They climbed upward, to the bright, and behind them Hadenth's fate was to fall, fall like a shadow from the world.

They soared above the heartland, the clear cockpit wall blindingly hot as they pointed to the sky. Anzi stared at the window as though still fighting her adversary. In a few moments she slumped against the bulkhead, closing her eyes, steadying herself.

The other ships sped away on their separate trajectories. They had launched. One ship ran toward the Inyx sway. It might not get far, but Quinn felt the tug of that ship.

He looked around the ship with something like disbelief. They had stolen a brightship from the very grasp of Lord Hadenth. Even if the worst happened, and they didn't survive, it would be a sweet ending. To take your enemy down with you.

He sat looking out, trying to shield his eyes from the slicing glints of light. When he looked away, confident that at least for now they weren't on a crash course, he saw Anzi gazing out the window with a strange expression. Well, she had never flown before.

"How's the view?" he said.

"It is hard to say."

She was staring at the crack in the window. Looking more closely, Quinn saw that lodged there was a four-inch talon, separated from its socket. The substance comprising the window pooled around it, encapsulating it.

Hadenth. In his mind's eye, Quinn saw the gracious lord falling onto a bright city plaza—or better yet, falling thirty thousand feet to the sea, with plenty of time to anticipate his landing.

CHAPTER TWENTY-EIGHT

Storm wall, hold up the bright,
Storm wall, dark as Rose night,
Storm wall, where none can pass,
Storm wall, always to last.

—a child's verse

THEY WERE FLYING NEAR THE ROLLING ENERGIES OF THE BRIGHT. Only a few thousand feet above, the sky appeared to boil, like a molten river streaming from some silver-throated volcano. The ship maintained distance from that boil. But they were flying across the Sea of Arising, without a destination.

Behind Quinn lay the littered path of his mistakes: his broken promise to Sydney, and to Johanna, to bring his wife's body home. And the crime he could never have imagined: the killing of a child. He tried to shove these things away, for now.

The bright stretched on, and everywhere.

Anzi stood by his side, gazing out the viewports. "We cannot land this ship at Bei's reach," she said. "It will cause a sensation among the scholars. It would implicate Bei."

He barely heard her. His mind was dredging for memories, searching for a glimpse of how to pilot the ship. Nothing new came to him. Chiron had guarded her maneuvers, especially when entering the bright.

Anzi's brow furrowed. "We could land in a nascence, though. No one would see us there. Then you could walk to the reach."

"Yes." Thank God she was clearheaded as always. A nascence was dangerous, though. On the way to Bei's reach, when he and Anzi had been aboard the sky bulb, they'd passed a nascence in the distance. Such a place was a temporary and forbidding root hair, fitfully sparking into and out of existence. If they could get to that nascence, and if it still existed, he could hike up the minoral to the veil. Then Anzi—setting out on foot and then by train—might have time to reach Yulin, to warn him of all that had transpired. They owed Yulin a warning, although the lords might already have seized him, if Wen An, the old woman scholar, had failed to evade the Tarig—and if she had revealed all she knew.

Despite all these complications, they had one great advantage. He and Anzi had a brightship, and the lords didn't. Although they might create others, it would take time. The lords had only one other choice for crossing the Entire's galactic-scale distances: they could travel on the Nigh. But they must still cross the primacy, a distance they would have to cover by the slow means they imposed on everyone.

Anzi broke his train of thought. She murmured, "When you come back, I will be in Ahnenhoon. It's a good place to go unnoticed."

After a long pause she said, "Or, I could go with you."

He didn't know what to say. There were a dozen reasons against it; the greatest being that if he died in the attempted crossing, who would be left except Anzi who knew Johanna's secret?

He didn't want to tell her no. He waited for her, watching her, with her stark white hair and alabaster skin—both elegant and inhuman. For all its strangeness, her face was familiar to him. He had come to know her better than he knew even those closest to him, like his own brother, or Lamar Gelde.

"I could come with you," she said again. "But then, who would warn my uncle?"

They were both silent then. Finally she turned and left, walking back into one of the curved arms of the crescent-shaped ship. He thought she had made her decision, and it oppressed her, as it did him.

Without the sound of engines, the ship was eerily quiet, as though they swam instead of flew. He couldn't remember how the craft propelled itself. Perhaps he had never known. The smooth bulkheads glowed like mother-of-pearl, the instrumentation hidden until touch retrieved it. He forced himself to concentrate, touching the bulkhead, bringing the instrumentation into view. It meant little to him, except to activate flight to and from the hangar.

Then the thought bloomed in his mind, like a floodlight in a dark museum: His only chance was to get the ship itself to help him.

Snatches of conversation from his excursions with Chiron came to him. The ships were sentient—not alive here, in this universe, but in another. The Tarig referred to the ship beings as *fragmentals*. He remembered fruitless rummaging in the archives for information on them.

Chiron had told him that the fragmentals lived in higher dimensions, traveling in the bright in the same way that the navitars guided ships on the River Nigh. The Tarig enslaved them in the four-dimensional universe, confining them to a useful form. The beings were compelled through *framing*, a process that shaped their hyper-forms into a lower-dimensional geometry.

This ship was an incomplete manifestation of its true self, caged and shaped by Tarig powers. They were like the navitars in that they were dreadfully altered. For the navitars, however, the alteration was by choice. Quinn didn't know how to fly such ship-beings, but they knew how to fly themselves.

He possessed only one inducement for this ship to do so: he could free them—this ship and the four others. Could they be persuaded? Could he communicate with them, and did they understand the Lucent tongue? To find out, he might try to unframe the ship. But that meant jeopardizing the stability of its shape. The more frames he removed, the more free will the sentient had, but also the more the ship's form would decay.

So Quinn sat in the Tarig-sized pilot chair and sweated out the decision, whether or not to attempt communication. If you let a tiger out of its cage, the creature might be grateful—or not. He sat for a time, looking out over the world outside, the Sea of Arising below, the bright above. On all sides they were surrounded by exotic matter, like wayfarers in a transient bubble of air, unable to touch the world.

He spoke to the ship, murmuring, "Help me." But he knew that a closely framed ship couldn't speak. The Tarig didn't want to hear cries of pain.

He touched the cool surface of the wall. A simple navigation display sprang to life.

What choice did he have? He could land the ship—possibly—and then what? No, to return home, to bring home what he'd learned, he had to use this ship to escape quickly to the far reach. Through the bright.

Touching the grid of the display, he called up the framing patterns. Chiron had said, *There are many frames to keep them in bounds.*

He canceled one pattern of lines, the outermost frame.

In their true form, the beings would appear in the three dimensions of the Entire as fragments, much like a human standing in a two-dimensional realm might look like two round circles, when viewed at ankle level. Chiron had told him these things, her black eyes lit with a dark fire, anticipating the dive into the bright, where she could taste the other dimension through the sensibilities of the ship. Because even the Tarig, for all their powers, couldn't directly perceive a higher dimension—and, being curious, they wished to.

As he sat waiting, it seemed that the air around him had thickened. He watched it turn cloudy, become tangible. "Help me," he repeated. The breath behind the words created vacuoles in the thick air.

He spoke again. His voice had become deeper, unrecognizable. "The brightships can go home."

He waited. Sweating, his face was slick inside the jellied air.

Anzi had come to his side. "What's wrong?"

"I have to ask for the ship's help, Anzi. I can't do it alone. I told you this."

She looked like she was standing in a league of water—like the interpreter who had died in Yulin's lake.

"I'm sorry," he said to her. "For everything."

"No, I'm sorry." She knelt at his side. Her arms were around his legs, as though she needed to hold on or she would float away.

He reached out his hand and erased the next frame.

Instantly, the navigational display moved into the air in front of him, in a heads-up display, freed from the bulkhead. Brilliant hues flashed, representing the frames. They flashed on, off, clamoring for his attention.

The ship was telling him which frames to remove.

"Take me to the minoral at Su Bei's reach," he said. Through the clotted air, bubbles issued from his nose. "Then I'll release the frames. And all the other ship frames."

The navigation display stopped flashing. Then one frame appeared as a hot, red line.

One more frame, was the implication.

Quinn thought hard. If this was a poker game, he had no idea what cards the ship held. Or even if the ship was in the game.

He touched the display, releasing the next frame.

Deep in his skull, a needle probe of light found a path. He heard a garbled sound of condensed words, unintelligible.

Another pattern in the display began flashing. The ship was treating him like a child: pick the pretty colored lines, it was telling him. He hesitated, as his mind filled with static, the cries of a muzzled ship.

His hand hovered over the lines. Then he released the next frame.

The ship walls blurred, and pustules appeared there, swelling convex then sinking, as though in rhythm with blood or breath. The chair melted into the floor, and Quinn sprawled down beside Anzi. Beneath him the deck undulated, but whether it was real or a visual disorientation, he couldn't tell. Anzi's face twisted in impossible contortions. They clung together in the middle of the cabin.

He heard a voice. *Daishenquinntitus*, it said.

Quinn looked at Anzi. She nodded. Yes, she could hear it, too.

His pulse pounded into the thick air; his sweat streamed into the gel, making rivulets. "We help each other," he said out loud.

Free of boundaries, Daishenquinntitus. Free us.

His heart caught on a snag. Those beings, caged all these years. He wanted to open the gate for them. But not yet.

"Without the frames, you'll kill us."

Frames kill us. Free of lords. Pain of the form. We die of the pain of this form.

It sent him a sample. A spike of pain slanted into his head, and he thrashed forward.

"Quinn!" Anzi whispered.

The pain had vanished, but the brightship had made its point. If it could send pain like that into him, it wouldn't be long before the ship had all it wanted.

Now the display showed a searing blue pattern. Before the ship could compel him, he said, "I want to go home, like you do. I am in pain here, also."

Daishenquinntitus in pain.

"Yes. Help me. Take me to the nascence." He pictured in his mind where it was, although he had only the vaguest idea. He turned to Anzi. "Think of the geography, Anzi. Think of where Bei's reach is."

Meanwhile, the ship was clamoring for freedom. The blue frame flashed on, flashed off.

"The nascence," Quinn insisted.

Daishenquinntitus free in the nascence.

"Yes," he told it. Had they agreed?

He thought so. A different display came up, a dizzyingly complex pattern. But the pattern was clear to him, as the ship-being spoke to him. It was a schematic for the other ships, four of them. A fifth schematic remained off to one side, representing the ship he and Anzi were on.

"Anzi," he said. "Hold on." He couldn't think of what else to say. They were gambling everything.

Quinn touched the pattern, moving his fingertips along the paths. He canceled each frame in turn.

Soon the ship icons began melting away. No longer framed, no longer coerced.

He thought he felt a sigh move through the ship. The other ships were free. Now they would choose their own destination, and that would be toward home. *God not looking at you*, Quinn thought, wishing them well, wishing them the blessings of obscurity.

The floor tilted. The ship had begun to climb.

Anzi murmured, "No one can live in the bright."

"They lied," he said, and then wished it were not the last thing he had said to her.

A leaping white foam reached down and swallowed them as the ship plunged into the bright.

He awoke to utter silence. The ship was down. He'd passed out, but how long had he been here, blacked out in the ship? Anzi was gone. The odor of powerful biologicals nearly overwhelmed his senses.

A wan light spilled from deeper in the ship. Even in the semidark, he saw that the former ship cabin was wobbling between forms. He was no longer in a brightship, but in the deformation of the fragmental. Half submerged in the walls were tubes pulsing with a flow of bright matter, humming like a struck tuning fork.

He went in search of Anzi, making his way down the former cabin, now a ribbed tunnel that thrashed to and fro, each twist evoking a muffled twang.

Ahead, he saw her walking toward him, but half in, half out of the tunnel walls.

He hurried to her and grasped her outstretched hand, then pulled. Stepping into his tunnel, she looked disheveled but unhurt, her white clerk's tunic stained yellow-brown, and her hair askew.

"The ship . . . ," she began.

"Reshaping," he said.

The rear of the cavity was thin enough to see through it, as though that portion of the ship was already abandoned. Through the thin walls they could see a blue-black storm raging. They were close to the storm wall. In the distance, lightning stabbed laterally, almost lacing the two storm walls together, where they converged at the end of the nascence.

He spoke aloud to the ship. "Is this the right place?"

There was no answer. He put his hand on the tunnel side, attempting to call up the navigational display, but the tunnel wall contracted from his touch.

"Brightship," he said. "Where are we?" When no answer came, he wondered if the ship, in deforming, had now lost the ability to communicate.

With a sucking sound, a tiny hole appeared in the floor nearby.

It grew. Below the hole, a short drop away, was solid ground, darkened to gray by the storm walls.

If this wasn't the right nascence near the right minoral, they wouldn't have another chance. It was time to go.

Quinn put his hand on Anzi's arm. "Are you ready?" And more to the point, "Are you sure, Anzi?"

Her clear, amber eyes were steady, looking into his. "Yes."

He took a deep breath and told her something she wasn't going to like. "I'm staying on board. This is how I'm going home. On the ship."

The look on her face was incredulous as she surveyed the chaotic surroundings.

The ship had put the idea into his mind. As Quinn had lain unconscious on the deck, the being had said, *You will pass through to the home place in this conveyance, this unframed.*

It was a risk. He didn't know how long the being would cohere as a vehicle. As well, he didn't know if the ship-being could survive the passage, or live in the Rose, in space. But this idea appealed far more than waiting at Bei's reach for a safe moment to cross over. The Tarig might easily arrive long before that moment.

Anzi's gaze hardened into amber stone. "This ship will unravel. It could kill you."

"At least it'll be quick." He said it lightly, but she didn't smile.

Stubbornly, she held his gaze. The ship shuddered, and a moan came needling in from some unseen throat.

The hole in the floor was now a yard wide, rippling at the edges. Ozone-charged air flooded in, refreshing the stench of the interior.

It was becoming unpredictably hard to say good-bye. They had awoken suddenly, and now she must simply jump down, and leave.

Again the moan from far away.

Into his mind came the clear voice: *Kill the Tarig.*

It was an odd piece of advice at such a time, but Quinn thought that were he the ship, revenge on the lords might well be his first free thought. And it was a relief that the being could still communicate. They would need to, once in the Rose.

"Anzi," he said.

Her expression softened as she gave up on argument. "Look for me at Ahnenhoon," she said, barely audible.

Then she crouched beside the hole. And jumped down.

The ship was propped up on its jointed struts, allowing her to exit through the underbelly. There was something he'd meant to do or say, when the time came. He'd forgotten what. It was all happening too fast, and he was half-stupid from the transit of the bright.

Outside the ship he glimpsed a motion as Anzi jumped. It was the glinting view of a long bronze leg.

"Anzi!" he shouted. She was looking up at him instead of protecting herself. He scrambled out of the egress hole, dropping to the ground and drawing his knife.

They stood on a splintered plain, between glowering storm walls that tossed lances of light back and forth. A tall, segmented bronze body stood fifteen yards away. The clothes and some of the skin had ripped from his body. The Tarig's blood was red. It didn't seem right.

Hadenth, it must be he. But how?

Although his lips were gone, Hadenth opened his mouth. Out came a sound of a body gone mad. A low moan, issuing from what was left of his throat.

Knife drawn, Anzi was moving off to one side, to spread their attack.

Quinn moved away from the ship to avoid becoming trapped there. As he did so, Hadenth lifted his arm. Out came a talon, clicking into place.

The storm walls leaned in toward each other, squeezing the sky into a lightning-filled crack. The air was crushed into a stillness.

He tried to judge Hadenth's strength. One human and one Chalin against a Tarig—that was no contest. But a Tarig who had ridden outside the ship through the bright? If the creature was half-dead, they had a chance.

Hadenth watched him impassively with one eye, the other eye tracking Anzi. But he hadn't moved yet. Perhaps he couldn't move.

It was in that frozen moment that Quinn noticed a strange formation on top of the ship. It looked like Lord Ghinamid, sleeping on his bier. But that made no sense.

Quinn edged in a circular pattern around Hadenth, goading him to move. As he did so, he looked once more at the ship. Extruding from the hull was a mold in the shape of a Tarig. The side was split, where Hadenth had emerged. The ship had encapsulated the lord. *Kill the Tarig*, the ship had said. Yet the ship itself may have been incapable of such an act.

Again, the awful sound trickled from Hadenth's lips. The creature stepped forward, his long legs jerking him toward Quinn, his hand still outstretched. His reach was long.

"Come to us," Hadenth said, as blood welled up with each word. "No death. You will stay now. Alive, ah?"

As assurance, the talon snapped back in, but the hand remained out.

"Yes, I stay alive. You die, though." Quinn came at him, lunging with the Going Over blade. Hadenth stepped into his path, making no attempt to evade. His arm swept out, thrusting into Quinn's shoulder. The jolting blow sent Quinn to his knees.

That clarified the issue of Hadenth's strength.

Anzi was moving in even as Quinn was falling, bringing her blade up into Hadenth's back, where it stuck, thrust upward toward whatever organ lay where his heart should be. At the impact, Hadenth leaped high, turning to strike Anzi in the chest with his foot.

She fell, blood flying from her neck; then she lay on the sand. Red soaked into the white of her tunic. Quinn fought with his emotions to focus, focus, on Hadenth.

The lord crouched next to Anzi. The burnished bronze of his skin was blistered black, especially on his arms, where he might have tried to cover his face when the bright scalded him. But there were huge scabs where his skin had already begun healing. Hadenth was growing in strength with every moment. But now he crouched, panting.

Seizing the moment, Quinn came at Hadenth, howling, forgetting strategies, lessons, and warnings. Hadenth was rising up to meet him, but too slowly, as Quinn slashed his knife in a lightning motion across Hadenth's eyes. It wasn't a firm cut, but it creased the lord's nose and cheek with red. The Tarig rose to his full seven feet, pivoting toward his assailant, sending out a circle of blood as he did so. Snapping his foot into Quinn's path, Hadenth knocked Quinn's feet out from under him, sending him sprawling.

Even with his mouth full of dust, Quinn managed to keep the grip on his knife. But now he felt Hadenth approach, felt his footfalls on the sand, next to his ear.

Quinn rolled over, yanking his knees toward his chest, and, seeing an opening in the creature's defenses, sent his feet crashing into Hadenth's groin, where his phallus had curled into a tight spiral. The blow buckled Hadenth, bringing his upper body forward so that he lost his balance and crashed heavily.

That was when Quinn realized that Hadenth didn't know how to fight. Why should he? When had anyone but Titus Quinn ever assaulted a Tarig?

He collected his thoughts. *When overmatched*, Ci Dehai had said, *be content with small harms. Small adds up to large.*

He began circling Hadenth, forcing him to turn and turn. The creature was off balance, pivoting on one foot. Quinn lunged, striking for the hands. Swift as a sparrow, he darted his arm out, and back, and before Hadenth understood that he was wounded, his left hand suffered a deep cut. Turning as he swept by, Quinn slid his knife along Hadenth's back.

Quinn wouldn't commit to a large action that could open him to a Tarig mortal blow. He would parry and strike, stinging and maiming.

He circled again. The Tarig had learned nothing, turning to watch, waiting for Quinn to choose the moment.

Hadenth faced him dead-on, both arms held ready to attack. A foolish posture. Again Quinn darted in, slashing at the upraised hands, cutting him.

Then, as Hadenth saw Quinn spiraling in for another cut, he began backing away.

The lord was afraid. The Tarig walked backward, arms raised, ready for the major assault that never came. Quinn advanced, feinting a lunge, following him.

Quinn slashed at Hadenth's hand, taking three of his right hand's four fingers. The talons now hung useless.

Hadenth kept backing up. Quinn followed. Slowly, step for step, he matched the lord's pace.

Hadenth could no longer fight. His hands, wrists, and lower arms were strips of gore. But he was still upright, still walking backward, walking toward the storm wall that hovered behind, roaring with dark light. It was impossible to tell exactly how close they were to the wall. Tendrils of silver wriggled out to surround Hadenth, to stab at Quinn. It jolted him. Walking forward now was like advancing into a line of spears.

Quinn could go no farther as Hadenth receded from him.

"You do not kill us," Hadenth said.

Quinn stood locked in place, watching the Tarig move toward the wall. Quinn said, "You need to die."

"You do not kill us," Hadenth said.

Kill yourself then, Quinn urged.

And Hadenth did. He turned, and walked deliberately into the wall, into that jumping land of sometimes wall and sometimes not. His form grew indistinct, wavering, then burning. A blistering tear appeared where Hadenth's body appeared to rend the billowing fabric.

He was gone, leaving behind the odor of singed meat.

Around Quinn the nascence sputtered like a fire crackling in grease. Quinn staggered back across the sand toward the ship. The fragmental was now twitching and shuddering as though nervous to leave. "A moment more," Quinn said to it.

He found Anzi, propped up against one of the ship's legs, or piers, whatever they were. She had gotten that far, and watched his fight. He knelt by her side.

Her eyes were open. "You are bleeding," she said.

"Hadenth's blood."

He took out his knife and cut her tunic at the neck. Carefully, he ripped the tunic fabric all the way to Anzi's waist. When he got to skin, the news was good. The wound was not deep, though it was still bleeding, a gash straight up the middle of her sternum and ending at her throat just shy of a mortal wound. He used his own shirt to make a bandage to bind her up.

"You fought well," she said. "Ci Dehai would be proud." By her look, she was, also.

"He killed himself," Quinn said wonderingly.

"He was a flame in the storm wall," she murmured, and then she closed her eyes—in exhaustion, or savoring the memory.

The ship supplied water, and Anzi drank. After a half hour she declared herself ready to make the several day trek to a train station.

It was nonsense. They argued. He would help her walk down to the train, then come back.

She refused to budge in that case.

Eventually, he saw there was no winning. She was going alone, and perhaps she was right to try.

Behind them, the ship flowed alarmingly into and out of higher dimensions. He had to hurry.

Helping Anzi to her feet, he said, "Now Yulin can release the gardeners." He had never forgotten their awful sentence, to remain within Yulin's garden walls because they knew of a stranger who shouldn't have been there.

She shook her head, brushing the sand from her leggings. "Still thinking of gardeners." But she smiled.

They stood a moment in silence.

"The walls," Anzi said, gazing at the coiling dark side of the nascence. "They hold us. But burning the Rose to do so." The look on her face was bleak, deepened in shadow by the blue storm. It was an irreconcilable contest. One world lived at the expense of the other.

She turned to him. "Go home now, Quinn."

He nodded, whispering, "And you."

Then he remembered the thing he had wanted to do when the time came for them to part. He reached under his jacket and removed the cord on which the heartchime hung. He placed it around her neck. "Stay away from the Ascendancy," he said, smiling. "If this thing screams, you're too close."

Her hand closed around the chime. "Once was enough," she said.

Then she turned, and began her walk down the nascence. It was not the custom in the Entire to say good-bye. You never knew in such long lives when you might meet again.

The minoral was near. In the distance he could see a land where the view opened up, and the world was permanent. She didn't turn around again, for which he was glad.

When she was only a small white blur, wavering in the charged air, he turned and entered the ship.

Afterward, he remembered little of punching through the wall. One moment what was left of the ship was picking up speed down the minoral, aiming—he knew, but could not see—for the fold where the two walls met: Bei's reach.

In the minutes before takeoff he had conveyed to the fragmental all he could of how to identify the solar system. God above, even the *galaxy*. Finally, almost despairing of saying the right things, he advised, *Look for radio transmission sources.*

What is radio?

Before he had time to answer, the ship rose from its landing space. They were under way.

He remembered hoping that no travelers were in the minoral to witness this. He remembered thinking that Anzi would be pausing in her trek, watching the brightship speed away, up the minoral. He wondered what it looked like to her, what it had become as it prepared to go between realms.

He found himself trusting this creature. The fragmental had waited for him during the fight with Hadenth, when it could have simply slipped into the side wall of the nascence. Since coming to the Entire, Quinn had become an optimist. It was what the Entire did for you. Gave you hope—not that life would be necessarily better, but that, given the long hours, eventually you would have time to do what you must.

They sped toward the junction in the wall.

And then he was unconscious.

He dreamed the ship said, *Cannot hold the form.*

He dreamed that he responded, *Now you tell me.*

Immobilized and helpless, he was spinning. Around and around, stretched out, his feet moving clockwise and his head following, like a baton. Set adrift.

He remembered looking down at Small Girl, her face under a foot of water. Immobilized. Helpless.

Dead.

He remembered the girl in his backyard looking up the barrel of his shotgun. *Sorry we bothered you. We just wanted to see you for real.*

Here I am, then.

Ready or not.

Going home.

CHAPTER TWENTY-NINE

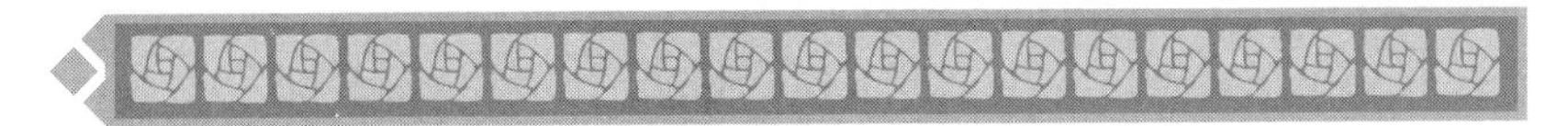

If the day brings grief,
It will ebb.
If the ebb brings joy,
It will burn away.
—from *The Twelve Wisdoms*

SYDNEY CROUCHED ON THE ROOF OF THE BARRACKS, imagining the steppe-land that surrounded her. Flat and dry. A limitless flat and dry. She came to the roof to lighten her heart, but the joy of this grand roamland had seeped away the last few days.

It had been forty days since Riod had taken command of the herd. Priov was dead, but the mares had yet to fully endorse his successor. If it had been breeding season, Riod might have earned more loyalty from the mares, but Priov had picked his challenge time carefully, and the mares who remained were skittish and demanding.

Two mares had defected to Ulrud the Lame's herd, along with Akay-Wat's former mount, Skofke. Good riddance, Mo Ti had growled, if they have no stomach for free bond and for Riod.

But an interval ago the riders of those mares had come limping into camp, having walked the long distance from Ulrud's herd. These were among the growing numbers of riders who were used to a free-bond status, and meant to keep it. Noting their approach, Akay-Wat had let out a whoop, and thundered out with her new mount, Gevka, to welcome them. Her prosthetic leg helped her to grip Gevka's back in a vise, transforming her into a superb rider.

It was time for Akay-Wat to accept her mission to go to Ulrud's herd. But the Hirrin delayed, avoiding Sydney, keeping to herself.

Sydney noted all this with detachment. She hardly cared about mares and chieftainship after the news about Titus Quinn had reached the encampment. She was weary of the herd and its politics.

The steppe called to her. She clambered down from the roof on the side of the barracks facing away from camp, and set out walking. She had no clear goal, except quiet—especially the quieting of her mind. The steppe had always revived her, with its scoured horizon and clean smells. She had seen its vista from Riod's mind so often, its image was burned into her mind. Perhaps it would renew her today, if she walked carefully and didn't step in a vole hole.

Despite her hope for peace, the quiet of the land brought her thoughts crowding for attention. Three days ago, the news had begun filtering through the roamlands, leaping from mind to mind, from encampment to encampment. *Titus Quinn. Returned.*

Normally the Inyx sensed little from the outside world. It had always seemed normal to Sydney that the mounts kept their concerns local, as hers were. But some Inyx were fighting in the war, and even as distant as these kin were, their hearts could be read. Thus came the shocking tale.

The human man Titus Quinn had returned. Hiding in the Ascendancy for a time—it was unclear how long—he had gone on a killing rampage and then destroyed the brightships, every single one. Having done all this, he eluded his pursuers, nor was he yet in custody. It was a tale almost past believing.

He had spared one ship for his own escape. Where had he gone with it? No one knew, but many thought he had returned to the Rose.

Oh, Cixi, she thought. *Cixi, he has left me.* Who else but Cixi would know and care? Cixi, who had sheltered her, and protected her from the fiends. Cixi, who had seen her cry the last tears that she would ever shed.

As she walked, the bright cooled toward ebb, making her trek more bearable, but her feet were beginning to hurt. What she wouldn't give for fine boots, so that she could walk forever.

There hadn't been time for Cixi to send a report to her about this event. But from Inyx glimpses, the story came that Titus had murdered a Tarig child and a Tarig lord. Sydney had no idea why her father would kill a child, and how he could kill a lord. Perhaps he had been hiding in the Magisterium all these thousands of days, and had only now found a way to escape. Maybe he had grown tired of Lady Chiron at last. Or perhaps he had heard that Johanna was dead, and decided the Entire held little interest for him now. For any or all of these reasons he might have decided to run, and then, having been discovered, he killed those who tried to prevent him.

Of course, Johanna wasn't dead. The rumor that it pleased the Tarig lords to spread was that, because of her lost child, she had died of grief. This sentimental story had taken root and spread until all had heard it. And although it was a lie—as Cixi had assured her—Sydney no longer thought about Johanna. Nor about Titus. Until now.

The pack on Sydney's back grew heavy, and she considered leaving it behind. But the pack stayed on. In it, as always, was her journal containing the record of her Entire days. Perhaps her days were over, now. She felt tired enough with her life.

She sat by a scraggly tree, leaning against it for a few moments' rest. Then, weary of thinking, she slept.

When she awoke, Mo Ti's voice came to her: "Mistress."

"Mo Ti." She rose to her feet, still weary. No shared sight came to her from his mount. Mo Ti was on foot.

Remaining silent, he put a water flask in her hand. She drank as he lowered his bulk to sit beside her.

Eventually she whispered, "Mo Ti."

"My lady?"

"Look at the sky." After a pause she added, "Do you see a brightship?"

"No, Lady, there is no brightship."

"But have you looked in all directions—down the Long Gaze of Fire, and toward the heartland?

"Mo Ti has looked."

"No one there, then." She felt dispassionate, but curious. Where was Titus now? But there was no figuring such things out. She rose, and started to walk again. At her side, the big man matched her steps.

He said, "Mo Ti also watches for the caravan that brings your eye surgeon."

Her surgeon was coming. The beku caravan bringing her Chalin surgeon would be here in ten days. The Tarig had agreed with Riod's demand, eager to curry Inyx favor. The mantis lords would have to find a new gulag for their misfits, though. Once the riders were sighted, many individuals would come to the sway to ride freely with the Inyx. But it no longer seemed such a fine thing to her.

"Where are you going?" Mo Ti asked.

"Walking."

"Walking where?"

She kept silent. She didn't know where.

His hand was on her arm, stopping her. She felt like a twig, like a steppe mouse. He could stop her, or carry her home, so insubstantial she was compared to him.

"My lady. This person is not worthy of your sorrow."

"But I'm not sad, Mo Ti. I feel nothing, truly." She heard the tenderness in his voice, and it hurt her that he was troubled on her account. How was it possible for such a mountain of a man to imagine one girl's sorrow? He had never seemed so fanciful, before.

She began to walk again, but he still held her arm, restraining her.

"Let me go, Mo Ti."

"No."

She thought about this a moment. Had he ever told her no before? She tested his resolve by twisting her arm in his hold. Tight as a vise. "I forbid you to bring me back to the encampment," she said, her calm beginning to tatter at the edges.

"Very well. Then we'll stand here together."

"We'll get thirsty."

"Yes."

She stood, her arm pinioned in his gentle grip. But when she tried to move, his fingers tightened. They stood like this a while, forged together. She lifted her face to the bright, to gauge the time. Moving into Twilight Ebb. But it was a guess. Of all the Entire's inhabitants, only she and Johanna had no instinctive sense of bright-time.

Over thousands of days Sydney had come to think of herself as Chalin.

Cixi was her mother. The Rose held nothing that Sydney loved anymore. She hardly remembered the Rose. She was of the Entire. But today, standing on this plain, she knew she belonged to neither one place nor the other. This must be why she felt so untethered from the world, and from herself.

Mo Ti handed her the water flask. She refused it. She was starting to get used to not needing water.

She tried freeing her arm again. "Let me go, Mo Ti."

Surprisingly, he did. But he put something new in her hands. It was a knife.

"Dying of thirst is a hard way to go," he said. "I recommend the knife. With a nice deep cut, it will all be over quickly. Very efficient. Unless you're afraid of the knife."

Ugly words from one she'd thought was a friend. Resentment surged. "Have I ever been afraid of a knife?"

"No. But that was during fights, when your blood is worked up, and you throw away caution. It's not true courage."

How could he say such things to her? It was a bitter betrayal, to call her a coward, to push a weapon on her and urge her to use it on herself. Had he been waiting for a moment of weakness to take control of the herd? Was it all a ruse, this friendship?

Stripping off the scabbard, she stood, pointing the knife in his direction. "Do you mean to kill me, Mo Ti?"

"Mo Ti doesn't care."

She gripped the knife, trembling with anger. "Don't care? All your high-sounding plans, and urging me on? To raise the kingdom?" Her fury built, and she advanced on him.

"Mo Ti doesn't care for a young girl who quits."

"I'm not quitting!" She was just walking on the steppe, and it was no crime to walk. Why was he against her?

His soft voice came to her, maddeningly smug. "Standing alone here under the bright, no food or water. Yes, quitting." He added. "Like Akay-Wat, like a gutless Hirrin."

She hurled herself at him, lunging with the knife, knowing that she would miss, but hoping to shut him up.

Missing him, she spun around, and charged at him again.

This time he caught her, and grabbing her wrist, shook the knife free from her hand. In a fury, Sydney struck him in the chest. His huge arms came around her, leaving little room for her flailing arms, but she attempted to beat on his torso. She twisted back and forth to free herself while pummeling him over and over again. Eventually her hands lost their feeling.

When she was quiet at last, Mo Ti sank to his knees, taking her with him. Then, kneeling in his embrace, she began to cry.

He put his hand on the back of her head and held her close to his chest, and her face grew so hot with crying, she thought it must be swelling up. She grew weak with crying. Mo Ti didn't move, except to caress the back of her head.

Then, for a long time, she was silent, dazed. By the feel of the bright on her skin, it must have fallen into Deep Ebb.

Her mind shut off, and perhaps she slept.

After a time she became aware that she was lying in Mo Ti's arms, stretched out on the ground. He dabbed at her face with his kerchief and the remains of the water.

Stirring, she sat up. Mo Ti was there; he would always be there. More loyal than her former family. More important. "I will rejoin the herd, Mo Ti. But first take me, love me."

He dried her face with his kerchief. "Mo Ti loves you," he said. "But that is not how he serves you."

"It's best for us to be bonded, Mo Ti. After this."

"My lady. Mo Ti is a eunuch."

She touched his face. The bulging cheekbones, the heavy brow. Truly life was cruel. Yet wonderful as well. Then she clung to him again.

At last she said, "We will walk back, now."

"Yes, Lady."

And they walked back to camp, taking a long time to get there, because, of course, she wasn't going to enter the barracks yard being carried.

The next day, Akay-Wat left the encampment, riding out on Gevka just as the bright began its waxing phase. Before she left, the Hirrin had knelt by

Sydney's bunk, waking her and whispering, "Someday I am coming home, yes." It was becoming impossible for Akay-Wat to imagine living without this woman of the Rose. She hoped her assignment of preaching free bond would soon be over.

Stirring, Sydney sat up. "Yes. Then you'll be my high officer."

"High officer?" Akay-Wat said, stupefied.

"Who has been braver?"

Akay-Wat never thought she would hear this word applied to herself, much less from Sydney. She felt her long throat tighten with emotion. "This Hirrin is still afraid, mistress."

"So am I, Akay-Wat. Just don't tell anyone."

Akay-Wat thought of her parents, long dead in the war at Ahnenhoon, and thought how she had at last earned the right to be their progeny. She wished that they were alive to see this day.

Now came the next brave thing: leaving. She would miss Sydney, who now had become queen of the sway. *Queen* was perhaps too strong a word. But Sydney was a great personage, and someday, Akay-Wat thought, she would have the whole of the roamlands under her dominion. The key was free bond, of course.

The Hirrin pressed her mobile lips into Sydney's hand. Then she walked out of barracks, her newly fashioned leg striking the floor and adding a new rhythm to her gait.

Later, when Sydney at last climbed from her bed, she found a skinned vole carcass at her feet. A present from Takko. She'd smelled him nearby, when he deposited his present there. She was willing to use Puss's real name as long as he behaved.

Taking the carcass to the fire pit, she roasted it to a crackling finish.

Around the fire pit, her barracks-mates prepared their meals, talking of yesterday's rides and of free bond. A few mounts stood next to their riders, sharing morning thoughts. Their bodies and faces were familiar to Sydney: Mo Ti the Chalin, Adikar the Ysli, Takko the Laroo, and many others, including the mounts themselves. Each one was outrageous of shape and of culture, stinking for lack of bathing, and wary of leadership. But as they talked and shared tidbits of food, it seemed to Sydney that they were linked in a new way, in a shared life—connected by their mounts to each other.

Feng was absent from their midst, having slunk off to another herd. And now Akay-Wat was gone, an emissary to Ulrud's herd, to tell her story of how she had lost her leg to the old bonds and now rode better and freer.

Late in the ebb, Mo Ti woke Sydney. "A ship," he said.

She rose, shoving her feet into her boots. Riod's thoughts came to her from the yard, alarmed. Accompanying Mo Ti outside, she tried to breathe normally, but her chest seemed too small to draw air. Above her the bright stretched over the roamlands, and a trail marked the passage where a ship had cleaved the sky. That trail came from the heartland.

Mo Ti said, "I have talked with this new arrival, my lady. It is your surgeon."

"Surgeon?" Her surgeon was to arrive by caravan, not brightship.

Riod urged her to mount. His thoughts were chaotic, but his instinct was to have Sydney on his back.

Mo Ti spoke to both of them. "The Tarig have sent one of their own to do the surgery."

A breeze blew across Sydney's face, chasing away old hopes. She let it cool her.

Then she murmured, "It was a Tarig who blinded me." She climbed onto Riod's back. "We will send this mantis lord away." Mo Ti had her by the ankle, and Sydney jerked her foot, wrestling to free herself. "I won't let them touch me."

"But you must."

Now Riod turned his displeasure on Mo Ti, and it was a standoff of wills.

Mo Ti said, "Let them think they have your gratitude. Take their gift. You need it to win the herds, to make Riod strong. To raise the kingdom."

Mo Ti's hand was still on her foot as she sat astride Riod. He was waiting for her to say what she would do—not just today, this awful moment, but forever.

"What do I want, Mo Ti?" she almost cried to him.

"Sight. Power. Revenge."

She listened to the summation as Riod stomped beneath her, his hide trembling with agitation.

"You know me, Mo Ti."

"Yes, Lady."

She took a breath, drawing it deep. Then: "Yes, if I have to, I'll take their help." Riod shook his head in agitation, twisting the horns on his neck back and forth. But at last he moved forward, bearing her through the camp, past the stirring herd, out onto the steppe where the brightship waited—a new kind of ship, it seemed to Sydney, different-looking than the one that had brought her here so long ago. So the Tarig were replenishing their fleet. Mo Ti followed, mounted on Distanir.

If the fiend's hand falters, I will kill him, Riod sent.

"Yes, beloved," she said. "Do so."

CHAPTER THIRTY

APRIL IN PORTLAND WAS COLD THIS YEAR, scoured with wind gusting off the river. Lamar Gelde tucked his face into his neck scarf as much as possible and trudged across the parking lot to Minerva Building 919. His reserved parking place was long gone, of course.

Damn the wind. His face felt like it might fall off. An expensive misfortune if so, since he'd spent liberally on mitochondrial enhancements. For skin tone. For turkey neck, and drooping eyelids, and the other little insults of age. His face hurt as he entered the lobby. The docs said he'd be supersensitive to temperature changes.

Walking into the high-security area, he held up his hand, catching the beam of the tideflow, using the day pass Stefan Polich had stranded to him. It must have been a top-drawer security pass, because people were practically bowing to him as he went by. He looked around, wishing for a motorized conveyance, but Minerva wasn't built for the feeble.

Entering the savant warehouse, he silvered his palm for directions to Rob Quinn's cubicle. It was almost like the old days, when his access to the beam was absolute. But as he passed the workstations of the minor savant-tenders, no one recognized him.

When he finally found Rob, the man was flexing his fingers, using digit commands instead of a keyboard. Fancy. But he looked like a man trying to touch a real life, instead of the one he had.

Lamar coughed. Rob turned around.

"Spare a minute?"

Rob nodded. "Didn't expect to see *you*," he said by way of greeting for his father's old friend. Rob stood and waved for Lamar to follow him out of the warren and then down a corridor.

Lamar's legs protested. "Jesus, Rob, I've already walked my limit."

Rob stopped dead. "Okay, fine, let's talk here." He looked resentful. Well, he'd heard about Stefan's threats and blackmail. No doubt he didn't like being a pawn. But truth to tell, Rob *was* a pawn, and always would be. He was a forty-year-old savant tender. Couldn't get much more marginal than that.

"What's wrong with your face?" Rob asked, squinting at him.

"Had a little procedure." *Wrong with my face?* Took twenty years off him, his surgeon said. Pushing away his annoyance, Lamar said, "It's Titus. He's back."

Rob's mouth compressed, holding in his emotions. "Back?"

"Yes. He's been through hell, but he'll live."

"How much hell?"

Lamar shrugged. "You'll have to ask him."

"I mean, how bad is he?"

"He's weak, dehydrated, disoriented, and bleeding from internal capillaries. He's in shock, and he might lose a couple of toes from frostbite."

"Christ."

"Not quite, but he'll work that angle, I'm sure." Lamar smiled, hoping that Rob would join him.

He didn't. Rob shook his head, trying to track this news. "It's only been ten days."

A flock of techs were thumping down the hall, and Lamar waited for them to pass out of earshot. "Time is different in the adjoining region. Remember? And he's been adrift in space for several days."

"Where?"

"Look, I need to sit down." He looked around for a chair, but the corridor was as clear as a twenty-year-old's arteries.

Rob led him a few steps down the corridor, where they entered a storeroom containing surplus furniture, including a couple of executive chairs. Lamar sighed as he got off his feet. He fished in a pocket for a PopUp tab, swallowed it, trusting that it would give him enough kick to get through the conversation.

He began: "Two days ago we got a call they'd found him." Actually, Stefan Polich got the call, and would never have brought Lamar into this if he could have helped it. "Your brother was wrapped in a body capsule like a worm in a cocoon. Orbiting some moon of Uranus—Cressida, if you want the specifics. Cressida's nothing more than a radio relay station, so it took a while to spot him, even though his capsule was emitting regular pulses of light. Normally, even that would have taken weeks to notice, but the intensity of this light was special. More like supercharged lightning or something."

His body or the chair creaked as he changed positions. "He was unconscious, and the capsule was losing heat. If they hadn't found him when they did, he'd be dead. An EoSap mining vessel was extracting methane down on Uranus, and pulled him in. They were afraid to open the capsule, because of how it looked. But thank God they did."

"What did it look like?"

"That's just the thing. It wasn't really like an escape capsule. It was like a transparent sarcophagus, in his exact shape. The material—and they've got no idea what material it is—replicated his shape, down to the features on his face. By rights, they should have left it for the experts. But they were a bunch of middies, and they were curious. And one of them said they saw his eyelids flutter, so they opened it. Saved his life."

"Someone had to," Rob said with a bite in the tone. "Where is he now?"

"On board a Minerva in-system ship. They picked him up from the mining vessel yesterday. He insists on seeing you before he'll talk to anyone." He cut a glance at Rob. "He wants to be sure you're all right." The whole blackmail business made him sick. Threatening Rob and then young Mateo. It never would have happened in the old days.

Rob stood. "Let's go, then."

"We're talking *Mars*, Rob. He's headed to a hospital there."

"Mars?" Rob had never left the Pacific Northwest, much less the Earth. He shrugged. "Better get started, then."

Lamar stood, his legs protesting. He looked Rob in the eyes. "Christ, but I'm sorry about Stefan—and Helice—how they've handled things."

Rob's jaw worked a little before he answered. "How *they've* handled things? Minerva's hiding this huge scientific discovery, and using Titus as a guinea pig. And you're doing their bidding, Lamar. Even against people that would have called you family."

"Rob, I'm just—"

"No. See, you're the messenger, Lamar. You run interference for Stefan and Helice and the gang." He sneered. "They shoot messengers, you know?"

He walked out, leaving Lamar to hobble after him. Lamar wanted to set the record straight. Wanted to say that he'd talked Quinn into the mission in the first place because he knew the man had to go back. Anybody who knew him knew that much. It was only the naïve who had hoped Titus would get on with his life.

But Rob clung to his opinions. Like most middies, he knew just enough to draw the wrong conclusions.

Muttering, he followed Rob, waiting for the PopUp pill to kick in.

Birdsong and green grass. It seemed wrong.

Five stories underground at the Sinus Meridiani hosplex, Quinn sat on a bench in the park, waiting for Helice Maki. His gaze was stuck on a nearby bed of flowers. Yellow flowers with little ruffs around the collar. Over there, orange exotics, with five petals, like trumpets.

He wondered if he used to know the names. The game of tag he'd played with his memories in the Entire sometimes had the effect of blurring even things he knew he knew. But he was still healing from the brightship crossing, a passage that had nearly killed him, despite the protective measures of the ship-being. The fragmental had encapsulated him as best it knew how before fleeing the limited dimensions of its prison. He hoped it had made it home.

By his feet rested a small leather satchel containing his possessions: some hospital toothpaste, several changes of underwear, and an extra set of eye scrims to cover the Chalin amber. They'd taken his clothes—the Chalin silks—and Ci Dehai's knife, but he wouldn't need those things for a while.

He was ready to go home.

He hoped that Helice Maki saw the wisdom in letting him go, now that they'd had him for seven weeks and he'd told them all he knew. Well, not quite all. He left out the mistakes he'd made, his visit to the Ascendancy, and the enemies he'd drawn to himself. The story he stuck by was that his memories of the Entire had returned, and he'd managed by virtue of his deep knowledge of the realm to remain undiscovered by the Tarig while making allies with the Chalin leader Yulin. And the Tarig lord who wanted converse with the Rose.

In all that he'd told his interrogators, Johanna's story had been the biggest sticking point. Helice and her minions had rejected it at first, but the topic always returned. *Something* had to power the Entire, with its unnatural needs. But how likely was it that Johanna would be privy to such a volatile secret? Very likely, Quinn argued. She lived among the Tarig, and she had reason to seek out such a danger. The debriefing team hammered at the story, at the logic of it, at the ways around it.

For one thing, the timing didn't work. Johanna had said the Rose had one hundred years left. How could the Rose collapse so quickly, faster than light speed? Unfortunately, they figured out a way. It could be a quantum transition to a lower phase state, they said. Since matter always tries to reach the lowest energy state—much as water always tries to flow downhill—if the Rose was not already at the lowest-energy state possible, it could make a sudden quantum leap, dissolving all matter into a chaotic plasma of subatomic particles. And we'd never know what hit us. A theory only. But could the Tarig do it?

Quinn had not the slightest doubt. The recent collapse of a few star regions that had so perplexed astronomers was a Tarig beta test, of course.

The engines at Ahnenhoon were coming online.

So while Quinn rested and recuperated at home, Minerva would be searching for a way to disable those engines. It was the kind of problem the techs relished: an engineering challenge—unlike the twisted issues of culture and politics of the Entire.

In the midst of Minerva's endless debriefing, Rob had come to visit, saying all was well with Mateo and Emily and Caitlin. He'd actually cried when he saw Titus. That put a lump in Titus's throat, and they'd shaken hands. *Get yourself home*, Rob had said.

He wanted to. He was tired of Helice Maki and Booth Waller, and the others who formed the drill team. Drilling for truth, drilling for a better version that wouldn't muck up their business plan. A route to the stars. Use the River Nigh. Negotiate with the Tarig for the correlates, for travel rights. There must be something the Tarig wanted.

Oh yes. They wanted the Rose.

There were a few bad days when Helice had insisted that others needed to go over. To confirm his story. To probe for options. But they would never last; they'd be spotted immediately. Language. Even if they learned the Lucent tongue, they'd speak with an accent. They'd make mistakes, and they'd be dead. Eventually Helice gave up. The two of them looked at each other hatefully. Minerva needed him. And, the truth was, he needed Minerva—for the harness, for the way over.

The way over. Already he was homesick, for all the things he'd left behind in the Entire. For the Entire itself. He sat gazing at the yellow flowers. They made him uneasy. Overembroidered, too fancy.

A noise from behind, and Quinn turned, seeing Helice Maki.

She walked toward him: petite, athletic, cheerful. For a sharp moment he missed Anzi—her directness, her quiet wisdom.

"They said I'd find you here," she chirped.

"And here I am."

She sat cross-legged in the grass, to face him.

He gestured at the flowers. "What are those yellow things, do you know?"

"Daffodils."

"Yes, daffodils." He thought the name lacked the elegance of *rose*.

He mused: "Ever think how strange flowers are? They go way beyond what's necessary to attract insects. It's like someone went on a creative binge."

"Evolution *did* go on a binge. It's full of excesses, experiments."

He thought how it was that the Tarig had usurped evolution in their domain, copying the products of Rose evolution. Among the marvels that Quinn brought home was the tantalizing glimpse of the other self-knowing creatures of the Rose universe: beings like the Hirrin, the Gond, and the Jout. What they called themselves on their own worlds, and where those planets were, the human race had yet to discover. But they waited out there, for contact, if routes could be found.

Helice interrupted his thoughts. "No flowers in the Entire, huh?"

"No." He gazed past her, past the flowers. "Somehow, you don't end up missing them."

She watched him carefully. "You've changed."

"Have I?" His face was that of another man, but he figured she didn't mean the cheekbones and the golden eyes.

"Yes. You're not as edgy."

"No, Helice, I'm real edgy. It's just that I'm a little tired right now. Tired of talking to you and Booth and the boys. But you still need to be careful around me." He watched her with a steady gaze until she broke eye contact.

"Quinn, I know we're putting you through a hell of a debriefing—"

He held up a hand. "Don't apologize. I'm nowhere near ready to hear an apology from you." He shrugged. "Maybe when I see Mateo again and count fingers and toes, maybe then I'll be ready."

Helice winced inwardly. She was well aware that she hadn't handled Quinn well. But he *had* come back, even with the daughter still incarcerated among the Inyx. Helice was sure he'd made some sort of bid for Sydney over there, although he wouldn't admit it.

Envy gnawed at her. He sat there, having been to a place of wonders, a landlocked galaxy of impossible skies and improbable creatures. The things he'd described—the bright, the exotic river, the flying Adda, the Tarig, the sways with their cultures, the city in the sky—these things had flooded her mind for weeks. She dreamed of it. And loathed Titus Quinn for going there first. More, she hated Quinn's blithe summation of her chances in that place: *You wouldn't like the Entire, Helice. You wouldn't be at the top of the feeding chain. Believe me.*

Now, sitting here with him in the garden, she glanced uneasily at the bag near his feet. "Going somewhere?"

"Home. I need to go home."

"Yes, soon. We've got just a few more—"

He was shaking his head. "No. Today. I'm going home today. Ship leaves in three hours. I'll be needing a seat."

She stood up. She hadn't released him yet. How could she? He knew more than he had told, oh, much more. "I'll make you a deal. Give us one more week, and this time, tell us the rest it. No holding back."

Slowly, he rose to his feet. "Actually, I *have* told you all the important stuff. The rest is personal."

They faced off, with Helice trying very hard to control her irritation. That he would consider anything about that universe *personal*. She began with great restraint: "You still belong to Minerva, Quinn. We have the harness, the platform. If you want to go back where your daughter is, you'll need to prove you're a good advance man. You'll need to be, at a minimum, truthful."

He picked up his satchel and put it gently on the bench, a movement so tight and controlled that she thought he might strike her. "Maybe you haven't been paying close attention, Helice. We need a reliable way to go to and from. Your lab module and harness won't be the doorway. Not even close."

"Maybe not," she countered, "but for now, you still need that harness—and us."

He looked at her like she wasn't very bright. "I know a Tarig lord who will open a nice, big door. The one we need to send ships through, to find routes that will take us all the places we want to go. Without that door, we've got no routes, no converse, no salvation."

He held up a hand to forestall her response. "And I'm the one who knows this Tarig lord, and the only one who's got a chance in hell of bringing the correlates home."

They locked gazes, and by his expression, he knew that he held the upper hand. This has-been pilot with his tattered past and bad manners.

His face was hard and calm. It made her want to see him waver, but, instead, his words came like little cuts: "You see why you're going to get me on that Earth-bound ship today? You see why I don't need you?"

He cocked his head in curiosity. "You are following the argument, aren't you, Helice?"

It made her ill to acknowledge that he held that kind of power over her. Barely audible, she said, "Yes."

"Well, then."

She looked into his wrong-looking eyes, falsely blue, tinged at the edges with gold, a little halo that reminded one that he now had Chalin eyes. "I'll get you on that ship." The words filled her mouth with a sour taste.

He nodded. "Good. Maybe then we can start to overlook how much we despise each other. Worth a try." He hoisted the pack.

Blocking his path, she said, "You aren't ever going to let it go, are you? How I've handled things."

"Did you think the Entire was going to improve my character?" An ironic smile crept across his face.

That caused her to smile a bit in return. He was still a handsome man when he smiled, despite the surgery, and despite that scar down his cheek that he claimed a Tarig child had given him. Another personal matter, he'd said.

They held eye contact for a time, understanding each other. It was all out in the open now, as to who was in charge.

From nearby came the trill of a bird, singing for the pure joy of it, or perhaps locked in a deadly struggle for nesting territory.

The sound made Quinn eager to be back home, far from Helice and Minerva. He badly needed a long walk on the beach.

He looked at Helice with her weird dark hair and gaudy clothes, and felt like a different species from her. He wasn't a Rose elite. He was once, a long and strangely twisted time ago. But he'd passed by the right education when he became a pilot, passed on membership in the corporations that controlled the knowledge of the world, controlled it because they could bloody well *understand* it.

Well, if he wasn't in their ranks, so be it. It was the other world where he had to be an expert.

And was.

Later that day he took the last empty berth on a homeward-bound ship. Through the viewing port, he stared out at the black deeps of the Rose and, for the first time in his life, found the sight very strange.

CHAPTER THIRTY-ONE

TWO SEAGULLS FOUGHT OVER A CLAM IN THE SURF, dropping the trophy in the process, climbing into the sky with angry squawks.

Heading back to his cottage, Quinn followed his outgoing footsteps, now deforming in the wet sand, becoming larger, more misshapen. Above him, a few cirrus clouds rode the blue, like the remnants of a larger blanket. The sky needed a blanket of clouds. It was vastly empty and deep, and it seemed miraculous that its airy substance held in place or did any worldly good.

Except for a steady wind off the ocean, the day was warm, and Quinn carried his shoes, walking barefoot, pleased that he'd kept all ten toes. And this time, kept his memories.

His thoughts kept returning to the tunnel in the adobe wall, the one it must surely have taken him years to carve, to direct the material to conform. He had wondered how he'd spent his time, how he'd conformed to Tarig society—what there was of it—and hated the picture he'd conjured, of indolence and comfort. And since he couldn't remember much of that sort of life, he'd been left imagining ugly scenes of extravagance and dissolution.

But, in reality, he'd been working in his room.

Chiron had been curious. *What do you do in there, all by yourself?*

Read, walk in my garden.

Come to us.

Tomorrow, perhaps. He remembered an expression crossing her face: disappointment, a flash of anger. Sometimes he was able to keep her at bay.

Now, far from the bright city—it wasn't even possible to think how far—he sat on a log tossed up by the latest storm. The beach, with its relentless surf and strong horizon, was the best place in the Rose.

In the distance, a figure was approaching, following the strand of the retreating tide. Caitlin waved.

He waited for her, glad to see her, grateful at how few questions she'd had for him about his journey. One of them had been, "What did you do with that door knocker?"

"Buried it," he'd answered. The face had been Hadenth's, although he couldn't have known it then.

When Caitlin arrived, he saw that she had a string bag full of beach glass and shells.

"Find stuff?" he asked.

"The tide always leaves something." She retied her bandana to keep the hair from whipping in her face. "Feel like soup?"

"Yeah, most of the time," he said.

She smiled. "I mean, homemade soup and bakery bread."

He stood up, grabbing his shoes. "Sure. Long as I can dunk the bread."

"Dunking and slurping flatter the cook."

She led the way. "The kids spent all morning running those trains, Titus. I'm scared to death they'll break something."

"Don't be. If it breaks, I'll fix it."

Caitlin lengthened her stride to keep pace with him, but then found that he had stopped. He was looking out at the ocean.

"Are you okay?" she asked.

He didn't answer, but continued looking outward. Caitlin figured he wasn't seeing a thing. She stood by his side a few moments watching the waves bulk up near the shore.

"Titus, are you sure you want two brats to take care of for a whole week?" She and Rob were leaving the next day for a long-overdue vacation to fish in the Gulf of Mexico.

"Yes. I'll take them in the kayak without life jackets, and teach them how to make homemade bombs." He turned a heart-stopping smile on her. The smile hadn't changed, although the whole family was still adjusting to the altered features. But she liked the new Titus. Less glib, more relaxed. If he got any better, she'd have to join a nunnery.

They resumed walking, this time in silence, until they spied the cottage. Rob waved from the porch.

Caitlin waved back. To forestall anyone joining them prematurely, she planted her feet in the cool sand and looked up at him. "How old would she be, Titus?" She knew that Sydney was always on his mind.

"How old? Nearly twenty, I think. . . . She'll be grown. When I bring her home." He looked out toward the horizon, thrashing in the distance. "I'm afraid she'll look exactly like a young Johanna."

Caitlin sighed. "That would be wonderful. And hard."

"About sums things up." His expression suddenly changed, and Caitlin followed his gaze to the nearest dune, where Mateo had appeared.

"Uncle Titus!" Mateo waved, summoning his uncle to see his latest beach find.

Titus turned to her. "Can lunch wait?"

Getting her nod, he headed off to the dune where Mateo waited. "We'll be just a second," he said.

"Take your time, Titus," Caitlin called after him.

ABOUT THE AUTHOR

KAY KENYON grew up in northern Minnesota, where winters are long and books, particularly science fiction books, could take you away—the farther, the better. She was in thrall to the alien worlds of authors like Silverberg, Le Guin, and Herbert. She never lost that early love of alternate worlds, but creating her own would have to wait through several careers in the real world. After professions in TV and radio copywriting, acting in commercials, and promoting urban transportation alternatives, she at last turned to fiction writing. Since then she has published six science fiction novels, including *Tropic of Creation*, *The Seeds of Time*, *Maximum Ice*, and *The Braided World*. The latter two were short-listed for the Phillip K. Dick and John W. Campbell awards, respectively. Her short stories have appeared in such recent anthologies as *I, Alien*; *ReVisions*; *Live without a Net*; and *Stars: Stories Based on the Songs of Janis Ian*. Kenyon's work has been translated into French and Russian. *Bright of the Sky* launches her first series, The Entire and the Rose. She is president of a writing conference, Write on the River, in eastern Washington State, where she lives with her husband. You can visit her Web site at www.kaykenyon.com.